THE INDEPENDENCE OF MISS MARY BENNET

COLLEEN McCULLOUGH

The Independence of Miss Mary Bennet

HarperCollins*Publishers*

HarperCollins*Publishers*
77–85 Fulham Palace Road,
Hammersmith, London W6 8JB

www.harpercollins.co.uk

Published by HarperCollins*Publishers* 2008
1

A catalogue record for this book
is available from the British Library

ISBN: 978 0 00 727183 2

This novel is entirely a work of fiction.
The names, characters and incidents portrayed in it are
the work of the author's imagination, and, while
historical characters make appearances in the book,
this is a fictionalised account.

Printed and bound in Great Britain by
Clays Ltd, St Ives plc

Mixed Sources
Product group from well-managed
forests and other controlled sources
www.fsc.org   Cert no. SW-COC-1806
© 1996 Forest Stewardship Council
FSC

FSC is a non-profit international organisation established
to promote the responsible management of the world's forests.
Products carrying the FSC label are independently certified
to assure consumers that they come from forests that are managed
to meet the social, economic and ecological needs
of present and future generations.

Find out more about HarperCollins and the environment at
www.harpercollins.co.uk/green

For Bruni
Composer and diva
As beautiful a person inside as she is outside

ONE

The long, late light threw a gilt mantle over the skeletons of shrubs and trees scattered through the Shelby Manor gardens; a few wisps of smoke, smudged at their edges, drifted from the embers of a fire kindled to burn the last of the fallen leaves, and somewhere a stay-behind bird was chattering the tuneless nocturne of late autumn. Watching the sunset from her usual seat in the bay window, Mary felt a twisting of her heart at its blue-gold glory, soon to be a memory banked inside the echoing spaces of her mind. How much longer? Oh, how much longer?

Came the rattle and tinkle of the tea tray as Martha bore it in; she deposited it carefully on the low table flanking the wing chair in which the mistress of Shelby Manor slumbered. Sighing, Mary turned from the window and took her place, setting a delicate cup in its frail saucer, then another for herself. How lucky they were to have Old Jenkins! Still harvesting an occasional cucumber from his frames. And how lucky that Mama relished cucumber slices atop her bread-and-butter! She would wake to see the treats sitting on a sprightly doily, and care not that the cake was three days old.

"Mama, tea has arrived," said Mary.

Bundled in shawls and wraps, the little round body jerked; its little round face puckered up peevishly, scowled at being roused. Then the faded blue eyes opened, saw the cucumber atop the bread-and-butter, and a preliminary joy began. But not before the everyday complaint was uttered.

"Have you no compassion for my poor nerves, Mary, to wake me so abruptly?"

"Of course I do, Mama," Mary said perfunctorily, pouring milk into the bottom of her mother's cup, and tilting the fine silver teapot to pour an amber stream on top of the milk. Cook's girl had done well with the sugar, broken it into good lumps; Mary added one of exactly the right size to the tea, and stirred the liquid thoroughly.

All of which occupied her for perhaps a minute. Cup and saucer in her hand, she looked up to make sure Mama was ready. Then, not realising she had done so, she put her burden down without removing her eyes from Mama's face. It had changed, taken on the contours and patina of a porcelain mask from Venice, more featureless than expressionless. The eyes still stared, but at something far beyond the room.

"Oh, Mama!" she whispered, not knowing what else to say. "It came all unaware." She closed those eyes with the tips of her fingers, eyes that somehow seemed to contain more knowledge of life than ever they had during that life, then kissed Mama's brow. "Dear God, You are very good. I thank You for Your mercy. How afraid she would have been, had she known."

The bell cord was in reach; Mary tugged it gently.

"Send Mrs Jenkins to me, Martha, please."

Armed with plenty of excuses — what *more* could the sour old crab ask for than out-of-season cucumber? — Mrs Jenkins came in girded for battle. But the look Miss Mary wore banished her anger at once. "Yes, Miss Mary?"

"My mother has passed away, Mrs Jenkins. Kindly send for Dr Callum — Old Jenkins can go in the pony and trap. Tell Jenkins to saddle the roan, pack his needs and be ready to ride for Pemberley as soon as I have written a note. He is to have five guineas from your jar for his journey, for he must make all haste. Good inns, good hired horses when the roan cannot carry him farther."

Mary's voice held its usual composure; no huskiness, no tremor to betray her feelings. For nigh on seventeen years, thought Mrs Jenkins, this poor woman has listened to her mother's megrims and woes, moans and complaints — when, that is, she wasn't listening to shrill outpourings of delight, triumph, self-congratulation. Saying just the right thing, competently averting an attack of the vapours, jockeying Mrs Bennet into a better mood as briskly and unsentimentally as a good governess a wayward child. And now it was over. All over.

"Begging your pardon, Miss Mary, but will Jenkins find Mr Darcy at home?"

"Yes. According to Mrs Darcy, Parliament is in recess. Bring me Mama's pink silk scarf, I would cover her face."

The housekeeper bobbed a curtsey and left, a prey to many doubts, fears, apprehensions. What would become of them now, from Father to young Jem and Dora?

The scarf properly draped, the fire stoked against the coming night of frost, the candles lit, Mary went to the window and sat on its cushioned seat, there to reflect on more than this visitation from Death.

Of grief she felt none: too many years, too much boredom. In lieu of it, she fastened upon a growing sense of becalm, as if she had been transported to some vast chamber filled by a darkness that yet was luminous, floating on an invisible ocean, not afraid, not diminished.

I have waited thirty-eight years for my turn to come, she thought, but not one of them can say that I have not done my duty, that I have not tipped my measure of happiness into their cups, that I have not stepped backward into obscurity crying one word of protest at my fate.

Why am I so unprepared for this moment? Where has my mind wandered, when time has hung so heavily upon me? I have been at the beck and call of an empty vessel called Mama, but empty vessels hardly ever manage to scratch up an observation, a comment, an idea. So I have spent my time waiting. Just waiting. With a squadron of Jenkinses to look after her, Mama did not *need* me; I was there as a sop to the proprieties. How I hate that word, propriety! An ironbound code of conduct invented to intimidate and subjugate women. I was doomed to be a spinster, the family thought, with those shocking suppurating spots all over my face and a front tooth that grew sideways. Of course Fitz felt that Mama had to be chaperoned by a member of the family in case she took to travelling to Pemberley or Bingley Hall. If only Papa had not died two years after Lizzie's and Jane's weddings!

Think, Mary, think! she scolded herself. Be *logical*! It was the boredom. I had no choice but to dream the weeks, the months, the years away: of setting foot on the stones of the Forum Romanum; of eating oranges in a Sicilian orchard; of filling my eyes with the Parthenon; of pressing my cheek against some wall in the Holy Land that Christ Jesus must have touched, or leaned upon, or brushed with His shadow. I have dreamed of roaming free along foreign shores, dreamed of sampling the cities of sunnier climes, the mountains and skies I have only read about. While in reality I have lived in a world divided between books, music, and a Mama who did not need me.

But now that I am free, I have no wish to experience any of those things. All that I want is to be of use, to have a purpose. To have something to do that would make a difference. But will I be let? No. My elder sisters and their grand husbands will descend upon Shelby Manor within the week, and a new sentence of lethargy will be levied upon Aunt Mary. Probably joining the horde of nurses, governesses and tutors who are responsible for the welfare of Elizabeth's and Jane's children. For naturally Mrs Darcy and Mrs Bingley enjoy only the delights of children, leaving the miseries of parentage to others. The wives of grand men do not wait for things to happen: they make things happen. Seventeen years ago, Mrs Darcy and Mrs Bingley were too busy enjoying their marriages to take responsibility for Mama.

Oh, how bitter that sounds! I did not mean that thought to shape itself sounding so bitter. At the time, it was not. I must be fair to them. When Papa died they were both new mothers, Kitty had just married, and Lydia — oh, Lydia! Longbourn went to the Collinses, and my fate was manifest, between the spots and the tooth. How smoothly Fitz handled it! Shelby Manor purchased together with the services of the Jenkinses, and the fledgling maiden aunt Mary eased into her task as deftly as a carpenter dovetails two pieces of wood. Mama and I removed ten miles the other side of Meryton, far enough away from the odious Collinses, yet close enough for Mama to continue to see her cronies. Aunt Phillips, Lady Lucas and Mrs Long had been delighted. So was I. A huge library, a full-sized fortepiano, and the Jenkinses.

So whence this sudden bitterness against my sisters now it is over? UnChristian and undeserving. Lord knows Lizzie at least has had her troubles. Hers is not a happy marriage.

Shivering, Mary left the window to huddle in the chair on the far side of the fireplace from her still, utterly silent companion. She found herself watching the pink silk scarf, expecting it to puff with a sudden breath from underneath. But it did not. Dr Callum would be here soon; Mama would be taken to her feather bed, washed, dressed, laid out in the freezing air for the long vigil between death and burial.

Starting guiltily, she remembered that she had not summoned

the Reverend Mr Courtney. Oh, bother! If Old Jenkins has not returned with the doctor, Young Jenkins would have to go.

"For one thing I refuse to do," she said to herself, "is send for Mr Collins. I have been over *that* for twenty years."

"Elizabeth," said Fitzwilliam Darcy as he entered his wife's dressing room, "I have bad news, my dear."

Elizabeth turned from the mirror, brows arched higher over her luminous eyes. Their customary sparkle faded; she frowned, rose to her feet. "Charlie?" she asked.

"No, Charlie is well. I have had a letter from Mary, who says that your mother has passed away. In her sleep, peacefully."

The stool in front of the dressing table refused to help her; she sagged sideways onto its corner, almost fell as she scrambled for balance, and found it. "Mama? Oh, Mama!"

Fitz had watched her without going to her aid; finally he moved from the doorway, strolled across the carpet to rest one hand on her bare shoulder, its long fingers pressing her flesh lightly. "My dear, it is for the best."

"Yes, yes! But she is only sixty-two! I had fancied she would make very old bones."

"Aye, coddled like a Strasbourg goose. It is a mercy, all the same. Think of Mary."

"Yes, for that I must be thankful. Fitz, what to do?"

"Set out for Hertfordshire first thing in the morning. I will send to Jane and Charles to meet us at the Crown and Garter by nine. Best to travel together."

"The children?" she asked, grief beginning as shock went. What were the old, when there were young to fill the heart?

"They stay here, of course. I'll tell Charles not to let Jane cozen him into taking any of theirs. Shelby Manor is a commodious house, Elizabeth, but it will not accommodate any of our offspring." Reflected in her mirror, his face seemed to harden; then he shrugged the mood off, whatever it had been, and continued in his level voice. "Mary says that she has sent for Kitty, but thinks Lydia is better left to me. What a truly sensible woman Mary has become!"

"Please, Fitz, let us take Charlie! You will ride, and I will make the journey alone. It is a long way. We can drop Charlie back at Oxford on the way home."

His mouth slipped a little awry as he considered it, then he gave his famous regal nod. "As you wish."

"Thank you." She hesitated, knowing the answer, but asking the question anyway. "Do we hold this dinner tonight?"

"Oh, I think so. Our guests are on their way. Your mourning weeds can wait until tomorrow, as can the subject." His hand left her shoulder. "I am for downstairs. Roeford is sure to arrive at any moment."

And with a grimace at mention of his least esteemed Tory ally, Darcy left his wife to finish her toilet.

A tear escaped, was whisked away by the haresfoot; eyes swimming, Elizabeth fought for control. How splendid a political career could be! Always something important to do, never the time for peace, companionship, leisure. Fitz did not mourn Mrs Bennet's passing, she knew that well; the trouble was that he expected her to feel the same indifference, heave a thankful sigh at the lifting of this particular burden, part shame, part embarrassment, part impotence. Yet that shallow, idiotic, crotchety woman had borne her, Elizabeth, and for that, surely she was entitled to be loved. To be mourned, if not missed.

"I want Mr Skinner. At once," Darcy said to his butler, busy hovering over the first footman as he divested Mr Roeford of his greatcoat. "My dear Roeford, how splendid to see you. As always, first into the fray." And without a backward glance, Darcy led his obnoxiously early guest into the Rubens Room.

The curt but civil command had Parmenter fleeing in search of the third footman the moment his master disappeared. Something was amiss, so much was sure. But why did Mr Darcy want that forbidding man at this hour?

"Run all the way, James," Parmenter instructed, then went back to the hall to await more timely guests. Six of them appeared half an hour later, glowing with anticipation, exclaiming at the cold, speculating that the new year would come in hard and freezing. Not long after, Mr Edward Skinner stalked through the front door. He went straight to the small library — with never a please, thank you, or kiss my foot, the Pemberley butler thought resentfully. Valued he might be and speak like a gentleman he might, but Parmenter remembered him as a youth and would have gone to the stake maintaining that Ned Skinner was no gentleman. There were perhaps twelve years between his master and Ned, who therefore was no by-blow, but *something* existed between them, a bond not even Mrs Darcy had been able to plumb — or break. Even as Parmenter thought these things he was on his way to the Rubens Room to nod at Mr Fitz.

"A difficulty, Ned," said Fitz, closing the library door.

Skinner made no reply, simply stood in front of the desk with body relaxed and hands by his sides loosely; not the pose of a minion. He was a very big man, five inches taller than Darcy's six feet, and was built like an ape — massive shoulders and neck, a barrel of a chest, no superfluous fat. Rumour had it that his father had been a West Indian blackamoor, so dark were Skinner's complexion, hair and narrow, watchful eyes.

"Sit, Ned, you make my neck ache looking up."

"You have guests, I'll not delay you. What is it?"

"Whereabouts is Mrs George Wickham?" Darcy asked as he sat down, drawing a sheet of paper forward and dipping his steel-sheathed goose quill nib into the inkwell. He was already writing when Ned answered.

"At the Plough and Stars in Macclesfield. Her new flirt has just become her latest lover. They've taken over the best bedroom and a private parlour. 'Tis a new location for her."

"Is she drinking?"

"Not above a bottle or two. Love's on her mind, not wine. Give her a week and things might change."

"They won't have a chance." Darcy glanced up briefly and grinned sourly. "Take my racing curricle and the bays, Ned. Deliver this note to Bingley Hall on your way to Macclesfield. I want Mrs Wickham reasonably sober at the Crown and

Garter by nine tomorrow morning. Pack her boxes and bring them with you."

"She'll kick up a fine old rumpus, Fitz."

"Oh, come, Ned! Who in Macclesfield will gainsay you — or me, for that matter? I don't care if you have to bind her hand and foot, just have her in Lambton on time." The swift scrawl ceased, the pen went down; without bothering to seal his note, Darcy handed it to Ned Skinner. "I've told Bingley to ride. Mrs Wickham can go in his coach with Mrs Bingley. We are for the charms of Hertfordshire to bury Mrs Bennet, not before time."

"A monstrous slow journey by coach."

"Given the season, the wet weather and the state of the roads, coach it must be. However, I'll use six light draughts, so will Bingley. We should do sixty miles a day, perhaps more."

The note tucked in his greatcoat pocket, Ned departed.

Darcy got up, frowning, to stand for a moment with his eyes riveted sightlessly on the leather-bound rows of his parliamentary Hansards. The old besom was dead at last. It is a vile thing, he thought, to marry beneath one's station, no matter how great the love or how tormenting the urge to consummate that love. And it has not been worth the pain. My beautiful, queenly Elizabeth is as pinched a spinster as her sister Mary. I have one sickly, womanish boy and four wretched girls. One in the eye for me, Mrs Bennet! May the devil take you and all your glorious daughters, the price has been too high.

Having but five miles to cover, the Darcy coach-and-six pulled into the courtyard of the Crown and Garter before the Bingley contingent; Bingley Hall was twenty-five miles away. Hands tucked warmly in a muff, Elizabeth settled in the private parlour to wait until the rendezvous was completed.

Her only son, head buried in a volume of Gibbon's *Decline*, used his left hand to grope for a chair seat without once lifting his gaze from the print. Light reading, he had explained to her with his sweet smile. Nature had given him her own fine features and a colouring more chestnut than gold; the lashes of his downcast lids were dark like his father's, as were the soft brows above.

At least his health had improved, now that Fitz had yielded to the inevitable and abandoned his remorseless campaign to turn Charlie into a satisfactory son. Oh, the chills that had followed some bruising ride in bad weather! The fevers that had laid him low for weeks after shooting parties or expeditions to London! None of it had deflected Charlie from his scholarly bent, transformed him into a suitable son for Darcy of Pemberley.

"You must stop, Fitz," she had said a year ago, dreading the icy hauteur sure to follow, yet determined to be heard. "I am Charlie's mother, and I have given you the direction of his childhood without speaking my mind. Now I must. You cannot throw Charlie to the wolves of a cavalry regiment, however desirable it may be to give the noble son and heir a few years in the army as polish — *polish*? Pah! That life would kill him. His sole ambition is to go to Oxford and read Classics, and he must be permitted to have his way. And do not say that you loathed Cambridge so much you bought yourself a pair of colours in a hussar regiment! *Your* father was dead, so I have no idea what he might have thought of your conduct. All I know is what suits Charlie."

The icy hauteur had indeed descended, had wrought Fitz's face into iron, but his black eyes, gazing straight into hers, held more exhaustion than anger.

"I concede your point," he said, tones harsh. "Our son is an effeminate weakling, fit only for Academia or the Church, and I would rather a don than a Darcy bishop, so we will hear no more of that. Send him to Oxford, by all means."

A cruel disappointment to him, she knew. This precious boy had been their first-born, but after him came nought save girls. The Bennet Curse, Fitz called it. Georgie, Susie, Anne and Cathy had arrived at two-year intervals, a source of indifference to their father, who neither saw them nor was interested in them. He had done his best to alter Charlie's character, but even the might and power of Darcy of Pemberley had not been able to do that. After which, nothing.

Cathy was now ten years old and would be the last, for Fitz had withdrawn from his wife's life as well as her bed. He was already a Member of Parliament, a Tory in Tory country, but after Cathy's birth he took a ministry and moved to the front benches. A ploy that freed him from her, with its long absences in London, its eminently excusable reasons to be far from her side. Not that she lost her usefulness; whenever Fitz needed her to further his political career, she was commanded, no matter how distasteful she found London's high society.

* * *

Lydia arrived first, stumbling into the parlour with a scowl for that strange man, Edward Skinner, as he gave her a hard push. Elizabeth's heart sank at the sight of her youngest sister's face, so lined, sallow, bloated. Her figure had grown quite shapeless, a sack of meal corsetted into a semblance of femininity, crepey creases at the tops of her upthrust breasts revealing that, when the whalebones were removed, they sagged like under-filled pillows pinned on a line. A vulgar hat foaming with ostrich plumes, a thin muslin gown unsuited for this weather or a long journey, flimsy satin slippers stained and muddy — oh, Lydia! The once beautiful flaxen hair had not been washed in months, its curls greenish-greasy, and the wide blue eyes, so like her mother's, were smeared with some substance designed for darkening lashes. They looked as if she had been beaten, though George Wickham had not been in England for four years, so she was at least spared that — unless someone else was beating her.

Down went Charlie's book; he moved to his aunt's side so quickly that Elizabeth was excluded, took her hands in his and chafed them as he led her to a chair by the fire.

"Here, Aunt Lydia, warm yourself," he said tenderly. "I know that Mama has brought you warmer wear."

"Black, I suppose," said Lydia, giving her older sister a glare. "Lord, such a dreadful colour! But needs must, if Mama is dead. Fancy that! I had not thought her frail. Oh, why did George have to be sent to America? I *need* him!" She spied the landlord in the doorway, and brightened. "Trenton, a mug of ale, if you please. That frightful man kidnapped me on an empty stomach. Ale, bread-and-butter, some cheese — now!"

But before Trenton could obey, Ned came back with a big cup of coffee and put it down in front of her. A maid followed him bearing a tray of coffee and refreshments enough for all.

"No ale," Ned said curtly, dipped his head to Mrs Darcy and Mr Charlie, and went to report to Fitz in the taproom.

It had been a regular circus, getting Mrs Wickham away. She was on her third bottle, and the callow pup she had found to warm her bed had taken one look at Ned Skinner, then decamped. Assisted by the terrified landlord of the Plough and Stars and his grim-faced wife, Ned had proceeded to force several doses of mustard-and-water down Lydia's throat. Up came the wine bit by bit; only when he was sure no more of it was still to come did Ned cease his ruthless ministrations. The landlady had packed two small boxes of belongings — no decent protection from the cold in it, she said, just this ratty wrap. Lydia's luggage strapped where the tiger would have perched, Ned had tossed his weeping, shrieking captive into the small seat and hustled Mr Darcy's racing curricle out into the cruel night with scant regard for his passenger.

Dear Charlie! Somehow he persuaded Lydia to eat a bowl of porridge and some bread, convinced her that coffee was just what she wanted; bearing a somewhat restored Lydia on her arm, Elizabeth went to the bedroom wherein Mrs Trenton had laid out fresh drawers and camisole, petticoats, a plain black wool dress bearing a frill hastily tacked on at Pemberley to make it long enough for Lydia, the taller of Elizabeth by half a head.

"That disgusting man!" Lydia cried, standing while Mrs Trenton and Elizabeth stripped her, washed her as best they could; she stank of wine, vomit, dirt and neglect. "He dosed me to make me puke my guts out just as if I were one of his whores!"

"Mama is dead, Lydia," Elizabeth reminded her, giving the filthy corsets to Mrs Trenton between two fastidious fingers, and nodding that she could manage alone now. "Do you hear me? Mama died peacefully in her sleep."

"Well, I wish she could have chosen a better time!" The bloodshot eyes widened, curiously like two glass marbles in that scrubbed, pallid face. "How she used to favour me above the rest of you! I could always bewitch her."

"Do you not grieve?"

"Oh, I suppose I must, but it is near twenty years since I last saw her, after all, and I was but a mere sixteen."

"One forgets," said Elizabeth, sighing, and deliberately shutting out the knowledge that, upon Papa's death, Fitz had severed all the ties that bound the sisters, made it impossible for them to see each other unless he approved. Not a difficult task; they were all dependent upon him in one way or another. In Lydia's case, it had been money. "You have spent more of your life with George Wickham than with Mama and Papa."

"No, I have not!" snapped Lydia, glowering at the dress. "First he was in the Peninsula, now he is in America. I am an army wife, not even allowed to follow the drum. Oh, but fancy! Mama gone! It beats all understanding. This is a dreadful dress, Lizzie, I must say. *Long sleeves!* Must it be buttoned so high? And without my stays, my bosoms are around my waist!"

"You will catch cold, Lydia. Shelby Manor lies at least three days' away, and while Fitz will ensure that the coach is as warm as possible, it is seventy years old, full of draughts."

She gave Lydia a muff, made sure the black cap beneath the severe bonnet was tucked over her sister's ears, and took her back to the parlour.

Jane and Charles Bingley had come in their absence, having set out from Bingley Hall four hours earlier. Charlie had gone back to Gibbon; Bingley and Darcy stood by the fireplace in stern conversation, and Jane sat slumped at the table, handkerchief pressed to her eyes. *How far apart we have drifted, that even in this unhappy hour we are separated.*

"My dearest Jane!" Elizabeth went to hug her.

Jane threw herself into those welcoming arms, wept afresh. What she was saying was unintelligible; it would be days before her tender feelings were settled enough to permit lucid speech, Elizabeth knew.

As if he owned some extra sense, Charlie put his book down and went immediately to Lydia, guiding her to a chair with many compliments about how much black suited her, and gave her no opportunity to snatch a mug of ale from the table where a jug of it had appeared to sustain the men. A snap of Fitz's fingers, and Trenton whisked the jug away.

"Pater?" Charlie asked.

"Yes?"

"May I travel in Uncle Charles's coach with Aunt Lydia? Mama would be more comfortable with Aunt Jane for company."

"Yes," Darcy said brusquely. "Charles, we must go."

"Is Ned Skinner to ride with us?" Charles Bingley asked.

"No, he has other business. You and I, Charles, will be able to avail ourselves of an occasional gallop. The party will put up at the Three Feathers in Derby, but you and I will have no trouble reaching my hunting box. We can rejoin the ladies in Leicester tomorrow night."

Bingley turned to look at Jane, his face betraying his anxiety, but he was too used to following Fitz's lead to raise any objections to leaving Jane in Elizabeth's hands. There was no denying that griefstricken ladies in need of succour were better served by sisters than husbands. Then he cheered up; Fitz's Leicestershire hunting box was just the ticket to break the monotony of a two-hundred-mile journey to Shelby Manor.

Only her sisters and their husbands could be accommodated at Shelby Manor; the rest of the extended family would be at the Blue Boar and Hertford's other good inns, Mary knew. Not that she had any say in such matters. Fitz would, as always, be arranging everything, just as he communicated with the various persons who saw to the running of Shelby Manor and even such minor things as the payment of her own pin-money. Fitzwilliam Darcy, the centre of every web he encountered.

It had been Fitz who had ensured that his mother-in-law would be extremely comfortably isolated far from all her daughters save Mary, the sacrificial goat; somehow people did not care to earn his displeasure even when, like Kitty, they had little to do with him. Poor Mama used to pine to see Lydia, but never had so much as once, and Kitty's very cursory visits ceased long ago. Only Elizabeth and Jane had continued to come during the last ten years, but Jane's constant delicate condition usually forbade her going so far. Be that as it may, in June Elizabeth always descended on Shelby Manor to take her mother to Bath for a holiday. A holiday, Mary was well aware, designed chiefly to give her, Mary, a holiday from Mama. And oh, what a holiday it always was! For Lizzie brought Charlie with her and left him to keep Mary company. No one dreamed the mischief she and Charlie got into: the games they played, the places they went, the things they did. Definitely not the sort of things commonly associated with maiden aunts shepherding nephews!

Coming from London, Kitty arrived the day after Mama's death, tearful but fairly composed. She had done most of her weeping en route, soothed and commiserated by Miss Almeria Finchley, her indispensable lady's companion, who would have to have a truckle-bed in Kitty's room, Mary decided.

"Kitty will not like it, but she will have to lump it," said Mary to Mrs Jenkins.

To Kitty's face Mary tried to be more tactful. "I declare, Kitty, you are more elegant than ever," she said over tea.

Knowing this to be the truth, Lady Menadew preened. "It is mostly a knack," she confided. "Dear Menadew was top-of-the-trees himself, and enjoyed my taking the way I did. Mind you, Mary my love, it was a great help to have stayed at Pemberley with Lizzie for two years before Louisa Hurst brought me out. Lord, that fusty girl of hers!" Kitty giggled. "The chagrin when it was I made the excellent marriage!"

"Wasn't Menadew considered past it?" Mary asked, her blunt speech unimproved by seventeen years of caring for Mama.

"Well, yes, in years perhaps, but not in any other respect. I took his eye, he said, because I was clay just crying out to be a diamond of the first water. A delightful man, Menadew! Exactly the right kind of husband."

"So I imagine."

"Though," Kitty said, pursuing this theme, "he expired at precisely the proper moment. I was turned out in the first stare and he was beginning to be bored."

"Didn't love enter into it?" Mary asked, never before having been in her sister's company alone for long enough to satisfy her curiosity.

"Lord, no! The wedded state was very pleasant, but Menadew was my master. I obeyed his every command. Or whim. Whereas life as a widow has been unadulterated bliss. No commands or whims. Almeria Finchley doesn't plague me, and I have the entrée to all the best houses as well as a large income." She extended one slender arm to display the cunning knots of jet beads ruching its long sleeve. "Madame Belléme was able to send this around before I left Curzon Street, together with three other equally delectable mourning gowns. Warm, but in the height of fashion." Her blue eyes, still moist from her last bout of tears, lit up. "I fear only Georgiana as a rival. Lizzie and Jane are quite frumpish, you know."

"Jane I will grant you, Kitty, but Lizzie? One hears she is quite the jewel of Westminster."

Kitty sniffed. "*Westminster!* And not even the Lords, to boot! The Commons — pah! 'Tis no great thing to queen it over a bundle of dreary MPs, I assure you. Fitz likes her weighed down with diamonds and rubies, brocades and velvets. They have a certain magnificence, but they are not fashionable." Kitty eyed Mary speculatively. "Now that Lizzie's amazing apothecary has cured your suppurating spots and her dentist has dealt with your tooth, Mary, you have a distinct look of Elizabeth. A pity the improvements came too late to find you your own Lord Menadew."

"The prospect of lifelong spinsterhood has never dismayed me, and a face is a face," said Mary, unimpressed. "To be free of my aches and ailments is a blessing, but the rest is nothing."

"My dear Mary," said Kitty, looking shocked, "it is a *good* thing that your looks have improved so, now that Mama is dead. You may not wish for marriage, but it is far more comfortable than the alternative. Unless you wish to exist at the beck and call of other people, which is what will happen if you move to Pemberley or Bingley Hall. No doubt Fitz will make some sort of provision for you, but I doubt it will extend to luxuries like a lady's companion and a smart carriage. Fitz is a cold man."

"Interesting," said Mary, offering the cake. "Your reading of his character is much the same as mine. He dispenses his fortune according to necessity. Charity is a word in a lexicon to him, nothing more. Most of the stupefying amount he has spent upon us Bennets is to alleviate his own embarrassments, from George Wickham to Mama. Now that Mama is gone I doubt he will be as generous to me. Especially," she added, the thought popping into her unruly mind, "if my face no longer brands me an appropriate maiden aunt."

"I know Sir Peter Cameron is hanging out for a wife," said Kitty, "and I do think he would suit you — in no need of a fat dowry, bookish and kind."

"Do not even entertain the idea! Though I cannot say I am looking forward to Pemberley or Bingley Hall. Lizzie cries a lot, Charlie tells me — she and Fitz see little of each other since he went on the front benches, and when they are together, he is cold to her."

"Dear Charlie!" Kitty exclaimed.

"I echo that."

"Fitz does not care for him," Kitty said with rare insight. "He is too soft."

"I would rather say that Fitz is too hard!" snapped Mary. "A kinder, more thoughtful young man than Charlie does not exist."

"Yes, sister, I agree, but gentlemen are peculiar about their sons. Much and all as they deplore over-indulgence in wine, dice, cards and loose women, at heart they think of such pursuits as wild oats, sure to pass. Besides which, that rat of a female Caroline Bingley slanders Charlie, who she early divined was Fitz's Achilles heel."

Time to change the subject, thought Mary. It did not do to mingle her sense of loss with a far more important grief, her love for Charlie. "We may expect the Collinses tomorrow."

"Oh, Lord!" Kitty groaned, then chuckled. "Do you remember how you mooned over that dreadful man? You really were a pathetic creature in those days, Mary. What happened to change you? Or are you still sighing for Mr Collins?"

"Not I! Time and too little to do cured me. There are only so many years one can fritter away on inappropriate desires, and after Charlie came to stay that first time, I began to see the error of my ways. Or at least," Mary admitted honestly, "Charlie showed me. All he did was ask me why I had no thoughts of my own, and wonder at it. Ten years old! He made me promise to give up reading Christian books, as he called them, in favour of great thoughts. The kind of thoughts, he said, that would prick my mind into working. Even then he was quite godless, you know. When Mr and Mrs Collins came to call, he *pitied* them. Mr Collins for his crassness and stupidity, Charlotte for her determination to make Mr Collins seem more tolerable." Lizzie's smile lit Mary's face — warm, loving, amused. "Yes, Kitty, you have Charlie to thank for what you see today, even to the spots and the tooth. It was he who asked his Mama what could be done about them."

"Then I wish I knew him better than I do." Kitty looked mischievous. "Did he perhaps remark on your singing?"

That provoked an outright laugh. "He did. But the thing about Charlie is that he never leaves one bereft. Having told me that I did not sing, I screeched, and advised me to leave song to nightingales, he spent a full day assuring me that I played pianoforte as splendidly as Herr Beethoven."

"Who is that?" asked Kitty, wrinkling her brow.

"A German man. Charlie heard him in Vienna when Fitz was there trying to restrain Bonaparte. I will play you some of his simpler pieces. Charlie never fails to send me a parcel of new music for my birthday."

"Charlie, Charlie, Charlie! You love him very much."

"To distraction," Mary said. "You see, Kitty, he has been so kind to me over the years. His visits lit up my life."

"When you speak in that tone, I confess I am a trifle envious. Dearest Mary, you *have* changed."

"Not in all respects, sister. I still tend to say what I am thinking. Especially to Mr Collins." She huffed. "When I thought him looking for a *beautiful* wife I was able to excuse his choosing inappropriate females like Jane and Lizzie, but when he asked for Charlotte Lucas, the scales began to fall from mine eyes. As plain and unappetising as week-old pound cake is Charlotte. I began to see that he was not a worthy recipient of my affections."

"I do not pretend to have your depth of intellect, Mary," said Kitty in a musing voice, "but I have often wondered at God's goodness to some of His less inspiring creations. By rights Mr Collins ought to have barely scraped along, a penurious clergyman, yet he always prospers through no merit of his own."

"Oh, it was not easy for him between Lizzie's marriage to Fitz and Papa's death, when he inherited Longbourn. Lady Catherine de Bourgh never forgave him — quite what for, I do not know."

"I do. Had he been to Lizzie's liking, she would have wed him instead of stealing Fitz from Anne de Bourgh," said Kitty.

"Well, her ladyship's long dead, and her daughter with her," said Mary on a sigh.

"And that is more evidence of God's mysteriousness!"

"What *are* you wittering about, Kitty?"

"The attack of influenza that carried off both de Bourghs so quickly after Colonel Fitzwilliam's marriage to Anne! Or should I say, General Fitzwilliam? He fell heir to Rosings and that huge fortune in time to be respectably widowed before someone else took dear Georgiana's fancy."

"Huh!" Mary emitted a snort of amusement. "Georgiana had no intention of settling for anyone except the Colonel — or the General, if you prefer. Though I cannot approve of unions between first cousins. Their eldest girl is so stigmatised that they have had to shut her away," said Mary.

"The Bladon blood, dear. Lady Catherine, Lady Anne, and Lady Maria. Sisters all."

"They married very rich men," said Mary.

"And rightly so! They were the daughters of a duke," Kitty protested. "Their papa was very high in the instep — the merest whiff of Trade was enough to kill the old gentleman. That was the General's father — turned out to have made his fortune in cotton and slaves."

"How ridiculous you are, Kitty! Is your life nought but gossip and gallivanting?"

"Probably." The fire was dying; Kitty pulled the bell cord for Jenkins. "Do you really expect the Collinses to travel twelve miles to condole?"

"It is inevitable. Mr Collins can scent a tragedy or a scandal a hundred miles away, so what are twelve? Lady Lucas will come with them, and we can expect to have Aunt Phillips here constantly. Only an attack of her lumbago prevented her coming today, but a good cry will cure it."

"By the way, Mary, must Almeria sleep in my room? She has a tendency to snore, and I know there is a nice bedroom at one end of the attic. She is a lady, not an abigail."

"I am keeping the attic room for Charlie."

"Oh! Will he come?"

"Undoubtedly," said Mary.

It was not custom for women to attend funerals, either in the church or at the graveside, but Fitzwilliam Darcy had decreed that this social rule should be ignored on the occasion of Mrs Bennet's obsequies. With no sons among her offspring and five daughters, attendance would be far too thin unless the rule were relaxed. So notification had gone out to the extended family that the ladies would be in attendance at church and graveside, despite the objections of persons like the Reverend Mr Collins, whose nose was rather out of joint because he would not be officiating. Thus Jane's sisters-in-law, Mrs Louisa Hurst and Miss Caroline Bingley, came down from London to be present, while Mrs Bennet's cronies, her sister Mrs Phillips, and her friends Lady Lucas and Mrs Long, made the shorter journey from Meryton to attend.

And there they are together at last, the five Bennet girls, thought Caroline Bingley after the funeral service was over and before the procession to the grave began.

Jane, Elizabeth, Mary, Kitty and Lydia ... Twenty years of living in limbo, thanks to them and their fabled beauty. Of course it had faded, dimmed — but so had her own considerable good looks. Jane and Elizabeth had embarked upon the stormy seas of their forties; but then she, Caroline, had already survived those tempests and looked now at her fearsome fifties. As did Fitz, they were much the same age.

Jane looked as if God had grafted the head of a twenty-three-year-old upon the body of a forty-three-year-old. Her face, with its tranquil honey-coloured eyes, rich unlined skin, exquisitely delicate features, was surrounded by a mass of honey-gold hair. Alas, twelve pregnancies had taken their toll of her sylphlike figure, though she had not grown fat; merely thickened in the waist and dropped in the bosom. In her, the Bennet type was decided; all five of them were some shade of fair, no surprise considering their fair parents.

Elizabeth and Mary had the best Bennet hair, thick, waving, as much red as gold, though it could be called neither; to herself, Miss Bingley called it ginger. Their skins inclined to ivory and their large, slightly sleepy eyes were a grey that could turn to purple. Of course Elizabeth's features were not as perfect as Jane's — her mouth was too wide, too full in the lips — but for some reason that still eluded Miss Bingley, men found her more alluring. Her excellent figure was swathed in black fox, whereas Mary wore dismally plain black serge, a shocking bonnet and even worse pelisse. Caroline was fascinated by her, for she had not seen Mary in seventeen years, an interval of time that had transformed Mary into Elizabeth's equal. Or she would have been, had her naturally generous mouth not retained its prim severity: it alone proclaimed the spinster. Did she still have that ugly overlapping tooth?

Kitty she knew very well. Lady Menadew of the wheaten hair and cornflower-blue eyes, so elegant and fashionable that she enjoyed a sublime widowhood. As good natured as she was frivolous, Kitty looked twenty-six, not thirty-six. Ah, how brother Charles had gulled them! Curse Desmond Hurst! When his port bill had outrun his pocket, he had applied to Charles for assistance. Charles had agreed to pay, on one condition: that Louisa gave Kitty Bennet a London season. After all, Charles had said reasonably, Louisa was bringing out her own daughter, so why not two? Caught, Desmond Hurst had traded the port bill (and many other bills) for Kitty's London season. But whoever would have believed that the minx would walk off with Lord Menadew? Not one of the Marriage Mart's biggest prizes, but extremely eligible despite his advanced years. While dearest Posy (as Letitia was called) did not catch a husband at all, and went into a long decline — fainting fits, vapours, starvation.

Lydia was another matter. It was she who looked well into her forties, not Jane. What age was she? Thirty-four. Caroline could well imagine the shifts her family must have resorted to in order to stop Mrs Wickham drowning herself in a bottle. Had they not endured the same with Mr Hurst? Who had succumbed to an apoplexy eight years ago, enabling Caroline to quit Charles's houses in favour of the Hurst residence in Brook Street, there to dwell with Louisa and Posy, and indulge more freely in her favourite pastime — pulling Elizabeth Darcy and her son to pieces.

She swallowed the lump in her throat as Fitz and Charles emerged from the church, their mother-in-law's small coffin balanced on their shoulders, with the diminutive Mr Collins and Henry Lucas on its back end; it gave the polished rosewood box an interesting but not precarious tilt. Oh, Fitz, Fitz! Why did you fall in love with her, marry her? I would have given you *real* sons, not a sole specimen as ludicrous as Charlie. A devoté of Socratic love, everyone is convinced of it. Why? Because the breathtaking degree of his beauty makes him look the sort, and I spread the calumny as a truth my intimacy with that family makes eminently believable. To brand the son with an affliction so far from his father's heart is a way of punishing Fitz for not marrying me. You would think Fitz would see through the ploy, always starting, as it does, with something I have said. But no. Fitz believes *me*, not Charlie.

Her long nose twitched, for it had picked up nuances of trouble on this unwelcome trip to bury the empty-headed old besom. All had not been well in the Darcy ménage for a while, but the mood was increasing — markedly so. Fitz's air of aloof hauteur had grown back; during the early years of his marriage it had all but disappeared, though some instinct told her he was not the blissful man he had been at the altar. Hopeful, perhaps. Still aspiring to conquer — what? Caroline Bingley did not know, beyond her conviction that Fitz's passion for Elizabeth had not resulted in true happiness.

Down through the graveyard now, the black-clad mourners threading between the haphazard monuments, old as the Crusades, new as still-sinking soil. Miss Bingley and Mrs Hurst walked with Georgiana and General Hugh Fitzwilliam, not in the forefront of the congregation, but somewhere at its middle. Goodbye, Mrs Bennet! The silliest woman ever born.

Standing well back, Caroline let her gaze roam until it encountered Mary's; there it stopped, startled. The violet orbs of the maiden sister rested in derision upon her face, as if they and the apparatus behind them *knew* what she was thinking. What had happened to those eyes, now so intelligent, expressive, alert? She was leaning on Charlie, who held her hand: an odd pair. Something about them hinted at a divorcement from this maudlin parody, as if their persons stood there while their spirits cruised among other worlds.

Do not be ridiculous, Caroline! she told herself, and inched her rump onto the edge of a convenient stone; that frightful mushroom, the Reverend Mr Collins, was preparing to add a few words of his own to an already overly long service. By the time that Caroline had unobtrusively adjusted her weight in some relief, Mary and Charlie had returned to who they actually were. Yes, Caroline, a ridiculous notion. As well that Louisa and I bespoke the carriage for immediately after the funeral; to have to exchange civilities with all five Bennet sisters at Shelby Manor is not an enthralling prospect. If our coachman springs the horses, we can be back in London by nightfall. But if I am invited to Pemberley for this summer's house party, I shall go. With Louisa, of course.

TWO

All save the Pemberley party had gone before the beginning of December, anxious to be home in plenty of time for a Christmas spent with children and loved ones. This was especially true of Jane, who loathed being away from Bingley Hall for as many as one night, except for visits to Pemberley, fairly close at hand.

"She is increasing yet again," said Elizabeth to Mary with a sigh.

"I know I am not supposed to be aware of such things, Lizzie, but can't *someone* tell brother Charles to plug it with a cork?"

The crimson surged into Elizabeth's face; she put both her hands to her cheeks and gaped at her spinster sister. "*Mary!* How — how — oh, how do you know about — about — and how can you be so indelicate?"

"I know because I have read every book in this library, and I am tired of delicacy about subjects that lie so close to our female fates!" said Mary with a snap. "Lizzie, surely you can see that these endless pregnancies are killing poor Jane? Why, brood mares have a better life! Eight living children and four either lost at five months or stillborn! And the tally would be larger if Charles did not sail to the West Indies for a year every so often. If she is not prolapsed, she ought to be. Has it escaped your notice that those she has miscarried or borne dead have all been *after* the living ones? She is worn out!"

"Dearest Mary, you must not speak so crudely! Truly it is the height of impropriety!"

"Rubbish. No one is here save you and me, and you are my most beloved sister. If we cannot be frank, what is the world coming to? It seems to me that no one cares about a woman's health or welfare. If Charles does not find a way to have his pleasure without causing Jane to increase so frequently, then perhaps he should take a mistress. Immoral women do not seem to increase." Mary looked brightly interested. "I ought to find some man's mistress and ask her how she avoids babies."

Speech utterly failed Elizabeth, so mortified and at a loss that she could do nothing but stare at this apparition, no more her young sister than some female out of the hedgerows. Was there perhaps some gross peculiarity in Mama's ancestry that had suddenly come out in Mary? *Plug it with a cork!* Then from a time far away and a place long gone, her sense of humour came to Elizabeth's rescue; she burst into laughter, laughed until tears streamed down her face.

"Oh, Mary, I do not even begin to know you!" she said

when she was able. "Pray assure me that you do not say such things in other company!"

"I do not," said Mary with an impenitent grin. "I just think them. And confess it, Lizzie, don't you think the same?"

"Yes, of course I do. I love Jane with all my heart, and it grieves me to see her health declining for no better reason than the lack of a cork." Her lips quivered. "Charles Bingley is the dearest man, but, like all men, selfish. It is not even that he is trying for a son — they have seven already."

"Odd, is it not? You bearing girls, Jane boys."

What *had* happened to Mary? Where was the distressingly narrow and imperceptive girl of Longbourn days? Could people change so much? Or was this dangerous emancipation from female constrictions always there? What had inspired her to sing when she could neither hold a note nor keep a tune nor regulate the volume of her voice? Why had she pined for Mr Collins, surely the most unworthy object of any woman's love ever put upon the earth? Questions to which Elizabeth could find no answers. Except that now she could better understand Charlie's affection for his Aunt Mary.

A huge guilt washed over her; she, no less than Fitz, had thoughtlessly sentenced Mary to the caretaking of Mama, a task that, given Mama's age, could well have lasted another seventeen years. They had all expected it would last a minimum of thirty-four years! Which would have made Mary fifty-five when it ended — oh, thank God it had come to an end now, while Mary had some hope of carving a life for herself!

Perhaps, she thought, it is not wise to isolate young women as Mary had been isolated. That she possessed some intelligence had been generally accepted in the family, though Papa had sneered at its direction, between the books of sermons and the gloomily moral works she had chosen to read as a girl. But had that been forced upon Mary? Elizabeth wondered. Would Papa have given her a free rein in his own library? No, he would not. And Mary had trotted out her pedantic observations upon life because she had no other way of gaining attention from the rest of us. Maybe the singing was a way to gain our attention too.

For a long time now I have looked back upon my childhood and girlhood at Longbourn as the happiest years of my life; we were so close, so merry, so *secure*. Because of the last, that security, we forgave Mama her idiocies and Papa his sarcastic attitude. But Jane and I shone the brightest, and were well aware of it. The Bennet sisters were layered: Jane and I considered the most beautiful and promising; Kitty and Lydia empty-headed jesters; and Mary — the middle child — neither one thing nor the other. I can see shades of that Mary in this one; she is still a merciless critic of frailties, still contemptuous of material things. But oh, how she has changed!

"What do you remember of our years at Longbourn?" Elizabeth asked, seeking answers.

"Feeling a misfit, chiefly," said Mary.

"Oh, a misfit! How awful! Were you at all happy?"

"I suppose so. Certainly I did not repine. I think I was absorbed in a goodness I could not see in you or Jane, or in Kitty and Lydia. No, do not look alarmed! I am not condemning any of you, but rather myself. I thought you and Jane were obsessed with making rich marriages, while Kitty and Lydia were too undisciplined, too wild. I modelled my own conduct on the books I read — how dreadfully prosaic I must have been! Not to mention boring, for the books I read were boring."

"Yes, you were prosaic and boring, though it is only now that I understand why. We left you no other recourse, the four of us."

"The pustules and the tooth did not help, I confess. I saw them as a punishment, yet I had no idea what my crime had been."

"No crime, Mary. Just unfortunate afflictions."

"It is you I have to thank for ridding me of them. Who could ever have believed that something as banal as a small teaspoon of sulphur every two days would cure the spots, and that extraction of the tooth would allow the others to grow into place perfectly?" She got up from the breakfast table, smiling. "Where can the gentlemen be? I had thought Fitz wanted to make an early start."

"Charlie's fault. He went ratting with Jem Jenkins, and Fitz has gone to find him."

The queries swarmed inside Mary's head, all of them crying for satisfaction. Ask, and ye shall know, she thought.

"What kind of man is Fitz?"

Elizabeth blinked at such bluntness. "After nineteen years of marriage, sister, I confess I do not know. He has such — such exalted ideas of who and what the Darcys are. Perhaps that is

35

inevitable in a family that can trace itself back to the Conquest and before. Though I have sometimes wondered why, given this centuries-old pre-eminence, there has never been a title."

"Pride, I expect," said Mary. "You are not happy."

"I had thought to be, but entering the married state is to commence a voyage into the unknown. I suppose I thought that, given Fitz's love for me, we would settle to an idyllic life at Pemberley, our children around us. But I was not aware of Fitz's zeal, his restlessness, his ambitions. His secrets. There are elements in his nature that elude me." She shivered. "And I am not sure I wish to know what those elements are."

"It grieves me to see you so blighted, Lizzie, but I am glad we have had this opportunity to talk. Is there a definite element to Fitz that worries you most?"

"Ned Skinner, I would have to answer. That is a very strange friendship."

Mary frowned. "Who is Ned Skinner?"

"If you had come to Pemberley, you would know. He is Fitz's general manager, overseer, factotum. Not his steward — Matthew Spottiswoode is steward. Ned travels a lot for Fitz, but what he does exactly, I do not know. He lives in a beautiful cottage on the estate, has servants of his own, and his own stables."

"You called it a friendship."

"It is, a very close one. That is the mystery. For Ned is not Fitz's equal in society, which under ordinary circumstances would disbar him from friendship. Yet they are close."

"Is he a gentleman?"

"He speaks like one, yet is not one."

"Why have you never mentioned him?"

"I suppose the subject has never come up. I have not had any opportunity in the past to speak with you so openly."

"Yes, I know. Mama was always there, or Charlie. How long has Fitz been close with this Ned Skinner?"

"Oh, since before he married me. I remember him as a young man lurking in the background, looking at Fitz with adoration. He is a little younger than I —"

Elizabeth cut off whatever else she might have been going to say when Fitz walked in, bringing a rush of cold air with him. Still a fine-looking man, Mary thought, even at fifty. Everything a young, sheltered female could have wanted in a husband, from circumstances to presence. Yet she remembered Jane's saying once, with a sigh, that Lizzie had not loved him as she, Jane, loved her dear Mr Bingley. A true Jane statement, holding no condemnation or disapproval; just something about Lizzie's setting eyes on the glories of Pemberley and thinking much better of Mr Darcy thereafter. When he had renewed his addresses in the wake of Lydia's scandalous elopement, Lizzie had accepted him.

"Mary, a word before I go," Darcy said, then turned to his wife. "Are you ready, my dear?"

"Yes. Did you find Charlie?"

"Naturally. Encumbered with a dozen rats."

Elizabeth laughed. "I hope he washes his hands. I want no fleas in the coach."

"He has gone to do so. After you, my dear Mary." And he stood aside for her with his customary chill courtesy, thence to follow her to the library, a genuine one stocked with thousands of books.

"Sit down," he said, going to the business side of the desk with the calm authority of one whose purse had paid for it and all the rest of Shelby Manor. Knees suddenly weak, Mary sank onto the client's chair and faced him, chin up. Just because her knees gave way did not mean her backbone would!

For a moment Fitz said nothing more, simply gazed at her with a trace of puzzlement. Then, "How like Elizabeth you have become. It was the pustules, of course. Fortunate that they did not pock your skin." The physical niceties over, he embarked upon her other deficiencies. "I never heard a worse voice, nor one more prone to give vent in song. My hair still stands on end at the memory."

"You should have informed me of its lack, brother."

"It was not my place." He folded his hands together in front of him, their pose indicating their owner's indifference. "So, Mary, your duty is done." The cold black eyes bored into hers, gradually taking on a tinge of uncertainty when she neither withered nor shrank. "At the time that your father died, Charles Bingley and I decided that you should be adequately recompensed for your willingness to stay with your mother. Your father was not in a position to leave you anything, preferring to bequeath his unentailed capital to Lydia, in greater need. You, he understood, would put Charles Bingley and me in your debt by caring for your mother at a distance remote from the North."

"Insulate you from her idiocies, you mean," said Mary.

He looked taken aback, then shrugged. "Quite so. For which service, we have funded you to the tune of five hundred pounds per year. Eight and a half thousand pounds in all."

"It is certainly true that lady's companions are not so well paid as I have been," said Mary tonelessly.

"However, Shelby Manor must now be sold in the same manner as it was bought — whole and entire, including the books in the library and the services of the Jenkins family. A buyer has been found already, not least because of the Jenkinses. I must therefore uproot you, sister, for which I am very sorry."

"Lip service," she said, snorting.

A soft chuckle escaped him. "The years may not have wrought destruction upon your face or figure, but they have coated your tongue with more acid than syrup."

"For which, blame the exhaustion of a religion picked to bare white bones, and the enticements of far too much leisure. Once I had Mama properly trained — which was not difficult — the hours of my days sat upon me heavily. To change the metaphor, you might say that the creaking gate of my mind received lubrication from the contents of this excellent library, not to mention the company of your son. He has been a bonus."

"I'm glad he's good for something."

"Let us not quarrel about Charlie, though I take leave to tell you that every day you do not appreciate his quality is yet one more day proves you a fool. As to me, I, myself, what do you propose doing with them now their task is ended?"

His colour had risen under her scathing words, but he answered civilly. "You should come to us at Pemberley, or to Jane at Bingley Hall — your choice, I imagine, will depend upon whether you prefer girls or boys."

"At either place it would be an empty existence."

The corners of his mouth turned down. "Have you any kind of alternative?" he asked, sounding wary.

"With over eight thousand pounds, a measure of independence."

"Explain."

"I would prefer to live on my own."

"My dear Mary, ladies of your station cannot live alone!"

"Whyever not? At thirty-eight, I have said my last prayers, brother. Take myself an Almeria Finchley? Pah!"

"You don't look your thirty-eight years, and you know it. Shelby Manor has sufficient mirrors to show you. Is it Lady Menadew you wish to join?"

"*Kitty?* I would kill her in a month, and she me!"

"Georgiana and the General have housed Mrs Jenkinson ever since Anne de Bourgh died. She would be pleased to keep you company in — what? A commodious cottage, perhaps?"

"Mrs Jenkinson sniffles and sighs. Her tic douloureux is at its worst in winter, when it is harder to elude a companion."

"Then some other suitable female! You *cannot* live alone."

"No female, suitable or unsuitable, from any source."

"What *do* you want?" he demanded, exasperated.

"I want to be useful. Just that. To have a purpose. I want self-esteem of the proper kind. I want to stand back and look at something I have done with pride and a sense of accomplishment."

"Believe me, Mary, you have been useful, and will be useful again — at Pemberley or Bingley Hall."

"No," she said, meaning it.

"Be sensible, woman!"

"When I was a girl, I had no sense. It was not inculcated in me because I had no example to follow, including my parents as well as my sisters. Even Elizabeth, who was the cleverest, had no sense. She did not need sense. She was charming, witty, and full of sensibility. But to have sensibility is not to have sense," said Mary, fairly launched. "Nowadays, brother Fitz, I have so much sense that you cannot bully or cow me. To have sense is to know what one wants from life, and I want to have a purpose. Though I admit," she ended rather pensively, "that I am not quite sure yet what my purpose will be. What it will *not* be is to live with either Lizzie or Jane. I would be underfoot and a nuisance."

He gave up. "You have a month," he said, getting to his feet. "The bill of sale for Shelby Manor will be signed then, and your future must be decided. Banish all thought of living alone! I will not permit it."

"What gives you the right to dictate to me?" she asked, spots of colour burning in her cheeks, her eyes glowing purple.

"The right of a brother-in-law, the right of your senior in years, and the right of a man owning *sense*. My public position as a Minister of the Crown, if not my private standing as a Darcy of Pemberley, makes it impossible for me to tolerate eccentric or otherwise-crazed relatives."

"What will eight and a half thousand pounds buy me?" she countered.

"A dwelling I will happily find you, provided that you live in it with proper decorum and propriety. In the country rather than the city — Derbyshire or Cheshire."

"Hah! Where you can keep an eye on your eccentric or otherwise-crazed sister-in-law! I thank you, no. Is the eight and a half thousand pounds mine, or is it put in trust for me? I want a direct answer, for I will find out the truth anyway!"

"The money is yours, safely invested in the four-percents. Kept invested, it will give you an income of about three hundred and fifty pounds a year," Fitz said, having no idea how to deal with this termagant. On the outside she was so like Elizabeth — did that mean Elizabeth harboured a termagant too?

"Where is it lodged?"

"With Patchett, Shaw, Carlton and Wilde in Hertford."

The look in her eyes gave him fresh pause: about to go to the door, he delayed. "You will kindly allow me to conduct your business, sister," he said, voice adamant. "I forbid you to do it yourself. You are a gentleman's daughter, allied to my own family. It would not please me were you to defy me. In the new year I expect you to give me a satisfactory answer."

Apparently put in her place, she followed him out of the room and down the hall to the front door, where Lizzie and Charlie had assembled, together with Hoskins, the dour woman who maided Elizabeth with fierce possessiveness.

Mary took Charlie's face between her hands, smiling into his dark grey eyes tenderly. A beauty almost epicene, yet below it lay no feminine streak at all, if his self-absorbed father had only one-tenth of the brain the world accorded him to see it. Do not despise Charlie, Fitz! she said silently, kissing Charlie's smooth cheek. In him lies more of a man than you will ever be.

Then it was Lizzie's turn, and the party sorted itself out; Darcy astride a dappled grey horse as proud as Lucifer, Lizzie and Charlie in the coach with heated bricks, fur rugs, books, a basket of refreshments, and Hoskins. Hand up in a wave, Mary stood on the top step until the lumbering vehicle, its six gigantic horses making light of their load, disappeared around the bend all drives had, and so out of her life. For the time being, at any rate.

Mrs Jenkins was weeping; Mary eyed her in exasperation.

"No more tears, I beg you!" she said severely. "Shelby Manor will go to Sir Kenneth Appleby, I am sure of it, and Lady Appleby will prove as pleasant a mistress as he a master. Now get my own boxes from the attic and start preparing my belongings for packing. Not a crease, not a speck of dust, nothing chipped or dirty. And send Young Jenkins for the chaise. I am going out."

"To Meryton, Miss Mary?"

"Heavens, no!" cried Miss Mary, actually *laughing*! And it so soon after her mother's death! "I am going to Hertford. You may expect me home for tea. Home!" she repeated, and laughed again. "I do not have a home. How emancipating!"

Not having much to do, Mr Robert Wilde got up from his chair and moved to the window, there to gaze out at the muted bustle of the high street. No one had asked him to draw up a will or consulted him about some matter requiring the deftness of a lawyer's touch, and a natural industry had long since reduced the assortment of pleated, red-taped files to perfect readiness. As today was not market day, the view offered him more pedestrians than wagons and carts, though there went Tom Naseby in his gig, and the Misses Ramsay perched upon their plodding ponies.

There he is again! Who the devil is that fellow? asked Mr Wilde of himself. Hertford was a very small capital of a very small county, so the stranger had been noticed by all and sundry — black–avised and big as a bear was the verdict of all who saw him. Sometimes he was mounted on a massive thoroughbred whose leggy lines contradicted the rider's low appearance and garb, or else he was leaning against a wall with muscular arms folded, as now. The mien of a villain, Mr Wilde decided. His under-clerk had informed him that the fellow was staying at the Blue Boar, spoke to no one, had sufficient money to buy the best dinners, and had no inclination to avail himself of one of Hertford's few trollops. Not an ill-looking villain, nor a very old one. Yet who was he?

A chaise came down the slight hill, drawn by two pretty greys, with Young Jenkins riding postilion: the Shelby Manor equipage, a familiar sight. Miss Mary Bennet was in town to shop or visit. When it stopped in front of his door Mr Wilde was surprised; though he managed all Shelby Manor's business, he never had been permitted to meet the beautiful Miss Bennet, though he had seen her often enough. Mr Darcy had called on his way north to Pemberley — the last of several visits — but had said nothing about sending Miss Bennet to see him. Yet lo! here she was! She emerged clad in black from head to foot, her glorious hair quite hidden by a black cap and hideous bonnet. Her handsome face wore its customary composed expression as she trod up the steps to his front door, there to ply its knocker.

"Miss Bennet, sir," said his clerk, ushering her in.

By this time Mr Wilde was standing the correct distance away, his hand out to touch her fingertips, all the shake propriety allowed. "My condolences upon the death of your mother, Miss Bennet," he said. "I was *at* the funeral, of course, but did not condole in person."

"I thank you for your sentiments, Mr Wilde." She sat down stiffly. "You look a little young for a senior partner."

"I doubt there ever was a Patchett," he said with a smile, "Mr Shaw and Mr Carlton are deceased, and my father handed the practice to me a full five years ago. I do assure you, Miss Bennet, that I have served my articles and am fully conversant with a solicitor's duties."

This rather unprofessional statement did not thaw the lady's expression; clearly she was impervious to charm, of which dubious asset Mr Wilde knew he owned much. He coughed an apology.

"You are the custodian of a sum of money due to me, is that correct, sir?"

"Why — er — yes. Forgive me, Miss Bennet, while I find your particulars." And he ran a hand across a shelf of files marked B until a fat folder caught his attention, was removed.

He sat down at his desk, untied its red tape, and perused it. "Eight and a half thousand pounds, invested in the four-percents."

Tucking her gloved hand back inside her muff, Miss Bennet looked relieved. "How much interest has it accrued?" she asked.

His brows rose; ladies did not usually betray such a vast knowledge of financial matters. Back he went to the papers. "As of last quarter-day, one thousand and five pounds, nineteen shillings, and fourpence," he said.

"In toto, nine and a half thousand pounds," she said.

"That is correct, give or take a pound."

"How long will it take to withdraw it from the Funds?"

"I could not advise that, Miss Bennet," he said gently.

"No one asked you to, sir. How long?"

"Some weeks. Perhaps the middle of January."

"That will be satisfactory. Kindly commence the process, Mr Wilde. When my money is free, deposit it in the Hertford bank. You will arrange that I can draw upon it from any bank anywhere in England." She paused, nodded. "Yes, England will suffice. Scotland, I believe, has its own laws and customs, and Ireland is full of Papists. Wales I regard as a part of England. Further to my needs, sir, I understand that Shelby Manor is already sold, and I must vacate it. It would suit me to vacate before Christmas, rather than after. Kindly find me a small furnished house here in Hertford, and rent it for six months. I will be travelling by next May, and will no longer need a Hertford residence."

His jaw had dropped; he cleared his throat, about to utter reasonable persuasions, then decided not to bother. If ever he had seen determination writ upon a face, he saw it now in Miss Mary Bennet's. "With servants?" he asked.

"A married couple, one maid above stairs, a cook and below stairs maid, if you please. I do not intend to entertain, and my needs are simple."

"And your lady's companion?" he asked, making notes.

"I will not have one."

"But — Mr Darcy!" he exclaimed, looking horrified.

"Mr Darcy is not the arbiter of my destiny," said Miss Bennet, chin out-thrust, mouth a straight line, heavy-lidded eyes anything but sleepy. "I have myself been a dreary female for long enough, Mr Wilde, not to want another foisted on me as a reminder."

"But you cannot *travel* unattended!" he protested.

"Why not? I will avail myself of the services of the maids at the various hostelries I patronise."

"You will provoke gossip," he said, plucking at straws.

"I care as little for gossip as I do for idleness, and have been prey to both for far too long. I am not a helpless female, sir, though I am sure that you, like Mr Darcy, thus regard all of womankind. If God has seen fit to release me to do His work, then God will be my helpmate in everything, including the attentions of the unworthy and the importunities of men."

Terrified of so much iron purpose and quite unable to find any argument likely to deflect Miss Bennet from her chosen path, Mr Wilde gave up, only resolving that he would write to Mr Darcy at once. "All shall be done," he said hollowly.

She rose. "Excellent! Send word to me at Shelby Manor when you have found me a house. What little property I have, Jenkins can move. It will give the poor fellow something to do. With my mother gone, he is rather at a loss for occupations."

And out she sailed.

Mr Wilde went back to the window in time to see her step into her chaise, her profile through its glass pane as pure and sculpted as a Greek statue. Lord, what a woman! She would petrify Satan. So why, asked Mr Wilde of himself, have I fallen in love with her? Because, he answered himself, I have been half in love with the vision of her for years, and now this one meeting tells me she is unique. Suitable ladies are inevitably boring, and I have, besides, a penchant for mature women. She enchants me!

Oh, what a dance she will lead her husband! No wonder Mr Darcy looked disapproving when he broached the subject of Miss Mary Bennet and her tiny fortune. A fortune not imposing enough to form a decent dowry, nor sufficient, really, for a gentlewoman to exist upon without help. Mr Wilde had gathered that Mr Darcy wished her to retire to Pemberley, but such were very evidently not the lady's plans. And what did she plan to do with her money, stripped of its potential to earn more? Uninvested, it would not last her into old age. The best alternative for Miss Bennet was marriage, and Mr Wilde very much wanted to be her husband, no matter how frightful the dance she led him. She was a nonpareil — a woman with a mind of her own, and not afraid to speak it.

The chaise drew off; not a minute later, the hulking fellow who had been lounging against a nearby wall was riding his black thoroughbred behind it. Not precisely like a guard or escort, yet somehow tied to it, for all that Mr Wilde suspected its occupant was unaware that she was being followed.

The letter to Mr Darcy had to be written, and immediately; sighing, Mr Wilde seated himself. But before he had dipped his pen in the standish, he had brightened; she would be in town for the winter … Now how did one get around the fact that she would be unchaperoned? No gentleman callers. A man of some resource, Mr Wilde mentally reviewed their mutual acquaintances and resolved that Miss Bennet would be invited to all manner of parties and dinners. Festivities whereat he might attend his awkward beloved.

A nice young man, Mr Robert Wilde, but rather hidebound was Mary's verdict as the chaise bowled along; one of Fitz's minions, to be sure, but not subserviently so. Her stomach rumbled; she was hungry, and looked forward to a good tea in lieu of any luncheon. How easy it had been! Authority, that was all it took. And how fortunate that she had an example for her conduct in that master of the art, Fitzwilliam Darcy. Speak in a tone that brooks no argument, and even the Mr Wildes crumble.

The idea must have been there all along, but Mary had not felt its presence until that interview this morning in the library. "What *do* you want?" Fitz had asked, goaded. And even as she spoke of needing a purpose, of having something useful to do, she had known. If the many eyes of Argus could see into every putrid English corner, then the two humble eyes of his disciple

Mary Bennet could bear witness to all the perfidies he wrote about so briefly, and set down what she saw at far greater length than he. I shall write a book, she vowed, but not a three-volume novel about silly girls imprisoned in castle dungeons. I shall write a book about what lies festering in every corner of England: poverty, child labour, below-subsistence wages …

The landscape went by outside, but she did not see it; Mary Bennet was too busy thinking. They set us to embroidering, pasting cut-out pictures on screens or tables, thumping at a pianoforte or twanging at a harp, slopping watercolours on hapless paper, reading respectable books (including three-volume novels), and attending church. And if our circumstances do not permit of such comfort, we scrub, cook, drag coals or wood for the fire, hope for leftovers from the master's dinner table to eke out our own bread-and-dripping. God has been kind enough to exempt me from drudgery, but He does not need my tapestry chair covers or tasteless pictures. We are His creatures too, and not all of us have been chosen for bearing children. If marriage is not our lot, then something else quite as important must be.

It is men who rule, men who have genuine independence. Not the most miserable wretch of a man has any notion how thankless life is for women. Well, I have thirty-eight years on my plate, and I am done with pleasing men as of this morning. I am going to write a book that will make Fitzwilliam Darcy's hair stand on end far stiffer than ever it did for my singing. I am going to show that insufferable specimen of a man that dependence on his charity is anathema.

The fire was roaring when she entered the parlour, and Mrs Jenkins came in a moment later with the tea tray.

"Splendid!" said Mary, sitting in her mother's wing chair without a qualm. "Muffins, fruit cake, apple tarts — I could ask for nothing better. Pray do not bother with dinner, I will have a large tea instead."

"But your dinner's a-cooking, Miss Mary!"

"Then eat it yourselves. Has the *Westminster Chronicle* come?"

"Yes, Miss Mary."

"Oh, and by the way, Mrs Jenkins, I expect to be gone a week before Christmas. That will give you and Jenkins ample time to set the house in order for the Applebys."

Bereft of speech, Mrs Jenkins tottered from the room.

Six muffins, two apple tarts and two slices of cake later, Mary drained her fourth cup of tea and opened the thin pages of the *Westminster Chronicle*. Ignoring the usual ladies' fare of court pages and obituaries, she turned to the letters, a famous and prominent feature of this highly political newspaper. Ah, there it was! A new letter from Argus. Devouring it avidly, Mary discovered that this time its author was attacking the piecemeal transportation of the Irish to New South Wales.

"They have no food, so they steal it," said Argus roundly, "and when they are caught, they are sentenced to seven years' transportation by an English magistrate who knows full well that they will never be able to afford to return home. They have no clothes, so they steal them, and when they are caught, they suffer the same fate. Transportation is as inhuman as it is inhumane, an exile for life far from the soft green meadows of Hibernia. I say to you, Peers of the Lords, Members of the Commons, that transportation is an evil and must stop. As must cease this senseless persecution of the Irish. Not that this evil is confined to Ireland. Our English gaols have been emptied, our own poor indigent felons sent far away. Hogarth would scarce recognise Gin Lane, so denuded is it. I say to you again, Peers of the Lords and Members of the Commons, abandon this cheap solution to our country's woes! It is as final a solution as the graveyard, and as loathsome. No man, woman or child is so depraved that he or she must be sent into a permanent exile. Seven years? Make it seventy! They will never come home."

Eyes shining, Mary laid the paper down. Argus's attention to phenomena like transportation did not thrill her as did his diatribes against poorhouses, workhouses, orphanages, factories and mines, but his fiery passion always inflamed her, no matter what his subject. Nor could the comfortably off ignore him any more; Argus had joined the ranks of the other social crusaders, was read and talked about from the Tweed to Land's End. A new moral conscience was blossoming in England, partly thanks to Argus.

Why shouldn't I make a difference too? she asked herself. It was Argus who opened my eyes; from the day I read his first letter, I was converted. Now that I am freed from my duty, I can march forth to do battle against the pernicious ulcers that eat away England's very flesh. I have heard my nieces and nephews speak to beggars as they would not speak to a stray dog. Only Charlie understands, but it is not his nature to go crusading.

Yes, I will journey to see England's ills, write my book, and pay to have it published. Publishers pay the ladies who write the three-volume novel, but not the authors of serious works: so said Mrs Rowtree, that time she gave a lecture in the Hertford library. Mrs Rowtree writes three-volume novels and has scant respect for serious books. Those, she informed us, have to be funded by the authors, and the publication process costs about nine thousand pounds. That is almost all I have, but it will see my book published. What matter if, my money exhausted, I turn up on Fitz's doorstep to claim the shelter he has offered? It will be worth it! But I do not trust Fitz not to think of a way to stop me spending my money if it is invested in the Funds, so I will breathe a sigh of relief when it is safely banked in *my* name.

"Dearest Charlie," she wrote to her nephew the next morning, "*I am going to write a book!* I know that my prose is a poor thing, but I remember once or twice your saying I had a way with words. Not a Dr Johnson or a Mr Gibbon, perhaps, but after reading so many books, I find that I can express my thoughts with ease. The pain of it is the realisation that none of my thoughts thus far has been worthy of commitment to paper. Well, no more! I have a theme would adorn the humblest pen with laurels.

"I am going to write a book. No, dearest boy, not a silly novel in the mode of Mrs Burney or Mrs Radcliffe! This is to be a *serious* work about the ills of England. That, I think, must be its title: *The Ills of England.* How much help you have been!

Was it not you who said that, before anything can bear fruit, all the research must be done? I know you meant it for the rigours of *Prolegomena ad Homerum* but for me it entails the inspection of orphanages, factories, poorhouses, mines — a thousand-and-one places where our own English people live in impoverishment and misery for no better reason than that they chose their parents unwisely. Do you remember saying that of the urchins in Meryton? Such a neat aphorism, and so true! Were we offered the chance, would we not all choose kings or dukes for fathers, rather than coal-lumpers or jobless on the Parish?

"How wonderful it would be, were I, busy doing my research, to light upon some awesomely grand personage deep engaged in crime and exploitation? Were I so lucky, I would not flinch from publishing a chapter upon him, complete with his august name.

"When I have assembled all the facts, the notes, the conclusions, I will write my book. Around the beginning of May I will set out on my journey of investigation. Not to London, but to the North. Lancashire and Yorkshire, where, according to Argus, exploitation is most vicious. Mine eyes yearn to see for themselves, for I have lived circumscribed and circumspect, passing the wattle-and-daub hovels in the hedgerows as if they did not exist. For what we see and accept as a part of life when children has not the power to shock us later on.

"By the time that this reaches you at Oxford, I imagine I will have moved to a house in Hertford; believe me when I say that

I will not mourn at quitting Shelby Manor. As I write this, the first flakes of snow are falling. How quietly they blanket the world! Would that our human lot were as peaceful, as beautiful. Snow always reminds me of daydreams: ephemeral.

"Do you mean to go to Pemberley at Christmas, or are you staying in Oxford with your tomes? How is that nice tutor, Mr Griffiths? Something your mama said made me think he is more your friend than a strict supervisor. And though I know how fond you are of Oxford, have a thought for your mama. She would dearly love to see you at Pemberley at Christmas.

"Write to me when you have time, and remember to take that restorative tonic I gave you. A spoonful every morning. Also, my dearest Charlie, I am tired of being addressed as *Aunt* Mary. Now you are eighteen, it seems inappropriate for you to defer to my spinster station by calling me your aunt. I am your *friend*.

"Your loving Mary."

Stretching, Mary lifted the pen above her head; oh, that felt better! She then folded the single sheet of tiny script so that it had only one free edge. There in its middle she dropped a blob of bright green wax, taking care not to besmirch it with smoke from the candle. Such a pretty colour, the green! A swift application of the Bennet seal before the wax solidified, and her letter was ready. Let Charlie be the first to know her plans. No, more than that, Mary! said a tiny voice inside her head. Let Charlie be the *only* one to know.

When Mrs Jenkins bustled in, she handed her missive over. "Have Jenkins take this into Hertford to the post."

"Today, Miss Mary? He's supposed to mend the pigsty."

"He can do that tomorrow. If we're in for heavy snow, I want my letter safely gone."

But it was not Jenkins who lodged her letter with the post in Hertford. Grumbling at the prospect of a tediously slow errand, Jenkins decided to drop into the Cat and Fiddle for a quick nip to fortify himself against the cold. There he found that he was not the only patron of the taproom; cosily ensconced in the inglenook was a huge fellow, feet the size of shutters propped upon the hearth.

"Morning," said Jenkins, wondering who he was.

"And to you, sir." Down came the feet. "Wind's coming round to the north — plenty of snow in it, I hazard a guess."

"Aye, don't I know it," said Jenkins, grimacing. "What a day to have to ride to Hertford!"

The landlord came in at the sound of voices, saw who had arrived, and mixed a small mug of rum and hot water. Hadn't he said as much to the big stranger? If Jenkins has to go out, he will come here first. As Jenkins took the mug, the landlord winked at the stranger and knew he would be paid a crown for a tankard of ale. Queer cove, this one! Spoke like a gentleman.

"Mind if I share the warmth?" Jenkins asked, coming to sit in the inglenook.

"Not at all. I am for Hertford myself," said the stranger, finishing his tankard of ale. "Is there aught I can do for you there? Save you a trip, perhaps?"

"I have a letter for the post, 'tis my only reason for the

journey." He sniffed. "Old maids and their crotchets! I ought to be fixing the pigsty — nice and close to the kitchen fire."

"Do the pigsty, man!" said the stranger heartily. "It's no trouble for me to hand in your note."

Sixpence and the letter changed hands; Jenkins settled to sip his hot drink with slow relish, while Ned Skinner bore his prize as far as the next good inn, where he hired the parlour.

Only in its privacy did he turn the letter over and see the bright green wax of its seal. Christ almighty, green! What was Miss Mary Bennet about, to use green wax? He broke the seal very carefully, unfolded the sheet, and discovered writing so fine that he had to take it to the window to read it. Giving vent to a huff of exasperation, he had no idea that he was not the first man to suffer this emotion over Miss Mary Bennet. He took a sheet of the landlord's paper, sat at the desk and began to copy the letter word for word. That took three sheets in his copperplate hand; Ned Skinner had been well schooled. Still, it was done. He picked away every remnant of the green wax, frowning at the landlord's stick of red. Well, no help for it! Red it would have to be. The blob in place, he swiped his own signet across it in a way that rendered the sender's identity unintelligible. Yes, it would suffice, he decided; young Charlie was not observant unless his eyes were filled with the ghost of Homer.

Pausing in Hertford only long enough to dispose of the letter, Ned hunched down in the saddle and rode for Pemberley. Out of this Lilliputian southern world at last! Give me Derbyshire any day, he thought. Room to *breathe*. The snow was beginning to drive rather than fall, and would get worse, but Jupiter's strength belied his looks, he could forge through a foot and more with Ned up.

Having little to do and nothing save snow to see, Ned turned his mind inward. An interesting woman, Miss Mary Bennet. As like Elizabeth as another pea, and not, he knew now, pea-brained. Addle-pated, yes, but how could she be aught else, given the circumstances of her life? Naive, that was the right word for her. Like a child set loose in a room made of thinnest glass. What might she shatter were she not restrained? If she had selected London for her crusade, all would have been well. But the North was a dangerous place, too close to home for Fitz's comfort. And the trouble with naiveté allied to cleverness was that it could too easily be transformed to worldly shrewdness. Was Mary Bennet capable of making that leap? I would not bet my all against it, Ned thought. Some of what she had to say to her pretty-boy nephew in her letter was not so much worrying as a nuisance; it meant he would have to keep an eye on her without letting her know that he was keeping an eye on her. Though not, he thought, heaving an inward sigh of relief, until May.

Of course Mary Bennet's nuisance value could not keep his mind occupied for very long; rigging his muffler to shield his lower face as much as possible, he passed to a more agreeable reverie, one that always made the dreariest, longest journey of little moment: his mind's eye was filled with the vision of a weeping, toddling little boy suddenly lifted up in a pair of strong young arms; of cuddling against a neck that smelled of sweet soap, and feeling all the grief drain away.

*   *   *

The snow had isolated Oxford from the North; Charlie could not have gone home for Christmas even had he wanted to. Which he did not. Much as he adored his mother, an advancing maturity had rendered his father less and less tolerable. Of course he knew full well that he, Charlie, was Pater's chief disappointment, but could do nothing about it. At Oxford he was *safe*. Yet how, he wondered, gazing at the snowdrifts piled against his walls, can I step into Pater's shoes? I am no Minister of the Crown, no ardent politician, no conscientious landlord, no force to be reckoned with. All I want is to lead the life of a don, an authority upon some obscure aspect of the Greek epic poets or the early Latin playwrights. Mama understands. Pater never will.

These unhappy thoughts, so familiar and answerless, were banished the moment Owen Griffiths pushed open his study door; Charlie turned from the window, eyes lighting up.

"Oh, the boredom!" he exclaimed. "I'm stuck in the middle of the stuffiest Virgil you can imagine — say that you have a better task for me, Owen!"

"No, young sir, you must unstuff Virgil," said the Welshman, sitting down. "However, I do have a letter, delayed a month by the snows." And he held it up, waved it just beyond Charlie's reach, laughing.

"A plague on you! It is not my fault I lack your inches! Give it to me at once!"

Mr Griffiths handed it over. He was indeed tall, and well built for one who had espoused Academe; the result, he would say unabashedly, of a childhood spent digging holes and chopping wood to help his farmer father. His hair was thick, black and worn rather long, his eyes were dark and his features regular enough to be called handsome. A certain Welsh gloom gave his face a severity beyond his years, which numbered twenty-five, though he had little cause for gloom once Charlie had arrived at Oxford. Mrs Darcy had been searching for a tutor able to share a good house with her son as well as guide him through his in-college studies. All expenses paid, of course, as well as a stipend generous enough to enable the lucky man to send a little money home if his parents were in need of it. The miracle of being chosen from among so many hopeful applicants! A memory that still had the power to deprive Owen of his breath. Nor had it done his academic career any harm to secure this position; the Darcy wealth and influence extended to the upper echelons of power in Oxford's colleges.

"Odd," said Charlie, having broken the letter's seal. "It is Aunt Mary's handwriting, but the wax isn't green." He shrugged. "With so many people at Shelby Manor, perhaps the green wax was all used up." He bent his head, absorbed now in what his aunt had to say, his growing look of mingled horror and despair giving Owen a pang of apprehension.

"Oh, Lord!" Charlie cried, putting the letter down.

"What is it?"

"A conniption fit — an attack of some feminine peculiarity — I don't know how to describe it, Owen. Only that Mary — I am to call her plain Mary in future, she says — has well and truly taken the bit between her teeth," said Charlie. "Here, read."

"Hmmm" was Owen's comment. He raised an eyebrow.

"She doesn't know what is entailed! It will kill her!"

"I doubt that, Charlie, but I see why you're concerned. It is the letter of a sheltered woman."

"How could she be aught else than sheltered?"

"Does she have the money for this quest?"

That gave Charlie pause; his face screwed up in the effort of remembering something unconnected to Latin or Greek. "I am not sure, Owen. Mama said she had been provided for, though I fancied she deemed the provision niggardly in view of Mary's sacrifice. See? She says she is living in Hertford — because Shelby Manor has been sold, I suppose. Oh, it is too bad! Pater could afford a dozen Shelby Manors to house Mary for the rest of her life!" He wrung his hands together, anguished. "I don't know her circumstances! And why didn't I ask? Because I couldn't face a scene with my father! I'm a coward. A weakling! Just as Pater says. What is wrong with me, that I cannot face him?"

"Come, Charlie, don't be so hard on yourself. I think you cannot face him because you know it will accomplish nothing, perhaps even make a situation worse. As soon as the post is moving again, write to your mother. Ask her what Mary's situation is. She is not travelling until May, so you have a little time."

Charlie's brow cleared; he nodded. "Yes, you're right. Oh, poor Mary! Where does she get these zany ideas? Write a book!"

"If her letter is anything to go by, she gets her ideas from Argus," Owen said. "I admire the man immensely, but he is no friend of the Tories or your father. I would keep this from him if you can. It never crossed my mind that ladies read the *Westminster Chronicle*, least of all your aunt." His eyes twinkled. "Whom, I note, you have no difficulty in calling plain Mary."

"Well, I have always thought of her as plain Mary, you see. Oh, how I used to look forward to those holidays with her at Shelby Manor! Mama used to take Grandmother to Bath once a year, and I stayed with Mary. The fun we had! Walking, going out in the trap — she could talk about anything and was game for anything from climbing trees to pot-shotting pigeons with a catapult. With Pater snapping at my heels when my schoolmasters were not, my weeks with Mary remain the most wonderful part of my childhood. She loves geography most, though she is no mean historian. It amazed me that she knew the common and botanical names of all the mosses, ferns, trees and flowers in the woods." Charlie's perfect teeth flashed in a grin. "I add that — spread this no farther, Owen! — she was not above tying up her skirts to paddle down a stream in search of tadpoles."

"A side to her that you alone were privileged to see."

"Yes. The moment others were around, she turned into an aunt. A *maiden* aunt, prim and prissy. Having seen them splash through many a stream, I can vouch for her legs — very shapely."

"I am intrigued," said Owen, deeming it time he reverted to a tutor. "However, Charlie, the weather has set for some days, and Virgil is still stuffed. No Horatian odes until he is as empty as an English pillow case drying on a line. Virgil now, a letter to your mama later."

THREE

At first the winter passed more delightfully than Mary expected. Though she could receive no gentleman callers, Mrs Markham, Miss Delphinia Botolph, Mrs McLeod and Lady Appleby came often to her house, privately deploring its musty atmosphere and dark outlook, not to mention privately speculating as to why dear Miss Bennet had no lady's companion. Enquiries met with a stone wall; Miss Bennet simply said she had no need of one, and changed the subject. However, if a carriage was sent for her or she hired one of her own, she could attend dinner parties and receptions. There were always enough unattached gentlemen, and Mr Robert Wilde had dropped unsubtle hints that he would very much like it were he to be seated beside Miss Bennet at a dinner table, or care for her on other kinds of occasion.

Wriggled brows and winks flew from face to face; it was no mean thing for a thirty-eight-year-old female to charm such an eligible bachelor as Mr Wilde. Who seemed not to care that he was her junior by a good six or seven years.

"Clever of him," said Miss Botolph, whose sixty years meant she experienced no pangs of jealousy. "One hears that she has an adequate income, and if he snares her, it will elevate his station. She is Darcy of Pemberley's sister-in-law."

"I could wish she dressed better," said Lady Appleby, a keen reader of ladies' fashion magazines.

"And I, that she did not come out with those truly peculiar remarks," from Mrs Markham. "I do believe she was seen in deep conversation with a gypsy."

The object of these observations was seated on a sofa with Mr Wilde in attendance, her plain black gown so old that it had a greenish hue, and her hair scraped into a bun without a single curl to frame her face.

"What did you learn from the gypsy?" Mr Wilde was asking.

"Fascinating, sir! It seems they believe themselves the descendants of the Egyptian pharaohs, and are doomed to wander until some paradise or prophet arrives. What he was really trying to do was to separate me from my sixpences, but he did not succeed. His eyes hungered for gold or silver, not food. I went away convinced that his tribe, at least, is neither impoverished nor discontented. He said they liked their life. I did learn that they move on when they have fouled their camp site with rotten food and bodily wastes. A lesson some of our own hedgerow people should learn."

"You say they like their life. But you do not like yours."

"That will change in May," said Mary, nibbling a

macaroon. "This is very good. I must ask Mrs McLeod for her cook's recipe."

"That's a relief!" cried Mr Wilde, forgetting that it was not polite for new acquaintances to contract words.

"A relief. In what way?"

"It says that there will be an end to your travels. That one day you will command the services of your own cook."

"I do that now."

"But do not entertain. Therefore, no macaroons."

"I am reproved."

"Miss Bennet, I would never dream of reproving you!" His light brown eyes grew brighter, gazed into hers ardently, and his whirling mind quite forgot that they were in Mrs McLeod's drawing room with ten other people. "On the contrary, I ask for nothing more of life than to spend it at your side." He took the plunge. "Marry me!"

Horrified, she wriggled down the sofa away from him in a movement so convulsive that all eyes fixed on them; all ears had been flapping far longer.

"Pray do not say it!"

"I have already said it," he pointed out. "Your answer?"

"No, a thousand times no!"

"Then let us speak of other things." He took the empty plate from her nerveless fingers and smiled at her charmingly. "I don't accept my congé, you understand. My offer remains open."

"Do not hope, Mr Wilde. I am obdurate." Oh, how vexatious! Why had she not foreseen this inappropriate declaration? *How* had she encouraged him?

"Will you be at Miss Appleby's wedding?" he asked.

And that, concluded the satisfied onlookers, is that — for the time being, at any rate. Sooner or later she would accept his offer.

"Though if she plays too hard to catch," said Miss Botolph, "she may find her fisherman has waded far upstream."

"Do you know what I think, Delphinia?" asked Mrs Markham. "I think she does not give tuppence for matrimony."

"From which I deduce that her situation is easy and her way of life settled," Miss Botolph answered. "It was certainly so for me after my mama died. There are worse fates than a comfortable competence and a maiden existence." She snorted. "Husbands can prove more of a sorrow than a blessing."

An observation that the married ladies chose to ignore.

Argus put down his pen and viewed his latest effort with a slightly cynical eye. Its subject was actually rather silly, he thought, but comfortably off English folk, particularly those who lived in cities, were incredibly sentimental. Not the most vivid, emotive prose could move them to pity the lot of a chimney sweep, but if one substituted an animal for the human being — ah, that was quite a different matter! Many a tear would be shed when this letter appeared in the *Westminster Chronicle*! Pit ponies, no less. Permanently blind from a life spent underground, their poor shaggy hides furrowed with whip marks …

It amused him to do this sort of thing occasionally, for Argus was not what he seemed to his readers, who in their fantasies pictured him starving in a garret, worn to bones by the sheer force of his revolutionary ideals. Ladies of Miss Mary Bennet's kind might dream of him as a fellow crusader against England's ills, but in truth his epistolary zeal was fired by his desire to make life uncomfortable for certain gentlemen of the Lords and Commons. Every Argusine letter caused questions to be raised in both Houses, provoked interminable speeches, obliged Lord This and Mr That to dodge a few rotten eggs on that perilous trip between the portals of Parliament and the cabins of their carriages. In actual fact he knew as well as did the most conservative of Tories that nothing would improve conditions for the poor. No, it was not that which drove him; what did, Argus had decided, was a spirit of mischief.

Closing his library door behind him, he sallied into the spacious hall of his house in Grosvenor Square and held out a hand for his gloves, hat and cane while his butler draped a fur-collared cape about his broad shoulders.

"Tell Stubbs not to wait up," he said, and ventured out into the freezing March night wearing his true guise; Argus existed only in his study. His walk was very short; one side of the square saw him reach his destination.

"My dear Angus," said Fitzwilliam Darcy, shaking him warmly by the hand. "Do come into the drawing room. I have a new whisky for you — it takes a Scot to deliver a verdict on a Scotch whisky."

"Och, I'll give my verdict happily, Fitz, but your man knows his Highland malts better than I do." Divested of cloak, cane, hat and gloves, Mr Angus Sinclair, secretly known as Argus, accompanied his host across the vast, echoing foyer of Darcy House. "Going to try again, eh?" he asked.

"Would I succeed if I did try?"

"No. That is the best part about being a Scot. I don't need your influence, either at Court or in the City, let alone the Houses of Parliament. My wee weekly journal is but a hobby — the bawbees come from Glasgow coal and iron, as you well know. I derive much pleasure from being a thorn in the Tory paw, stout English lion that he is. You should travel north of the Border, Fitz."

"I can tolerate your weekly journal, Angus. It's Argus who is the damnable nuisance," said Fitz, leading his guest into the small drawing room, blazing with crimson and gilt.

No doubt he would have continued in that vein, except that his ravishing wife was coming forward with a brilliant smile; she and Mr Sinclair liked each other. "Angus!"

"Each time I see you, Elizabeth, your beauty amazes me," he said, kissing her hand.

"Fitz is making a bore of himself again about Argus?"

"Inevitably," he said, heart sinking a little at her use of "bore". Too tactless.

"Who is he?"

"In this incarnation, I know not. His letters come in the post. But in his original, mythical incarnation, he was a huge monster with many eyes. Which, I am sure, is why the anonymous fellow chose his pen name. The eyes of Argus see everywhere."

"You *must* know who he is," said Fitz.

"No, I do not."

"Oh, Fitz, do leave Angus alone!" Elizabeth said jokingly.

"Am I making a *bore* of myself?" Fitz asked, a slight tinge of acid in his voice.

"Yes, my love, you are."

"Point taken. Try the whisky, Angus," said Fitz with a tight smile, holding out a glass.

Oh, dear, Angus thought, swallowing a potion he detested. Elizabeth is going to embark upon yet another of her poke-gentle-fun-at-Fitz essays, and he, hating it, will poker up stiffer than any iron implement ever forged to tame a fire. Why can she not see that her touch isn't light enough? Especially given its object, thinner-skinned by far than he pretends.

"Do not say you like it, Angus!" she said with a laugh.

"But I do. Very smooth," Angus lied valiantly.

A reply that mollified Fitz, but did not raise him in his hostess's esteem; she had been hoping for support.

It was a private dinner; no other guests were expected, so the three of them sat at one end of the small dining table in the small dining room, there to consume a five-course meal to which none of them did justice.

"I publish Argus's epistles, Fitz," Angus said as the joints were removed and the syllabubs came in, "because I am so tired of this waste." His rather crabbed hand swept the air above the table. "It is *de riguer* to serve me a gargantuan dinner, though I do not need it, and have eaten but a wee bit of it. Nor has either of you made greater inroads. All of us would have been content with a loaf of bread, some butter, some jam, some cheese and a winter apple. Your staff and all their relatives wax fat on your leavings — so, probably, do the ravens in the square gardens."

Even knowing Fitz's detestation of excessive loudness, Elizabeth could not help her burst of laughter. "Do you know, Angus, you and my sister Mary would get along together famously? That was exactly the kind of remark sets people's backs up, but you care as little for our feelings as she would."

"Whose wife is she?"

"Nobody's. Mary is unmarried."

"A spinster enamoured of Argus!" Fitz snapped.

Startled, Elizabeth's eyes flew to his face. "How do you know that?" she asked. "I certainly do not."

She had taken care to say it lightly, almost jokingly, but he would not look at her, and his face had gone very impassive. "I know it from Mary, of course."

"Does she live in London?" Angus asked, shrewd blue eyes taking note of the sudden tension between them.

"No, in Hertford," said Elizabeth, rising. "I will leave you to your port and cheroots, but do not, I beg you, linger over them. There will be coffee in the drawing room."

"You're lucky in your wife, Fitz," Angus said, accepting a port. "The most beautiful, vital creature."

Fitz smiled. "Yes, she is. However, there are other ladies equally entrancing. Why not espouse one yourself? What are you, forty? And unmarried. London's most eligible bachelor, they say."

"I beg to differ about the ladies. Elizabeth is unique." Angus puffed at his slender cigar. "Is the spinster sister in her mould?

If she is, I might try my luck there. But I doubt it, else she'd not be a spinster."

"She was called upon to look after their mother." Fitz grimaced. "Mary Bennet is a silly woman, forever quoting someone else's noble Christian thoughts. Though at her last prayers years ago, she has found a new god to worship — Argus." Darcy leaned both elbows on the table and linked his hands together; a habit of his to make other men think him relaxed, unworried. "Which leads me back to that vexed subject. It will not do, Angus, to keep on publishing this fellow's pathetic crotchets."

"If they were in truth pathetic, Fitz, you would not be half so perturbed. It's not London eating at you, is it? London has always been a stew, and always will be a stew. No, you fear some revolution in the North — just how far do your interests go?"

"I don't dabble in things beneath the notice of a Darcy!"

Angus roared with laughter, unoffended. "Lord, what a snob you are!"

"I would rather say I am a gentleman."

"Aye, an occupation all of its own." Angus leaned back in his chair, the hundred candles of an overhead chandelier setting his silver-gilt hair afire. The creases in his lean cheeks deepened when he smiled; they made him look impish. Which was how he felt, more intrigued with Fitzwilliam Darcy tonight than ever he had been. There were undercurrents he had not suspected — was that perhaps because Elizabeth was on a rare visit to the south? Most of his acquaintance with her had taken place at Pemberley during the house parties Fitz enjoyed having; she was, for all her beauty, not fond of the fleshpots of London society. A Court reception had brought her, and he counted himself fortunate that Fitz's curious fixation upon Argus had produced things like an intimate dinner for three.

"It is no good," he said, tossing back the last of his port. "Argus will have his forum for debate as long as I own the *Westminster Chronicle* — and you do not have sufficient money to buy me out. That would take the funds of a Croesus."

"What a pleasant dinner," Elizabeth said to her husband after their lone guest had departed. She commenced to climb the left-hand fork of the stairs above a splendid landing halfway up, Fitz by her side, helping her with her train.

"Yes it was. Though frustrating. I cannot seem to get it through Angus's head that it is Argus and his like will bring us down. Ever since the American colonists started prating about their democratic ideals and the French started cutting off the heads of their betters, the lower classes have been rumbling. Even here in England."

"A nation of shopkeepers, Bonaparte called us."

"Bonaparte has failed. Sir Rupert Lavenham was telling me that his grand army is lost in the Russian snows. Hundreds of thousands of French soldiers frozen to death. And he has left them to their fate — can you believe that, Elizabeth? The man is an upstart, to have so little honour."

"No honour at all," she said dutifully. "By the way, Fitz, when did Mary tell you she was enamoured of Argus?"

"When I saw her in the library the morning we left. We — er — had a little falling out."

They had reached her door; she stopped, her hand on its lever. "Why don't you tell me about these things?"

"They are not your affair."

"Yes, they are, when they involve my sister! What kind of falling out? Is that why she is living in Hertford? Did you make her feel she is not welcome at Pemberley?"

His dislike of being criticised made him answer sharply. "As a matter of fact, she absolutely refused to come to Pemberley! Or even to have a companion! It is the height of impropriety to live unchaperoned! And in Hertford, under the eyes of the people who have known her for years! I have washed my hands of her, frittering away her jointure on some quest put into her head by the letters of that fool, Argus!"

"Not a very generous jointure at that," she countered, eyes flashing. "As I know for a fact that brother Charles contributed a full half of it, Mary has cost you less per year than you spend on stabling your carefully matched curricle horses! And I do not mean the bays plus the greys, I mean one team only! Two hundred and fifty pounds a year! You pay your valet that much, and your horse master more! When it comes to yourself, Fitz, you spend. But not on my poor — literally as well as metaphorically — sister!"

"I am not made of money," he said stiffly. "Mary is your sister, not mine."

"If you are not made of money, why do you spend it on fripperies like emeralds? I have no lust for jewels, but Mary needs more security than you have given her. Sell these emeralds and give the money to Mary. After seventeen years, she will have no more than nine and a half thousand pounds all told. If she chooses to live on her own, she can afford no conveyance, or do more than rent. Do you expect her to pay for the lady's companion? Obviously! You are *shabby*!"

To have his conduct called shabby roused him to a rare anger; his lips drew back to bare his teeth. "I can take no notice of you, Elizabeth, because you speak in ignorance. Your idiotic sister has withdrawn her money from the four-percents, thus will have no income. Had I dowered her better, she would simply have more money to waste. Your sister, madam, is crazed."

Gasping, Elizabeth fought for control; if she lost it, he would dismiss her rage as worth less than it was. "Oh, Fitz, why have you no compassion?" she cried. "Mary is the most harmless creature ever born! What can it matter if she — if she goes off in some peculiar way? If she refuses to be chaperoned? It was your determination to be rid of our mother that made Mary whatever she has become. And how could you predict what she would do, with Mama dead? You predicted nothing, simply assumed that she would go on being what she had been as a girl, and *cheated* her of an old age comfortable enough to live as you made sure our mother would. Why did you do that for our mother, then? Because untrammelled she was too dangerous — she might turn up at some important political reception and make you a laughing-stock with her silliness, her loud and thoughtless remarks. Now you visit Mama's conduct upon poor Mary's head! It is unforgivable!"

"I see that I was right not to tell you what transpired."

"Not to tell me was unconscionable bad form!"

"Good night," he said, bowing.

And off down the shadowed hall he strode, his figure as straight and well-proportioned as it had been twenty years ago.

"And don't bother to write me one of your self-excusing and self-pitying letters!" she shouted after him. "I will burn it unread!"

Trembling, she entered her suite of rooms, profoundly glad that she had told Hoskins not to wait up. How dared he! Oh, how dared he!

They never quarrelled; he was too high in the instep, she too desirous of peace at any price. Tonight had been the first time they had exchanged bitter words in years. Perhaps, she thought, teeth chattering, we would be happier if we did quarrel. Yet even as angry as he had been tonight, he would not demean himself beyond what he deemed the conduct of a gentleman. No shouting, though she had shouted; no hands bunched into fists, though hers had been. His façade was unbreakable, for all that it had nearly broken her. Did his marriage satisfy his ideas of marriage? On her side, who could have dreamed the nightmare marriage would be?

What she harkened back to in her memories was the period of her engagement. Oh, the way he had looked at her then! His cold eyes lit from within, his hand finding any excuse to touch hers, his kisses soft on her lips, the conviction he gave her that she was more precious to him than all of Pemberley. They would always exist in a haze of perfect bliss: or so she had believed.

A belief shattered on her wedding night, a humiliation she endured only because so had God ordained procreation. Had Jane felt the same? She had no idea, could not ask. These intimacies of the bed chamber were too private for confidences, even with a most beloved sister.

Breathless with the anticipation of hours spent tenderly kissing and fondling, she had found instead an animal act of teeth and nails, hurtful hands, grunts and sweat; he had torn her nightgown away to pinch and bite her breasts, held her down with one hand while the other poked, pried, fumbled at the core of her. And the act itself was degrading, unloving — so horrible!

The next day he had apologised, explaining that he had waited too long for her, could not help himself, so eager was he to make her his. A shamefaced Fitz, but not, she realised, on her behalf. It was his own loss of dignity concerned him. A man had needs, he had said, but in time she would understand. Well, she never had. That first encounter set the pattern of the following nine years; even the thought that he might come to her in the night was enough to make her feel sick. But after the fourth girl in a row, his visits stopped. Poor Charlie would have to assume the burden of a position his very nature found repugnant, and her girls — such dear, sweet souls! — were as afraid of their father as they were of Ned Skinner.

The emeralds would not part company at the back of her neck. Elizabeth tore at them, heedless of how she pulled out tendrils of hair by the root. Oh, *wretched* things! More prized than the welfare of a sister. There. Free at last. But if only she were free! Did Mary realise that no husband meant at least a modicum of independence? To Elizabeth, dependence was galling.

Perhaps, she thought, crawling into the vast confines of her bed, I never loved Fitz enough. Or else there was not enough Lydia in me to respond to him the way a Lydia would. For I have grown sufficiently to realise that not all women are created the same: that some, like Lydia, actually welcome the grunts, the sweat, the stickiness; while some, like me, loathe them. Why can there not be a middle path? I have so much love to give, but it is not the kind of love Fitz wants. During our engagement I thought it was, but once I was his at law, I became a possession. The principal ornament of Pemberley. I wonder who his mistress is? No one in London knows, otherwise Lady Jersey or Caroline Lamb would have tattled it. She must be from a lower situation, grateful for the crumbs he throws her. Oh, Fitz, Fitz!

She cried herself to sleep.

Mr Angus Sinclair walked home to spend another hour in his library, but not in writing incendiary prose under the *nom de plume* of Argus. Angus — Argus. What a difference one wee letter made! He plucked a fat folder of papers from under a number of others on his desk, and settled to studying its contents afresh. It was made up of the reports of several of his agents on the activities of men he had christened the "nabobs of the North" — the ultimate owners of factories, foundries, workshops, mills and mines in Yorkshire and Lancashire.

Prominent among them was Mr Charles Bingley of Bingley Hall, Cheshire. Boon companion of Fitzwilliam Darcy. Yet the more Angus thought about it, the more curious that friendship became.

What did the colossal snob and the captain of trade and industry have in common? On the surface, a friendship that should not exist. His enquiries had revealed that they had met at Cambridge, and had been grafted to each other ever since. A youthful thing like an inappropriate crush on one side and a lofty condescension on the other? A wee Socratic fling, bums up? No, definitely not! Bingley and Darcy were nothing more nor less than firm friends. What they had in common must be less obvious … Bingley's grandfather had been a Liverpool dock worker; it was his father had carved out an empire of chimneys spouting dense black smoke into the Manchester air. While Darcy's grandfather had contemptuously refused a dukedom because, so rumour had it, he could not be the Duke of Darcy. Shires only for dukes.

Something binds that pair together, thought Angus, and I am positive it rejoices under the title of Trade and Industry.

"Yes, Angus," said Mr Sinclair aloud, "the answer must be the only logical one — that the illustrious Fitzwilliam Darcy is Charles Bingley's silent partner. Fifty thousand acres of Derbyshire peaks, moors and forests must yield Fitz ten thousand a year, but he also has many fertile acres of Warwickshire, Staffordshire, Cheshire and Shropshire. Why then is he said to have an income of a mere ten thousand a year? It must surely be twice that from the land alone. What other smokier, machine-driven activities contribute to how many thousands more?" He grunted. "Och, man, you're tired and not thinking properly!"

The situation appealed to him enormously because, sensible Scot that he was, he failed utterly to understand why any man should be ashamed of dirtying his hands. Trade and industry bring rewards enough to transform the grandson of a Liverpool docker into a gentleman. What is wrong with having no ancestors? How Roman that is! New Men versus the Old Nobility, and never the twain shall meet. Except in Bingley and Darcy. Though would that twain meet if Bingley had a desire to be socially prominent in certain London circles? He did not, never had. A man of the North, he kept a London residence only because friendship with Fitz made it necessary.

His eyelids drooped; some time later Angus sat up with a jerk to find that he had nodded off, and laughed softly. He had dreamed of a skinny, hatchet-faced female clad like a governess and marching up and down outside the Houses of Parliament carrying a placard that said REPENT, YE EXPLOITERS OF THE POOR! How Argus would love that! Besides which, however, no ladies ever marched up and down outside any Westminster building. The day they did that, he thought wickedly, the whole pile would tumble down.

Was she a skinny, hatchet-faced female in the garb of a governess? he wondered as he closed the folder and put it back where it belonged. If Elizabeth's sister, then surely not! Yet what spinster owned beauty? None, in his experience. She bore the Christian name of Mary, but how was he going to find out what her surname was? Then a memory surfaced: of Fitz saying Mary Bennett — one t or two? Two. One left the name looking the victim of amputation. Miss Mary Bennett ... Who lived in Hertford, a mere skip from London. How old was she?

The vision of Elizabeth had haunted him for ten years, and to find that she had an unmarried sister was irresistible. Yes, he would have to see Miss Mary Bennett, enamoured of Argus! Poor Elizabeth! A wretchedly unhappy creature. Well, what woman could be happy married to Fitz? One of the coldest men Angus had ever met. Though exactly how did one define cold, when applied to human beings? Fitz was not devoid of feelings, certainly. He had feelings — strong ones, too. The trouble was that they existed beneath an exterior made of ice. And Elizabeth had probably thought she could melt that ice when she married him. I have read, Angus mused, of a volcano covered in snow and glaciers, yet still, in its depths, a boiling pit of white-hot lava. And that is Fitz. God spare me from the day of the eruption! It will be devastating.

On his way to bed Angus notified the under-butler on duty that he would be going out of London for two weeks on the morrow; would he kindly inform Stubbs of that fact at once?

When commencing a mission to collect facts for Argus personally, Angus Sinclair's practice was to go first to the local legal chambers. Just because this was a mission to discover what sort of woman Elizabeth's spinster sister was did not mean a different approach. A Ned Skinner might have preferred taprooms and stables, but Angus knew lawyers were like a maypole: all the threads connecting a district came together in them. Of course this was only true in small towns, but England was a place of small towns and villages. Big towns and cities were a result of that new phenomenon, industry on a scale undreamed of in the days of Charles Bingley's grandpa.

Conveyed into the courtyard of the Blue Boar, there to deposit his chaise, his baggage and his valet, Angus discovered from the landlord that Patchett, Shaw, Carlton and Wilde was the firm of solicitors patronised by Hertford's best people, and that the man to see was Mr Robert Wilde.

In Mr Robert Wilde he found a younger, more presentable, less hidebound man than he had expected, and decided to appear frank. Of course his name had been recognised; Mr Wilde knew him for a hugely rich fellow from north of the Border as well as the proprietor of the *Westminster Chronicle*.

"I am a great friend of Fitzwilliam Darcy's," Angus said easily, "and have learned that he has a sister-in-law residing in Hertford. A Miss Mary Bennett — is that one t, or two?"

"One," said Mr Wilde, liking his visitor, who had a great deal of charm for a Scotsman.

"As I feared, an amputation — no, no, Mr Wilde, I am being whimsical! It is not on Mr Darcy's behalf that I am here. In actual fact I'm on a trip into East Anglia, and Hertford being on my way, I thought to call on Miss Bennet with news of her sister Mrs Darcy. Unfortunately I left in such a hurry that I did not think to obtain Miss Bennet's address. Can you furnish it?"

"I can," said Mr Wilde, eyeing Mr Sinclair with some envy: a striking-looking man, between the silvering sandy hair above an attractive face, and the fashionably tailored apparel that shouted his means and his social pre-eminence. "However," he said smugly, "I am afraid that you will not be able to pay her a call. She does not receive gentlemen."

The blue sailor's eyes widened, the fine head went to one side. "Indeed? Is she a misanthrope? Or indisposed?"

"Perhaps a little of the misanthrope, but that is not the reason. She has no chaperone."

"How extraordinary! Especially in one connected to Mr Darcy."

"If you had the privilege of knowing her, sir, you would better understand. Miss Bennet is of extremely independent turn of mind." He heaved a sigh. "In fact, she is fixated upon independence."

"You know her well, then?"

The Puckish cast of Angus's countenance lulled most of those who met him into confiding facts to him that were not, strictly speaking, any of his business; Mr Wilde succumbed. "Know her well? I doubt any man could say that. But I had the honour of suing for her hand some time ago."

"So I must congratulate you?" Angus asked, feeling a twinge of excitement. If Miss Bennet had elicited a proposal of marriage from this well set up and prosperous young man, then she could not be either skinny or hatchet-faced.

"Lord, no!" cried Mr Wilde, laughing ruefully. "She refused me. Her affections are reserved for a name in your own journal, Mr Sinclair. She can dream of no one save Argus."

"You do not seem cast down."

"Nor am I. Time will cure her of Argus."

"I am well acquainted with Mrs Darcy, also with another of her sisters, Lady Menadew. The most beautiful of women!" Angus exclaimed, throwing a lure.

Mr Wilde took it, hook and sinker. "I believe Miss Mary Bennet has the edge on both of them," said he. "She is in the mould of Mrs Darcy, but she is taller and has a better figure." He frowned. "She also has qualities more difficult to define. A very outspoken lady, particularly about conditions among the poor."

Angus sighed and prepared to go. "Well, sir, I thank you for the information, and am sorry that it will not be possible for me to convey Mrs Darcy's regards to her. Norwich calls, and I must take my leave."

"If you could stay in Hertford overnight you may meet her," Mr Wilde said, unable to resist the impulse to show his beloved off. "She intends to be at the concert this evening in the assembly rooms; Lady Appleby is taking her. Come as my guest and I will gladly introduce you, for I know that Miss Bennet is very fond of her sisters."

And so it was arranged that Angus would call at Mr Wilde's house at six. After a good lunch at the Blue Boar and a rather unstimulating stroll to see the attractions of Hertford, he presented himself at six to walk just across the high street to the venue.

There, half an hour later, he set eyes on Miss Mary Bennet, who came in with Lady Appleby just as an Italian soprano was about to launch into several arias from the operatic works of

Herr Mozart. Her garb was dismal in the extreme: depending on the governess, they dressed better. But there could be no diminishing the purity of her features, the glory of that wonderful hair, or the charm of her willowy figure. Entranced, he saw that her eyes were purple.

A supper was laid out after the concert, which was voted excellent, though privately Angus rated the musical talents of La Stupenda and Signore Pomposo mediocre. With Mr Wilde at his elbow, he was taken to meet Miss Bennet.

At the news that Mr Angus Sinclair was the publisher of Argus, she lit up like a Darcy House chandelier.

"Oh, sir!" she cried, stepping in front of Mr Wilde and thus excluding him from the conversation. "I can find no compliment lavish enough to bestow upon the publisher of such a one as Argus! If you but knew how his letters thrill me!" A gleam shot into those amazing eyes; Miss Bennet was about to ask questions maiden ladies were not supposed to upon first meetings. "What is he like? What does he look like? Is his voice deep? Is he married?"

"How do you imagine him, Miss Bennet?" he asked.

The question flustered her, especially since she had come to the concert in no expectation of more than music to while away the time. But to meet the publisher of Argus! Mind in a spin, Mary fought for composure. The proprietor of the *Westminster Chronicle* was not at all what she might have imagined had it ever occurred to her to wonder, so how could she find words to describe the god Argus?

"I see him as vigorous and dedicated, sir," she said.

"Handsome?" he asked wickedly.

She froze instantly. "I begin to think, Mr Sinclair, that you are teasing me. That my unmarried state and my advanced years make me an object of pity and amusement to you."

"No, no!" he cried, horrified at this prickliness. "I was merely trying to prolong our conversation, for the moment I answer your original questions, Miss Bennet, it is over."

"Then let us get it over, sir. Answer me!"

"I have absolutely no idea what Argus is like, literally or metaphorically. His letters come in the post."

"Have you any idea where he lives?"

"No. There is never a mark upon the exterior, and no kind of return address."

"I see. Thank you." And she turned her shoulder on him to speak to Mr Wilde.

The devastated Angus returned to his rooms at the Blue Boar, snapped Stubbs's head off, and sat down to scheme how he could further his acquaintance with Miss Mary Bennet. The most ravishing creature! Where did she get those awful clothes? How could she sully the ivory skin of her graceful neck with rough serge? How could she cram a black cap over that glorious hair? If Angus had ever dreamed of the one woman he would make his wife — he had not — he would have stipulated beauty and dignity, of course, but also a measure of ease in any situation. In other words, the gift of genteel chat, the ability to conjure up an expression of interest even if the subject, the occasion and the object were hideously boring. Prominent men needed such wives. Whereas his Mary — how could he be thinking of her so possessively after one short and disastrous encounter? — his Mary was, he suspected, a social imbecile. The beauty was there, but nothing else. Even Miss Delphinia Botolph, sixty if she was a day, had bridled and simpered when introduced to such a desirable bachelor as Mr Angus Sinclair. Whereas Miss Mary Bennet had turned her shoulder because he could not feed her frenzy for a figment of his own imagination, Argus.

He began to plot. First of all, how to meet his Mary not only again, but many times? Secondly, how to impress her with his undeniable assets? Thirdly, how to make her fall in love with him? In love at last, he found to his horror that things like social imbecility did not matter. Once he had snared her, he would have to paint Mrs Angus Sinclair as an eccentric. That is the best quality of the English, he thought: they have an affinity for eccentrics. In Scotland, not so. I am doomed to live out the rest of my days among the Sassenachs.

Ten years ago he had made the journey south from his native West Lothian to London. The Glasgow coal and iron had been in his family for two generations but, to a Scot as puritanical and logical as his father, wealth was no excuse for idleness. Newly graduated from Edinburgh University, Angus was bidden do something for a living. He had chosen journalism; he liked the idea of being paid to play, for he loved to write and he loved to pry into the affairs of other people. Within a year he was master of the innuendo and the allegation; so steeped was he in his profession that few, even among his closest friends, had any idea who and what he was. It had been exactly the right training for an Argus, for his work had taken him everywhere: a series of murders in a factory; fraud in government and municipal circles; robberies, riots and mayhem. In all walks of life, not least among the poor, the unemployed, and the unemployable. Sometimes he penetrated south of the Border into the haunts of the northern Sassenachs, and that had taught him that, no matter whereabouts in Britain he might be, ultimately everything stemmed from London.

When his father died eleven years ago, his chance had come. Leaving his younger brother, Alastair, to run the family businesses, Angus emigrated, reinforced with the huge inheritance of an elder son, and in the knowledge that income from the businesses would keep his pockets lined with gold. He had bought a house in Grosvenor Square and set out to cultivate the Mighty. Though he made no secret of the source of his money, he discovered that it mattered little because that source was, so to speak, in a foreign country. But he could not quite give up the journalism. Learning that no newspaper existed devoted entirely to the activities of the Houses of Parliament, he had founded the *Westminster Chronicle* and filled the gap. Given Parliament's lethargy and reluctance to meet any more frequently than necessary, a weekly journal sufficed. Make it a daily event, and soon much of its contents would be prolix and spurious. His spies had infiltrated every government department, from Home to Foreign, and the Army and the Navy were guaranteed to provide plenty of fodder for his paper's voracious maw. Naturally he employed half a dozen journalists, but nothing they wrote escaped his personal attention. Which still left him with time on his hands. Hence, a year ago, the genesis of Argus.

Oh, there had been a number of love affairs over the years, but none that had dented his heart. With the daughters of the Mighty it could be flirtation only, but his native shrewdness and considerable social skill had kept him out of the serious clutches of the many high-born young women who succumbed to his charms — and his money. The easiest way to rid himself of his more basic urges was to set up a mistress, though he took great care to avoid married Society ladies for that role; he preferred opera-dancers. None of these activities had imbued him with much respect for the female sex; women, Angus Sinclair was convinced, were predatory, shallow, poorly educated and, after a few months at most, hideously boring.

Only Elizabeth Darcy had captivated him, but at a distance. For one, she was incapable of seeing any farther than Fitz, and for another, beneath her attractions lay the temperament of a warm, maternal kind of creature. Whatever a man's scars, she would want to kiss them better, and Angus didn't think such a woman could keep him interested through half a lifetime of marriage.

Now to find that the woman of his heart was fixated upon his own creation was a blow both ironic and frustrating. No fool, Angus saw at once that, were he to confess his identity, she would scorn him as a dilettante. He did not practise what he preached, and had no intention of doing so, even for this new and painful emotion, love. Imbued with ardour, Mary took Argus at face value. Thus face value it would have to be.

Still, better to cross some bridges as he came to them; the first order of business was to get to know his Mary, make her like and trust him. What a hypocrite you are, Angus/Argus!

The next morning she was the recipient of a note from him asking her to walk with him. An activity, he was convinced, that could not offend her sensibilities. A gentleman escorting a lady through Hertford's public streets was irreproachable.

Mary read his letter and came to the same conclusion. Her plans for her mission of book-writing investigation were made as firmly as possible and the winter had long since begun to drag, despite the efforts of such determined individuals as Mr Robert Wilde, Lady Appleby, Mrs McLeod, Miss Botolph and Mrs Markham. How, she asked herself, could any person exist in such a pointless way? Concerts, parties, balls, receptions, weddings, christenings, walks, funerals, drives, picnics, visits to the shops, playing the pianoforte and reading; they were designed purely to fill in the huge vacancies in a female's life. Mr Wilde had his law practice, the married ladies had their husbands, children and domestic crises, but she, like Miss Botolph, existed in that fashionable new word, a vacuum. One short winter had been enough to teach her that the purpose she yearned for was vital to her wellbeing.

So, upon receipt of Angus's note, she met him in the high street eager to discover more about him, if not about Argus. After all, he did publish Argus! He was very personable, eminently respectable, and not to be sneezed at as a companion for the walk she would have taken anyway. His hair, she decided as they exchanged bows, was like a cat's pelt, sleek and glittery, and something in his features drew her. Nor was it disappointing to find that, in spite of her own height, he was much taller. If any fault were to be found in Mr Wilde, it was that he and she were on the same level. Miss Bennet liked the sensation of being towered over, a disturbing facet of basic femininity that Miss Bennet promptly buried.

"In what direction would you like to go?" he asked as he held out his arm for her to lean upon.

She spurned it with a sniff. "I am not decrepit, sir!" she said, striding out. "We will proceed up this way because it is but a short step into the countryside."

"You like the countryside?" he asked, keeping up.

"Yes, I do. The beauties of Nature are not obliterated by humanity's tasteless urban huddle."

"Ah, indeed."

Her idea of a short step, he learned, was more than a mile; beneath that awful dress two powerful legs must lurk. But at the end of the short step fields began to open up before them, and her pace slowed as she gazed about with delight.

"I suppose that Mr Wilde has informed you of my plans?" she asked, hopping nimbly over a stile.

"Plans?"

"To investigate the ills of England. I commence at the beginning of May. How extraordinary that Mr Wilde did not mention it!"

"It sounds an unusual aspiration. Tell me more."

And, liking the set of his far-sighted blue eyes, Mary told him what she intended to do. He listened without evidence of disapproval; rather, she thought, gratified, he took what she said seriously. And certainly, once she had finished, he made no attempt to dissuade her.

"Where do you intend to start?" he asked.

"In Manchester."

"Why not Birmingham or Liverpool?"

"Birmingham will be no different from Manchester. Liverpool is a sea port, and I do not think it wise to associate with sailors."

"As to sailors, you are right," he said gravely. "However, I still wonder at your choice of Manchester."

"So do I, sometimes," she said honestly. "I think it must be because I am curious about my brother-in-law Charles Bingley, who is said to have 'interests' in Manchester, as well as huge sugar plantations in Jamaica. My sister Jane is the dearest creature, and very devoted to Mr Bingley." She stopped, frowning, and said nothing more.

They had reached the perimeter of an apple orchard, beginning to foam with white blossoms; after such a cold winter, spring had come early and warm, and living things had awakened. The stone wall bordering the fluffy trees was low and dry; Angus spread his handkerchief on its top and indicated that she should sit.

Surprised at her own docility, Mary sat. Instead of joining her, he stood a small distance away from her, his eyes intent upon her face.

"I know what you will not say, Miss Bennet. That you are worried about your sister Jane. That if her husband is exploiting women and children especially, she will suffer a disillusion like to kill her love."

"Oh!" she exclaimed, gasping. "How perceptive of you!"

"I do read Argus's letters, you know."

Suddenly he stepped over the wall into the orchard, and snapped a branch off the nearest tree. "It is in full flower already," he said, presenting it to her with a smile that made her feel a little breathless.

"Thank you," she said taking it, "but you have deprived the poor tree of some of its fruit."

The next moment she was on her feet and walking swiftly in the direction of Hertford. "It is growing late, sir. My maid will be anxious if I do not return at the expected time."

He did not argue, merely ranged himself alongside her, and let her walk in silence. I am learning, he was thinking; do not dare court her, Angus! She is willing to be friends, but the slightest hint of wooing, and she closes with a nastier snap than a poacher's trap. Well, if a friend is what she wants, a friend I will be.

That was the first of enough excursions to cause flutters of hopeful expectation in the bosoms of Mary's female cronies, as well as gloom in the heart of Mr Wilde. What a catch! Angus's valet had triggered a chain of servant's gossip that, naturally, whizzed above stairs; Mr Sinclair had been going into East Anglia, had never intended spending over a week in Hertford. Yet here he was, dangling after Mary Bennet! Lady Appleby scrambled to give a dinner party at Shelby Manor to which

Mr Wilde was not invited, and Mrs Markham aired Miss Bennet's proficiency upon the pianoforte during a cosy evening in her drawing room. To his astonishment, Angus discovered that Mary's talent on the instrument was considerable; she played with unerring touch and true expression, though she was not fond enough of the soft pedal.

On Mary's side, try as she would, she could not resist her suitor's blandishments. Not that he ever said a word she could construe as romantic, or let his hand linger when it brushed hers, or gave her the kind of looks Mr Wilde did. His attitude was that of the brother she had never known; something like, she assumed, an older version of Charlie. For these reasons her sense of fairness said that she could not show him the cold shoulder, though, had she suspected what people were saying, Mr Sinclair would certainly have been dismissed forthwith.

And he, fearing for her, bit his tongue. After nine days he knew every minute aspect of her plans, and gained a better idea of why Fitz had spoken of her sneeringly. She was exactly the kind of female he most despised, for she lacked innate propriety and was too strong willed to take discipline. Not from any moral failing; simply that she did not see herself, an ageing spinster, as needing the full gamut of the proprieties. Young ladies were hedged around because they must go virgins to the marriage bed, whereas a thirty-eight-year-old spinster stood in little danger from masculine lusts or attentions. In that, of course, she was completely mistaken. Men looked at the sleepy-lidded eyes, lush mouth and spectacular colouring, and cared not a rush for her years or her appalling clothes.

Given her age and the years still to come, her means were not adequate for the kind of life she was entitled to; her house cost her fifty pounds to rent, her servants a hundred pounds in wages alone, to which had to be added their upkeep; Angus suspected that the married couple Mr Wilde had found cheated her, as did the cook. Her income did not permit of a riding horse or any kind of conveyance. If Angus understood anything about her, he did understand why she shrank from employing a lady's companion. Those females were uniformly dreary, ill-educated and stifling for such a one as Mary Bennet, whose vitality conquered the clothes and the life society decreed she must lead. What he could not know was what kind of person she had been until very recently, how successfully she had suppressed her aspirations. All in the name of duty.

The withdrawal of her nine thousand, five hundred pounds from the Funds was insanity — *why?* Her excuse to the ferreting Angus was that she might need it for her journalistic investigation, an arrant nonsense.

"I take it you will travel by post?" he asked her.

She looked scandalised. "*Post?* I should think not! Why, that would cost me three or four guineas a day, even for a single horse and a smelly chaise! Not to mention the half-crown I would have to pay the postilion. Oh, dear me, no. I shall travel on the stage-coach."

"The Mail, surely," he said, still thrown off balance. "There is a Manchester Mail every day from London, and while it may not pass through Hertford, it certainly does through St Albans. You would reach your destination the following night."

"After a night spent sitting bolt upright in a swaying coach! I shall travel north from Hertford on the stage-coach to Grantham, breaking my journey every evening to put up at an inn," said Mary.

"There is that to be said for it," said Angus with a nod. "A posting house will afford you overnight comfort as well as good food."

"Posting house?" Mary snorted. "I can assure you, sir, that I cannot afford to put up at a posting house! I will avail myself of cheaper accommodation."

He debated whether to argue, and decided against it. "Grantham is surely too far east," he said instead.

"I am aware of that, but as it is on the Great North Road, I will have several stage-coaches to choose from," she said. "At Grantham I will go west to Nottingham, thence to Derby, and so to Manchester."

Just how straitened were her circumstances? he wondered. Her nine thousand, five hundred pounds would not keep her into her old age, that was true, so perhaps her pride forbade her telling him that she knew she would have nothing more from Fitz, in which case, it made sense that she should scrimp on her mission of investigation. Yet why withdraw her money from the Funds?

Then one reason why occurred to him: because once it was deposited in a bank in her name she knew beyond a shadow of a doubt that it was *there*. To a Mary Bennet, investment in the four-percents was evanescent; her money might vanish in a puff of smoke, victim of another South Sea Bubble. Then a more sinister reason occurred to him: she was afraid that if she left it invested, Fitz might somehow deprive her of it. On their many walks she had talked of him freely, with scant respect and no love. She did not fear him, but she feared his power.

Angus did not fear Fitz or Fitz's power, but he did fear for Mary. Her indifference to clothes meant that she did not look what she was: a gentlewoman of *some* substance. Those who travelled on the stage-coach with her, Angus's racing mind went on, would take her for the most lowly sort of governess, or even a superior abigail. Oh, Mary, Mary! You and your wretched book! Would that I had never dreamed of a nonexistent man named Argus!

What did not occur to him, as she never once mentioned it, was that she expected to pay at least nine thousand pounds to a publisher to put her book into print. So in one way he had been right: the withdrawal of her money from the Funds was done because she feared the power of Fitzwilliam Darcy.

On the tenth day of his sojourn in Hertford, he decided that he could take no more. Better to stew about her fate in London sight unseen than continue to feast his eyes upon her while April's blossoms fell to the ground. Yet he could not say goodbye, did not dare face her again in case his resolution broke down and he made a declaration of love he knew was not returned. Apostrophising himself as a coward and a curmudgeon, he ordered his chaise for straight after breakfast and drove out of Hertford without telling his love that he was going, or leaving her a note.

The word of his departure flew faster than a bird from the

landlord of the Blue Boar to Mr Wilde's under-clerk and Miss Botolph's manservant, and thence, equally swiftly, to Mr Wilde and Miss Botolph. Who were on Miss Bennet's doorstep before the uncomfortably High vicar of St Mark's sounded the Angelus.

Mary heard their news impassively, though under her composure she was conscious of the sadness she always felt when Charlie's visits were over. She dealt with Mr Wilde's overt jubilation in the most dampening way, and assured the pair of them that she had been expecting Mr Sinclair's departure for some time. When Miss Botolph hinted heavily about disappointed hopes she was ignored; the rest of Hertford's upper stratum might have been anticipating a joyous Announcement, but Mary had not. To her, Angus was simply a good friend whom she would miss.

"Perhaps he will return," said Mrs McLeod toward the end of April.

"If he intends to, Sophia, he had better be quick," said Miss Botolph. "Mary is off on her travels very soon, though I do wish she was less secretive about them. And what is Mr Darcy about, to let her ride in the common stage?"

"Pride," said Mrs Markham. "A ha'penny to nothing, he has no idea she is journeying to Pemberley, though I note that her things have been packed and sent to Pemberley ahead of her."

"Is she at all cast down about Mr Sinclair?" asked Lady Appleby; living five miles out at Shelby Manor, she was always the last to know anything.

"Not a scrap cast down. In fact, I would say she is happy," said Mrs McLeod.

"The field is clear for Robert Wilde," said Miss Botolph.

Mrs Markham sighed. "She will not have him either."

FOUR

"I am going home to Pemberley," said Charlie ten days into May, "and I would very much like it if you came with me, Owen."

Dark brows raised, Mr Griffiths looked at his charge in astonishment. "You've finished the term, I know, but Pemberley? Your father will be there, and you dislike that."

"Yes, damn it! However, I cannot stay here."

"Why not?"

"Mary."

"Oh, I see. She has commenced her odyssey."

"Bound to have."

"But how can being at Pemberley help?"

"Closer to her targets. Besides, Pater will be aware of her every movement, if I know him. She may need a friend at court."

"Your mama did say that he was displeased at your aunt's plans, but do you think him likely to confide in you?"

"No." Charlie hunched his shoulders, his mobile face saying more than mere words could. "No one will deem it odd if I go home early, since I couldn't get there at Christmas. Pater will ignore my presence, and Mama will be ecstatic. If you're with me, we can do a bit of prowling in the direction of Manchester. 'Tis but a day's ride from Pemberley. We can pretend to walk the moors, or see the sights of Cumberland. There are reasons aplenty for absenting ourselves from Pemberley for days at a time."

The lad was fretting, anyone could see that, though how he thought he could pull the wool over his father's eyes escaped Owen's understanding. On the single occasion when he had met Mr Darcy, Owen had found himself torn between a strong detestation and a conviction that this was a man only fools would go up against. Of course the relationship between father and son was different from all others, but he could not help feeling that Charlie would do better to stay away. To be underfoot if Mr Darcy chose to apply discipline to his sister-in-law would make matters much worse; a year of listening to Charlie — a regular chatterbox when his head was not in a book — had \apprised Owen of a lot that Charlie had not intended to communicate. And ever since Miss Mary Bennet's letter, the correspondence between him and his mother had been profuse, each writing back to the other the moment a new letter arrived. Mr Darcy was extremely vexed; Mr Darcy had decided not to accompany Uncle Charles to the West Indies; Mr Darcy had delivered a crushing speech in the House against addle-pated do-gooders; Mr Darcy had suffered an attack of the migraine that felled him for a week; Mr Darcy suddenly switched from sherry to whisky before dinner; Mr Darcy had cruelly slapped dear little Cathy for playing a prank; and so on, and so forth.

These reports of affairs at Pemberley (and in London) had only served to throw Charlie into fits of apprehension that culminated in a migraine of his own on the very day when his *viva voce* was scheduled; clearly he had inherited his father's malady, if not his iron character.

"I cannot think it wise," Owen said, knowing that to say more would put Charlie's back up.

"As to that, I agree. Most unwise. Which doesn't make it a scrap less necessary for me to go. *Please* come with me, Owen!"

Visions of the wild, untamed Welsh countryside rose before his eyes, but there could be no refusing this behest; Owen put away his ideas of spending the summer tramping through Snowdonia out of his mind, and nodded. "Very well. But if things should become intolerable, I will not remain to be caught in the middle. Tutoring you is a godsend to me, Charlie, and I dare not run the risk of offending any member of your family."

Charlie beamed. "A done deal, Owen! Only you must let me pay the entire shot whenever we venture abroad. Promise?"

"Gladly. If my father and mother are right, every spare pound must go home. We have to find a good dowry for Gwyneth."

"No, really? An eligible match?"

"Extremely."

"It seems idiotic to me that a girl must be dowered when her betrothed is *extremely* eligible," said Charlie slyly.

"I echo that, but so it is nonetheless. With three girls to marry well, Father must shift to make it seem he can afford to dower them. Morfydd leaves the schoolroom next year."

In earlier days Elizabeth's natural good sense would have precluded her confiding in someone as unsuitable as her son, whose feelings were as strong as they were tender. As it was, she put such reservations away — she must talk to *someone*! Jane was poorly, also very low; Charles had gone off to Jamaica for a year and left her alone. His estates in that idyllic isle were extensive, and relied upon slave labour too heavily to permit manumission after a slave had served a number of years, he was saying now. When Jane had learned he kept several hundred slaves, she had been horrified, and made him promise that he would free them as soon as possible. Let them work for him as free men — in that, there was honour. But he had been obliged to inform her gently that those who slaved for him would refuse to continue working for him once freed. Explaining why had proved a task beyond him; Jane had no idea of the practical conditions that existed on sugar plantations in the West Indies, and would not have believed him had he told her. Floggings, fetters and short rations were expedients so far from her ken that she would have gone into a decline at the very thought that her beloved Charles engaged in them. What Jane did not know, her heart would not grieve about; that was Charles Bingley's credo.

Married to a franker man, Elizabeth did not harbour the same illusions; she was also aware that kidnapping Negroes from the steamy west coast of central Africa had become much harder than of yore, thus causing shorter supplies of fresh slaves as well as higher prices. In her opinion plantation owners ought to accept the inevitable and free their slaves anyway. But this, Fitz had said, was impossible because black men could work in tropical climates, whereas white men could not. An argument that to Elizabeth smacked of sophistry, though for the sake of peace she did not say so.

However, resistance and even rebellion among plantation slaves were growing, despite efforts to suppress them. For this reason Charles Bingley could not postpone his present voyage across the Atlantic. When Elizabeth had learned that Fitz proposed to go with him she had been surprised, but a little reflection had shown her why: Fitz was well travelled, but not west of Greenwich. His excursions abroad had been diplomatic, even including visits to India and China. Always east of Greenwich. A future prime minister ought to have first-hand experience of the whole world, not half of it. Not one to shirk his responsibilities, Fitz had seized upon his brother-in-law's trip as the perfect opportunity to apprise himself of affairs in the West Indies.

That someone as insignificant as Mary owned the power to deter her husband from his plans had not occurred to Elizabeth, so when Fitz announced that Charles would be going to Jamaica alone, she was astonished.

"Blame your sister Mary," he said.

Quite how the news of Mary's plans had become so public was a mystery to Elizabeth. First had come Charlie's letter in February, written in a pother of worry that had stimulated her own concern. Then she received a kindly note from Mr Robert Wilde, whom she did not even remember at Mama's funeral — local mourners had not been introduced. He begged that she would use her influence to persuade Miss Bennet not to go a-travelling in a common stage-coach, thus imperilling her safety as well as her virtue. Then Angus had dropped a line to the same effect! Missives from Lady Appleby and Miss Botolph were far less specific; both these ladies seemed more apprehensive about Mary's eccentricities than her projected travels, for they appeared to think that she was spurning some truly excellent offers for her hand. As, from a sense of delicacy, neither of them mentioned any names, Elizabeth was spared the news that Angus Sinclair was at the top of their list.

To add to her woes, Fitz had invited guests to Pemberley for as long as they wished to stay, which would not be above a week in the case of the Duke and Duchess of Derbyshire, the Bishop of London and the Speaker of the House of Commons and his wife. Probably true of Georgiana and General Hugh Fitzwilliam too, but Miss Caroline Bingley, Mrs Louisa Hurst and her daughter, Letitia/Posy, would probably stay the whole summer. How long Mr Angus Sinclair would stay she had no idea. Now here were two hasty lines from Charlie announcing his advent — with Mr Griffiths, if you please! Not that Pemberley was incapable of accommodating ten times that number in its hundred rooms; more that finding the army of servants to look after the guests and their servants was difficult, though Fitz never demurred at the cost of wages for temporary help. Besides this, the chatelaine of Pemberley was in no mood to devise the entertainments a house full of guests demanded. Her mind was on Mary.

It was not Fitz's habit to spend the spring and early summer at his seat; usually his house parties happened in August, when England's climate was most likely to become uncomfortably warm. In other years, he had vanished to the Continent or the East from April to July. For Elizabeth, May was ordinarily a delight of walks to see what had burst into flower, long hours spent in the company of her daughters, visits to Jane to see what her seven boys and one girl were up to. Now here she was, about to face that mistress of vitriol, Caroline Bingley, that embodiment of perfection, Georgiana Fitzwilliam, and that unspeakable bore, Mrs Speaker of the House. It really was too bad! She would not even have the leisure to find out what Charlie's life at Oxford was like — oh, how she had missed him at Christmas!

Arriving the day before the guests were due, Charlie made light of her apologies about having a full house and no time.

"Owen has not been in this part of England before," he explained ingenuously, "so we will be riding off for days on end — to a native of Wales and Snowdonia's heights, the Peaks of Derbyshire will not disappoint."

"I have put Mr Griffiths in the room next to yours rather than in the East Wing with the other guests," she said, gazing at her son a little sadly; how much he had changed during this first year away!

"Oh, splendid! Is Derbyshire to come?"

"Of course."

"Then bang goes the Tudor Suite, which would have been the only other place I could have let Owen lay down his head."

"What nonsense you talk, Charlie!" she said, laughing.

"Is it to be London hours for meals?"

"More or less. Dinner will be at eight exactly — you know what a stickler for punctuality your father is, so do not be late."

Two dimples appeared in Charlie's cheeks; his eyes danced. "If we cannot be punctual, Mama, I will cozen Parmenter into two trays in the old nursery."

This was too much; she could not resist hugging him, for all that he thought himself too old for that sort of conduct. "Oh, Charlie, it is good to see you! And you too, Mr Griffiths," she added, smiling at the young Welshman. "Were my son alone, I would worry more. Your presence will ensure his good behaviour."

"Much you know about anything, Mama," said Charlie.

"I presume that my son has made an appearance at Pemberley because he thinks to be closer to his Aunt Mary," said Mr Darcy to Mr Skinner.

"His tutor is with him, so he can't do anything too hare-brained. Griffiths is a sensible man."

"True. Whereabouts is his Aunt Mary?" Fitz asked, handing Ned a glass of wine.

They were in the "big" library, held the finest in England. It was a vast room whose fan-vaulted ceiling was lost in the shadows high above, and whose décor was dark red, mahogany and gilt. Its walls were lined with book-filled shelves interrupted by a balcony halfway up; a beautiful, intricately carved spiral staircase conveyed the browser heavenward, while sets of mahogany steps on runners made it possible to access any volume anywhere. Even two massive multiple windows crowned with Gothic ogives could not illuminate its interior properly. Chandeliers depended from the underside of the balcony and the perimeter of the ceiling, which meant the middle of the room was useless for reading. The pillars supporting the balcony bore fan capitals, and behind them in pools of candlelight were lecterns, tables, chairs. Fitz's huge desk stood in the embrasure of one window, a number of crimson leather chesterfields littered the Persian carpets on the floor, and two crimson leather wing chairs sat on either side of a Levanto marble fireplace sporting two pink-and-buff marble Nereides in high relief.

They sat in the wing chairs, Fitz ramrod straight because such was his nature, Ned with one booted leg thrown over a chair arm. They looked at perfect ease with one another, perhaps two old friends relaxing after a day's hunting. But the hunting was not animal, nor the friendship that of social equals.

"At the present moment Miss Bennet is in Grantham, awaiting the public stage-coach to Nottingham. It does not run every day."

"Grantham? Why did she not go west of the Pennines and come direct to Derby, if her destination is Manchester?"

"That would have necessitated that she travel first to London, and I don't think she's a very patient sort of woman," said Ned. "She's crossing the Pennines to Derby via Nottingham."

A soft laugh escaped Fitz. "If that doesn't beat all! Of course she was too impatient." Sobering, he glanced at Ned a little uncertainly. "You will be able to keep track of her?"

"Yes, easily. But with your guests arriving, I thought it better to come here while she's safely in Grantham. I'll go back to following her tomorrow."

"Has her progress been remarked upon?"

"Not at all. I'll give her this — she's a quiet soul — no idle chatter, no making a spectacle of herself. Were it not that she's such a fine-looking woman, I'd be tempted to say she needs no supervision. As it is, she draws the attention of all manner of men — drivers, postboys, grooms and ostlers, landlords, waiters, fellows on the roof and box. Those inside a coach with her are no danger — antiques or bear-led husbands."

"Has she had to cope with amorous advances?"

"Not thus far. I don't think it occurs to her that she is the object of men's lust."

"No, it wouldn't. Apart from her distressing eccentricity, she's a humble creature."

"It strikes me, Fitz," Ned said, keeping his voice dispassionate, "that you worry too much. What can the woman do to you, when all is said and done? It isn't as if anyone will take notice of her plaints, or listen if she tries to slander the Darcys, Argus and his letters notwithstanding. You're a great man. She's a nobody."

Fitz stretched his long legs out and crossed them at the ankles, staring into the ruby depths of his glass with a bitter face. "You were too confined to Pemberley to have known that family when it was together, Ned, that's the trouble. You didn't travel with me in those days. My concern over Mary Bennet has nothing to do with expediency — it's simply prudence. My reputation is my all. Though the Darcys are related to every king who ever sat upon England's throne, they have escaped the taint of more stupid men — men who snatched at huge honours, great commissions. Now, finally, after a thousand years of waiting, it lies in my power to advance the Darcy name in an absolutely unimpeachable way — as the elected head of England's Parliament. A duke? An earl marshal of the battlefield? A royal marriage broker? Pah! Mere nothings! England has never sunk so low as under the Hanoverians — petty German princelings with names longer than their ancestry! — but her Parliament has risen in exact step with the diminution of her sovereigns. A prime minister in this day and age, Ned, is *genuinely* pre-eminent. A hundred years ago it was still an empty title passed around the House of Lords like a port decanter, whereas today it is beginning to be based in the House of Commons. Existing at the whim of the electors, rather than embedded in an unelected oligarchy. As prime minister, I will deal with Europe in the aftermath of Bonaparte.

His Russian campaign may have finished him, but he has left the Continent in a shambles. I will mend it, and be the greatest statesman of all time. *Nothing* must be allowed to stand in my way."

Brows knit, Ned stared at him; for all their closeness over many years, this was a side of Fitz he did not know as well as he wanted to. "What has any of that to do with this woman?" he asked.

"Everything. There is a saying so old that no one knows who first uttered it: 'Mud sticks.' Well, I swear to you that not one minute particle of mud will besmirch the name of Darcy of Pemberley! My wife's family has been a constant thorn in my side for twenty years. First the mother, such an embarrassment that bitches like Caroline Bingley spread tales of her all over the West End, as witty as damning. How I writhed! So when the father conveniently died, I shut her away. Only to find that the Hydra had grown yet another head — Lydia. Her, I dealt with by removing her from all decent society and billeting her permanently in Newcastle. Then, after George Wickham was sent out of the country, I had you shepherd her elsewhere whenever she came too close to Pemberley. Though that head is not quite lopped off, it hangs by a strip of flesh and cannot lift itself. Now, just as my plans are nearing fruition, comes the Hydra's worst head to date — sister Mary. A wretched do-gooder!"

Folding his legs up, Fitz leaned forward, his lean face lit by a saturnine, very old anger. "Imagine if you will that this do-good woman with the face of a Botticelli angel writes her awful book, a book that perhaps accuses a Darcy of Pemberley of unspecified crimes. What would Society and the Parliament say? Mud sticks."

"I hadn't realised," said Ned slowly, "that you're so determined to go your own way."

"I tell you, I will be prime minister of these Isles!"

"Seriously, Fitz, let the woman write her book. No one will read it."

"How can you be sure? Beautiful women are *noticed*, Ned! What if Angus Sinclair should get wind of her book? A man of clout, a political creature with friends everywhere. Also the man who first started this brouhaha by making Argus famous."

"Fitz, you exaggerate! Why should her book have anything to do with the Darcys? She's after information about the plight of the poor. Honestly, it's a storm in a teacup."

"Some teacups can enlarge to hold an ocean." Fitz poured himself and Ned more wine. "Experience has taught me that the Bennet family is a perpetual catastrophe waiting to happen. I am not a prophet of doom, but whenever my wife's relatives rear their ugly Hydra heads, I cringe. They have a habit of destroying my luck."

"If they were men, they would be easier to deal with, I can see that." The dark face grew even darker. "The silence of men may be procured one way or another. But women are cursed difficult."

"I have never asked for murder."

"I know, and am grateful. However, Fitz, should it ever prove necessary, I am yours to command."

Fitz drew back in horror. "No, Ned, no! I can see the need to have some stubborn fool beaten within an inch of his life, but never the removal of that life! I forbid it."

"Of course you do. Think no more of it." Ned smiled. "Think instead of being prime minister, and of how proud I will be."

Angus Sinclair was the first of the guests to arrive, so eager was he to settle quickly into this staggering palace. His rooms were a suite decorated in the Sinclair tartan, a conceit Fitz had thought of when Angus had first visited nine years ago. A way of saying that he was welcome at any time, for however long. His man Stubbs was equally satisfied with his airless cubicle adjacent to the dressing room. One of the worst features of house parties in Stubbs's view was servant accommodation, usually a wearying walk involving many stairs away from the master's domain, and no top-of-the-trees valet cared to associate with a swarm of underlings. Well, such was not his lot at Pemberley, where, to his intense gratification, he knew that the top-of-the-trees valets and ladies' dressers even had their own dining room.

Leaving an unusually sanguine Stubbs to unpack, Angus went to the library, which always took his breath away. Lord, what would a member of the Royal Society say were he to see it? That none had, he could be sure, for Fitz did not mix in circles dedicated to the pursuit of knowledge and science.

Entranced, he wandered about peering at the spines of the many thousands of volumes, and yearned to have the organisation of its treasures. For it was clear that no one with an abiding love of books had ever put Appuleius with Apicius or Sophocles with Euripides and Aeschylus, let alone assembled all the voyages of discovery together half the room away from treatises on phrenology or the phlogiston theory.

In one alcove he found the Darcy papers, a big collection of poorly bound or even unbound screeds on land grants and acquisitions, tenants, properties elsewhere than Pemberley, citations from kings, codicils to wills, and many autobiographies of Darcy Royalists, Yorkists, Catholics, Jacobites, Normans, Saxons, and Danes.

"Ah!" cried a voice.

Its owner skipped nimbly between the chesterfields, a very young man with Elizabeth's beauty, a head of chestnut curls, and his own character, which Angus soon read as a combination of purpose and curiosity. This had to be the disappointing son, Charlie.

"Found the family skeletons, eh?" he asked, grinning.

"Years ago. But 'tis not bones annoy me. This place is a regular mess. It needs sorting, cataloguing and collating, and the family papers should be in a muniment room."

A rueful look appeared; Charlie nodded emphatically. "So I keep telling Pater, but he tells me I'm over-fussy. A great man, my father, but not bookish. When I'm older, I'll try again."

Angus touched the papers. "The Darcys have followed the true line, it looks like — York, not Lancaster."

"Oh, yes. Added to which, Owen ap Tudor was an upstart, and his son Henry a usurper to the Darcys. And how the Darcys of that particular time hated Elector George!"

"I'm surprised the Darcys are not Catholic."

"The throne has always meant more than religion."

"I beg your pardon!" Angus exclaimed, remembering his manners. "My name is Angus Sinclair."

"Charlie Darcy, heir to this daunting pile. The only bit of it I love is this room, though I'd take it apart, then put it together again more logically. Pater turned a much smaller room into his parliamentary library — his Hansards and Laws — and works there."

"Let me know when the day comes that you attack this room. I will gladly volunteer to help. Though what it most needs is its own wee sun to light it."

"An insoluble problem, Mr Sinclair."

"Angus, at least when we're not in lofty company."

"Angus it is. How odd! I never imagined the owner of the *Westminster Chronicle* as a man like you."

"What kind of man did you envision?" Angus asked, eyes twinkling.

"Oh, an immense paunch, a careless shave, soup stains on the cravat, dandruff, and possibly a corset."

"No, no, you can't have soup stains and dandruff in the same man as a corset! The first indicates indifference to appearance, whereas the corset indicates shocking vanity."

"Well, I doubt you'll ever have the dandruff or need the corset. How do you maintain your figure in a place like London?"

"I fence rather than box, and walk rather than ride."

They settled down on two chesterfields in close but opposite proximity and proceeded to lay down the foundations of a strong friendship.

I wish, thought Charlie wistfully, that Angus had been my father! His character is exactly what a father's should be — understanding, forgiving, unshakable, humorous, intelligent, unhampered by shibboleths. Angus would have taken me for what I am, and not belittled me as unworthy. Nor deemed me effeminate on no better grounds than my face. I cannot *help* my face!

While Angus thought Fitz's heir a far cry from the weedy and womanish weakling he had been led to expect. Though this was his ninth visit to Pemberley, he had never met Charlie any more than he had met the four girls; Fitz kept children, even those of seventeen, in the schoolroom. Now, looking at Fitz's heir for the first time, he grieved for the boy. No, Charlie didn't have the constitution of an ox or a sporting bone in his body, but his mind was powerful and his emotions admirable. Nor was he effeminate. If he set his heart on something, he would shift mountains to get it, yet never in a ruthless way, never riding roughshod over others. Were he my son, thought Angus, I would be very proud. People do not love Fitz, but they will love Charlie.

It was not long before Charlie confessed why he had invaded Pemberley during a stuffy house party.

"I have to rescue my aunt," he said.

"Miss Mary Bennet, you mean?"

Charlie gasped. "How — how did you know that?"

"I am acquainted with her a wee bit."

"Really?"

"Yes. I spent a few days in Hertford in April."

"But do you know she's taken the bit between her teeth?"

"Elegantly put, Charlie. Yes, I do. She confided in me."

"Who is this wretched Argus fellow?"

"I don't know. His letters come in the post."

At which point Owen entered the library, gaping at it with an awe he didn't feel for the Bodleian. As soon as he could be persuaded to abandon his explorations and join them, Charlie and Angus went back to the subject of Mary.

"Do you have to do things like promenade with Derbyshire and the Bishop of London?" Charlie demanded of Angus.

"Occasionally, yes, but by no means every day. I am familiar with the Peaks and quite enjoy the precipices and rocking stones, but my weakness is the caves. I am very fond of caves."

"Then you're the sort of fellow prefers getting wet through and covered in slime than getting overheated and covered in rubble. I do have an alternative occupation — you could ride with Owen and me in search of Mary."

"A far better idea! Count me in."

Charlie remembered that Angus had said he liked to walk rather than ride, and looked anxious. "Er — you *are* comfortable on a horse, I take it?" he asked.

"Quite comfortable, even atop your father's aristocratic prads."

"Capital! Owen and I are off to Buxton in the morning. The Plough and Stars in Macclesfield is famous for its luncheons and is the post house, so we intend to do Macclesfield as well. Coming?"

"I fear not," said Angus with regret. "I think tomorrow I must be on hand to welcome Derbyshire and the Speaker."

FIVE

Hertford did not have a coach terminus; the public conveyances that passed through it stopped to change horses at the Blue Boar — which was therefore a post house — at around about noon. Having two choices, either to go to London and there take a more direct route, or proceed north until she could find a vehicle going west, Mary had elected to go north, as she had told Angus. It did not seem logical to have to go south in order to achieve the opposite point of the compass.

Every aspect had been thought out, she could tell herself with satisfaction. The bulk of her belongings had gone via Pickford's carriers to Elizabeth at Pemberley for safekeeping, while what she took with her had been shaved down to as little as possible. Understanding that she might have to walk some distance carrying what she had with her, at least from time to time, she had shopped carefully for luggage. Boxes, which were actually small metal-bound trunks, were clearly out of the question, as were true portmanteaux, which could be carried, but were large and heavy. In the end she settled for two handbags made of stout tapestry; their bottoms held little metal sprigs that kept the fabric clear of water. One, larger than the other, had a false bottom in which she could put her dirty laundry until she could wash it. Apart from these two handbags, she had a black drawstring reticule in which she put twenty gold guineas (a guinea was worth slightly more than a pound, having twenty-one shillings to it rather than twenty), a phial of vinaigrette, her five favourite Argus letters, a coin purse for change, and a handkerchief.

In the handbags, carefully folded, went two black dresses shorn of frills and furbelows, camisoles, plain petticoats, nightgowns, under-drawers, one spare black cap, two spare pairs of thick woollen stockings, garters, handkerchiefs, rags for her menstrual courses, a spare pair of black gloves, and a mending kit. Each garment was as sparing in volume as she could make it. After some thought, she put a pair of bedroom slippers enclosed in a bag on top of her nightgowns in case the floor of her room should be cold or dirty. For reading she carried the works of William Shakespeare and the *Book of Common Prayer*. Her letter of credit was tucked in a pocket she had attached to each of her three dresses, so was always on her person.

She wore her third black dress, over which she was supposed to wear a cloak, but, despising cloaks as clumsy and inefficient, she had made herself a greatcoat like a man's. It buttoned down the front, came up to her neck, and down to her knees and wrists. Her bonnet was home-made too; even Hertford's milliners displayed nothing half so hideous in their windows. It had a small front peak that would not get in her or anybody else's way, and a spacious crown under which both cap and hair would fit comfortably. Firmly tied beneath her chin with stout ribbons, it would never blow off. On her feet she wore her only footwear, a pair of laced ankle boots with flat heels and no style whatsoever.

The reticule, she discovered as she waited at the Blue Boar for the northbound coach to arrive, was very heavy — who would ever have believed that nineteen gold guineas could weigh so much? She had drawn twenty from the bank yesterday, but tendered the twentieth at the stage-coach agency for a ticket in stages as far as Grantham. It indicated that she would break her journey at Biggleswade, Huntingdon, Stamford and, finally, Grantham. There she would have to buy another ticket, as she intended to leave the Great North Road.

The huge conveyance lumbered up at noon, its four light draught horses steaming, its cheap seats on the box and roof so full that the coachman refused to take more outside passengers. While the team was being changed Mary tendered her ticket to Biggleswade, only to be roundly sworn at; she was not on his passenger list.

"You go only as far as Stevenage," he growled angrily when she insisted that he honour her reservation. "There be a race meeting at Doncaster."

What this had to do with coaches to Grantham Mary did not know (or indeed, why gentlemen would wish to travel so far just to see horses race), but she resigned herself to alighting in Stevenage. In her youth she vaguely remembered that her elder sisters had occasionally travelled by stage or Mail coach, but such had never been her own lot. Nor, she knew from that time, did Jane or Elizabeth take a maid, though sometimes Uncle Gardiner gave them a manservant to guard them while they were on the Mail. Therefore she could see no impropriety in her own unaccompanied journey; she was, after all, quite an elderly spinster, not a beautiful young girl like Jane or Elizabeth at that time.

When she climbed into the coach cabin she discovered that the coachman had jammed four people on either seat, and that the two elderly gentlemen who flanked her were not chivalrous. They glared at her and refused to make room, but in Mary Bennet they mistook their mark. Neither timid nor afraid, she gave a determined thrust with her bottom that succeeded in driving a wedge between them. Braced as if in a very tight gibbet, she sat bolt upright and stared into the faces of the four passengers opposite. Unfortunately she was facing backward, which made her feel slightly sick, and it was only after some frantic searching that her eyes found a focus — a row of nails on the ceiling. How awful to be crammed cheek by jowl with seven strangers! Especially since not one of them bore a friendly expression or was given to talk. I shall die before I get as far as Stevenage! she thought, then stuck out her chin and settled to the business. I can do anything, anything at all!

Though the windows were let down, nothing short of a gale would dispel the sour stench of unwashed bodies and dirty clothes. In her fantasies she had gazed with delight out of the windows at the passing countryside, greedy to devour its beauties; now she found that impossible, between the swelling corporations of the gentlemen on either side of her, a huge box on the lap of the dame in the right opposite window, and an equally large parcel on the lap of the youth in the left opposite window. When someone did speak, it was to demand that the windows be shut — no, no, *no*! After a heated wrangle, the dame demanded a vote on the issue, and windows open won.

Three hours after leaving the Blue Boar, the coach pulled up in Stevenage. Not anything like as large as Hertford! Knees weak, head aching, Mary was liberated outside the best inn, but upon enquiry was directed to a smaller, meaner establishment half a mile away. A bag in either hand, she commenced to walk before she realised that she should first have ascertained the time of tomorrow's northbound coach. The sun was still well up; best turn around and do that now.

Finally she put her bags down on the floor of a little room in the Pig and Whistle; only then could she avail herself of something that had lurked in her mind for half the journey. Oh, thank God! There was a chamber pot underneath her bed. No need to traipse to an outhouse. Like all women, Mary knew better than to drink copious beverages while she travelled. Even so, iron control was necessary.

Not perhaps the most auspicious start, she reflected as she poked at greasy stew in a secluded corner of the taproom; the inn had no coffee room and no trays were available. Only her most forbidding expression had kept several tipsy drinkers at bay; not really very hungry, she ate what she could and went to her room, there to find that the Pig and Whistle did not close its taproom doors until well into the early hours. What a day to commence a journey! A Saturday.

The stage-coach she boarded at seven in the morning took her as far as Biggleswade, where a party with influence at the coach company in London had booked all its seats onward. The coachman kept his cabin passengers to three on either seat and the noon stop was an hour, time to drink a cup of scalding coffee, use the stinking outhouse, and stretch the legs. The woman in the left opposite corner talked incessantly, which Mary could have borne better had she not found herself the object of remorseless questions — who was she, where was she going, who had died to plunge her into mourning, what a lot of nonsense, to be investigating the plight of the poor! The only way Mary could stem the tide was to pretend to have a fit consisting of jerks and yammers. After that, she sat in peace. The Biggleswade inn was more bearable too, though she had to be up at five to board the stage to Huntingdon, then waited over an hour for it.

She was miles east of where she wanted to be, but knew that she would have to get to Grantham and a coach depot before she could turn west. Her first two days she had spent in the middle of the backward facing seat, but to her joy she was now luckier; she got a window seat facing forward. To be able to gaze out at the countryside was wonderful. The landscape was lovely, flat fields green with crops, coppices, snatches of forest that the coach trundled through in merciful shade; for May the weather was very warm, every day thus far a fine one. As they passed through an occasional village the children spilled out cheering and waving, apparently never tired of seeing the monstrous vehicle and its labouring horses. Labour the horses did; jammed with passengers, local mail and parcels, freight and luggage, the coach was immensely heavy.

The roads were shocking, but no one travelling them ever expected any other state. A coachman tried to avoid the worst of the potholes, but grinding along in the ruts was inevitable. Twice they passed carriages tipped into the ditch, and once some fellow in a many-caped greatcoat almost sent them into the ditch as he thundered past in a curricle drawn by two matched greys, grazing the wheel hubs and setting the coachman to cursing. Local carts, wagons and gigs were a nuisance until their drivers realised that if they did not get off the road in a hurry, they would be turned into kindling.

Those with the money to purchase a ticket on the stage-coach were not poor, though some were close to it. Mary's seat companion was a mere child going to governess two children near Peterborough; as she looked into that sweet face, Mary suppressed a shudder. For she knew as clearly as if she were a gypsy peering into a crystal ball that the two children would prove incorrigible. To hire this child said that the Peterborough parents had devoured many governesses. The woman of mid-age opposite was a cook going to a new position, but she was sliding down the ladder, not moving up it; her rambling conversation betrayed a fondness for the bottle and unclever fraud. How amazing! thought Mary as the miles ground by. I am learning about people at last, and suddenly I realise that my servants in Hertford cheated me, rightly deeming me an ignoramus. I may not yet have encountered any poor, but I am certainly receiving an education. In all my life, I have never before been inescapably exposed to strangers.

The poor walked from place to place, and there were many of them along the road to Huntingdon. A few carried a cloth in which were knotted bread and cheese; some swigged at bottles of gin or rum; but most, it seemed, lacked even food or inebriants. Their toes poked out of their flapping shoes, their children were barefoot, and their clothing was in filthy tatters. Women suckled babes and men made water openly, children squatted to empty their bowels exhibiting a chortling interest in what they produced. But shame and modesty are luxuries only those with money can afford, said Argus. Now Mary saw that for herself.

"How do they manage to live?" she asked a sensible-looking fellow passenger after he tossed a few pennies at a particularly ragged group of these wretched walkers.

"Any way they can," he answered, wondering at her interest. "'Tis not the season for work on the land — too late for sowing and planting, too early for harvest. Those walking south are going to London, those walking north probably to Sheffield or Doncaster. Hoping for a job of work in a mill or factory. None of these are on the Parish, you see."

"And if they find a job of work, they will not be paid enough to afford both food and shelter," she said.

"That is the way of the world, marm. I gave that lot my pennies, but I have not enough pennies for them all, and my shillings I must save for myself and my own family."

But it need not be the way of the world, she said silently. It need not be! Somewhere there are enough pennies. Somewhere, indeed, there are enough shillings.

The journey was very long. What had begun in Biggleswade at seven ended in Huntingdon at seven, the coachman smiling from ear to ear at the speed of his progress. So tired she felt light-headed, Mary discovered that the closest inexpensive inn was some distance away at Great Stukely. Well, nothing for it: tonight she would stay at the post house where the coach had stopped, since she was to board another at six in the morning for the wearisome leg to Stamford.

A meal of properly cooked roast beef, roast potatoes, French beans, peas and hot buttered rolls put new life into her veins, and she slept comfortably — if not for long enough — in a clean feather bed with well-aired sheets. However, half-a-crown was *dear*. All she could hope was that Stamford held a cheaper place.

The coach did not reach Stamford until nine that night, in a twilight that ordinarily would have enchanted her, perfumed and misty. As it was, the Grantham stage left early — why do they always leave early? I need to sleep, and I have learned that I cannot sleep sitting bolt upright in a smelly coach.

From Stamford to Grantham she found herself squeezed in between two selfish old gentlemen and facing two children sharing one seat. Since both were boys, and of quite the wrong age for a coach journey, they drove their mother to the edge of dementia and the other passengers to the edge of murder. Only a sharp crack around the shins from one old gentleman's cane saved four people from the hangman's noose, though the mother told him he was a heartless brute.

Grantham had a coach depot attached to a huge post house and was the centre for a network of stage routes; the town sat on the Great North Road that ran to York and finally to Edinburgh. The only trouble was, Mary learned, that east–west routes did not matter as much as north–south ones. No conveyance bound for Nottingham was due until the day after tomorrow, which left Mary on the horns of a dilemma: did she spend a day of inertia in this busy town at a decent inn, or frugally? Having severely suppressed a qualm of conscience, she elected the elegant post house alongside the depot, secured a room in the back sequestered from the noise of the yard, and ordered a tray of food. A whole two crowns poorer, Mary still couldn't feel very guilty. Not after those awful boys and their goose of a mother. And who could ever have dreamed that so many old gentlemen with huge paunches travelled long distances by stage-coach?

A full night's dreamless sleep did much to mend her temper and her headache. After ringing for hot water and a tray of coffee and rolls, she set out for a brisk walk to sample Grantham's attractions — not many, and not inspiring. The constant stream of traffic, however, she found fascinating, especially the post chaises, curricles, phaetons, carriages and barouches of the wealthy. Every vehicle going north or south went through the hub of Grantham because the horses kept by its posting inns were superior.

After a good luncheon she walked to the river Witham and stood upon its bank, only then realising why she felt a trifle flat.

Such a charming prospect! Willows, poplars, reeds, ducks and ducklings, swans and cygnets, the widening ripples of some fish kissing the water's surface — how much nicer it would be did she have company! Specifically, the company of Mr Angus Sinclair. Once the notion dawned, she acknowledged the fact that adventures were more satisfying if shared, from the horrors of the stage-coach to the sights of the countryside and its inhabitants. With Angus, the talkative and inquisitive lady could have been laughed at, those two dreadful little boys easier borne, the argument about whether the windows should be open or shut put in its proper perspective. The visions fell over each other in her mind, crying to be told to some dear friend, yet no dear friend was nigh to hear them.

I have missed Angus acutely, she admitted, not quite the same Mary after five days on the road in public coaches. I like the way his beautiful blue eyes sparkle with enthusiasm or humour, I like the way he watches out for me when we walk, I like his kind nature and his dry comments. Nor did he spoil it for me by speaking words of love — oh, I could not have borne that! Had he said them, I would have had to send him away. In the ordinary scheme of things I do not overly care for men. They are either overbearing and self-opinionated like

Fitzwilliam Darcy, or stuffed with romantic rubbish like Robert Wilde. But I do not think of Angus as a man. I think of him as a friend more satisfying by far than female friends, who care only for eligible marriages and *clothes*.

The ducks had gathered, expecting bread, and she had none; turning from the river with a sigh, Mary walked back to the inn and spent the rest of the day reading *Henry VI* — apart, that is, from spending half an hour devouring a steak-and-kidney pudding and a rhubarb tart with thick cream. Only six days into her journey, and she was losing weight! How could that be, when she had spent them sitting down? Yet another lesson for the student of humanity: that sometimes a sedentary occupation could be more gruelling than mixing mortar.

And hey-ho, back to the stage-coach on the morrow! Aware that she was heading west now, and that Nottingham was a much shorter distance from Grantham than Stamford, she had climbed into the conveyance in a sanguine mood, rested enough to be at the depot early, thereby securing a window seat. Unfortunately such desirous objects depended upon the coachman, and this day's coachman was a surly brute who stank of rum. Not five minutes after she was ensconced in her window seat, Mary found herself evicted from it to make room for a party of five men. As they were downy fellows up to every trick of travel, they had tipped the coachman threepence for the best seats. The sole female passenger, she was relegated to the middle of the backward facing seat, and was subjected to leers and pert remarks from the three opposite her and groping hands from the two flanking her.

When they realised that she had no intention of talking to them, let alone flirting with them, they judged her above herself and proceeded to make her journey the worst misery she had suffered to date. When the coach stopped to change horses she was imprudent enough to complain to the coachman, and got naught for her pains except to like it, or walk. Advice that the men on the roof and box thought brilliant: no help there. Everyone on this stage was drunk, including the coachman. A furious Mary took her place in the cabin afterward sorely tempted to hit the fellow on her right, stroking her leg; but some instinct told her that if she did, she would be overpowered and subjected to worse.

Finally Nottingham arrived. All but one of her companions shoved her aside in their hurry to alight, while the stroking one held back, bowing to her mockingly. Head up, she descended from the coach and went sprawling in a heap of reeking, watery manure; the stroking man had tripped her. She fell headlong, tearing the palms of her gloves as she tried to save herself, and her reticule flew to land feet away, its contents spilling out. Including her nineteen gold guineas. Bonnet dangling around her neck and half blinding her, she lay staring in horror at her precious coins, subsiding into more muck. What a slipshod place, an unruly little corner of her mind kept repeating: no one sweeps or cleans.

"Here, let me," said a voice.

In the nick of time. The glitter of gold had attracted much attention, including from the coachman and the stroking fellow.

The owner of the voice was a big man who had been watching the coach come in. He reached Mary before the others could, gave them a cold glance that saw them back away, then lifted her to her feet. Quick and lithe, he gathered up her guineas, her reticule and its other contents. The reticule was handed to her with a smile that transformed an otherwise menacing face.

"Here, hold it open."

Handkerchief, smelling salts, Argus's letters, coin purse and all nineteen guineas were dropped into it.

"Thank you, sir," said Mary, still gasping.

But he had gone. The driver had tossed her handbags into yet another pile of watery manure; Mary picked them up with an effort and walked out of the yard vowing that she would never again set foot in Nottingham.

The room she hired at an inn down a back street possessed a mirror that showed Mary what havoc the day's disaster had wrought. Her greatcoat and dress were soaked in horse urine and covered with remnants of manure; when she fished it out, she found to her horror that the sheet of paper authorising her to draw upon her funds from any bank in England was an illegible mess of run ink. How could that have happened, when her greatcoat should have shielded it? But it had not, nor had her dress. How much water did one of those huge horses produce? Gallons, it seemed. She was wet to the skin. Her palms were sore as well as dirty, and her tapestry bags were stained, damp on their bottoms — but not, thank God, wet.

Trembling, she sank onto the edge of the lumpy bed and buried her face in her hands. How dared those men treat her so? What was England coming to, that a gentlewoman of her age could not travel unmolested?

There was cold water in a ewer on a small table, and by now she had sufficient experience of cheap inns to know that this was the only water she would get. The dress was beyond wearing again until she could wash it, so she draped it over the back of a small chair to dry, and put her greatcoat on the larger chair that said this room was the best the inn could offer. In the morning she would roll dress and greatcoat together, wrap them in paper if she could beg some, and put them in the false bottom of the bigger bag. The water in the ewer would have to be for her own use, though she suspected that it would take a tub of hot water to rid her of the stink of horse excrement.

Dining in a corner of the taproom was positively congenial after such a day, especially when she discovered that the leg of mutton was fairly tender and the steamed pudding tasty. Let us hope, she said to herself, that my ordeal is over. Even if I have to pay half-a-crown or more a night at the best inn in town, I am doomed to travel by the public stage-coach. A hired carriage, even drawn by one horse and of the least expensive kind, still costs three guineas a day before gratuities. There is no point in writing my book if I cannot afford to pay to have it published. However, when I get to Derby I am going to put up at a place can offer me that tub of hot water.

* * *

Two coaches were waiting in the yard when Mary entered it at six the next morning, having had no sleep thanks to the ammoniac smell wafting off her own body. A dull ache at the back of her head ran through it and made her ears ring, her eyes water. There must be something in the Nottingham air, she decided, that makes people so unhelpful, so rude, for no one in the yard paid her any attention. Desperate, she grabbed at a fleeing groom's sleeve and forcibly detained him.

"Which is the coach to Derby?" she asked.

He pointed, twisted free of her grasp, and ran.

Sighing, she gave her two handbags to the coachman of the vehicle indicated. "How much is the fare?" she asked.

"I'll ticket you first stop. I'm late."

Praying that today would be more pleasant, she climbed up and occupied the forward facing window on the opposite side. Thus far she was the only passenger, a state of affairs she didn't think would last. But it did! Thank you, God, thank you! The coach, an old and smelly one pulled by four slight horses only, rolled out of the yard. Perhaps, she thought, developing a sense of humour, I am so fragrant that no one can bear my company. Which went to show how much Mary was changing; the old Mary had found little in life to laugh at. Or perhaps the new Mary was so beset by ill fortune that she thought it better to laugh than to cry.

The sheer luxury of having the cabin all to herself sent her mood soaring. She swung her feet onto the seat, put her head against a herniating squab, and fell asleep.

Only the cessation of movement woke her. Feet down, she stuck her head out of the window.

"Mansfield!" roared the driver.

Mansfield? Mary's geography did not extend to a list of every town in England, but it was extensive enough to tell her that Mansfield was not on the road from Nottingham to Derby. She scrambled out as the coachman was descending from the box.

"Sir, did you say Mansfield?" she asked.

"That I did."

"Oh!" she exclaimed, eyes gone as grey as the lowering sky. "Isn't this the coach from Nottingham to Derby, sir?"

He looked at her as if she were mad. "Marm, this is the stage to Sheffield. Derby was t'other one!"

"But the groom pointed me to this one!"

"Grooms point at the sun, the moon, the stars and stray dogs, marm. This is the Sheffield stage-coach, else it wouldn't be in Mansfield."

"But I don't want to go to Sheffield!"

"Happen you'd best get off, then. You owe me sixpence."

"Is there a coach back to Nottingham?"

"Not today, there ain't. But if you step inside yon inn and wait, happen you'll find someone going in that direction." He thought hard, grunted. "Or else going to Chesterfield. A lot of traffic between here and Chesterfield. From there you could get to Manchester, but knowing you, marm, you won't want to go to any of them places."

"I do want to go to Manchester! It is my ultimate destination!"

"There you are, then." Out came a callused paw. "Cough up sixpence, if you please. Right or wrong coach, it's sixpence from Nottingham to Mansfield."

Seeing his logic, she loosened the drawstrings of her reticule to give him the coin, and recoiled: the bag reeked! Her guineas! She had forgotten to wash them!

Off trundled the Sheffield stage-coach, the two men on its roof flat out and snoring. Judging by the clouds, they would soon be soaking wet. Mary walked into the taproom of a small, very respectable inn, resigned to accepting a lift from some farmer who would make her sit in the tray with his pigs. That would contribute an interesting overtone to her aroma!

The place smelled of strong soap, and the floor was still wet. The landlord's wife, wielding a scrubbing brush, got to her feet in a hurry.

"Be off with you, dirty creature!" she cried, nostrils flaring. "Go on, be off!" She waved the brush like a native his club.

"I will gladly depart, madam," said Mary icily, "if first you will furnish me with the name of an establishment from which I may secure transportation in the direction of Chesterfield."

Unimpressed, the woman eyed her contemptuously. "There's only one place for the likes of you! The Green Man. You stink the same."

"How may I find the Green Man?" As she asked, Mary found herself being hustled out into the road by a nerve-pinching grasp around her elbow. "Unhand me, you pitiless and worm-eaten female dog!" she cried, wrenching free. "Have you no charity? I have had a nasty accident! But instead of being kind, you are unkind. Female dog? That is a euphemism! I will call you what you are — a *bitch*!"

"Sticks and stones! A mile down that road," said the landlady, and shut the taproom door with a bang. Mary heard a bolt slide.

"It is easy to see that Eau de Cheval is not anyone's favourite perfume," said Mary to no one, and, a bag in either hand, set out down "that road".

A cottage stood to right and to left, but after them, the countryside went not to fields but to forest. Frowning, she looked up to find the sun, but no sun peered through the dense overcast. Unless the Green Man was very close, she was going to be drenched. She walked faster. Was she in truth heading west? Or did this road lead into the thickets and impenetrable glooms of Sherwood Forest? Nonsense, Mary! Sherwood Forest is long gone to a figment of the imagination, its great trees felled to make room for the country seats of newly enriched gentlemen, or else to form the strakes and ribs of His Majesty's ships of the line. Only small tracts of it remain, and those some miles east of Mansfield. My reading has informed me of these facts.

Even so, this nameless wood stretched away on either side, the ground coppered with dead leaves or bottle-green from clumps of bracken, and the road itself was as dim as twilight.

Came the sound of hooves clopping behind her; Mary turned to see if perhaps a pig-carting farmer was upon her, only to see a solitary rider astride a tall, fleet-looking bay horse. What do I do now? Pretend he does not exist, or ask him if I am going in the right direction? Then as he drew closer she went limp with relief. It was the kind gentleman who had picked her up in the Nottingham coach yard, retrieved her guineas.

"Oh, sir, how glad I am to see you!" she cried.

He descended from the saddle as easily as if it were but a foot off the ground, looped the reins around his left forearm, and stepped in front of her.

"I could not have asked for anything better," he said with a smile. "You have no luck, do you?"

"I beg your pardon?"

"I had no chance to steal your guineas in a busy coach station, but here? Like taking a rattle off a baby!"

Obeying an impulse, her hands dropped the bags and fastened tightly about her reticule. "Kindly forget what you have just said, sir, and permit me to find the Green Man," she said, chin up, eyes steady and unafraid. Yes, her heart was beating fast and her breathing had quickened, but they were prompting her to fight, not flight.

"I can't do that." The black hair, worn long enough to be tied back with a ribbon, stirred in a sudden gust of rainy air. "Besides, the Green Man is *my* ken — you'll get no succour there, just a trip to a bawdy-house. You're not young, marm, but you are uncommon pretty. Trust old Beatty's wife to throw you out! She's a Methodist, of whom there are many in these parts, more's the pity. Who are you, to have so much money? When you fell in the muck I thought you a sad apology for a governess, forever running from the master's amorous advances. Then I counted your guineas. Now I don't know what to think, except that the money is no more yours than it is mine. Stole it, you did."

"I did not! Step aside, my man!"

She may as well not have spoken. Head to one side, he looked her up and down in a considering way, eyes half closed, lips peeled back from equine teeth. "The question is, do I just take your guineas, or must I murder you? Were you bathed and better clad, might you be in fact a gentlewoman? If 'tis so, I'd best kill you. Otherwise when Captain Thunder is maybe caught one day, you'd bear witness against him, eh?"

Prudence commanded her to be quiet, not to betray her origins, but that low she had not sunk. "Is that your name, Captain Thunder? Yes, indeed, Captain Thunder, I would bear witness against you in a court of law! You deserve the gibbet as well as the gallows!"

Clearly she puzzled him, gave him pause; women were prone to scream the house down, not answer him back. Skinny, filthy, alone, yet not reduced to terror.

"Give me the money."

Her fists knotted over the reticule until their knuckles went white. "No! It is *my* money! I need it!"

The horse was patient and placid; when he laid hands on her the animal stood its ground as its reins were jerked about, apparently uninterested in the developing struggle. The plan Mary had been forming to set the horse plunging and kicking evaporated. Until now nothing in her life had revealed how physically strong she was; she surprised him with that strength as she fought to keep her money. He couldn't even bend her fingers back to break them, so convulsive was their grip on her reticule. Wiry and agile, she slipped from his hold. Off down the road she ran, yelling, but within yards he overtook her, gripping her shoulders cruelly.

"Bitch! Cow!" he said, swinging her around and taking her throat in his left hand. His right crushed her wrists together until, nerveless, they released her hold on the reticule. It began to fall, was scooped up.

Mary went quite mad. One foot lashed out at his shins, a knee tried to reach his groin, her nails clawed at his face and drew blood — how *dared* this brute rob her!

But he had not let go her throat. A roaring invaded her ears, his face in front of her goggling eyes grew darker, less distinct. All fight left her; just as a crashing blow landed on her brow, Mary lost consciousness.

Moaning, sick to her stomach, she woke to find she was crumpled at the base of a huge tree, almost hidden by its buttresses. Drear light percolated through the leaves from overhead, and it was raining. Had been raining for some time, if her soaked clothing was anything to go by.

About an hour elapsed before she managed to drag herself into a sitting position on one buttress, there to ascertain her injuries. A very sore and bruised throat, bruised wrists, a great swelling over her right brow, and a piercing headache.

When she felt able to stand she began to search for her bags and reticule, but in vain. No doubt Captain Thunder had taken them off the road and pitched them into thick bracken, probably well removed from her own site. Though no wind blew on the forest floor, her teeth were chattering and her skin chilly to the touch; she was cold and hurt, and everywhere she looked were massive trees. This was no secondary-growth forest, for its denizens looked a thousand years old. Perhaps it was Sherwood; in which case, she was miles from where she had been. Then good sense reasserted itself — no, this was not Sherwood! It was some other immensely old forest in a county famous for them. Probably not even very extensive, except that when one was in it, all concepts of dimension were lost.

If she was to live, she had to find shelter against the encroaching night. After walking a small distance she found a beech rotted from within. It offered her enough protection to shield her from the rain; squeezed into the narrow cavity, Mary felt her spurt of energy peter out, and lost consciousness again.

The blow to her brow had been more severe than she understood, and would plague her for days to come with lapses of consciousness; when next she roused, night prevailed. She had slipped to sit upon the ground, but at least it was not raining. Then she fell into a kind of coma, restless and haunted with horrible dreams, but when her eyes opened, they found daylight. An experimental walk told her that she was not well; her whole body was in pain, and she fancied she was running a fever. I am coming down with a chill, and I am hopelessly lost. What to do, what to do? If only my head would stop throbbing!

He had meant this, she was sure. Captain Thunder, some local highwayman whose headquarters lay at the Green Man. By abandoning her in the depths of the forest, he intended she would perish from starvation and exposure, thinking thus to absolve himself of guilt for her death. Well, Captain Thunder, she thought, I am not going to oblige you by tamely lying down and giving up! Somehow I will find my way to the road.

The nook in the beech tree that had sheltered her was soft, mossy — didn't moss grow on the north side of trees? And if it did, then the moss-free side was south. Only the woods lay left *and* right of the road! To walk south or north depended upon which side of the road he had chosen to dump her. Oh, the wretch! A true disciple of Satan! Eyes closed, Mary tried to put herself in the mind of a highwayman, and decided he would favour the left hand because that was the hand governed by Satan. But was left facing Chesterfield, or facing Mansfield? Mansfield, because the inn he frequented had been ahead of her, not behind her, when he accosted her. Therefore, said she, I will go south on the side of the trees not covered in moss.

How far would he have taken her? The trees did not allow a horse passage, so he would have had to carry her. Was he chivalrous enough to carry a lady as a lady ought to be carried — in his arms? No. Captain Thunder would have slung her over his shoulder, which meant he might have tramped as much as a mile inward from the road.

She marched along resolutely, but the pain in her bones was worse and the headache splitting. When she looked up, the lacy vault above wheeled ominously, and her legs seemed to drive through piles of wool. I am not going to die! she cried over the pounding of her heart. I am not going to die, I am not going to die!

Then in the distance she saw a break in the trees filled with sunlight — the road! She began to run, but her traitorous body was done with running; she tripped over a buried root and pitched flat out. The world went black. It is not fair! was the last thing she remembered thinking.

When she roused the next time she was across the withers of a horse, bent like a staple. She stirred and muttered unintelligibly, then realised that she was at the mercy of another captor, not a rescuer. Rescuers held a lady in their arms, captors put them across the horse's withers. I never knew England was so stuffed with villains, she tried to say. Whoever rode behind her lifted her head and shoulders and forced a fiery liquid down her gullet. Choking, spluttering, she flailed at him, but whatever he had made her drink set her bruised brain to whirling; back she slid into that world of darkness and nightmare.

Oh, she was *warm*! Exquisitely comfortable! Mary opened her eyes to find herself on a feather bed, a hot brick at her feet. Her limbs felt light, and she didn't smell of horse excrement. Someone had washed her thoroughly, even to, as her fingers discovered, her hair. The flannel nightgown was not hers, nor the socks upon her feet. But the pain in her body had diminished, and her headache was gone. The sole reminders of her ordeal were the bruises on her wrists, throat and brow, and the ones on her wrists, which she could see, had faded from black to a rather repulsive yellow. Which meant that considerable time had gone by. Where was she?

She swung her feet out of the bed and sat on its edge, eyes wide in the gloom. All around her were stone walls, not man-made, but natural; a gap in them was covered by a curtain, and a natural stone seat had a wooden plank across it with a hole — a commode of sorts. There were two tables, one piled with simple food, the other with books. Both had a chair tucked beneath them. But by far the most magical thing about this place was its lighting. Instead of candles, which she had believed to be the only form of lighting, glass lamps stood giving off a steady glow from a flame protected by a chimney. She had seen such chimneys before, when a candle needed protection from a wind, but never this broad, steady flame poking through a metal slot. Below the slot was a reservoir of some sort of liquid in which the wide ribbon of wick swam. One of these lamps, she thought, intrigued, gave off the same amount of light as ten candles.

Reluctantly abandoning her inspection of the lamps — there were four large and one small — she saw that a rug covered the floor and the curtain was of heavy dark green velvet.

Hunger and thirst asserted themselves. A jug of small beer sat upon the food table together with a pewter mug, and while Mary disliked beer of any kind, this, after her travails, tasted like nectar. She broke chunks off a crusty loaf, found butter, jam and cheese, and some slices of an excellent ham. Oh, that was better!

Stomach satisfied, function returned to her mind. Where was she? No inn or house had stone walls. Mary went to the curtain and pulled it aside.

Bars. Iron bars!

Horrified, she tried to see what lay beyond, but a massive screen blocked her view. And the only noise was a high, thin, shrill and constant howl. No sounds of human beings, or animals, or even plants. Under the howl was a heavy silence, as of a grave.

It was then that Mary realised her prison was under the ground. She was buried alive.

SIX

Derbyshire and his Duchess were to set off for their own seat on the morrow, so was the Bishop of London; Elizabeth made a special effort with the dinner on the night before. Her chef was French, but not from Paris; rather, he hailed from Provence, and could therefore be expected to produce an array of dishes that titillated the jaded palates of diners who sat at the best tables. There were still pockets of snow on The Peak itself, and Ned Skinner had gone west to the Welsh coast for shrimps, crabs, lobsters and swimmy fish, availing himself of the snow and ice on Snowdonia's lofty crags as packing. Fish that did not produce gastric upsets were all the rage, and here at Pemberley the theme could be fish in digestive safety.

Elizabeth chose to wear lilac chiffon, as she would not come out of mourning until November. No need for black during the second six months, but white was insipid and grey depressing. Easy for gentlemen, she thought; a black armband, and they could wear what they liked. Fitz would prefer her decked in her pearls, quite the best in England, but she preferred a collar of amethysts and wide amethyst bracelets.

At the top of the staircase she met Angus Sinclair and Caroline Bingley.

"My dear Elizabeth, you are the personification of your own gardens," Angus said, kissing her hand.

"That could be taken to mean sprawling and tasteless," said Miss Bingley, very pleased with her amber-bronze spangles and stunning yellow sapphires.

Elizabeth's hackles rose. "Oh, come, Caroline, can you honestly think Pemberley's gardens tasteless?"

"Yes, I can. I also fail to understand why Fitz's forebears did not use Inigo Jones or Capability Brown to lay them out — such an instinct for everything that is of the first mode!"

"Then you have not seen the daffodils smothering the grass beneath the almonds in full bloom, or the dell where lily of the valley are almost met by tendrils of weeping pink cherry," said Elizabeth tartly.

"No, I confess I have not. My eyes were sufficiently offended by beds of orange marigolds, scarlet salvia and blue somethings," said Caroline, not about to concede defeat.

Angus had regained his breath, and laughed. "Caroline, Caroline, that is not fair!" he cried. "Fitz has been trying to emulate Versailles, which does have some hideously mismatched flower beds. But I am all with Elizabeth — it is Pemberley's flowering glades that are the haunts of Oberon and Titania."

By this they had reached the bottom of the grand staircase and were entering the Rubens Room, sumptuously crimson, cream and gilt, its furniture Louis Quinze.

"Now this," said Angus, sweeping his arm around, "you cannot criticise, Caroline. Other gentlemen's seats may be littered with portraits of ancestors — most of them very badly executed — but at Pemberley one sees *art*."

"I find fat nudes repulsive," said Miss Bingley disdainfully, saw Louisa Hurst and Posy, and went off to join them.

"That woman is as sour as a Lisbon lemon," said Angus under his breath to Elizabeth.

In lilac her eyes were absolutely purple; they gazed at him gratefully. "Disappointed hopes, Angus dear. She so wanted Fitz!"

"Well, the whole world knows that."

Fitz entered with the Duke and Duchess, and soon a merry pre-prandial congress was underway. Her husband, Elizabeth noted, was looking particularly complacent; so was Mr Speaker, a great crony of Fitz's. They have been carving up the empire and Fitz is to be prime minister as soon as the crowned heads of Europe can deal with Bonaparte's abdication. I know it as surely as I know the bodies of my own children. And Angus has guessed, and is very unhappy, for he is no Tory. A champion of Whiggery is Angus, more progressive and liberal. Not that there is much in it; the Tories defend the privileges of the landed gentry, whereas the Whigs are more devoted to the entitlements of business and industry. Neither can be said to care about the poor.

Parmenter announced dinner, which necessitated a rather long walk to the small state dining room, decorated in straw-coloured brocade, gilt and family portraits, though not poorly executed — these were Van Dyke, Gainsborough, Reynolds and Holbein.

Charlie and Owen had arrived early enough to earn no censure from Fitz, secretly pleased. He had last set eyes on his son at Mrs Bennet's funeral, and he saw now that Charlie had grown both physically and mentally. No, he would never be entirely satisfactory, but he no longer looked like a bum-boy.

Elizabeth put Charlie on one side of the Bishop of London and Owen on the other; they could converse about Latin and Greek authors if such was their pleasure. However, it was not. With a scornful look at Caroline Bingley, his chief traducer, Charlie chose to entertain the entire table with stories of his adventures showing Owen the Peak District; the subject was irreproachable and the emphasis on gentle humour, just right to amuse such a disparate audience. No mention of sister Mary was made, though Elizabeth feared they had found no trace of her. If Manchester was her goal, she had not yet reached anywhere near it.

The lobster, plainly broiled and dressed only with drawn butter, had just been removed when a disturbance outside came to all ears in the dining room. Someone was screaming and screeching, Parmenter was shouting, and a confused babble of men's voices said that he had several footmen with him.

The double doors flew open; all heads at the table turned.

"Lydia!" said Elizabeth on a gasp, rising to her feet.

Her sister looked shocking. Somewhere she had been caught in a heavy shower of rain, for her flimsy dress was soaked, clung to her corsetted body shamelessly. If she had set out wearing a bonnet it had gone, nor did she have gloves, and it was obvious that she had ignored the conventions of mourning. Her dress was bright red — branding her a harlot — and cut very low. No one had done her hair, which stuck up wildly in all directions, and her face was a bizarre pastiche of mucus and smeared cosmetics. In one hand she clutched a piece of paper.

"You bastard, Darcy!" she shrieked. "You heartless, cold-blooded monster! Fucking bastard! Fucking bugger! *Cunt!*"

The words fell into a silence so profound and appalled that the women forgot to swoon at mention of them. As was the custom, Elizabeth sat at the foot of the table adjacent to the doors, while Fitz occupied its head fifteen feet farther away. At sight of Lydia he had tensed, but did not rise, and when she uttered the unutterable his face registered nothing but a fastidious disgust.

"Do you know what this says?" Lydia demanded, still at a shriek, and waving the paper about. "It tells me that my husband is dead, killed in action in America! You heartless, cruel bugger! Bugger! Bugger! *You* sent George away, Fitzwilliam Darcy, you and no one else! He was an embarrassment, just as I am an embarrassment, your wife's relatives that you wish did not exist!" Head thrown back, she emitted an eldritch wail. "Oh, my George, my George! I loved him, Darcy, I loved him! Nigh on twenty years we have been married, but always out of sight and out of mind! The moment

Bonaparte gave you an excuse, you used your influence to send George to the wars in the Peninsula, left me to exist as best I could on a captain's pay, for you refused to help me! I am your wife's sister!" Another of those awful wails. "Oh, my George, my George! Dead in America, his bones in some grave I will never see! You fucking bastard, Darcy! *Cunt!*"

Charlie had moved, but Elizabeth detained him. "No, let her say it all, Charlie. She has already said far too much. Try to stop her now, and we'll have a fight on our hands."

"I was so happy when he survived the Peninsular wars, my George! But that wasn't enough for you Darcy, was it? He was supposed to die in Spain, and he didn't. So you used your influence to send him to America! I saw him for less than a week between those two awful campaigns — now he's dead, and you can rejoice! Well, not for long! I know things about you, Darcy, and I am very much alive!"

Suddenly she collapsed. Elizabeth and Charlie went to her, helped her to her feet and out of the room.

"Heavens above, what a performance," said Caroline Bingley. "Where does your sister-in-law pick up her vocabulary, Fitz?"

That reminded the Duchess, Mrs Speaker and Posy of the words Lydia had used; the three of them fell to the floor.

"I imagine," said Fitz in a level voice after the ladies had been taken to their rooms, "that the covers are considerably reduced for the rest of what has been a memorable meal."

"Un-for-gettable," said Miss Bingley on a purr.

Angus chose to ignore all of it. "Well, I for one refuse to forgo the turbot," he said, determinedly cheerful.

Charlie came back looking very concerned, as Owen noted. "I bring Mama's apologies, Pater," he said to his father. "She's putting Aunt Lydia to bed."

"Thank you, Charlie. Do you stay to finish dinner?"

"Yes, sir."

He sat down, secretly feeling desperately sorry for his father. There was no excusing Lydia's conduct — oh, why did that nasty piece of work Caroline Bingley have to be present? The scene would be all over London the moment she returned there.

The Bishop of London was dissecting the etymology of obscenities for Owen's benefit, and welcomed Charlie's participation.

"Do you know the poetry of Catullus?" the Bishop asked.

Charlie's face lit up. "*Do* I?"

Having returned with his cartload of fish and crustacea, Ned Skinner was at home, and reported to Fitz in his parliamentary library as soon as the rather shattered guests had gone to their various suites.

"What possessed Parmenter and his minions to let her get as far as the dining room?" Ned asked.

"Fright. Apprehension. A reluctance to lay hands on the sister of their mistress, whom they love dearly," said Fitz with scrupulous fairness. "Besides, I imagine they had no idea what would happen in the dining room — she saved her choicest verbiage for my guests, the bitch. And she was drunk."

"Is it true? Is George Wickham dead?"

"The letter says so, and it's signed by his colonel."

"A pity then that she didn't go to America with him. She would undoubtedly have battened on to some colonial yokel and remained there. It baffles me why she's not poxed."

"It baffles me why she's never had children," Fitz said.

"Well, she doesn't fall easily, but when she does, she knows where to go to get rid of it. She's never sure who the father is."

Fitz grimaced. "Disgusting. As to why she didn't go with him to America, she was involved with his colonel at the time the regiment was shipped, and the fellow was desperate to shed her."

"Aye, she's a difficulty wherever she is."

"That's putting it mildly, Ned." Fitz beat his fists on his thighs, an angry and frustrated tattoo. "Oh, what an audience! And I with the prime ministership all but in my pocket! Derbyshire had promised to deliver the Lords, and the Commons has been inclined my way for a year now. The assassination of Spencer Perceval still reverberates, thanks to the Marquis of Wellesley, running everything. Oh, rot the woman!"

"Miss Bingley will spread tonight's tale far and wide."

"Anything to get back at Elizabeth — and me."

"And what of Sinclair? Will the *Westminster Chronicle* air your private troubles in its Whiggish pages?"

"He's a good friend, so I'll hazard a guess that he'll not put my private troubles in his paper."

"What exactly do you fear, Fitz?"

"More scenes of this nature, especially in London."

"She wouldn't dare!"

"I think she would dare anything. The booze has addled what few wits she ever had, and I feature in her mind as the chief villain. While ever she looks like something the cat dragged in, people will spurn her as crazed, but what if she cleans herself up, dresses respectably? As my wife's sister, she could manage to secure an audience with some powerful enemies."

"Saying what, Fitz? That you conspired to have her husband sent overseas to do his military duty? It won't wash."

Out came one shapely white hand to rest on Ned's sleeve. "Ah, Ned, what would I do without you? You demolish my fears with plain good sense. You are right. I will simply dismiss her as a madwoman."

"You'd best put her in a decent house. Line its walls with bottles, have a few men on hand to fuck her, and she'll give you no trouble. Though," Ned added, "I'd make sure she has what in Sheffield they'd call a minder. Someone strong enough to control her, persuade her not to go to London, for instance. I think comfort, clothes, men and booze will keep Lydia happy."

"Whereabouts? I sold Shelby Manor, though it's too close to London. Nearer here, yes?" Fitz asked.

"I know a place the other side of Leek. It housed a lunatic, so it should suit. And Spottiswoode can locate a minder."

"Then I may leave it to you?"

"Of course, Fitz."

The fire was dying; Fitz stacked it with wood. "Now it only remains to persuade my wife not to give her shelter for too long. Can you move quickly?"

"Depending upon Spottiswoode, I can be ready in five days."

Two glasses of port were forthcoming. "I repeat, Ned, that you are my saving grace. When you walked in tonight, I was almost on the verge of echoing Henry the Second's cry about Thomas à Becket — 'Will no one rid me of this meddlesome priest?' Substituting wench for priest."

"Things are never as bad as they seem, Fitz."

"What of the other sister?"

Ned scowled. "A different kettle of fish entirely. At first it was easy. She went from Hertford to Stevenage, thence to Biggleswade, Huntingdon, Stamford and Grantham. There, it seems she decided to head west to Nottingham. I traced her that far, and lost her."

"*Lost her?*"

"Don't worry, Fitz, she can't go far without being noticed, she's too pretty. I think she intended to take the stage-coach to Derby, but it left without her. The only other coach that morning was to Sheffield via Mansfield. It may be that she changed her mind about her destination — Sheffield instead of Manchester."

"I don't believe that for a moment. Sheffield has always been a manufacturing town — Sheffield steel and silver cutlery. Its practices are set in stone."

Grinning, Ned wriggled his brows expressively. "Then, knowing her, she got on the wrong coach. In which case, we will see her emerge either in Derby or Chesterfield."

"Have you time to look for her?"

"Fear not, yes. The house for Lydia is called Hemmings, and I'll have your solicitors deal with it. Leek isn't far from Derby."

It took a long time to calm Lydia down and persuade her that what she most needed was sleep. Elizabeth and Hoskins stripped her of her indecent apparel and put her into a bronze bath tub by the fire, there to wash her ruthlessly from the hair of her head to between her grimy toes. Warming pans had been put in the bed, and Hoskins had had a brilliant idea, though it was not one Elizabeth could like: a bottle of port. However, it did the trick. Still weeping desolately for the loss of her beloved George, Lydia went to sleep.

Fortunately Ned had gone when Elizabeth entered the small library; Fitz had his head bent over a pile of papers on his desk, and looked up enquiringly.

"She is asleep," said Elizabeth, sitting down.

"An unpardonable invasion of our home. She deserves to be whipped at the cart's tail, the harpy."

"I don't want to quarrel, Fitz, so let us avoid all such futile animadversions. Perhaps where we have always erred is in our estimation of Lydia's devotion to that dreadful man. Just because we think him dreadful does not make him so in her eyes. She — she *loves* him. In twenty-one years of rackety behaviour and feckless decisions, she has never swerved in her devotion to him. He taught her to drink, he rented out her body to those who could be of use to him, he struck her senseless with his fists when he was frustrated — yet still she loved him."

"Her loyalty would do credit to a dog," he said acidly.

"No, Fitz, don't disparage her! I think it admirable."

"Does that mean I've gone about you all the wrong way, my dear Elizabeth? Ought I to have turned you into a drunkard, rented you out to Mr Pitt, beaten you senseless to ease my frustrations? Would you then truly love me more than you do my possessions?"

"Don't be ridiculous! Why do you have to do that to me, Fitz? Belittle my compassion, sneer at my sympathy?"

"It passes the time," he said cynically. "I hope you're not cherishing hopes of keeping her here?"

"She must stay here!"

"Thereby preventing my using my seat as a valuable adjunct to my political career! You are my wife, madam, that is true, but it doesn't mean you are at liberty to foist guests on me who are social *and* political suicide. I have instructed Ned to find her a house not unlike Shelby Manor, at sufficient distance from us to posit no risk or threat," he said coldly.

"Oh, Fitz, Fitz! Must you always be so detached?"

"Since it is an excellent tool for a leader of men, yes."

"Just promise me that if Charlie should seek you out on this same errand, you'll treat him more kindly," she said, eyes sparkling with tears. "He means no harm."

"Then I suggest you deflect him, my dear. Especially as I begin to hope that Caroline Bingley's canards about his — er — proclivities are simply the product of her fevered imagination."

"I *loathe* that woman!" cried Elizabeth through her teeth. "She is a malicious liar! No one, including you, ever doubted Charlie's proclivities until she started whispering her poison in various ears — chiefly yours! Her evidence is specious, though you can never see that. She deliberately set out to traduce our son's character for no better reason than her own disappointed hopes! Not that she confines her malice to us — anyone who mortally offends her is sure to become her victim!"

He looked amused. "You make poor Caroline sound like Medea and Medusa rolled in one. Well, I have known her far longer than you, and take leave to inform you that you are mistaken. It is Caroline's nature to say what she thinks or has heard, not to fabricate lies. I invite her to our functions and house parties because not to do so would hurt Charles, who is our son's namesake. However, though I cannot summon up your unfounded indignation at her, I am beginning to believe that Charlie's looks and mannerisms belie his true nature. I daresay that both have been magnets to certain fellows whose proclivities are undeniable, but Ned says that he rejects their overtures adamantly."

"*Ned* says! Oh, Fitz, what is the matter with you, that you are more disposed to believe that man than your own wife?"

Seething, she said a stiff goodnight and left.

Charlie was waiting in her rooms, flirting outrageously with Hoskins, who adored him.

"Mama," he said, coming to her side as Hoskins slipped away unobtrusively, "have you seen Pater?"

"Yes, but I beg that you do not. His mind is made up. Lydia is to go to a Shelby Manor situation."

To her surprise, Charlie looked approving. "Pater is right, Mama. No one has ever managed to wean drunkards off the bottle, and Aunt Lydia is a drunkard. If you kept her here, it would wear you down. Poor little soul! What did George Wickham ever do, to earn such love?"

"We will never know, Charlie, because the only people who can see inside a marriage are the two people in it."

"Is that true of you and Pater?"

"For a child to ask, Charlie, is impudence."

"I beg your pardon."

"I take it that you and Owen have seen nothing of Mary?"

"Nothing. Today we rode to Chesterfield, thinking she might come that way, but she has not. Nor has she been seen in Derby. Tomorrow we think to ride toward Nottingham."

"Tomorrow the Derbyshires and the Bishop depart. You must be on hand to farewell them. The Speaker and Mrs Speaker go the day after. It will be Monday before you can search."

"When Fitz married Elizabeth, I knew I was going to have some sport," said Caroline Bingley to Louisa Hurst, "but who could ever have credited that the sport would grow better year by year?"

They were walking sedately across Pemberley's gargantuan front, their heads turned toward a stunning vista of the artificial lake. A zephyr breeze blew, just sufficient to tickle the surface of the water and turn Pemberley's reflection from a mirror image to a fairytale castle blurred by the approaching giant's footsteps. Not that all their attention was focused on the view; each of the ladies reserved a small corner of her mind for a different vision: that of the picture they themselves presented to any admiring gaze that might chance their way.

Mrs Hurst's slight figure was swathed in finest lawn, pale spearmint in colour and embroidered in emerald-green sprigs with chocolate borders, her hugely fashionable bonnet was emerald straw with chocolate ribbons, her short kid gloves were emerald, and her walking half-boots were chocolate kid. She wore a very pretty necklace of polished malachite beads. Miss Bingley, being tall and willowy, preferred a more striking outfit. She wore diaphanous pale pink organdie over a taffeta under-dress striped in cerise and black; her bonnet was cerise straw with black ribbons, her short gloves were cerise kid, and her walking half-boots black kid. She wore a very pretty necklace of pink pearls. If Pemberley needed anything to set off its glories, it needed them; they were convinced of it.

"Who, indeed?" asked Mrs Hurst dutifully; she was her younger sister's sounding board, and did not dare have thoughts of her own. One Caroline was all any family needed; two would have been utterly insupportable.

"Oh, the bliss of being present at that scene last night! And to think I very nearly refused Fitz's invitation to Pemberley this year! *The language!* How can I possibly convey its obscenity without employing the actual words she used? I mean, Louisa, is there a genteel sort of equivalent?"

"Not that I have ever heard of. Female dog does not begin to approximate those words, does it?"

"I will have to bend my mind to the problem, for I vow I will not be silenced by convention."

"I am sure you'll find an answer."

"I cannot allow people to think Lydia's language was less infamous than it actually was."

"Who will be the most shocked?" asked Mrs Hurst, moving the subject on.

"Mrs Drummond-Burrell and Princess Esterhazy. I am to dine at the Embassy when I return to London next week."

"In which case, sister, I doubt you need regale others. Mrs Drummond-Burrell will do your work for you."

A tall and stalwart form was marching toward them; the ladies paused in their stroll, reluctant to let motion destroy the effect they knew they were making.

"Why, Mr Sinclair!" Miss Bingley exclaimed, wishing she could extend her hand to be kissed, as Louisa was doing; an absurd shibboleth, that unmarried ladies could not have their hands kissed.

"Mrs Hurst, Miss Bingley. How fresh you look! Like two ices at Gunter's — one pink, one green."

"La, sir, you are ridiculous!" Miss Bingley said with an arch look. "I refuse to melt."

"And I fear I have neither the charm nor the address to melt you, Miss Bingley."

Louisa took her cue flawlessly. "Do you publish last night's scandalous goings-on in your paper, sir?"

Was that a flicker of contempt in those fine blue eyes? "No, Mrs Hurst, I am not of that ilk. When my friends have their private trials and tribulations, I stay mum. As," he continued blandly, "I am positive you will too."

"Of course," said Louisa.

"Of course," said Caroline.

Mr Sinclair prepared to move on. "What a pity we cannot hope for universal silence," he said.

"A shocking pity," Louisa said. "The Derbyshires."

"I concur," said Caroline. "The Speaker of the House."

And your own two viperish tongues, thought Angus as he tipped his hat in farewell.

He was meeting Fitz at the stables, but before he got there Charlie waylaid him, very cast down because he had to stay home.

"Are you available for a long ride on Monday?" Charlie asked. "Owen and I are for Nottingham. Best pack a change of raiment in your saddle bags in case we are delayed."

Angus promised, then walked off.

Mary's disappearance frightened him more than he had let anyone suspect; she was such a mixture of sheltered innocence and second-hand cynicism that, like a cannon loosed on the deck of a first-rater, she could go off in any direction, wreaking indiscriminate havoc. If she had adhered to her schedule, she ought to be in Derbyshire by now, so why wasn't she? Love, reflected Angus, is the very devil. Here I am in a lather of worry, while she is probably snug in some inn fifty miles south taking copious notes on farmers and the evils of enclosing common land. No, she is not! Mary is a stickler for being in the correct place at the correct time. Oh, my love, my love, where *are* you?

"Mr Sinclair?"

He turned to see Edward Skinner approaching, and frowned. An interesting fellow, deep in Fitz's confidence — a fact he had always known, yet somehow on this visit that fact was reinforced. Perhaps thanks to Mary and Lydia? Not an ill-looking man, if your tastes ran to massiveness and swarthiness. His eyes bore the same cool detachment as Fitz's, yet he was too old to be Fitz's by-blow — nearing forty, was Angus's guess.

"Yes, Mr Skinner?" he asked, giving Ned his due.

"Message from Mr Darcy. He can't bear you company today."

"Oh, too bad!" Angus stood still for a moment, then nodded to himself. "Well, no matter. I feel like a gallop to blow the cobwebs away, so I'll ride alone. Would you tell Mrs Darcy that I will be back in time for dinner?"

"Certainly."

A vain hope, that he could do anything significant in the time; it was already noon when Angus set out for Chesterfield, which he didn't reach. His horse cast a shoe, he was obliged to seek a blacksmith, and all he had for his pains was a headache from facing the setting sun as he returned.

"I know your mind is occupied with Mrs Wickham," he said to Elizabeth before dinner, "but I am more perturbed about Mary. I never met a person more meticulous, more addicted to the minutiae of timetables and schedules than Mary, yet she has disappeared in spite of informing me how she meant to go."

"I think you dwell upon it too much, Angus," Elizabeth said, her mind indeed preoccupied with hideous thoughts about Lydia. "Give Mary two or three more days, and she'll emerge from her hiding place unaware that she has caused consternation. She was ever thus, you know. Her meticulousness was usually to do with mere trivia, and her concentration upon the timing of events was not sensible. Life always surprised her, however hard she tried to strip it of its astonishments."

"You do not know her!" he said in tones of wonder.

She flushed, annoyed at his reaction. "She is my sister, sir. I do know her, and better than you."

He lifted his brows, leaving them to say without words that he did not agree, but Parmenter's announcing dinner saved them from a serious falling out.

On Monday, Angus, Charlie and Owen started for Nottingham shortly after seven, determined that they were going to find out whether Mary had been seen there. It was a logical place for one going north from Hertford to Manchester, given the stage-coach routes. If Huckstep the horse master was puzzled when they chose strong, steady horses rather than the goers Mr Charlie always rode, he knew better than to ask. Embarrassed that Mr Sinclair's last mount had cast a shoe, he made sure that would not happen today.

The distance from Pemberley to Nottingham was about fifty miles; by riding conservatively they hoped to reach the town in four or five hours without exhausting their steeds, though, said Charlie, "I warned Mama that we may not be back tonight. We are hot on the heels of the notorious Sheriff of Nottingham of Robin Hood's day, and may choose to spend the afternoon quizzing the locals."

"What *do* they teach at Oxford?" Angus demanded of Owen.

"Myths and legends, among other airy-fairy things. Was it not so at Edinburgh?"

"Very sedate, very down-to-earth. Is there a decent inn at Nottingham?"

"The Black Cat," said Charlie, who knew the country north of Birmingham intimately.

Their horses having held up very well, they reached Nottingham at noon, and ate luncheon at the Black Cat before setting out for the coach station posting house on foot.

And finally, news!

"Yes, sirs, I remember the lady," said Mr Hooper, manager of the stage-coach company in Nottingham. "She come in from Grantham last Thursday — one of them unfortunate journeys, I gather. Five louts shared the cabin with her, and I can imagine what a time she had of it! I was busy when the Grantham stage come in, but I run a decent sort of establishment here, and that were a coachload of bad trouble — them on the top were drunk and brawling. In fact, I sacked Jim Pickett the coachman for not running things shipshape. Threw the lady's bags in the dung pile. Hard to find coachmen that don't drink, and Jim drank. Well, he'll have no more rums on me!"

The three men listened in growing horror, but when Charlie would have interrupted the flow, Angus trod on his foot.

"Seems the lady wouldn't have nothing to do with them five louts," Mr Hooper went on, hardly drawing a breath. "So they got their own backs, they did. Tripped her when she was getting out — flat in the muck she went, poor lady! Knocked the wind clear out of her. Ruined her coat and dress — horse piss. I was told a man helped her up, dusted her off. But the muck ain't prone to be fixed by a dust-off. Her reticule went flying, but she got it back, and the man put her gold guineas back into it too. I only saw her a-going out of the yard — a regular mess."

Charlie's face was a study in grief; he gulped, held onto Owen's sleeve. "The curs!" he cried, almost in tears. "I — I cannot credit it! Five men picking on a defenceless woman in a public stage-coach? Wait until my father hears! There will be hell to pay from the highest to the lowest!"

A look of acute apprehension on Mr Hooper's face did not bode well for further information; Angus trod on Charlie's foot again. "Was that the last time you saw her, sir?" Angus asked.

"No. She come back at seven next morning — I were busy again, always am busy. London don't give me enough help, expect the whole thing to run like clockwork. Well, it don't." He fulminated for a moment, then returned to his tale. "Two stages. One bound for Derby, one for Sheffield. The lady got on the Sheffield coach and away she went. Looked fairly tuckered, she did. No coat, new dress, but it weren't no great shakes, and Len told me she stank of horse piss. Still, sir, she had gold in her reticule. Daresay she'll be right and tight."

A groan wrenched itself out of Charlie. "Sheffield! Oh, Mary, why Sheffield?"

"Something must have drawn her there," said Owen, trying to see the bright side. "A factory she heard of, perhaps?"

"So tomorrow we're for Sheffield," said Angus with a sigh. He dropped a guinea in the manager's hand. "Thank you, sir. You've been a great help."

Eyes round at the sight of the coin, Mr Hooper closed his fist on it; by the time he recovered his breath, the three gentlemen — terrific swells! — were walking away.

"Here!" he called after them, the guinea working magic on his memory. "Don't you want to know the rest, good sirs?"

They stopped in their tracks.

"The rest?" from Angus.

"Yes, the rest. My coachman told me yesterday. The lady got off in Mansfield. Turns out she thought she were on the Derby stage, not the Sheffield stage. My man had to charge her for the fare from Nottingham to Mansfield — sixpence — then went on to Sheffield without her. Last he saw of her, she were going into the Friar Tuck. Looking for transport to Chesterfield."

The richer by a second guinea, Mr Hooper could find no more to tell his auditors until long after they had gone. So enthused was he at the prospect of earning a third guinea that he trotted off to the Black Cat at once to impart his afterthought. Too late! The three gentlemen had ridden off.

"Oh, well, 'tain't important," said he to himself. Just that it was very peculiar to have *two* lots of enquiries about the same lady inside three days. Big, surly, black bugger, last Saturday's enquirer had been. Blotted out the sun. Did not bestow guineas — his idea of largesse had been a shilling. *A shilling*, and he the manager!

All of which left Mr Hooper with some questions of his own: who was this lady, why did she have gold in her reticule, who were the gentlemen in search of her, why were there two lots of them, and who was the pretty young man's dad?

They rode for Mansfield at once, Charlie having decided that their horses were rested enough to survive another fifteen miles. Neither Angus nor Owen disputed Charlie's authority in the matter of horseflesh; Owen's father was a farmer, but topnotch mounts were as far from his ken as they were from Angus's.

By six that evening they were dismounting in the yard of the Friar Tuck, and agreed that they would go no farther that day.

When they entered the inn they found its proprietor hovering expectantly.

"Your three best bed chambers, landlord," said Angus, every bone in his body aching; a London existence was not conducive to careering around the countryside with Charlie Darcy. His rump was very sore, but he could still sit down; heaving a sigh of content, he did so.

"It's too late for ale — your best wine, landlord!"

"Ask him, ask him, ask him!" Charlie kept muttering.

"In due time. First, we wet our whistles."

"Lord, I'm tired," said Owen.

"Cawkers, both of you." Charlie subsided with a scowl.

The cellars of the Friar Tuck yielded an excellent claret; after consuming two bottles of it, they repaired to their rooms to freshen up. In the kitchen Mrs Beatty, exhorted by Mr Beatty, was cooking what she termed a "tidy meal".

After doing the tidy meal justice, Angus finally broached the subject of Mary.

"We are in search of a lady," he said to the landlord. "We believe she came in on the Sheffield stage last Friday, it seems thinking she was on the Derby one. On learning her mistake, she alighted, apparently to seek some means of going to Chesterfield. Did you see her?"

"No, sir, I did not."

"I thought the Sheffield stage-coach stopped here?"

"It does. But I weren't here, sir. I was visiting my son at Clipstone, didn't get back until well after the Sheffield stage. It don't wait, sir, just sets down and picks up."

"Surely it changes horses here?"

"No, sir. It does that in Pleasley, two mile farther on. Another of my sons has the King John there, and we split it — he changes the northbound coaches, I change the southbound."

"And does your son in Clipstone have an inn?" Owen asked, fascinated at so much nepotism.

"Yes, sir. The Merry Men."

Charlie sat looking as if the world was ending. "If you did not see her, landlord, did anyone else?" he asked curtly.

"I could ask my wife, sir."

"Kindly do so."

"Is there a Robin Hood hostelry in the family?" Owen asked while Mrs Beatty was being sent for.

"How amazing of you to know that, sir! The Robin Hood belongs to my son Will, over in Edwinstowe, and the Lion Heart to my son John, in Ollerton. Though it's a tavern, not an inn."

Expecting praise for her dinner, Mrs Beatty bustled in engaged in a private debate — did they like the roast venison or the stew delicately flavoured with sage and lamb's kidneys? But the faces of her diners, she now discovered, did not belong to gentlemen with food on their minds. In fact, all three looked forbidding. She began to stiffen, some instinct telling her that she was in trouble.

"Matilda, did a lady get off the Sheffield stage on Friday?"

"Oh, *her*!" Mrs Beatty sniffed. "I would have to call her a woman, for a lady she was not."

Charlie yelped; Angus's foot had made contact with his already bruised toes.

"What happened to her, madam?" Angus asked, heart sinking.

"I sent her about her business, that's what! She *stank*! Dirtying my clean floors, and them not even dry! I'll have none of you, I said, and marched her out my door."

"Do you know where she went?" Angus asked, swallowing an ire quite as hot as Charlie's.

"Only that she wanted to go to Chesterfield, but first she needed a room. I sent her to the Green Man."

"Oh, Matilda!" cried Mr Beatty, looking horrified. "She was a *lady*! Our guests are in search of her."

"Happen they'll find her at the Green Man. Or Chesterfield by now," said Mrs Beatty, unrepentant. "She didn't look no lady to me. She looked like a dirty drab. Too pretty for her own good."

"Charlie, hold your tongue!" Angus snapped. "Then we go to the Green Man in the morning. Prepare an early breakfast."

"I wouldn't," said Mr Beatty.

"Wouldn't what?"

"Go to the Green Man. 'Tis a felons' haunt. Every rogue and thief on both sides of the Pennines congregates there. As well as the highwayman Captain Thunder." He rounded on his wife. "Which is why, Matilda, I take leave to say that you are a sour and bitter woman, to send a lady anywhere near the Green Man. You are always prating about God and you won't even let your daughters dance, but mark my words, God will punish you for your lack of charity! *Methodism!* Making it impossible for your daughters to find husbands outside of the church, and a more dismal lot than those young men I don't know! Well, this episode is the last straw for me! My daughters will wed men who like a drink and a dance!"

Deciding that discretion was the better part of valour, Angus yawned until his eyes watered and shepherded Charlie and Owen bedward before the domestic storm could break.

"There is no point in fretting, Charlie" were his final words to that indignant young man. "We'll be on our way early tomorrow, so get some sleep."

"Just as well I brought my pistols," Charlie said, eyes sparkling. "If the Green Man is half as bad as the landlord says, we may be glad of a pair of barkers."

"I'd feel better about that if I knew you could shoot."

"I can culp a wafer at twenty paces. Pater may deem me bellows to mend in a boxing ring, but he's seen me shoot too often to despise my skill with a pistol. In fact, he had Manton make me my own pair."

Angus's staunch façade fell once he was safely inside his room; surprised because he had felt no pain, he found that his nails had cut into the palms of his hands, he had clenched them so hard. Oh, Mary, Mary! Turned away as a common trollop by an imperceptive bigot like Mrs Beatty! Filthy from her fall — wherever she had stayed in Nottingham had not offered her a bath, probably not even hot water. Well, no doubt Nottingham's inns were stuffed with Mrs Beattys too. He had good reason to think that his Mary would not be intimidated, including by a pack of felons, but worry he must.

A state of mind Mr Beatty did not improve when he knocked softly on Angus's door a few minutes later.

"Yes, sir?" Angus asked irritably, clad in his nightshirt.

"I beg your pardon, Mr Sinclair, but I judged you the leader of your search party, and did not want to wait until the morning — we have a group of visitors arriving to view Sherwood Forest, and I may not get the time."

"What is it you want to say?" Angus asked, feeling a qualm.

"My wife told me that Captain Thunder was lurking last Friday noon when the Sheffield coach arrived. To do her a meed of justice, she was frightened, and very anxious to bolt the door. Though why she couldn't shout for the grooms I have no idea." He scratched his head, dislodging his wig. "After the coach went north to Pleasley she took a peek outside, and there was your lady walking down the road to the Green Man. Captain Thunder was following her, but at a distance. It seems that under her dirt the lady was very pretty, which, my wife being what she is, led her to make a false judgement. So she never called the grooms. Instead, she bolted the door."

"I see," said Angus quietly. "What can you tell me of this Captain Thunder, sir?"

"No good, and that is certain. Folks are afraid of him, and with reason. 'Tis said he is a murderer, though I never heard of him killing anyone he bailed up. Shot one courageous old geezer through the shoulder, but he lived."

"Then whom does he murder, Mr Beatty?"

"Rumour has it, women. The Green Man is a bawdy-house as well as an inn, and Captain Thunder has first choice of new light-skirts. If one goes all shrewish, like, 'tis said he kills her."

"Thank you." Angus shut his door.

He had no sleep that night.

When he stepped into the parlour to partake of breakfast, he still had not made up his mind how much of Mr Beatty's news to impart to Charlie and Owen. Only when he saw their fresh, rested faces did he decide to tell them virtually nothing. If Charlie went off half-cocked their troubles would multiply, but he needed to be sure that pair of Manton pistols were ready for use.

"I do not wish to sound unduly pessimistic," he said in the Friar Tuck stable yard amid the racket of unharnessing several carriages that had brought the sightseers, "but have you loaded your pistols, Charlie? For that matter, where are they? Can you reach them in a hurry if you have to?"

Grinning, Charlie lifted one saddle bag to reveal an elegant, silver-mounted pistol beneath it, a neat firearm ten inches long.

"There's one in the other holster too. They're loaded and almost ready to fire. Flick the frizzen up off the powder pan, cock the hammer, and pull the trigger. I assure you they'll not hang fire or flash in the pan — Manton don't make second-rate pistols."

"Good," said Angus, smiling apologetically. "There's more to you than meets the eye, Charlie."

"I'm not afraid to throw my heart over."

"Let us depart this chaos."

When Angus nudged his roan into a trot, Owen restrained him. "Since the Green Man is but a mile away, might it not be better to walk our horses that far? We should look for signs that Mary passed this way."

Seeing the sense in that, Angus reined in his steed to a walk and the three of them separated to spread across the road, Angus down the middle, Owen near the right ditch, Charlie near the left. The thickness of the woods to either side dismayed them; no chance of riding in to investigate.

Perhaps a half a mile from the Friar Tuck, Owen gave a loud whoop. "Hola! I see something!"

He swung from the saddle and hopped down into the ditch, hands scrabbling in the weed-choked grass, and came up holding a tapestry handbag. Angus opened it without a scruple upon sad women's under-things and the *Book of Common Prayer*. Her name was neatly written upon the front endpaper. Every item of clothing stank of horse excrement; he remembered Mr Hooper's saying that the coachman had thrown her bags onto the dung pile. Poor, poor Mary! Armed to fight the injustices of the world without dreaming that she too might fall prey to them.

"Well, that answers one question," he said, and tossed the bag back into the ditch; the book went into his saddle bag. "There's no point in carrying what's in there — we'll buy her much better at the nearest draper's."

"Oh, Lord, the villain must have set upon her!" Charlie said, blinking at tears. "I'll have his guts!"

"You'll have to share them with me," said Owen.

They could find no sign of the other handbag, but her plain black reticule was lying on the road just as the Green Man came into view around a bend.

"Empty," said Angus. "However, we'll keep it as proof, despite its aroma. See? She embroidered her name upon the lining. Black on black — her eyesight must be magnificent."

Perhaps because the hour was early and felons traditionally lay abed until noon or later, the Green Man looked the very picture of innocence. It was tucked into a pocket of land where the trees had been removed, had stables of a kind down a driveway to one side, and numerous dilapidated out-buildings that seemed to store everything from firewood to barrels and crates. The building itself was large, had a thatched roof and half-timbered walls; the Green Man had been sitting there for at least two centuries. Hens and ducks picked at the ground outside its entrance doors.

No one peered through its mullioned windows as they rode up; clearly the Green Man did not cater to pre-noon patrons.

"I'll go in alone," said Angus, preparing to dismount.

"No, Angus, I'll go," said Charlie with authority. "I'll allow you precedence in civilised places, but this is my country and I know how to go about things." He flipped the frizzen off one pistol, made sure the powder pan was well primed, tucked the weapon horizontally in his breeches waist and then carefully cocked it. "Angus, take the other pistol and stand watch. The frizzen's up, but it's not cocked."

Angus watched in horror at the youth's insouciance, carrying a cocked, primed pistol like that, especially after he draped his coat across it. A slip, a trip, and he would be a Mozart *castrato*. How familiar he must be with pistols! For himself, Angus made sure he held his pistol level, and made no attempt to cock it.

When Charlie entered, he had to bend his head, and blinked in surprise; he had grown inches this past year!

"Hola!" he called. "Anybody at home?"

Came the sound of someone moving, then the distinctive clop-clop of clogs, popular footwear in the North.

At sight of Charlie, the evil-looking fellow who appeared stopped abruptly, frowning at the expensive clothes and very beautiful face. "Yes, my pretty boy? Lost, are you?" He made an effort to smile, showing the rotten teeth of a rum drinker.

"No, I am not lost. I and my two companions are looking for a lady named Miss Mary Bennet, and we have reason to think that one Captain Thunder — a fearsome name! — set upon her between the Friar Tuck and this establishment."

"There be no ladies here," said the man.

"But might there be a Captain Thunder?"

"Never heard of the cull."

"That's not what people hereabouts say. Kindly fetch the fellow, landlord — if landlord you are."

"I be the landlord, but I don't know no Captain Thunder. Who might be asking?" His hand inched toward an axe.

Out came Charlie's pistol, absolutely level. "Don't bother with such antics, please! I am the only son of Mr Fitzwilliam Darcy of Pemberley, and the lady I am trying to find is my aunt."

The mere mention of "Darcy" and "Pemberley" worked upon the landlord so powerfully that his hand flopped to his side as if felled by a stroke. He began to whine. "Sir, sir, you be mistook! This is a respectable house that has no truck with bridle-culls! I swears to you, Mr Darcy, sir, that I ain't never heard of your aunt!"

"I'd be more prone to believe you if you admitted that you do know Captain Thunder."

"Only in a manner of speaking, Mr Darcy, sir, only in a manner of speaking. The cull is known to me in a like way to what he's known elsewhere in the district. He terrorises us! But I swears he brung no lady here! No woman of any kind, dear sir!"

"Where may I find Captain Thunder?"

"They say he got a house in the woods somewhere, but I don't know where, sir, honest! I *swears* it!"

"Then next time you see Captain Thunder, you may give him a message from Darcy of Pemberley. That his nefarious career is over. My father will hunt him down — from Land's

End to John o'Groats, if necessary. He will hang, but worse than that. His body will rot in a gibbet."

Charlie turned on his heel and left, the pistol still in his hand. At sight of him Angus sagged in relief; it seemed the young rascal did indeed know how to deal with Nottinghamshire villains. Concern for his aunt was honing him into the kind of man his father should have been, and was not; Fitz's iron strength was there, but without the coldness. How could Fitz be blind enough not to see what lay in his son?

"No luck," Charlie said tersely, remounting. "I doubt Mary was ever taken there. The rogue who is the landlord knows Captain Thunder very well, I hazard a guess, but isn't privy to all his business. Which makes sense. If he participated in the Captain's every scheme, he'd be entitled to at least a quarter share of the spoils, and the Captain is too fly for that."

"Then we're for Chesterfield?"

"Yes. I won't seek anyone official out — I'd rather sool my father onto the slugs of the constabulary from Nottingham to Leek to Derby and Chesterfield. If nothing else comes of it, Captain Thunder's career is at an end."

"What I haven't told you," Angus confessed, "is that Mr Beatty told me his wife saw the Captain lurking that Friday noon. And he followed Mary down the road toward the Green Man. He must have known she had guineas for the taking — but then, it seems that everyone in the Nottingham coach station knew that. Either the Captain was there to witness Mary's fall, or some paid informant told him. The woods hereabout were perfect for his purpose."

"Mrs Beatty deserves a dose of her own biblical retribution — may she be eaten by worms!" said Owen savagely.

"I agree," Angus said in soothing tones, "but the sentiment doesn't help us find Mary. I'll exhort Fitz to have the constables descend upon the Green Man armed with writs for the arrest of all in it, but like you, Charlie, I don't think Mary was ever there. The Captain didn't want to share his spoils, or tell a soul what he had done."

Owen had listened in growing horror. "Oh! Does this mean she's dead?" he blurted.

His question hung unanswered for a long time before Angus sighed. "We must pray she isn't, Owen. Somehow I can't see Mary giving up her life without a colossal struggle, and I don't mean a physical one. She would have striven to convince the cur that she was too important to kill with impunity."

Tears were rolling down Charlie's cheeks.

"How do we begin to search the woods for her, Charlie?" Angus asked, to give the young man something to think about.

One hand brushed the tears away. "We ride for Pemberley before we do anything else," he said. "My father will know."

Even taking into account an overnight trip to Sheffield, Ned Skinner was ahead of them by two full days. While Charlie (and perforce, Angus and Owen too) kicked his heels waiting to farewell Derbyshire and the Speaker of the House, he had ridden from Sheffield to Nottingham. His technique was different; while both Angus and Charlie tended to apply to the top echelons for information, Ned knew better. So upon reaching the freight depot and coach yard in Nottingham, he spoke very briefly with Mr Hooper, then located a groom who had seen what had happened with his own eyes. As it turned out, he was the same fellow whom Mary had accosted trying to find out which coach went to Derby. Without a scrap of surprise, Ned learned that the youth had maliciously directed her to the wrong conveyance, thinking it a huge joke.

"One day," said Ned, towering over the groom, "I will make sure you get your comeuppance, you thoughtless moron. The poor lady deserved the most tender compassion — a gentlewoman thrown upon the world. Were I not in a hurry, you'd get a beating right now."

Desperate to save his skin, the groom came out with a gem he had mentioned to no one, including Mr Hooper.

"I know who the man was that picked her up when she fell in the horse piss," he said.

Ned loomed even more menacingly. "Who?"

"A highwayman. Captain Thunder's his road name, but his real name's Martin Purling. He has a house hidden in the forest."

"I want directions — talk, you pathetic lump of inertia!"

The pathetic lump of inertia babbled so incoherently that he had to repeat himself several times.

Now what do I make of that? Ned wondered as he made his way to the Black Cat. A bridle-cull who gave her back her guineas? Why? The answer's simple — he couldn't rob her in Nottingham. Then the next morning she got on the wrong coach, but I'll bet he was following her no matter which stage she boarded. Nineteen guineas, the groom said — Miss Mary

Bennet, you are a fool! Captain Thunder would kill you for a quarter that sum!

It was too late to pursue his quarry that day, but next morning Ned was mounted on his beloved big black Jupiter, and riding at a canter.

Knowing more or less where Mr Martin Purling's domicile was, he didn't go anywhere near Mansfield or the Friar Tuck, though he headed in that general direction. The rutted cart track he took into the forest suddenly stopped, blocked by a huge clump of brambles, but Ned had been warned. Gloved, he dismounted and found a place where one set of the long, thorny canes grew from one side of the track and another set from the opposite side met it; dragging them apart was not very difficult for such a big man. Having ridden through it, he pulled the brambles back into place — no need to warn anyone of his presence quite yet.

Four hours from the Black Cat, brambles and all, he was at Captain Thunder's hideaway. What a hideaway! A snug cottage sat in a clearing like an illustration for a children's fairy tale. Thatched, whitewashed, surrounded by an exquisite garden in full early summer flower, it was so far from popular imagination of a highwayman's lair that, even if found, those who saw it would admire, then pass it by. The back yard held stables, a neat shed for firewood, and an outhouse; a clothes line flapping shirts and sheets, under-drawers and moleskin breeches spoke of some careful wife — now why had he assumed Mr Martin Purling would live alone? Clearly he did not. A complication, but not an insuperable one.

Even as Jupiter stopped at the barrier of a picket fence, a woman emerged from the house. What a beauty! Black hair, pale skin, vivid blue eyes smutted by black lashes and brows. Ned felt a pang of regret at the sight of her long legs, tiny waist, swelling bosom. Yes, she was a rare beauty. Not a light-skirt crying out to be murdered, either. Just, like Mary Bennet, a virtuous woman cursed by beauty.

"You're on the wrong road, sir," she said in a Londonish accent, eyeing Jupiter with appreciation.

"If this is the house of Mr Martin Purling, I am not."

"Oh!" she exclaimed, taken aback. "'E ain't 'ere."

"Have you any idea when he'll be back?"

"Tea time, 'e said. That's hours away."

Ned stepped from the saddle, tied the reins to the gate post, loosened Jupiter's girth, and followed the girl — she was more girl than woman — down the flagged path to the front door.

At it she turned to face him. "I can't let you come in. 'E wouldn't like it."

"I can see why."

So quickly she had no idea what was coming, he took both her wrists in his left hand, clamped his right over her mouth, and pushed her through the door.

The kitchen yielded meat twine to tie her up temporarily, with a long, narrow cloth for her mouth; the lovely eyes stared at him in terror above the gag, it never having occurred to her that anyone would tamper with Captain Thunder's property. Ned carried her into the parlour, dumped her in a chair, and drew up another close to hers.

"Now listen to me," he said, voice calm and level. "I'm going to remove your gag, but don't scream or shout. If you do, I'll kill you." He withdrew a knife from his pocket.

When she nodded vigorously, he removed the gag.

"Who are you?" he asked.

"Martin's wife."

"Legal, or common law?"

"What?"

"Did you have a wedding ceremony?"

"No, sir."

"Have you relatives in these parts?"

"No, sir. I am from Tilbury."

"How did you get here?"

"Martin bought me. I was going to the Barbary coast."

"A slave, eh?"

"Yes, sir."

"How long have you been here?"

"A twelvemonth."

"Do you go into town? Into the village?"

"No, sir. Martin does that, but in Sheffield."

"So no one knows you are here."

"No one, sir."

"Are you grateful to Martin for saving you from slavery?"

"Oh, yes, sir."

Satisfied, he put the gag back into her mouth, then went to the yard in search of something less cruel than meat twine to bind her, and found thin rope. Ideal. Poor soul. Her beauty was of an order that had made her stand out in a maritime village like Tilbury. Undoubtedly her parents, soaked in gin, had sold her for enough money to satisfy their liquid passion for months to come. Had she gone to the Barbary pirates, she would eventually have arrived in the harem of some Ottoman Turk, there to wither away from homesickness and a form of subjugation more alien than any in England. Poor soul. I hate to do it, but I must. For Fitz's sake, if for no other reason. No loose tongues, no matter how ill-born.

This time he trussed her so efficiently that she could not move, stuffed a small potato in her mouth behind the gag, and left her to watch the meeting between her Martin and this stranger.

Martin Purling returned shortly after three, whistling cheerfully. His horse, exactly the right kind for a highwayman, was put into its stable and rubbed down; then he strode up the back path toward the kitchen, calling for her.

"Nellie! Nellie, love! Whose is the black gelding? I hope he'll part with it, for I have a mind to own it. Do a hundred miles with a big man up, I'll warrant."

"The black gelding is mine." Ned appeared just inside the doorway with a pistol levelled at Captain Thunder's heart.

"Who are you?" Purling asked, displaying no fear.

"Nemesis." Ned's left hand came up holding a small sandbag, and struck the Captain on the nape of the neck. He went down, only stunned, but it was long enough for Ned to bind him hand and foot. Then he picked him up as if he weighed nothing and carried him into the parlour, where he was thrown into a chair some distance from Nellie. As he came around the first face he saw was hers, and he began to struggle, trying without success to free himself.

"Who are you?" Purling repeated. "I thought you were a fellow knight of the road, riding that horse, but you're not, are you?"

"No."

"It is despicable to be so cruel to Nellie."

"Probably two days ago, Mr Purling, you did far worse insult to a far greater lady than yon strumpet."

Enlightenment dawned; Captain Thunder nodded slowly, all his questions answered. "So my instincts were right. She's from an important family."

"I'm pleased to hear you employ the present tense."

But fright was creeping into the Captain's dark eyes; he was remembering how he had disposed of her. "Naturally I speak in the present tense! I am not a murderer of women, sir!"

"That's not what they say in Nottingham."

"Stories! The highways and byways of Derbyshire, Cheshire and Nottinghamshire are mine and mine alone. They have been for nigh on fifteen years. Time enough for Captain Thunder to have acquired a mythology. Well, the stories are false, sir! And who are you?"

"I'm Edward Skinner, Darcy of Pemberley's man. The lady you robbed of nineteen guineas is his sister-in-law."

The breath hissed through the Captain's teeth, his face mottled, he drummed his bound feet upon the floor. "Then what the hell was she doing on the common stage? How can a man sort the sheep from the goats if carriage folk ride in public coaches? Serves her right, the silly cow!"

"You have a bad temper, Captain. I'm astonished that no one has caught you in fifteen years, though this bolt-hole must be a help. What did you do with Miss Bennet?"

"Left her in the forest. She'll find the road."

"Today is Sunday. That must have been Friday, early afternoon. But no one has seen her, Captain, I assume because she didn't find the road. You never intended that she should. I'll wager you left her a mile inside the trees with no idea of direction. Did you harm her when you took her money?"

The Captain gave a bitter laugh. "I, harm *her*? Look at what she did to me!" Since he couldn't point, he waggled his head about. "The woman is a fiend! She went for me like a terrier with a rat! Choking her didn't work! I had to knock her out."

"Whereabouts did you abandon her?"

"Five miles east of here, on the north side of the road to Mansfield. If you look in my left pocket, you'll find all nineteen of her guineas. Take them. They've brought me naught but ill luck."

"Keep them."

Ned had primed his pistol, but didn't bother bringing the frizzen down to shield the powder pan; instead he cocked it, walked to the girl, put its muzzle against her head, and blew her brains out. It was done so suddenly it took time for the Captain to produce a thin scream of grief. The spent weapon went down on the table; Ned unearthed a second pistol from his other greatcoat pocket and proceeded to tip a few grains of powder into the pan to prime it, brought the hammer back, pulled the trigger, and shot Captain Thunder, also known as Martin Purling, in the chest.

"Never leave witnesses," he said to the parlour as he went about the business of cleaning both pistols, then reloading them; the weapons went into his pockets together with the tiny powder horn he used for priming. "Sorry about that," he said to Nellie as he prepared to leave, "but it was quicker by far than hanging. I hope you go somewhere fairer, but you, Mr Purling, are bound for Hell."

Jupiter ready to ride again, Ned mounted and rode off, being very careful to pull the brambles together. Any with business at Mr Purling's house would take one look, and run. No one would report their deaths.

An hour later he found Mary. She had tripped over that root and fallen not yards from the road. What he saw were her white face and red-gold hair; the rest of her blended into the shadows. He made light work of picking her up and carrying her to Jupiter, but when he reached the beast he put her down and conducted a careful examination. No, not desperately injured, but seriously, yes. A huge swelling over her right brow worried him most, the more so because she failed to rouse. What to do? Were she any other female, he would have taken her to the nearest doctor, but well he knew Fitz's dislike of gossip. Deciding that she would fare no worse for the ride to Pemberley, he put her across Jupiter's withers and mounted.

What he hadn't counted on was tainted meat in the pie he had had for breakfast at the Black Cat. Like many big and powerful men, he could work indefatigably for hours, even days, at a time. But that demanded good health, and he began to feel not quite himself just after he passed to the north of Chesterfield.

Jupiter disliked bearing a burden across its withers, but did so for Ned's sake. Just after darkness fell, Mary stirred. The consciousness she regained was confused and irritable; thinking him Captain Thunder, she tried to fight. Having, as he saw it, no alternative, he tipped neat cognac down her throat, and was only content when she slipped back into oblivion. Once Mary sagged, Jupiter neighed softly and settled down.

Not half an hour later he lost the ability to control his gut, pulled Jupiter up, threw the reins over its head, and lifted Mary down to lie on a soft patch of short, pungent grass and herbs. Tugging at his breeches, he went into a small copse of trees and endured some minutes of uncomfortable cramps and diarrhoea. Oh, what a bother! Lucky it hadn't made him heave, but the runs were bad enough. Tidying himself as best he could, he stood waiting to see if there was more to come, but apparently not. How long had he been? A glance at his fob watch reassured him; no more than ten minutes. How bright the stars were, out in the middle of nowhere! Even without a moon, he fancied he might have been able to read the larger print in a newspaper. Certainly he could see his watch face.

Jupiter was standing in a grateful nap when he returned to the bridle-path, but Mary Bennet had disappeared. Confounded, he stared at the squashed herbs where her body had rested — God, no! No, no, no! Where *had* she gone? Into the trees to relieve herself, as he had done? She could hardly go far in ten minutes, not in her parlous condition.

But she was nowhere in the grove, nowhere on the bridle-path, and nowhere within an easy walk in any direction. Trembling, Ned stopped to think things through without panicking, and decided it was time to mount Jupiter, from which elevation he could see better and farther.

Two hours later he put his head against Jupiter's mane in dull despair. Mary Bennet was nowhere to be found. And now he would have to report to Fitz that he had rescued Mary, only to lose her to some new, unknown peril. She had been stolen while she slept beside the bridle-path; nothing else made any sense, for walk off on her own two legs she had not.

"It is not your fault, Ned," Fitz said when Ned reached him before breakfast on that Monday. "I blame myself and no one else. I gave you Lydia *and* Mary. So terribly unfair!"

"'Twas not you who lost her."

"No, but how could you predict a bellyache? And why would you think her in danger on a deserted bridle-path well beyond Chesterfield? You are a rare man, Ned. You can plan well ahead, then seize the opportunity of a moment in a moment. I can trust you with these exceeding delicate matters, and in turn that leads me to overburden you. What undid both of us was a bellyache, but who could have predicted its outcome? Don't blame yourself. And I'm sorry."

"Don't be. As you say, who could have predicted a bellyache?"

He hesitated, then decided that he would have to tell Fitz about the fate of Captain Thunder and Nellie: a laundered version that would not upset Fitz's own principles.

"Captain Thunder and his light-skirt are dead. When I found their house, a rather wild mêlée ensued that proved me better prepared — and the better shot." He grinned sourly. "In fact, I begin to think that it's the element of surprise and the pistol already cocked and levelled have made Captain Thunder the terror of these parts for fifteen years. The poor girl threw herself in the way of the first ball to save her love. Blew her brains out. I managed to prime and fire my second pistol while the Captain was still fiddling with his powder horn. He took my ball in the heart. I doubt anyone ever goes near the place — they had even hidden the track to it with a formidable hedge of brambles. With your consent, I would rather not divulge the events. Especially because I have to deal with Lydia for the next few days. Could we simply let the pair of villains rot?"

There was no pleading in Ned's voice; Fitz considered his tale carefully, and decided he did not disapprove of the way Ned had handled things. Clearly it had been a matter of life and death, and the only other man he knew was as knacky as Ned over the exasperating business of getting a pistol ready to fire was Charlie. Even had their capture been peaceful, he could see where keeping the pair for the hangman's noose would cause unwelcome publicity. Mary was too involved, and now Mary was missing yet again, which necessitated a new search for her.

Fitz shrugged. "I agree, Ned. Let them rot." He poured Ned fresh coffee. "Today you must rest. Nurse your belly, yes, but most of all get a long sleep. Charlie, Angus and Owen Griffiths went out at seven this morning in search of Mary. They don't know your story, but they might find out something interesting. I predict that they won't return until tomorrow evening, which gives you plenty of time to recover. And yes, I could send someone to bring them home at once, but I would rather not. They will approach the task a different way than you, and we don't know who took Mary off you."

"As you wish, Fitz."

Fitz got to his feet, came around the table and gave Ned a warm hug. "I thank you for your splendid work, Ned. Were it not for you, Mary would have died in the forest. As it is, I think we may safely assume she is still alive. I am deeply in your debt."

"When do you want Mrs Wickham escorted to Hemmings?"

"Thursday, I hope. Spottiswoode has had a letter from the proprietress of the agency in York he uses, saying she has someone on her books, but first must thoroughly check the woman's recommendations. Now go home and sleep."

Ned rested his cheek against Fitz's hand on his shoulder, then got up wearily. He departed glowing, despite his sense of failure. Fitz had hugged him, the love was still there. Could anything destroy it? This business had been the most acid test of it, yet still it survived. Oh, Fitz, what would I not do for you?

All of Elizabeth's time had been taken up in caring for Lydia, whose health was quite broken down. Nor did she see why she should be shifted from Pemberley, where there was always someone else to do the irksome tasks like keeping herself and her clothing clean. Who knew what other premises would yield?

"Lydia, in your heart of hearts you must know," Elizabeth said, secretly sharing her sister's sentiments about removal. "Pemberley is Fitz's seat, famous enough to seem a pinnacle of social achievement. An invitation to stay here is an aspiration fulfilled. He needs Pemberley to further his political career. You did untold damage when you burst into the dining room mouthing disgusting obscenities and accusing Fitz of murder. Your audience included some of the most important people in England — *and* Caroline Bingley, who remains in residence here. She will use your behaviour to belittle and denigrate Fitz. How can you blame him for wanting to be rid of you?"

"Easily," said Lydia sulkily. She surveyed herself in a mirror. "What dreadful clothes you wear, Lizzie! I want money to buy new things — fashionable things. And I refuse to wear black!"

"You may have the money and the clothes, but not here. Fitz has found a nice house called Hemmings, outside Leek. There you may live in the same sort of comfort as Mama did at Shelby Manor. You may shop for apparel in Stoke-on-Trent or Stafford — Fitz has given you accounts at certain modistes in both towns. Your companion, Miss Mirabelle Maplethorpe, has a list of the shops."

Lydia sat up straight. "*Companion?* What can you mean, Lizzie, companion? I have no need of one!"

"I think you do, dearest." Oh, what a wretched situation! Fitz had been happy to explain matters to Lydia himself, but that would have led to such ructions! So Elizabeth had begged to tell Lydia the news herself, thinking it best she wear the witch's hat. She tried again. "My dear, your health is not what it should be. That means you must have company, if only until you build up your health. We have engaged a respectable lady to look after you — part nurse, part companion. As I have already said, her name is Miss Mirabelle Maplethorpe. She hails from Devonshire."

Scrubbed clean of its paint, Lydia's face looked curiously bald, for her fairness was extreme enough to extend to her brows and lashes, absolutely colourless. The puffiness had vanished; she had had no further access to wine or other intoxicants since Hoskins had given her port, and that had been six days ago. Which meant Lydia had now reached craving point, and was ripe for mischief.

"I want two bottles of claret with my lunch," said Lydia, "and I warn you, Lizzie, that if I do not get it, I will create a scene that will pale the last one to insignificance. Is Fitz afraid of Caroline Bingley, then? Well, not as afraid as he will be of me!"

"No wine," said Elizabeth, iron in her voice. "Gentlewomen do not drink to excess, and you were born a gentlewoman."

"*This* gentlewoman drinks! Like a fish! And I am not the only one! Why do you think Caroline Bingley and Louisa Hurst are so prim and proper? Because they drink — in secret!"

"You know nothing about either lady, Lydia."

"It takes one to know one. Is Fitz really afraid of Caroline? He won't be after I get through with her!"

"Lydia, compose yourself!"

"Then give me claret with my lunch! And if you think that I am going off tamely to Leek or anywhere else with a dragon for my companion, you are mistaken!"

"You go tomorrow, Lydia. Fitz insists."

"He can insist until he turns in his grave, I will not go!"

Elizabeth fell to her knees, tried to take the clammy, restless, plucking hands in hers. "Lydia, please, I beg you! Go to Hemmings willingly! If you do not, you will go anyway. That fearsome man Ned Skinner is to escort you, and he puts up with naught. Try him, and you'll be treated as he treated you when Mama died. For my sake, Lydia, please! Go willingly! Once you are ensconced at Hemmings, what you do will be your affair provided you are quiet and discreet. I am led to believe that there will be plenty of wine, though you will not be permitted to entertain men."

"What a mouse you are, Lizzie! Did the jewels, Pemberley and enough pin-money to buy the Royal Pavilion strip you of all spirit? Fitz snaps his fingers, and you scurry, squeaking. Once you used to stand up for yourself, but no more. You are a bought woman. Well, I would rather be an army wife than the chatelaine of Pemberley! Oh, George, George!" The tears began to pour down her face, her body rocked. "I am a widow at a mere thirty-five! *A widow!* Doomed to black crepe and veiled bonnets! Well, I won't! How can I find another husband if I'm shut up at Fitzwilliam Darcy's dictate? Do you really want to be rid of me? Then send me to Bath!"

"To become the talk of that place? No," said Elizabeth, more iron erupting from beneath her pity and grief. A bought woman! Was that how her friends from Longbourn days saw her? Head turned by the material things Fitz could give her? "You will go to Leek and live at Hemmings with Miss Maplethorpe, there to drink yourself silly if such is your desire! Accept it, Lydia. The alternative, I have been informed, is to see you dumped in Cornwall with nothing more than the clothes you stand up in."

The lids dropped over Lydia's pale blue eyes, shielding her thoughts from her sister. "Let me hear this from Fitz."

"Lydia insists upon hearing her fate from you," Elizabeth said to her husband in the small library.

"I take it she doesn't like her fate?"

"'Like' is too mild a word. She's full of wild threats, and wants to go to Bath to live." The smoky eyes turned up to his, full of an agonised pleading. "Couldn't she be allowed that, Fitz? In no time she would become a joke to all and sundry, and no one would heed her."

"A joke who is known to be my sister-in-law. No, Elizabeth, she cannot go to Bath, and that is final. She goes to Hemmings."

"I fear it won't hold her."

"What do you mean?"

"She'll venture out in search of men. There is a side to Lydia that I don't understand, and it involves lovers. The drink is only part of her trouble. She is — on heat."

"Indelicate, coming from you, wife, but a very good description. I would prefer to call her a strumpet."

"I don't believe it can be so lightly dismissed."

"Oh, grow up, Elizabeth! Your family always showed a lack of propriety. That Kitty turned out so well was a minor miracle, but not one I can hope for with Lydia. She always was self-willed, and would go to any lengths to achieve what she willed. I knew George Wickham very well, and I can tell you that eloping with Lydia wasn't his idea. She was crazed about him, and could see only one way to keep him — an elopement. George consented to the marriage only because I agreed to pay his debts. And have been paying his debts ever since, thanks to the identity of his wife."

"Yes, Fitz, I understand all that," Elizabeth said steadily, "but it is past history. You won't keep Lydia at Hemmings."

"Miss Maplethorpe comes highly recommended. Most of her work has been with the mentally afflicted, and so I regard Lydia."

A cold sweat broke out on Elizabeth's brow. "I cannot permit you to imprison my sister, sir."

"That will not be necessary, madam. Miss Maplethorpe will not attempt to limit Lydia's drinking, which will answer, I believe. She'll be too drunk to go in search of lovers." His eyes had turned to obsidian, a black, hard glitter. "It is a year since the Prime Minister was assassinated in the very halls of the Commons, and things have been in flux ever since, with Wellesley guarding the bone. I am within an amesace of becoming Mr Perceval's true successor, and I am not going to be cheated of office by a trollop like your sister!" The cold fire died out of his eyes. "I suggest you go back to Lydia and explain the facts more harshly than, it is apparent, you have thus far."

"Oh, Fitz, what is this passion to be prime minister? Couldn't you abandon public life in favour of your family? Of me?"

He looked astonished. "Family and wife are excellent in their place, but they cannot fulfil an ambitious man's aspirations. I am determined to be prime minister and lead my country to a position of unparalleled power and respect. Our British reputation was severely damaged when we conceded the war in America to the rebels of the thirteen colonies, and we seem unlikely to win this fresh conflict there. However, we have beaten Bonaparte, and that must outweigh all else. Our navy rules the oceans, but strong action must be taken to turn our army into a body of soldiers even the French would quail to meet." His chest swelled, he looked invincible. "I intend to turn Britain into *Great* Britain!"

"Hear, hear!" Elizabeth cried, clapping derisively. "I am so pleased you think me excellent in my place. Of late I have come to realise that you are every bit as proud and conceited as I thought you when first you came into Hertfordshire!"

"It's true that I had no basis for self-satisfaction in those days," he said stiffly, "but the situation has changed. I knew well that I was marrying beneath me — oh, the follies of youth! Were I to have it to do all over again," he said deliberately, "I would not marry you. I would have married Anne de Bourgh, and fallen heir to the Rosings estate. I do not grudge it to Hugh Fitzwilliam, but by rights it was mine."

White faced, she swayed, but righted herself without the help he probably would not have given her. "I thank you for that frank explanation," she said with a stiffness quite the equal of his. "Would you prefer that I removed myself from Pemberley and your life? One of your minor estates would suit me very well."

"Don't be a fool!" he snapped. "I am simply trying to deal with the damnable nuisance your family represents. Lydia will go to Hemmings tomorrow, and very willingly. Not a difficulty, my dear. Ned will dangle a bottle of some lethal liquor under her nose, and she, donkey that she is, will follow it into the carriage."

"I see."

"However, I have another embarrassment looming. Namely, your sister Mary. She's disappeared."

"*Disappeared?*" Oh, what other shocks would he produce?

"Yes. Somewhere between Chesterfield and here."

"What are you doing about it?"

"If you had paused in your ministrations to Lydia, Elizabeth, you might have learned much from our son. Yes, we've all been worried about her, but he and Angus — and Ned, independently of them — have established beyond a doubt that she's been abducted. Charlie can tell you the story."

"He has grown in all sorts of ways, Fitz," she said, sidetracked.

"I am not blind! I'm very pleased at what Oxford and young Griffiths have done for him."

"I suspect Angus has had some influence too."

Fitz laughed. "That is an alliance of mutual affection, my dear Elizabeth. Angus hopes to be your brother-in-law. Were it to come about, the last threat your family represents would be no threat at all, and I would have the *Westminster Chronicle* in my pocket."

"As to the union of Angus and Mary, I rejoice, but if you think that would put his newspaper at your political disposal, then you very much mistake your man. As well as my sister."

Elizabeth quit the library and left her husband to his dreams of grandeur. Leopards don't change their spots, she thought. Oh, but you fooled me, Fitz! I genuinely thought I had cured you of your pride and conceit. And when you began to assume the leopard's hide again, I blamed it on my inability to give you the sons you wanted. But it was never that, I see now. The leopard has stayed the leopard throughout our twenty years together. While I, if I may believe Lydia, have turned into a mouse. A *bought* mouse.

SEVEN

Some days had passed, but Mary had no idea how many, for the lump on her brow seemed to have provoked a series of faints or comas from which she recovered slowly. Sheer exhaustion had entered into it too, and being deprived of daylight, she had no way of knowing how regularly she woke to drink, eat, use the commode.

The velvet curtain was drawn back to reveal a gap in the iron bars that confined her, formed when a section was let down to make a shelf. Stacked on this she would find fresh food, small beer, a jug of water for her ablutions, and a tin with a pouring spout containing an oily liquid. The last, she soon discovered, was to replenish the reservoirs of her lamps. Terror of being plunged into utter darkness stimulated her dazed mind into deducing this, after which she learned how to do the filling: take off the glass chimney, unscrew the metal centre holding the wick, and pour new oil on top of what remained in the glass reservoir. The little lamp burned for longer than the big ones, and she found to her relief that, when she held its weak flame to the wick of a big lamp, it kindled readily.

Twice she had found clean nightgowns and socks on the shelf, once a clean robe, but never outer wear of any kind. She was warm enough, as the chamber never seemed to grow freezingly cold any more than it grew very hot. About the temperature of a cool spring day, she concluded.

If only she had some way to gauge the passage of time! The highwayman must have taken her fob watch; they were expensive and not easily come by. Hers had been a gift from Elizabeth, greatly appreciated. No external elements penetrated her prison apart from that tiny, moaning whine, which she no longer consciously heard. If it reminded her of anything, it was of a window left carelessly open a crack in a high wind, but if there was a window behind that gigantic screen, she could not see it — and doubted its existence besides. Windows meant light, and she had none.

Rummaging among the books on the second table brought steel pens into view, as well as several pencils; there was a standish containing black ink and red ink, and a shaker full of sand for blotting. Also several hundred sheets of paper, hot-pressed and with the ragged edges that spoke of a pure linen-cotton mixture. The titles of the books were interesting yet uninformative: Dr Johnson on the poets of his time, Oliver Goldsmith, Sheridan, Defoe, Richardson, Marlowe, Spenser, Donne, Milton; also works on chemistry, mathematics, astronomy and anatomy. Nothing popular, nothing religious.

Nothing that her swimming brain could compass. Time, it was evident, was best expended in curative sleep.

Finally there came an awakening that saw her mind alert, her bruises faint, and the swelling on her brow vanished. Having eaten, drunk, and used her peculiar commode, she took up a pencil and made a series of seven strokes upon the smooth wall at the back of her cell, adjacent to what looked like iron hinges set into it. Since no one had left her clean sheets as yet, she decided that no more than a week had gone by since she had been put here, for whoever had put her here apparently believed in cleanliness, and that meant clean sheets would be forthcoming.

Though the oil that fuelled them had an elusive aroma, the burning wicks of her lamps gave off no smoke of any kind, nor made it hard to breathe. She took the chimney off her little lamp and toured the cell to see if a stray puff of air caused its flame to wobble, but none did. Even when held over her commode hole, it remained steady. What was down there? No cesspit, certainly, for no odour of human wastes floated out of it. When she thrust the flame down into the hole, it revealed something unexpected: not a narrow vent, but a broad round vertical tunnel, like a well. Her light had not the power to illuminate its bottom, but as she bent close above the wooden seat she heard what sounded like swiftly running water. So that was why the privy did not smell! The matter she voided tumbled free to be borne away on a stream.

A river? She remembered dearest Charlie talking about the caves and underground rivers of the Peak District, and suddenly knew where she was. Imprisoned in the caves of the Peak District of Derbyshire, which meant not very far from Pemberley. *But why?* Instinct said that her virtue was not threatened, and Captain Thunder had stolen everything she possessed, so it was not money either. Unless she had been kidnapped and was being held for ransom? Ridiculous! replied common sense. Nothing on her person gave away more than her name, which was not Darcy, and her condition would have told her captor soon enough that she was a nobody, most likely a governess. Who could know of her connection to Darcy of Pemberley? The answer was no one. So whatever her captor's reason for this abduction, it was not ransom.

Yet for this unknown captor she did have a purpose, else he would not have succoured her, striven to keep her alive. Not rape and not ransom, so what?

It was while she was replacing the chimney on her little lamp that she saw him, sitting comfortably on a straight wooden chair on the far side of her bars — how long had he been watching her? She put the lamp down and faced him, her eyes busy.

A little old man! Almost gnomish, so small and wizened was he, his legs crossed at the knees on spindled shanks ending in open brown sandals. He wore a heath-brown, cowled robe cinched around the waist with a thick cream cord, and on his breast sat a crucifix. Had the colour been a browner brown, he might have been a Franciscan friar, she thought, staring at him intently. His wrinkled, buffeted scalp was bald everywhere, even around his ears, and the eyes surveying her with equal interest were so pale a blue that their irises were only marginally darker than their whites. Rheumy eyes, yet with an unnerving quality because they seemed always to look sideways. His thin blade of a nose was beaky and his lips a thin, severe line, as of a martinet. I do not like him, thought Mary.

"You are intelligent, madam Mary," he said.

No, said Mary to herself, I refuse to display any sign of fear or confusion; I will hold my own against him.

"You know my name, sir," she said.

"It was embroidered on your clothing. Mary Bennet."

"*Miss* Mary Bennet."

"Sister Mary," he corrected.

She pulled the chair out from under her book table and set it exactly opposite his, then sat down, knees and feet primly together, hands folded in her lap. "What leads you to think me intelligent?"

"You worked out how to replenish the lamps."

"Needs must when the devil drives, sir."

"You are afraid of the dark."

"Of course. It is a natural reaction."

"I saved your life."

"How did you do that, sir?"

"I found you at death's door. You had, Sister Mary, a mortal swelling of the brain that was squeezing the life-juice out of you. The gigantic fellow who had you was too ignorant to see it, so when he went about his business, my children and I stole you. I had developed a cure for just such a malady, but I was in sore need of a patient to try it out on. You nearly died — but nearly only. We got you home in time, and while my children bathed you and made you comfortable, I distilled my cure. You have been the answer to many prayers."

"Do you belong to an order of monks?" she asked, fascinated.

He reared up in outrage. "*A Roman? I?* Indeed, no! I am Father Dominus, custodian of the Children of Jesus."

Mary's brow cleared. "Oh, I see! You are the leader of one of the many outlandish Christian sects that so afflict northern England. My Church of England newsletter is always inveighing against your like, but I have not read of the Children of Jesus."

"Nor will you," he said grimly. "We are refugees."

"From what, Father?"

"From persecution. My children belonged to men who exploited and ill-treated them."

"Oh! Mill and factory owners," she said, nodding. "Well, Father, you stand in no danger from me. Like you, I am the enemy of men like them. Release me, and let me work with you to liberate *all* such children. How many have you freed?"

"That is no business of yours, nor will it be." His eyes drifted past her shoulders to gaze at her prison walls. "I saved your life, which therefore belongs to me. You will work for me."

"*Work* for you? Doing what?"

Apparently in answer, he stretched out his hands to her; they were crabbed with age and some disease had swollen their joints. "I cannot write," he said.

"What is that to the point?"

"You are going to be my scribe."

"Write for you? Write what?"

"My book," he said simply, smiling.

"I would be glad to do that for you, Father, but of my own free choice, not because you keep me a prisoner," she said, feeling the stirrings of alarm. "Unlock the door. Then we can come to some mutually satisfactory arrangement."

"I think not," said Father Dominus.

"But this is insane!" she cried, unable to stop herself. "Keep me prisoner to act as a scribe? What book could be so important? A retelling of the Bible?"

His face had assumed a patient, long-suffering expression; he spoke to her now as to a fool, not an intelligent person. "I do not despair of you, Sister Mary — you are so nearly right. Not a retelling of the Bible, but a new Bible! The doctrines of the Children of Jesus! It is all here in my mind, but my hands cannot turn my thoughts into words. You will do that for me."

Off the chair he sprang with a laugh and a whoop, ducked around the corner of the screen, and was gone.

"How fortunate that I am sitting down," said Mary, looking at her hands, which were shaking. "He's mad, quite mad."

Her eyes smarted; tears were close. But no, she would not cry! More urgent by far was to review that bizarre conversation, try to construct a footing, if not a foundation, upon which to base the talks sure to come. It was indeed true that northern England was the breeding ground of all kinds of peculiar religious sects, and clearly Father Dominus and his

Children of Jesus fitted into that mould. Nothing he had said revealed a theology, but no doubt that would come, if he meant to write his beliefs down in the form of a religious text. His name for himself and the name he had given her smacked of Roman Catholicism, but he had denied that strenuously. Perhaps as a child he had been exposed to Papism? "Children of Jesus" had rather a puritanical ring; some of these sects were so heavily concentrated upon Jesus that God hardly ever got a mention, so perhaps there was some of that in it too. But were there actually any children? She had seen none, heard none. And what kind of cures did he practise? To speak of a swelling of the brain with such authority argued a medical background. And the statement about their being refugees was illogical; if he had taken his children from mill and factory owners, those men were more likely to seize upon new children than search for escapees. The source of children was almost limitless, so Argus said; having borne them, their parents were only too happy to sell them into labour, especially if they had no parishes.

"Hello?" said a little girl's voice.

Mary lifted her head to see a small figure clad in a heath-brown, cowled robe staring at her through the bars of her cage.

"Hello," said Mary, smiling.

The smile was returned. "I have something for you, Sister Mary. Father Dominus said you would be pleased."

"I would be more pleased to know your name."

"Sister Therese. I am the oldest of the girls."

"Do you know the number of your years, Therese?"

"Thirteen."

"And what do you have for me that will please me?"

The child didn't look her age, but nor did she appear poorly nourished or weighed down by fear. When she attained full maturity her nose and chin would be too large for prettiness, but she had a certain charm of colouring, this being light brown of eye, skin and hair. Two small hands clasped a tripod stand which they put on the shelf; a kettle with steam curling out of its spout stood upon the ground next to her, and was lifted up in its turn. Then came a small china teapot, a cup and a saucer, and a little jug of milk.

"If you take the chimney off one of your lamps and put it under the stand, it will bring the kettle to the boil, and then you may make a pot of tea," said Sister Therese, producing a tin of tea leaves. "Father Dominus says tea will do you no harm, but you are not to ask for coffee."

"Therese, that is wonderful!" Mary cried, setting a lamp beneath the tripod and putting the kettle on its top. "Tea! So refreshing! Thank Father Dominus for me too, please."

Therese turned to go. "I will be back later with your clean sheets, and will collect the kettle then. You can empty the leaves down the privy and keep the pot and stand."

"Wait!" Mary called, but the little brown-robed girl was gone. "I will talk to her when she comes back," she said, and went about making herself a much needed cup of tea.

Is this the carrot for the donkey? she asked herself as she sat sipping the scalding liquid. "Oh, this is so good! Father Dominus keeps an excellent sort of tea."

Therese returned some time later; Mary gave her the kettle, but dallied about it, eager to learn what she could from this little member of the sect.

"How many children does Father have?" she asked, making a show of wiping the outside of the kettle.

The wide eyes looked into hers trustfully. "He says, fifty, Sister Mary. Thirty boys and twenty girls." A shadow crossed her face, of grief or fear, but she squared her shoulders and drew a deep breath of resolution. "Yes, fifty."

"Do you remember your bad master?"

Bewilderment! Sister Therese frowned. "No, but Father says that is usual. Brother Ignatius and I were the first, you see. We have been with Father a long time."

"Do you like your life with Father?"

"Oh, yes," she answered, but automatically; it was not a question aroused emotion in her. "Please, may I have the kettle?"

Mary handed it over. Hasten slowly, she thought. I have a strong feeling that there will be more than enough time to quiz her.

Not a prisoner in the way she, Mary, was a prisoner, she was forced to conclude. Therese had the run of wherever they were, so much was sure. Nor was she inclined to escape. Her life seemed to be the only one she knew, which set Mary to wondering. Mill and factory owners didn't enslave very young children, who were too much trouble; they might take on an eight-year-old, but Argus said nine or ten was the ideal age for a child to commence a life of unpaid labour, existing for the food scraps and sordid shelter offered in return. Therefore Therese should recollect a life before being rescued: why didn't she?

The need for exercise had driven her to pacing her cell — four double steps encompassed its dimensions. By walking thus for what she judged to be at least two hours, Mary tired herself out sufficiently to sleep when her eyelids grew heavy. When she woke she ate — the bread was always fresh, she noted — and sat down with John Donne to pass this dreadful inertia.

Which didn't last very long; Father Dominus appeared.

"Are you ready to start work?" he asked, seating himself.

"In return for the answers to some questions, yes."

"Then ask."

"Describe my situation when you took me more fully, Father. Where exactly was I? With whom was I?"

"I know not the identity of your captor," he said readily, "but he was big enough to suffer from some glandular anomaly, I concluded." He tittered. "He had a bellyache, and set you down to relieve it. I happened to be gathering medicinal herbs in the vicinity, and had Brother Jerome and our hand cart with me — the water in a spring nearby is unique, and I intended to fill my jars there. But you were fitting, and any fool could see you were not epileptic by nature. Brother Jerome put you on the hand cart and — away we went! That is all."

"Are you a physician, Father?"

"No. I am a druggist — an apothecary. The finest in the world," he announced in ringing tones. "I cannot cure epilepsy, but I can keep it in abeyance, and that is more than anyone else can say. Some of my children are epileptic, but I dose them and they do not fit. Just as some of my children have been riddled with worms, parasites, flukes. But no more! I can cure almost anything, and what I cannot cure I can keep controlled."

"From what did Therese suffer?"

"*Sister* Therese, if you please! As an infant, gin instead of milk, as a small child, lack of food. It affects their memories," he said, sounding glib. "Now may we begin?"

"Begin what, precisely?"

"The story of my life. The story of the Children of Jesus. The fruits of my labours as an apothecary."

"I am sure I will be consumed with interest."

"It matters not, Sister Mary. Your task is to take down my dictation with a pencil on this cheap paper," he said, producing a thick wad of it that went down on the shelf with a faint clang.

"My pencils will blunt," she said.

"And you would like a knife upon which to sharpen them, you imply. But I have a better idea, Sister Mary. Each day I will give you five sharpened pencils in exchange for blunted ones."

"I would appreciate a shelf for the books," she riposted. "This table is not overly large, Father, and I would like to move it closer to the bars to take dictation. Books should not lie on a floor to get damp and mildewy."

"As you wish," he said indifferently, watching her transfer the books to the ground and move the table closer to him.

"Is your new Bible also an autobiography, then, Father?"

"Of course. Just as the Old Testament is the story of the doings of God among men, and the New Testament the story of the doings of Jesus among men, so the Bible of the Children of Jesus is the story of God's younger son — I — among men and the children of men," Father Dominus explained.

"I see." Mary sat down, pulled several sheets of cheap paper toward her, and picked up a pencil.

"Here!" cried the old man with a faint screech. "*One* sheet at a time, madam! It is too difficult to bring in my supplies to permit of wanton waste by anyone."

"Sir," she said with like irony, "my pencil will go through one sheet of this paper, for the table surface is quite rough. I intend to use the dozen or so sheets under my writing sheet as a cushion. If you are a man of science, you should know that without needing to be told."

"It was another test of your intelligence," he said loftily. "Now commence, as follows: 'God is the darkness, for God existed before the coming of light, and is not Lucifer the Bringer of Light? He was Lucifer first, Satan only afterwards. He falls every day in the person of the Sun, does battle with God through the darkness, and rises every morning on another bootless journey into nothing. The scales, he thinks, are evenly matched, but God knows better. For long after light is a spent force, the darkness will continue, and the darkness is God.

"'This revelation burst upon me when, in my thirty-fifth year, I chanced upon the Primal Cave, the Omphalos, the Navel, the Universal Womb, that place I still call the Seat of God, His dwelling place. For where in this world of light is God to be found? Only when I chanced upon the Seat of God did I understand at last. There, in a blackness so profound mine eyes shrivelled for the lack of even one mote of light to see, there, in the silence so profound mine ears shrivelled for the lack of even one whisper, there, I stepped into the very belly of God. I was one with Him, and underwent the first of what were to be many revelations as He unfolded His darkness to me layer upon layer.'"

Father Dominus ceased while Mary's pencil laboured to catch up and her mind, reeling, kept a part of itself for her own thoughts and reactions.

"Layer," she wrote, and stopped, instrument poised, eyes on the seamed face and its smeared pale eyes with the pinpoint pupils. Why are they pinpoint? that exclusive-to-self segment of her mind asked. Has he drugged himself with something? The subject suggested it, certainly, yet — was it possible that he couldn't see much? That it was not the crabbed hands forbidding his authoring his own treatise, but the quality of his vision?

Say nothing derogatory, Mary! Say nothing that mocks him, or otherwise impugns his theology. "I am humbled," she said, "to be the scribe of such a mind, Father."

"You see it?" he asked, leaning forward eagerly.

"I see it."

"Then we will go on."

And go on he did, at great length; as the pages piled up to the right of her makeshift scribe's cushion, Mary's knees began to shake and her hand to cramp. Finally, when he paused for breath, she put her pencil down.

"Father, I can write no more today," she said. "I have a

writer's cramp, and given that you want all of this transcribed in a fair, copperplate hand, I must beg you to stop."

He seemed to come back into himself from a different place, blinked, shivered, parted his thin lips in a mirthless smile. "Oh, that was wonderful!" he said. "So much easier than trying to get meaning out of looking at words."

"What do you call this theology?" she asked.

"Cosmogenesis," he said.

"Greek roots, not Latin."

"The Greeks *thought*. Those who came after imitated."

"I look forward to our next dictation, but there is no need to lock me up," she tried again. "I need exercise, for one thing, and pacing a cell is not adequate. A shelf for my books, please."

"Think yourself lucky that I have given you the means to make a cup of tea," he said, rising to his feet.

"You are a bad master, Father Dominus, no better than those from whom you took your children. You feed me and shelter me, but deny me freedom."

But she said it to empty air; he had gone.

She sat on her bed to give her body a change of posture as well as substance, and tried to come to grips with the fantastic drivel he had spoken. To Mary, a staunch adherent of the Church of England, he was apostate, worse than any heretic, for he talked of God as no Christian ought, and thus far Jesus had not even entered the theological world he painted. Which meant he had little in common with almost all the sects northern England could boast. If she, who never counted the cost of saying what people didn't want to hear, had kept a tight rein on her thoughts and striven mightily not to offend him, she had done so because, by the end of their very long session, she had become convinced he was absolutely mad. Remained only for him to say that he was God, or perhaps Jesus, and her judgement would be irrevocable. Logic had no part in his way of looking at things, which seemed to be purely for his own comfort or convenience or aspirations. Though what his aspirations were, as yet she had no idea. He claimed to be God's *younger* son!

Privately she put his age at somewhere around seventy, but if she erred, it was on the younger side, not the older. He had been well looked after, whether by his children or by others was moot; it was even possible that he was eighty. So had he always been a madman, or was it a symptom of old age? Though he was not senile in any way; his memory was excellent and his reasoning powers acute. It was more that his reason was not reasonable nor his memory unwarped. What she had been exposed to was a person whose self owed nothing to the ethics and structure of English society. Were there really fifty children, thirty boys and twenty girls? Why had Therese's face changed when she spoke those numbers? How rigorously would the little girl be quizzed by Father Dominus as to what questions Sister Mary asked? She had a duty to the child not to put her in harm's way, and perhaps that expression had hinted at dread punishments.

* * *

So Mary went gently with Therese, whom she could interrogate about less perilous things than numbers and punishments. Since Father Dominus had made no secret of his caves, Mary concentrated upon that aspect of her imprisonment. According to Therese, there were many, many miles of caves, all interconnected by tunnels; speaking with awe, Therese told her that Father Dominus knew every inch of every tunnel, every cavern, every nook and cranny. One system was called the Southern Caves, another the Northern Caves; Mary and the Children of Jesus lived in the Southern Caves, but the work went on in the Northern Caves, which also contained God's Temple. What exactly the work consisted of took time to elucidate, but gradually Mary pieced it together from Therese and a new friend among the Children of Jesus, Brother Ignatius. He had appeared with an awl, a screwdriver, some screws, several iron brackets and three planks of wood.

It was then that Mary learned what the iron hinges in her far wall were: a second cowled youth, tall and slender, had helped Brother Ignatius carry his load inside — but only after he had stood Mary against the wall and closed the hinges on her ankles to form fetters. Then, having used a rule to mark the screw holes for the brackets, he took himself off and left Ignatius to do the actual work. Brother Ignatius was shorter than the other lad, whom he called Brother Jerome, but more powerfully built, and very close to puberty. When Mary asked his age, he gave it as fourteen.

"Therese and I be the eldest," he confided, screwing his screws into the soft rock.

"Why did Brother Jerome measure and mark, if he wasn't to help you in aught else?" Mary asked.

"Can't read nor write," said Ignatius cheerfully. "Jerome's the only one of us who can."

She suppressed a gasp. "*None* of you can read or write?"

"'Cept Jerome. Father brought him from Sheffield."

"Why hasn't Father taught you?"

"We be too busy, I expect."

"Busy doing what?"

"Depends." Ignatius set a plank on two brackets, wiggled it and nodded. "Nice and level. Jerome's a fussy one."

"Depends?"

The rather dull brown eyes clouded with the effort of remembering something uttered a few seconds before. "Might be pounding powder, or steeping herbs, or filtering, or distilling, or thickening, or putting in a dab of colour. Blue's for liver, lavender's for kidneys, yaller's for bladder, mucky green's for gallstones, red's for heart, pink's for lungs, brown's for guts." His mouth opened to say more, but Mary stopped him hastily.

"Medicaments?" she asked.

"What?"

"What does filtering mean?" she countered. "Or distilling?"

He shrugged his broad and sturdy shoulders. "Dunno, 'cept we does 'em, and that's what they're called."

"He did say he was an apothecary," said Mary to herself. "Do you make potions and elixirs for Father Dominus, is that it?"

"Aye, that's it." He began to stack her books on the bottom shelf, and put what volumes were left on the middle one. "There, Sister Mary! You can fit as many again."

"I can indeed. Thank you, Brother Ignatius."

He nodded, gathered up his tools and prepared to leave.

"Just a moment! I am still fettered."

"Jerome will come back for that. He's got the keys."

Off he went, leaving Mary to wait what seemed an eternity for Brother Jerome to unlock the hinges binding her ankles.

This lad, she thought looking down on his head, which displayed the bald spot of a tonsure on its crown, this lad is very different from Brother Ignatius. His eyes, almost as light as Father Dominus's, were sharp and intelligent, and displayed that peculiar lack of emotion people usually call "cold". That he was fond of inflicting pain became evident as he unlocked her, grazing her flesh on the iron until he drew blood.

"I wouldn't, Brother Jerome," she said softly. "Your master needs me healthy, not laid low with some infection from a wound."

"'Twas you did it, not I," he said, disliking the threat.

"Then watch that you — or I! — do not do it again."

"I hate him!" said Therese through her teeth after Jerome had gone. "He's cruel."

"But Father Dominus's pet, am I correct?"

"Yes, they're thick," she said, but would say no more.

"What kind of work do you girls perform for Father Dominus?"

"We bottle the liquids, put the pills in boxes, fill the tins with ointment, label everything, and make sure the corks are tight in the bottles," she said, as if by rote.

"And this work keeps twenty of you busy?"

"Yes, Sister Mary."

"Father Dominus's cure-alls must be famous."

"Oh, yes, very! Especially the choler elixir and the horse ointment. We have a special arrangement for those."

"Special arrangement?"

"Yes, with an apothecary's warehouse in Manchester. They go there, and then to shops all over England."

"Does Father have a brand name?"

"A what?"

"A name that every different kind of product you make has in common. Father Dominus, for instance?"

Therese's brow cleared. "Oh, I know what you mean! Children of Jesus. Everything is called Children of Jesus this or that."

"I have never heard of it."

"Well, lots must have, or we wouldn't be so busy."

When Father Dominus appeared, Mary was able to hand him forty pages of exquisitely neat, handwritten manuscript. The hand that plucked it from the shelf trembled slightly; the sheaf of paper went up to his eyes and there was pored over, his face registering an awed delight that was not, she divined, counterfeited in any way. "But this is *beautiful*!" he cried, looking up before tucking the top sheet under all the others.

"You write straight across the page, and have marginated perfectly without ruling it."

So he does see something, she thought, but not the sense of the words; she had deliberately put the pages out of numerical order. He can see the straightness and apparently a pencil line, but only if he holds a page five inches from his nose.

"A publisher will be happy," she said. "Where do we begin today? Is it to be darkness, lightness, or how God has formed caves?"

"No, no, not today! I must take this and read it properly. I will see you tomorrow, Sister Mary."

"Wait! If I am to be idle this day, give me exercise!"

Not long afterward, Brother Ignatius appeared carrying a coil of thin rope and two lanterns. Grinning like a conjurer about to pull a rabbit from a hat, he made a trumpeting noise and produced her boots from behind his back.

"Exercise!" carolled Mary, leaping off her chair.

"Of a sort," he said. "Father will allow me to take you down to the river and back, but you'll need your boots — 'tis very wet in places. But I dasn't let you keep the boots — they're to go back to him after I lock you up again. And please don't think of running away," he said as he unlocked the door and came into her cell, loosening the rope. "There's none place to go, and without a lantern it's God's Insides. I have to tie one end of this around you and the other around me, and we got a lantern each. The oil lasts long enough to do the round trip with a rest by the river, but there's naught in it after that."

"I won't try to escape, I promise," said an ecstatic Mary, allowing him to knot the rope around her waist while she laced up her boots.

Hoping to see what lay beyond the screen, she was disappointed to find herself led into the maw of a tunnel that, had she known it was there, she could actually see; she had dismissed it as a dense black shadow. At first the path, illuminated by his lantern in the lead and hers coming on behind, was dry and strewn with rubble, but perhaps ten minutes into the downward-sloping tunnel appeared the first puddle, and after that the floor grew steadily moister. At the end of half an hour Mary found herself standing on the bank of a rushing turbulence, a considerable body of water that formed the bulk of the floor in a cavern so vast that the puny light from their lanterns gave the merest hint of its dimensions. Now she could see what Charlie had sometimes talked about! Great glistening fingers pointed down from above, their encrusted surfaces glittering and sparkling; an occasional formation that looked for all the world like semi-translucent, scintillating cloth was flung across the abyss like a shawl; long crystal whiskers sprouted out of pools or from some source hidden in the shadows.

"*Beautiful!*" she breathed, stunned.

Now I begin to understand how Father Dominus formulated his bizarre concept of God. To be caught down here lightless might well trigger insanity, nor would the kindling of a tiny light remove the terror from such an immensity. I pray I am never lost down here.

"It be pretty," said Brother Ignatius, "but we got to go back now, Sister Mary."

Tramping upward was harder work, but Mary relished it; if she did not exercise, she would not keep up her strength.

"How long have you been with Father Dominus?" she asked.

"Dunno. Don't rightly remember being anywhere else. Me and Therese are the oldest, been with Father the longest."

"So Therese said. Also that Father brought Jerome from Sheffield. Do you come from Sheffield too?"

"Dunno. Jerome's a special case, Father says. Reads 'n' writes."

"Did you suffer a bad master?"

"A bad what?"

"A bad master. A nasty man who whipped you to make you work."

"Father Dominus don't whip" was the answer, sounding puzzled.

"What do you eat?"

"Fresh bread we bake. Butter 'n' jam 'n' cheese. Roast beef for dinner on Sundays. Stew. Soup."

"What kind of soup?"

"Depends. Good, but."

"Who cooks?"

"Therese. Camille helps, so do the other girls in turns."

"So you don't starve."

"What's starve?"

"Feeling hungry from too little food."

"No."

"What do you drink?"

"Small beer. Hot chocolate on Sundays."

"Do you get pudding?"

"Treacle tart. Steamed pud. Rhubarb tart. Cream."

"Have you cows?"

"No. Jerome brings the milk 'n' cream."

"Do you have a day of worship?"

"Worship?"

"Saying hello to God. Thanking Him for His kindness."

"No. We thank Father."

Well, that was interesting! So Father Dominus's god was his god, did not belong to the children. Apparently they belonged to Jesus, though it would be interesting on their next walk to ask Brother Ignatius what he had been taught about Jesus.

But when Father Dominus appeared the next day Mary feared that she might not be allowed to walk again. The Founder of Cosmogenesis was not pleased with his secretary.

"You put my pages out of order!" he accused, still standing.

"Oh, my goodness, did I?" asked Mary, looking blank. "I *do* apologise, Father. Not having a watch or a timepiece of any kind, I am afraid that I become confused. I was sorting the pages out to make sure that every single one was free from error, and you caught me unaware. I gathered them together in such a hurry that I forgot I hadn't collated them. Pray forgive me, please!"

His pose relaxed a little, though his face did not soften. "As well for you, then, that you had numbered the pages," he said stiffly. "A pity that you cannot print, as in a genuine book."

"The only persons who ever did that, Father," she said, her temper tried, "were medieval monks. I do not say I could learn to do it, but do you have the time to permit me to learn?"

"No, no, no! Today we work. Begin as follows: 'Light is evil, created by Lucifer to his own image. God has no eyes, but Lucifer took two sparks off his body and made them into eyes so that he could see his own beauty. That is the evil of light — its beauty, its seductiveness, its capacity to dazzle, to daze and numb the mind, throw it open to Lucifer to work upon.'" He stopped to look at her. "You have Lucifer's hair," he said. "I warn you, Sister Mary, that I saw the devil in you even while you lay comatose upon that bank. Yet God gave you to me to answer my prayers, and forewarned is forearmed. You proved the efficacy of my treatment for oedema, and now you serve me as a scribe. But I know your origins! Never forget that!"

Then back he went to his dissertation upon Lucifer, a jumble of hatred for the ordinary phenomenon of light that served to convince her that, in losing his sight, Father Dominus's profound experience in the cave during his thirty-fifth year had translated into a rejection of the world he could no longer see save poorly. There were people throughout the globe who revered caves, even thought of them as the home of their god, but few had gone on from that concept to loathe and fear God's most thrilling creation, light. All the near-infinite shades of grey had bled out of Father Dominus's philosophy, leaving him with the black of God and the white of Satan, whom he called Lucifer because of its Latin meaning — Bearer of Light. The pitiless creed of a fanatic, and every religion had those. But not extreme enough for Father Dominus, whose mind besides was an original one.

What must he have been like in his thirty-fifth year, hale and hearty and brimful of genius? Those lamps! His nostrums and elixirs, his energies and enthusiasms. Once, she was sure, a truly extraordinary man. But now, a mad one. Old, near-blind, relying upon the adulation of a small group of children to plump out a juiceless heart. Even the adulation was second-rate; he wanted no developed mind among his worshippers, so had deprived them of letters and numbers, taught them an apothecary's cant without ever explaining what the words meant, set himself up as being far above them — and left his minion, Brother Jerome, to apply the more unpleasant aspects of discipline, thus deflecting fear and loathing onto Jerome as if it had no origins in him.

Jerome ... The odd one out, the foreigner brought in from Sheffield at, Mary presumed, a more advanced age than any of the other children. Therese and Ignatius insisted that they remembered no previous master, good or bad, and said flatly that none of the children did. A potion that obliterated memory in them? That was possible, of course. Or did he never steal them from bad masters?

These caves! In other places those who lived in them were called troglodytes, but they were entire communities from the very old to newborn babes, not an artificial group like the Children of Jesus. From Therese she had learned that her own prison cell was quite close to the kitchen in which Therese and her little helpers made bread, stews, roast beef, tarts, soups, puddings. No Child of Jesus grew ill, or wasted away from consumption; provided they did their work in the laboratory (one of the big words he had taught them without explaining what it meant) if they were boys or the packing room if they were girls, they were free to roam from the Southern to the Northern Caves, and even outside if they chose.

"Brother Jerome's too busy to take notice," said Ignatius. "We go where we want."

"Then why hasn't anybody ever seen you?" Mary asked.

"It be the dark of God," said Ignatius simply.

"You mean the night time?"

"Dark, yes."

"But don't you love the day?"

Brother Ignatius shuddered. "No, daytime's *awful*! Hurts our eyes, Sister Mary, like red-hot pokers."

"Yes, of course it would. I had not stopped to think about that," Mary said slowly. "I daresay that my eyes would hurt too, after so many days immured in lamplight. If you do go outside in the dark of God, where do you go? What do you do?"

"Run around, play chasings. Skip with a rope."

"And no one sees you?"

"Ain't no one to see," he said, deeming her dense. "Them's the moors outside the Northern Caves. We don't go outside the Southern." He looked conspirational, leaned closer and spoke in a whisper. "We ain't staying in the Southern Caves, moving everything to the others. Father says there be too many busybodies in the south — cottages going up everywhere."

"How do you get your supplies, Ignatius? The food? Coal for fires? Substances for the laboratory? The tins, boxes and bottles?"

"Dunno, exactly. Brother Jerome does it, not Father. We got a cave full of donkeys. Sometimes Brother Jerome goes off with all the donkeys and comes back loaded up. The boys unpack the donkeys — coal, all sorts of stuff."

"And Father Dominus stays with you all the time?"

"No, he goes out a lot, but while Lucifer is in the sky. He takes the orders and collects the money. If Lucifer is there, he walks, but if he goes out in the dark, Brother Jerome drives him in the donkey trap."

"What is money, Ignatius?"

He rubbed his tonsure, where the scalp was quite glossy from much rubbing. "Dunno, Sister Mary."

EIGHT

Angus, Charlie and Owen returned to Pemberley on Tuesday after dark, too late for dinner. Accepting Parmenter's offer of food for a little later, they sought Fitz out in the small library.

Fitz listened in something of a quandary, not sure how much of Ned's story he should tell them.

His mood was bitter, mostly because of Elizabeth, who he knew was a tender creature, yet, yet … Something about her brought out the worst in him, made him say things to her that no wife would relish hearing, least of all Elizabeth. It was not her fault that her relatives were such a ramshackle lot. In fact, what puzzled him more and more as time went on was how Mr and Mrs Bennet had ever produced five such disparate offspring. Two absolute ladies in Jane and Elizabeth; a nonentity in Mary; and two blatant trollops in Kitty and Lydia. The miracle lay in Jane and Elizabeth, who simply did not belong in the Bennet litter basket. From whom had they got their refinement, their propriety? Not from their mother, or from their father. Nor from Mrs Phillips, their aunt who lived in Meryton. The Gardiners had only visited once in each year, so could have had no real influence. It was as if a gypsy had put Jane and Elizabeth in place of two trollop-babies. Changelings, not Bennets.

Yet marriage to one meant marriage to the whole family. That, he had not fully understood, thinking to spirit his wife away to Derbyshire and make sure she never saw her family again. But she hadn't seen it that way. She *wanted* to remain in contact with them!

With a huge effort he dragged his thoughts away from his wife and listened to Charlie, whom Angus was letting speak for them; he spoke well too, neither illogically nor emotionally.

"I do not believe that Mary ever entered the Green Man," he was saying, "though she definitely encountered Captain Thunder. Here." He laid out the reticule. "Empty. We found it on the road, and one of her handbags in the ditch nearby. The cur who claimed to be the landlord of the Green Man says that Captain Thunder has a house in the woods, but no one knows whereabouts. There is a reward on his head, and he cannot be sure that one of his fellow villains will not betray him. In the end we decided it was best to seek your advice and help before doing anything else."

"Thank you, Charlie," said his father, very pleased at how the young man had handled things. Of course Angus would have been a steadying influence, but only if Charlie did not resent him. Clearly he and Angus had got along together very well, and it had not escaped him that Angus had consented to let Charlie enter the Green Man alone.

He got up to pour chambertin. "They say this is Bonaparte's favourite wine," he said, handing glasses around. "Now that the French are desperate for foreign currency, we are seeing some very good wines again, and I think I shall move in the House to lighten the import duty on cognac." He sat down and crossed his legs. "You have done well, the three of you," he said, with a special smile for Owen. "Knowing that by the time you would be able to set out, the trail would be cold, I put Ned Skinner on the problem, too. In many ways he's more skilled at this sort of thing than you, but his investigations haven't advanced us much beyond yours — no mean feat on your parts."

Too concerned to hear what Ned had learned to bother with compliments, Charlie leaned forward. "Did he find Captain Thunder?"

"Yes, he did. And your deductions are correct. Captain Thunder did indeed set upon Mary and rob her, but he didn't take her to the Green Man. He left her in the midst of the forest, presumably there to wander in circles until she died. However, Charlie, your aunt is made of sterner stuff than most ladies. How she managed to find the road I do not know, just that she did. Ned found her not yards away from it."

"Oh, bravo!" Charlie cried, face transfigured. "So she's safe? She's well?"

"As to that, neither Ned nor I can hazard a guess," Fitz said, frowning. "Ned had had a very heavy day of it, and by the time he found her, he was not feeling himself. A bellyache, he thinks due to bad food at the Black Cat."

The others were hanging on Fitz's words, eyes round.

"Mary was unconscious, and continued in her faint. She had been badly beaten, including a blow to the head. When Ned asked Captain Thunder for the details, he was informed that she had put up a terrific fight."

Growls and imprecations greeted this, but Fitz continued.

"Ned put Mary across Jupiter's withers, and rode for home. But as he approached the beginning of the Peaks he had to answer an urgent call of nature — the bad food had caught up with him. Not knowing how long he might be, he put Mary down on the bank beside the bridle-path he was travelling, and went into a grove of trees. When he returned, Mary was gone."

"*Gone?*" asked Angus, paling.

"Yes, vanished. Ned's watch told him that he had been away for ten minutes, not a second longer."

"Ten minutes?" Charlie asked. "How could she vanish in just ten minutes?"

"How, indeed? Ned searched as only Ned can, and I do assure you that his bellyache did not interfere with his thoroughness. He could find no trace of her. He mounted Jupiter and looked from that height, as well as farther afield. To no avail. She had been spirited away as a conjurer deals with his assistant at a circus."

"Captain Thunder!" Charlie cried, pounding his thigh.

"No, Charlie. Whoever it was, Captain Thunder it was not.

By that time his corpse was cold. Ned killed him in a struggle after he found the fellow's house."

"How did he find it if none knew its whereabouts?" Owen asked.

"He was told where it was by a spy in the Nottingham coach yard who must sniff out likely victims and share in the proceeds."

"Could she have regained consciousness and walked off?" Angus asked, hating to see Charlie's pain, and hating to feel his own. Oh, Mary! You and your fool crusade!

"Ned says not, and I believe him. The injuries to her wrists and even her throat did not matter, but the blow to her head was severe enough to cause prolonged unconsciousness. If she roused, which is possible, she would have been confused and stumbling, not fleet of foot. Ned scoured every inch of the countryside for five miles in all directions. One must assume that she did not walk off, but was carried."

"*Why?*" asked Angus, despairing.

"I do not know."

"*Who?*" asked Owen. "Who would do such a thing?"

"At first I thought whoever took her must have acted on some chivalrous impulse, perhaps thinking that Ned was on foul business. Since Chesterfield is the nearest town, I had extensive enquiries made there yesterday, hoping that a woman had been brought in and the mayor or the sheriff notified. But no one had brought in a woman. I had my people ask every doctor, with the same result. So whoever did steal Mary was not acting chivalrously. He has some nefarious scheme in mind.

Were she known to be my relative, I would have thought, kidnapping, and have been waiting for a ransom demand. None has come. Because, I believe, no one knew who Mary was. Her condition was parlous. She was filthy and badly bruised."

"And all this because of a bad breakfast at the Black Cat?" cried Charlie. "Well, I know that place can produce bad food, but to find her, only to lose her again —!"

"I agree."

"So what do we do now, Pater?"

"We make the whole matter public — with reservations, of course. We post notices that Miss Mary Bennet is missing, whereabouts she was last seen, and what her possible condition is. We say that she is Mrs Fitzwilliam Darcy's sister, and we offer a reward of one hundred pounds for information leading to her retrieval. As Mary is very like Elizabeth in the face, I will have Susie take a pen-and-ink sketch from Elizabeth's portrait, and include that in the notice. As well as going up in every town hall and village hall, I will put the notice in all the newspapers of the region."

"And I will put an article in the *Westminster Chronicle* that describes the perils a gentlewoman may face travelling by the public stage," said Angus. "Its readers are scattered throughout England."

"Thank you," Fitz said, inclining his head regally. He turned to his son. "If you like, Charlie, you may take a party of Pemberley men back to the bridle-path where the abduction occurred. Ned can give you directions." He looked grim. "The thing is that the bridle-path in question is neither well known nor well travelled. It is basically a short cut to Chesterfield from Pemberley." He lifted a warning finger. "I do not need to tell you that we say nothing about the fate of Captain Thunder."

"Agreed, Pater."

"Choose men who know the southern Peaks."

"Of course."

"Now go and eat some dinner, please. What do you think of my chambertin?"

"Smooth and fruity," said Angus glibly. "Bonaparte has a good palate. Not unusual in a Frenchman," he added demurely.

Fitz sneered contemptuously. "The man is no Frenchman! He is a Corsican peasant."

The groom in the Nottingham coach station was a loose end that had to be tied, Ned Skinner realised, cursing his own lack of foresight. Why hadn't he lingered long enough to discover the fellow's name and origins? Because you had no idea how important they would be, he apostrophised himself wrathfully as he readied the light carriage and Jupiter for the journey to Hemmings with Lydia Wickham. Clearly the groom was Captain Thunder's spy in Nottingham, took the highwayman's gold in return for information about people who used the stage-coach. Not all such were on the verge of poverty; some could have afforded a private chaise, but thought that drew them to a highwayman's attention, never dreaming of his network of informants. Shipments of coin to provincial banks also went by stage-coach, and the contents of some of the parcels were valuable. The groom in Captain Thunder's pay knew the movements of every vehicle passing through the Nottingham depot, Nottingham being a big city with many industries, and therefore wealthy.

The journals carrying the advertisement about Mary with its hundred-pound reward would be published shortly, and the groom could not be allowed to read one or hear of it. Did he, he would be off in a trice to lay his information, and Ned Skinner's neck might come into danger. For who could forget him, at his size? The last thing Fitz needed was to have his factotum thrown into a cell on suspicion of *anything*, no matter how easy to clear up.

Thus Ned did not enjoy his Thursday, spent conveying Mrs Lydia Wickham to her new home, Hemmings.

Lured into the carriage by a bottle of cognac, Lydia had proceeded to drink at a rate that saw her stuporose by the time she passed through Leek. Hemmings sat ten miles beyond the town, a small mansion in ten acres of park. Its stables had been stocked with a barouche and two matched chestnuts, and a pony for a trap. Very much the kind of residence Shelby Manor had been, except that, despite the looming darkness, Ned's sharp eyes noted iron bars over the ground floor windows. Yes, of course! The last inhabitant of Hemmings had been a raving lunatic, but Ned had been present when Fitz told Matthew Spottiswoode to see that the bars were removed, so why? Still … he closed his eyes in thought, trying to see how he could put this omission to best use. The bars could not stay there, so much was sure, as Mrs Darcy and Mrs Bingley were bound to pay their sister visits, but ... Yes, it might work!

He knew Miss Mirabelle Maplethorpe very well, and had no doubt that she would be up to the task of caring for Lydia. It had taken some shifting to procure her the position of Lydia's lady companion, but he had succeeded and none the wiser, including Fitz.

Miss Maplethorpe opened the door herself. "Ah, Ned."

"I have your charge, Mirry."

"We are ready. Bring her in," said Miss Maplethorpe, a tall, strapping woman of about forty whose face was debatably the reason why she was still single; it resembled the Judy in a Punch-and-Judy show. Poor Mirry! Rarely had face and occupation been so perfectly reconciled.

"She's out to it. The only way I could get her here without binding her hand and foot was to give her a bottle of cognac."

"I see." Her glacial eyes surveyed him ironically. "You are quite big enough to carry her, Ned."

"True. But I do not fancy wearing a coat of puke all the way home. It's due to come up — she's a puker."

"Then wait a moment." She left him on the step while she went somewhere deeper into the house, reappearing with two men who looked more like boxers than footmen.

"Come on, boys." And he led them to the carriage, opened its door. "You are here, Mrs Wickham. Hop to it!"

If she did not do that, she did move off the seat, put a foot on the step down, and fell in a heap, giggling. As Ned had prophesied, up came the cognac together with the contents of a hamper. The two men stepped back hastily.

"A hand under either arm, boys — look sharp!"

When Ned Skinner commanded, he was obeyed, puke or no puke. Still giggling and gagging, Lydia was half-dragged, half-carried into her new home, Miss Maplethorpe watching grimly.

"Best of luck, Mirry," said Ned. "Return the carriage and men to us tomorrow. Mr Darcy's orders."

He went to Jupiter and remounted.

"Cheer up, old boy," he said to the horse as he rode away. "Just ten miles to Leek, then we'll put up for the night."

Shortly after dawn he was on the road again, not to ride toward the north and Pemberley, but cross-country, keeping well clear of main roads and even, when possible, side roads too. He knew exactly where he was going; it lay some twenty miles from Leek, on the outskirts of Derby.

In no hurry, he let Jupiter choose their pace, a treat for the big black horse that it relished.

At the prescribed spot beneath a signpost, he found his informant, a groom at a shady sort of hostelry in Sheffield, and a man who looked horsey enough to be instantly at ease among others of the same calling. Occasionally he did this kind of job for Mr Skinner, whom he had known for a long time, and feared, and respected.

"Well, Tom?" Ned asked, reining in alongside him.

"No trouble, Mr Skinner. His name is Ezekiel Carmody — Zeke for short. He works six days a week at the coach station, sleeps in the barn there. Sundays he goes home. His dad's got a farm outside Nether Heage — big place, breeds coach horses."

"The name of the farm?"

"Carmody."

"Thank you, Tom." Five guineas changed hands. "Go home now."

And off went Tom, well satisfied.

The news was better than Ned had hoped for. With a name like Ezekiel, the groom was obviously a Methodist; to spend Sundays at home would have been mandatory. But I doubt, thought Ned, that the family knows their church-going son Zeke is hand-in-glove with a highwayman. Well, and who could blame a young fellow? No money to call his own with such a father, I'll be bound; dad's horses sold to the coach companies and Zeke's wages garnished for family and church. No hope for a pint or a penny light-skirt. It's a story I chance upon time and time again.

Gauging his progress accurately, Ned approached the Carmody farm at one o'clock — dinner hour. He found the main gate down the fourth lane he tried, with the name written upon it proudly: CARMODY FARM. Using his eyes to best advantage, he decided there was no other entrance worth taking if the farmstead itself was the goal; yes, this was the way Zeke Carmody would come. What kind of transport the groom would use Ned could not know; very likely he cadged a ride with someone going this way from Nottingham. But Ned took a bet with himself that Zeke walked the last quarter-mile of his weekly trip home.

On Saturday, while Jupiter dozed in its stall with oats in its manger, Ned worked very privately on a curious device: a post to which was attached a horseshoe of a size worn by light draughts, the kind of horse drew the extremely heavy public coaches.

On Saturday evening at ten o'clock he mounted Jupiter and set out for Carmody Farm, at first on the main roads, deserted at this hour. It was fifty miles as Jupiter went, but many a horseman rode a hundred and more miles in a day — couriers, ministers with a widely scattered flock, commercial travellers, those going in a hurry to a sickbed or a deathbed. There was no moon to speak of, but dense clouds of stars lit his way, and Jupiter was sure-footed.

They made good time; he reached his destination before dawn, and settled down to wait in the shadows beneath trees with pendulous leafy branches, not far from the farm's main gate. His post-and-shoe untied from the saddle, Ned put that and some other things beside him. He was very much on his mettle, blaming himself for the loss of Mary Bennet, and determined that he would leave nothing for any nosy constable to unearth.

Zeke Carmody knew whereabouts Captain Thunder's house was located, and his tongue wagged. Though the part of Ned that understood Zeke's needs pitied his lot, which had to be death, not for a millionfold such pity would he have stilled his hand. Fitz was in danger through his, Ned's, bungling, and that was all that mattered.

A cheery whistle from the end of the lane alerted him. Ned rose to his feet, stretching, and waited in the lee of the bushy trees for his quarry. As the groom passed, Ned swung the post and struck him on the side of his head. He fell without a whimper to sprawl in the lane. Moving quickly, Ned pulled the body under the trees, where he had spread out a sheet of canvas. Once the body was arranged on the canvas to his satisfaction, he put the horseshoe against the wound with accuracy and deliberation, and hammered the end of the post with a stone purloined from Farmer Carmody's field. One imprint of the shoe was enough; looking at the pulped mess, he judged that anyone would deem the injury the result of contact with a big horse. Then he wrapped the body in the canvas, picked it up, carried it some distance down the lane, and emptied it out of its wrapping and into a field where four light draught horses grazed, their hooves and hairy skirts above muddied from a recent shower of rain.

No one had come out of the house, no dog barked. Breathing quite normally, Ned folded the canvas carefully to contain the very little blood, and dismantled his instrument of murder. The shoe was flung far into the field, the post tucked inside the canvas. He kept to the shadows until he reached the little road that led to Nether Heage; there he straightened and walked swiftly to Jupiter, grazing nearby. After saddling a horse delighted to see him, he mounted and rode away. In the far distance a church bell was tolling, but no one saw Ned Skinner, now cantering toward the road to Chesterfield.

Undoubtedly there were other grooms Captain Thunder used as sources of information — post house inns were ideal — but they could not matter. It was Ezekiel Carmody who had spoken to the gigantic fellow on the gigantic horse, told him whereabouts the Captain lived. With Zeke the victim of a shocking accident, no one was left who could connect Ned Skinner to the highwayman. It was always best to tidy up. The shire constables were a dozy lot, but ...

The news that Mary had been abducted by parties unknown left Elizabeth winded, not least because Fitz had chosen to make his news public in the Rubens Room after dinner, just before Charlie, Angus and Owen had returned. Though Elizabeth had been aware of her disappearance for some time, Fitz hadn't taken his wife to one side beforehand and told her privately of this abduction. Instead, he told her in the presence of Caroline Bingley and Louisa Hurst — and Louisa's daughter, Letitia/Posy, perhaps the most vapid and cheerless girl of Elizabeth's acquaintance. So she had no alternative other than to suppress her anger until a more appropriate moment to unleash it on Fitz's chilly, unfeeling head. Under the shield of Caroline's exclamations, Louisa's faintness and Posy's squeaks, she sat with a red spot burning in each cheek, but so composedly that no one could have assumed she did not already know. Pride, Elizabeth! You too have pride.

Her husband went on to explain the measures he proposed taking, much the same as he had outlined to Charlie, Angus and Owen: the notice, the reward, Susie's pen-and-ink sketch, the style. He told them of Captain Thunder's part in the business, and the insoluble mystery of her disappearance while she was under Ned Skinner's care. He made no intimation that the Captain was responsible for this second disappearance, though he did not mention the Captain's death at Ned's hands. Only that it could not have been the Captain who kidnapped her.

"Shall you tell Susie of the sketch, or shall I?" she asked.

"I shall. I know what I want," said Fitz.

"When do you ever not know what you want? I must go to Bingley Hall first thing tomorrow to tell Jane."

"Oh, do let me keep you company!" cried Caroline. "Twenty-five miles there, and twenty-five miles back again. You will need a truly sympathetic hand to hold."

And Elizabeth literally saw red: a scarlet veil descended in front of her eyes. "I thank you, madam," she said with a bite, "but I would rather hold the devil's hand than yours. It is more honestly malign."

A collective gasp went up. Caroline sprang to her feet, Louisa flopped sideways in her chair, and Posy pitched forward onto the floor. Elizabeth sat with a sneer on her face, enjoying every moment of it. The *bought* mouse had suddenly turned into a large rat, and oh, it felt so good! After one amazed glance at her, Fitz fixed his gaze on a splendid Rubens nude above the fireplace.

"Pray excuse me, I am very tired," said Caroline, with a venomous glare at Elizabeth, who returned it with a purple flash Miss Bingley's brown orbs could not equal.

"I will come too, dear," said Louisa, "if you help me with poor little Letitia. What a demonstration of ill breeding!"

"Yes, get yourselves away!" Elizabeth said fiercely.

"About the only thing I can be thankful for, Elizabeth," Fitz said at her bedroom door, "is that Charlie, Angus and Mr Griffiths were not present to hear you insult Miss Bingley with such vulgar coarseness."

"Oh, a pox on Caroline Bingley!" Elizabeth opened her door and marched inside, her arm in position to slam it in Fitz's face.

But he wrenched it from her and followed her, face as white as hers was red. "I will not hear you speak to one of my guests so — so contemptuously!"

"I will speak to that woman in any terms I please! She is a liar and a mischief-maker, and they are *compliments* compared to some of her other characteristics!" said Elizabeth, ending with a hiss. "Abominable! Reprehensible! Malicious! Cunning! Meretricious! I have suffered Caroline Bingley for twenty years, Fitz, and I am done with it! Next time you invite her to Pemberley or Darcy House or anywhere else I happen to be, kindly inform me in time for me to shift my person from her neighbourhood!"

"This is the outside of enough, madam! You are my wife, and in the eyes of God sworn to obey me! I *order* you to treat Caroline civilly! Do you hear me? *I order you!*"

"Do you know what you can do with your orders, Fitz? You can put them where the monkey puts his nuts!"

"Elizabeth! Madam! Are you as stark a lunatic as your younger sister? How dare you speak to me so disgustingly!"

"What a sanctimonious prig you are. At least I will say this for Caroline Bingley," said Elizabeth in pensive tones, "what one sees is what one gets. No false façade. Just a dripping sponge soaked in vitriol. Whereas you, Fitzwilliam, are the most duplicitous, the most underhanded of men. How dare you break the news to me that Mary has been abducted in front of two harpies like Caroline and Louisa? Have you no feelings? No compassion? No grasp of what is due to a wife as well as a sister? What was to stop you taking me to one side and telling me privately? What excuse can you tender for such cold-hearted stupidity? I could not even *react*! Had I, it would have been all over the best houses the moment Caroline returns to London. With a titter here, a sly look there, and everywhere an innuendo! Oh, cruel, Fitz! Abominably cruel!" Visibly shaking, Elizabeth ran down, could find nothing more to say.

He stepped into the breach. "Of course your criticisms of me are not a new phenomenon, I am aware of that. You first took delight in apostrophising me as — er — conceited, arrogant, proud and ungentlemanly twenty-one years ago. I congratulate you upon finding a new set of epithets. They leave me unwrung. As to why I did not apprise you privately of Mary's missing state, blame yourself. I dislike women's vapours and tears. Our marriage does not stand upon a rock, madam, it moves around on shifting sands. Sands that you have created. You do not obey me, though it is a part of your marriage vows. You lack a proper disposition, and your language is the height of impropriety. What's more, your conduct is growing rapidly worse. I can no longer be sure that you will comport yourself with any more decency than your sister Lydia."

"Whereas I suppose you find nothing to fault in your telling me that you wished you had never married me?" she asked, eyes blazing.

His brows rose. "I spoke the truth."

"Then I think we should end this farce of a marriage, sir."

"Death will do that, madam, nothing else." He walked to the door. "Do not antagonise me further, Elizabeth. I will engage to soothe Caroline's feelings by telling her that you are not yourself. A slight dementia brought on by worry for your sisters. She is aware of the weakness that runs through your family, so my tactful explanation will suffice."

"I have not asked you to make a hypocrite of yourself by being sweet and reasonable to Caroline Bingley! In fact, I ask you not to bother! You are branding the Bennets!" she cried as he opened the door. "Lydia, Mary, now me!"

The door shut behind him with an audible snap. Legs giving way, Elizabeth staggered to the nearest chair and sat with her head between her knees, fighting dizziness. Oh, Fitz, Fitz! Where have we gone wrong? Who is your mistress? Who, who?

Her heartbeat began to slow, her head to clear. Elizabeth got herself out of her dove-grey silk gown, the jewels, the underwear, and into her gauzy nightgown. Why do I bother with such fripperies when Fitz never comes near my bed? Because they are comfortable is why. The flannel of my youth chafed and itched.

Somewhere outside a fox shrieked, an owl screamed. Oh, Mary, where are you? Who would have braved the wrath of Ned Skinner? And what is Fitz keeping from me? How has Lydia settled into her house, Hemmings?

*　　*　　*

After eating a bread roll crisp from the oven and drinking a cup of hot chocolate, Elizabeth set out the next morning for Bingley Hall and her sister Jane. Who had suffered yet another miscarriage — a mercy. Since Charles had written that he would be away at least another twelve months, perhaps Jane would recover her health before the whole business started again. What had Mary said? That she wished Charles would plug it with a cork. How mortified Fitz would be at such plain speaking from a maiden lady!

Bingley Hall lay in five thousand acres outside the village of Wildboarclough, well south of Macclesfield. It had been a happy purchase for one seeking to advance his social station from plutocrat to aristocrat, and had fallen to Charles for a good price thanks to Fitzwilliam Darcy, who stood as guarantor not for his wealth (that was proven) but for his respectability, his propriety. Charles Bingley would not use the wrong fork or put the port decanter on the table! The land was well tenanted and Charles an excellent landlord, but the chief glory of the estate was its mansion, a large white building of central pile and two wings. Its beautiful and imposing Palladian façade dated it to the seventeenth century.

The boys were off somewhere — the youngest was now eight — which meant they knew their mother needed peace and quiet. The only girl, Priscilla, had come after William, Percival, Robert, James and Marcus, so there was no hope that Prissy, as she was universally called, would turn out in a feminine mould. Since Hugh and Arthur were her juniors, she had two brothers to dominate and bully, and hared about with quite as much vigour as her brothers, leaving havoc in her wake and a mountain of darning in the housekeeper's mending basket.

"She's always more difficult when Charles is away. He knows exactly how to deal with her," said Jane, having gone through the Bingley litany for her sister's delectation as soon as she arrived. Which she did in time for breakfast, served at ten o'clock, and dreading how to broach the subject of Mary.

William walked in, not to dine, but to pay his respects, for he viewed his favourite aunt with great affection; Aunt Elizabeth was uniformly loved, Aunt Louisa was tolerated, and Aunt Caroline feared. A year older than Charlie, he was a handsome young man who resembled his father and seemed likely to follow him into the labyrinthine corridors of plutocracy. Since he had elected Cambridge, he and his cousin never saw each other apart from Christmas, for which Elizabeth was glad. They would never have got on together. Charlie was brilliant, William a plodder. Charlie's looks were spectacular, William's orthodox. Charlie didn't notice girls — or boys, curse Caroline's slanders! — whereas William liked to break hearts and keep tally of his conquests.

However, he did not stay long, and none of the others appeared in his place, not even Prissy.

"You're not eating, Lizzie," said Jane with disapproval. "I swear that you are as slender today as you were when you married, so you have no excuse. Have some bread-and-butter."

"Just coffee, thank you. I ate at Pemberley."

"That was hours ago. What is this I hear about Lydia?" Jane asked, pouring coffee.

"*Lydia?*" For a moment Elizabeth stared blankly — oh, too much had happened in the past few days! How could she possibly have forgotten Lydia? So she ploughed through that story first, while Jane listened in horror.

"Oh, it is too bad! Can't you tell me the exact words she used to Fitz?"

"Believe me, I can't. The foulest-mouthed soldier doesn't say That Word — he would be flogged within an inch of his life. Truly, Jane, she used the worst words in the English language! And she was so drunk! Coaxing her with a bottle was the only way we could elicit co-operation from her."

"Then she must be shut away," said Jane with a sigh.

"So Fitz has decided, and what he decides is the law. Still, much and all as I condemn his highhandedness, I must confess I too can see no alternative other than to shut her up as Mama was. Her new address is Hemmings, ten miles the other side of Leek. Perhaps sixteen or seventeen miles from Bingley Hall. As soon as I can, I'll visit her."

"Let us go together. What is today, Wednesday? Shall we plan for this Friday?" asked Jane.

"We cannot," said Elizabeth miserably. "Lydia isn't the sum of my news. In fact, I've come for quite a different reason."

"Tell me, please!"

"Mary has disappeared, we fear abducted."

As Jane was still sadly pulled down after miscarrying, she fainted. Brought around by the hartshorn and vinaigrette, she began to weep, and half an hour passed before Elizabeth could calm her enough to give her the details.

"I came because I didn't want you seeing it in a journal," she concluded. "Fitz even had the notion of including a sketch of me because I look like Mary. There is a reward of one hundred pounds, large enough to stimulate a good search."

"Lizzie, this is dreadful! Oh, poor Mary! All those years of looking after Mama, and now this. What was she about, to travel on the common stage?"

"We don't know, even Angus Sinclair. Were it not for him and a disjointed letter she wrote to Charlie last year, we would be even more ignorant. They seem to think that she embarked upon some kind of investigation of the poor, with the intention of writing a book. Perhaps the stage-coach journeys were a part of it."

"That would fit," said Jane, nodding. "Mary never had a particle of sense, for all her goodness and piety. I thought her much improved when I saw her at Mama's funeral, but perhaps the improvement was only skin deep — the festering spots gone, I mean. For surely her lack of good sense won't have improved. She was a sad case."

"No, I believe the improvement went all the way to her core. Certainly Ned Skinner admired her spirit, and he isn't a susceptible man. She fought back when she was set upon, and she managed to find her way out of a dense forest. The real abduction took place on a bridle-path, not a road, and far from any big town. So Fitz has ruled out footpads or another highwayman. Whereas I begin to think of a madman, Jane."

"A Bedlamite, you mean? But the nearest Bedlam is surely the one in Manchester."

"Yes. Fitz is making enquiries to see if any inmate has escaped recently. From the Birmingham Bedlam too."

They discussed the matter until every possibility had been exhausted, by which time Jane looked exhausted too.

"I confess that I'm glad Charles will be away for another year. You need time to recuperate," said Elizabeth.

"He has a mistress in Jamaica," said Jane, sounding quite her usual self. "Children by her as well."

"Jane! No!"

"Yes."

"Who told you that?"

"Caroline. She was very angry — the girl is a mulatto, which offends Caroline's sense of fitness. It means the children are also tainted, poor little things."

"Oh, I knew I was right to put my foot down about that *bitch* of a woman!" cried Elizabeth. "Jane, Jane, I beg of you, don't grieve! Charles loves you, I would stake my life on it!"

The beautiful honey-coloured face broke into a smile that put dimples in its cheeks. "Yes, Lizzie, I know Charles loves me. I never doubt it for a single moment. Gentlemen are — well, *strange* in some ways, is all. Charles's business interests in the West Indies require his presence there every eight or nine years, and he's always away for months, sometimes a year or more. I would far rather that he had a decent woman as his mistress than flitted from woman to woman. I don't want to accompany him on these trips, so how can I repine? I simply hope that he provides properly for this woman and their children. When he comes home this time, I'll talk to him."

Elizabeth was staring, amazed. "Jane, you are a saint. Even a mistress doesn't have the power to shake you or your marriage. What did you say to Caroline when she told you?"

"Much what I've just said to you. You're too hard on poor Caroline, Lizzie. Some people are so stuffed with malice that it bursts from them like a jet of water from a fountain. Caroline is such a one. I used to think that her poison was reserved for you and me, but it isn't. It's for anybody who offends her. Like Charles's mulatto mistress, like Charlie, Prissy, and quite a few ladies in London."

Elizabeth took the opportunity. "Do you happen to know the identity of Fitz's mistress, Jane?"

"Lizzie! Not Fitz! He's far too proud. What's given you this idea? It isn't true."

"I think it must be. My resolution is crumbling — I don't know how much longer I can keep up this charade," Elizabeth said, her throat aching. "Very recently he informed me that he desperately regretted marrying me."

"No! I don't believe that! He was so passionately in love with you, Lizzie. Oh, not like Charles and me. We were cosy and comfy — passion was secondary to love. With Fitz, it was the very opposite. I mean that he had great passion, an overriding and unquiet passion. What have you done to disappoint him? If he said that to you, then you have disappointed him, and dreadfully so. Come, you must have some idea!"

Eyes closed, Elizabeth got to her feet and made a huge show of putting on her tight kid gloves, one finger at a time. When she opened the eyes, they were dark and stormy. Jane shrank away, terrified.

"The one person I have always been able to count on, Jane, was you. Yes, I use the past tense, for I see that I was mistaken. My husband treats me disgracefully! And I have done nothing to disappoint him! On the contrary. It is he who disappoints me. Last night I offered to leave him, but he won't even let me do that! Why? Because he would have to answer questions about the wife who left him! What an obsequious crawler of a wife you must be, Jane! No wonder you can excuse little peccadilloes like mistresses."

She peered through the window, ignoring Jane's fresh bout of tears. "I see my carriage has come. No, don't bother getting up, finish your snivelling in peace. I can find my own way."

And out she stalked, outraged, quivering, to weep all the way home to Pemberley. There she went straight to her rooms and told Hoskins to draw the curtains.

"Convey a message to Mr Darcy that I am laid low with the migraine, and will not be able to say farewell to Mrs Hurst, Miss Bingley, and Miss Hurst."

"I don't wish to pry, Elizabeth, but are you quite well?" Angus asked the next morning when he found his hostess walking her favourite path through the woods behind Pemberley's river.

She indicated the dell in which they were standing with one hand. "It's difficult to be down in spirits, Angus, when there is such beauty within half a mile of the house," she said, trying to deflect him. "It's too late for flowers, but this spot is perfect at all times of year. The little brook, the dragonflies, the maidenhair ferns — delicate beyond imagination! Our gardener says that such tiny, lacelike leaves and fronds are peculiarities of the maidenhair that grows in this dell only. I know people who go into ecstasies over peacock feathers, but I would rather a frond of this exquisite fern."

But Angus was not to be deflected. "We live in an age when the personal is exceeding private, and no one is more aware than I that ladies don't confide in gentlemen apart from their husbands. However, I claim the privileges of one who would enter your family. I'm in love with Mary, and hope to marry her."

"Angus!" Elizabeth smiled at him in absolute delight. "Oh, that is good news! Does she know you love her?"

"No. I did not declare my suit when I stayed in Hertford for ten days because I could see that she wasn't ready for proposals of marriage." His eyes twinkled. "The local solicitor tried his luck, and was turned down most emphatically, though he is young, affluent and handsome. I took my cue from him, and presented myself to Mary as naught save a good friend. It was the right ploy, in that she held nothing back from me about her ambitions and her ardent devotion to Argus the letter writer. In one way, girlish dreams, yet in another, valid aspirations. I listened, offered what advice I thought she would take, and mostly held my tongue."

Elizabeth found a mossy boulder and sat on it. "I would be so happy to welcome you into my family, Angus. If you did not declare your suit, I'm sure your instincts were right. Mary has never had a high opinion of men, but how could she resist a man as personable and intelligent as you?"

"I hope not forever," he said, a little wistfully. "I have gained her trust, and hope to gain her love." Which was all he could say; the identity of Argus had to remain his secret.

"Why did you choose her to love?" Elizabeth asked.

His brows flew up. "*Choose?* That's a strange word to couple with love! I don't believe there's much if any choice about it. I'm rich, I'm not decrepit, and my face is generally thought to be appealing to women. I say these things only to reinforce what is said about me in Society — that I can have my pick of eligible females. So why Mary, who is far from eligible? If it had a visible beginning, I suppose that was her beauty, which not even her dreadful clothes can disguise. But after I scraped an acquaintance with her, I found a prickly, misanthropic, fiercely independent soul who burns with the desire to make her mark on English thought. One cannot call her a philosopher; she hasn't been grounded in its disciplines or educated in its theories or steeped in its evolution. But I could see that the seventeen years she cared for her mother had allowed her an unparalleled exposure to books normally kept away from women, and had imbued her with an almost frantic desire to be freed from customary female restraints. Ignorance is the best friend and ally of custom, particularly those customs foisted on lesser beings like women and blackamoors. Well, Mary lost her ignorance, she became *educated*. And had sufficient sense to understand that without experience, her education was still lacking. It is all of this, I believe, that led her to embark upon her project. When she settles down, I think she will espouse not the cause of poverty, but the cause of universal education."

"But why travel on the stage-coach, why stay at inferior inns?"

"I don't quite know, but I suspect it may have been in order to appear an impoverished governess. People don't talk to their betters, Elizabeth, therefore Mary resolved not to seem a better."

"How remarkably well you know this Mary! You tried to tell me that I didn't know her at all, and I reproved you. But I was the ignorant one, not you," Elizabeth said, sighing.

Angus pulled a face. "There's one factor I failed utterly to take into account," he said, "and that is her natural attraction for disaster. For that, I can find no logical explanation. The very poorest of governesses travel by public coach and stay at mean inns, but they aren't set upon or abducted. Even the wee bit we know of her journey from Grantham to Nottingham confirms this tendency — she was harassed by five yokels, who pitched her into the mire of a coach yard and laughed at her plight. Her adventures are appalling! What caused them to be so? Her beauty? The guineas in her purse? That prickly misanthropy? Or simply a combination of everything?"

Elizabeth frowned. "She never got into trouble as a girl, though my father despised her. He persisted in lumping her with Lydia and Kitty as one of the three silliest girls in England. Which wasn't really fair. She persisted in singing atrociously at functions, but while everyone, including Papa, complained about it behind her back, no one ever told her to her face. Which indicates that her mind heard the notes as true, rather than demonstrates stupidity. Mary wasn't the kind of girl who excited admiration, but she wasn't silly. She was earnest, hard-working and scholarly. Qualities that made her dull, though Lydia would have said, boring."

She got up and began to walk, as if suddenly very uncomfortable. "In fact," she went on, "the worst one could say of Mary then was that she had an inappropriate and unreciprocated passion for our cousin, the Reverend Mr Collins. The most frightful man I have ever met. But Mary mooned and moped in his presence so obviously that I, for one, decided that our cousin wanted a beautiful wife. Mary's face was covered in suppurating spots, and her teeth were crooked." She laughed. "He didn't get a beautiful wife. He married Charlotte Lucas — a very plain but eminently sensible woman. And when he did, Mary very quickly got over him."

"Oh, I imagine that what attracted Mary to your cousin was his calling. She told me that in those days she was very religious." Unwilling to torment himself to the point of tears, Angus returned to the subject of Elizabeth herself. "Well, there's nothing we can do for Mary at this moment beyond Fitz's measures, so let us change the subject. I'm more concerned about you, my dear. I esteem your friendship greatly, just as I do Fitz's. But only an unobservant man of low intelligence could fail to see that you're unhappy."

"Purely on behalf of Lydia and Mary," she parried.

"Rubbish! You have offended Fitz."

"I am always offending Fitz," she said bitterly.

"Is it to do with Caroline Bingley? I was told what you said."

"She's a secondary issue."

"You did offer her an unpardonable insult."

"And would be glad to do so again. My friendship with you is a mere ten years old, Angus, but I have had to put up with Caroline Bingley for twenty-one years. Fitz's friendship with Charles Bingley is of such a nature that he's prepared to suffer Caroline. So I've sat mumchance under her insults for so long that I suppose there came a straw that broke my back. I lashed out. Yet so hypocritical is our English society that veiled insults are tolerated, whereas frankness never is. I was frank."

"How much does Charlie have to do with this?" Angus asked, thinking that it would do Elizabeth good to be — frank.

"A great deal. She sowed the seeds of discord between him and his father by implying that Charlie's tastes in love are Socratic. And she spread it all over London! Instead of blaming Caroline, Fitz blamed Charlie. It is his face, of course, and the silly effect it has on some men who are indeed Socratic. But he'll grow out of his youthful beauty — it's beginning to happen now, in fact. If this business of Mary's has anything to recommend it, it is that Fitz and Charlie are getting on together at last. Fitz is beginning to see that the reputation Caroline gave Charlie is underserved."

"Yes, you would be better off if Caroline were not a part of your lives," Angus said. "However, she is Jane's sister-in-law."

Squaring her shoulders, Elizabeth marched on without seeing anything around her. "I may have offended Fitz unforgivably, but at least I have made it impossible for Caroline to be anywhere I am. That is why Fitz is so angry."

"Well, Lizzie, a lot of people in London have put up with Miss Caroline Bingley because you and Fitz do — you're leaders in Society far beyond Westminster. When these people notice that Caroline no longer has the entrée to a Darcy function, I predict that invitations to the best houses will cease. In a year's time, Caroline and poor Louisa will have to retire to Kensington, with all the other tabbies."

Elizabeth burst out laughing. "Angus, no!"

"Angus, yes."

"Thank you for cheering me up so splendidly! The thought of Caroline and Louisa relegated to Kensington is delicious."

"Yet she isn't the crux of the matter between you and Fitz?"

"It's easy to see that you're a journalist — pick, poke, pry, chip, hammer, chisel."

"That is no answer, Elizabeth."

"I think Fitz has a mistress," she blurted.

Jane's response had been instinctive and horrified; his was calm and considered. "Absolutely not."

"Why?"

"The Darcy pride. Also, Fitz is in the vanguard of what he calls 'moral improvement' — a shocking prude, your husband! If he had his way, he would legislate a man's right to a mistress out of existence. But since he cannot do that — even archbishops have mistresses — he will make the punishment for harlotry more far-ranging as well as more severe. His first order of business will have been to make sure his own life is above any suspicion. No Augean stables for Fitzwilliam Darcy! He intends to crack down on mistresses as well as common prostitutes." Angus took her arm and tucked it through his own. "As proprietor of the foremost political paper in the kingdom, my dear, I am in a position to know everything about every important man. Whatever is going on between you and Fitz is very much your own business, but I can assure you that there is no third party involved."

When they came beneath the small library windows, Fitz emerged to join them.

"I see you're feeling better," he said to Elizabeth.

"Thank you, yes. Visiting Jane turned out to be rather a wearying ordeal. She was upset about Lydia, but Mary's plight left her prostrate. I came home with a frightful headache."

Angus released Elizabeth's arm, bowed to her, and walked away in the direction of the stables. The sound of Charlie's whoop came clearly; both parents smiled.

"You missed Caroline's departure," Fitz said.

"The headache was quite genuine, if you are implying that it was a ploy."

"Actually, no, I was not," he said in tones of surprise. "I knew where you were going, and what your reception would be. The Bingley ladies understood. They know Jane too."

"I hope you don't think I regret what I said to Caroline," Elizabeth said, voice hard. "My detestation of that — that sad apology for a woman has reached its zenith, and I cannot bear to see her. In fact, I don't know why I didn't do this years ago."

"Because it involved an unforgivable insult."

"Sometimes the thickness of a hide makes an unforgivable insult necessary! Her conceit is so monumental that she believes herself to be perfect."

"I dread telling Charles Bingley, and won't spare you."

"Do your worst," she said, sounding unperturbed. "Charles isn't a fool. The vagaries of family gave him a malignant sister, and he knows it well. When those same vagaries gave you unacceptable relatives by marriage, you removed them from your life. What is so different about my removal of Caroline Bingley? Sauce for the gander, Fitz." She shot him a minatory look. "Why did you provide so poorly for Mary? You're immensely rich and could easily have afforded to compensate her properly for the seventeen years of peace she gave you. Instead, you and Charles agreed on a paltry sum."

"I had naturally thought that she would come to live with us at Pemberley or Jane at Bingley Hall," he said stiffly. "Had she, over nine thousand pounds would have yielded her an income well in excess of her needs."

"Yes, I do understand your reasoning," she said. "However, when she refused those alternatives, you should immediately have settled a much larger sum on her. You did not."

"How could I?" he asked indignantly. "I insisted that she think about her situation for a month, then come back to me. But she never did come back to me — or inform me of her plans. Just hired an unsuitable house in Hertford and lived without a chaperone. What was I to make of that?"

"Since Mary is a Bennet, the worst." Nodding regally — thus depriving him of the opportunity to do so — Elizabeth walked into the house and left him to go wherever he pleased.

At a loose end after the unsatisfactory conclusion to their investigations, Angus, Charlie and Owen scattered like balls on a billiards table. Angus returned to the company of those in his own age group, Charlie suffered a fit of guilty conscience and went to his books, and Owen decided to explore Pemberley.

Charlie could understand a stranger's desire to see peaks, tors, rocking stones, gorges, cliffs, tormented landscapes and caves, but, having grown up at Pemberley, never thought it worth a tour of its sights.

The Welsh countryside was wilder than Derbyshire, at least in its north, so the Welshman took profound delight in the lush woods that lay between the palace — he could never think of it as a mere house — and the tenant farms that lay in the Darcy purlieu.

What fascinated him were the English oaks, incredibly old and massive. His reading had led him to believe that none had survived the ship-building that started with the eighth Henry, or the huge increase in house and furniture construction, but clearly the oaks of Pemberley's woods had never experienced the axes, saws and wedges of tree-fellers. Well, he thought, within the bounds of this mighty estate, the King's word would not count for half as much as the word of a Darcy, especially were the King a pop-eyed German nobody.

The situation among the Darcys fascinated him too, for he was as sensitive as educated, and could feel the tensions that tugged at civilities like a strong tide at an old jetty. It went without saying that he adored Mrs Darcy, though closer and longer exposure to Mr Darcy had softened his initial detestation. If one was a great man, he reflected, one probably knew it, and acted not the part but the essential truth of it. Angus said Mr Darcy would be prime minister, possibly shortly, and that made him a demigod. However, he would not be easy to live with.

The good thing was that Charlie and his father were building a rapport that certainly had not existed when Charlie first went to Oxford. Most of that was due to maturation, but some of it to the lad's natural tendency to see all sides of a question — a quality that made his scholarship formidable. The year away had seen him move farther from his mother, and that too was a good thing. She was a reminder of a painful childhood that he was rapidly outgrowing.

"Ho there!" said a young and very imperious voice.

Startled, he looked around, but could see no one.

"Up here, dolt!"

Thus directed, his gaze found an oval face framed by a mop of disordered chestnut curls; two eyes of a colour he could not discern glared at him.

"What happens now?" he asked, having three sisters of his own. For Charlie's sister she certainly was, with that hair.

"You get me down, dolt."

"Oh, are you stuck, scruff?"

"If I were not, dolt, you wouldn't know I was here."

"I see. You mean you would have pitched stones or nuts at me from your hiding place."

"Nuts at this time of year? You are a dolt!"

"How are you stuck?" he asked, beginning to climb the oak.

"My ankle is wedged in a crevice."

"That's the first elegantly phrased thing you've said."

"A fig for elegant phrases!" she said scornfully.

"Oh, dear. Definitely inelegant." His face was now level with her feet, and he could see the wedged ankle. "Take hold of a stout branch with both your hands and give it all your weight. Once your legs aren't bearing your weight, bend your knees. My, you have got it stuck!" When he lifted his head he realised that he was looking straight up her skirts, and gave a cough. "When you're free, kindly gather up your skirts. Then I may help you down while preserving your modesty."

"A fig for modesty!" she said, starting to go limp at the knees.

"Just do as you're told, scruff." He put his hands around her lower leg and eased the foot sideways until it came free.

Instead of preserving her modesty by bunching her skirts around her closely, she gave a wriggle that perched her on his shoulders, then slid down his length and eventually reached the ground. There she waited until he stood beside her.

"I must say, dolt, that you did that deedily."

"Whereas you, scruff, behaved with a complete lack of propriety." He looked at her closely. "You're not a scruffy schoolgirl, though you act like one. What are you, sixteen?"

"Seventeen, dolt!" She stuck out a grubby hand, its nails

bitten to the quick. "I'm Georgie Darcy, but I quite like being called a scruff," she said, smiling.

"And I'm Owen Griffiths, but I don't like being called a dolt." He shook her hand. Her eyes, he discovered now, were a light green, the colour of new leaves; he had never seen their like before. She was, of course, beautiful. No child of those parents could be ugly.

"Charlie's Oxford tutor! I'm glad to meet you, Owen."

"I think it should be Mr Griffiths," he said gravely.

"I know it should be, but that makes no difference."

"Why do we guests never meet you?"

"Because we are not yet out. Schoolroom misses with Mr Darcy for father are sequestered." She looked wicked. "Would you like to meet the Darcy girls?"

"Very much."

"What time is it? I was stuck up that tree for ages."

"Tea time in a schoolroom."

"Then come and have tea with us."

"I think I should ask Mrs Darcy first."

"Oh, pooh, nonsense! I'll take the blame."

"I suspect you take the blame often, scruff."

"Well, I'm not a very satisfactory daughter," she said, the curls bouncing as she engaged in a complicated skip down a flagged path. "I come out next year, when I am eighteen, but Mama despairs of my taking."

"Oh, I am sure you will take," he said with a smile.

"As if I care! They will lace me into stays that push up my bosoms, style my hair, smear lotion all over my face, make me use a parasol if I go into the sun, forbid me to ride astride, and generally make my life a misery. All to procure a husband! I can do that *without* a London season because I have ninety thousand pounds settled on me. Did you ever hear of a man who demanded to look at the teeth of a filly worth half that much?"

"Er — no. Except that I don't think the age of a filly is in much doubt, so he probably wouldn't look anyway."

"Oh, you are the kind of man who throws cold water!"

"Yes, I fear I am."

She gave another skip. "They will bully me into simpering and forbid me to say what I think. And it will all be wasted, Owen. I don't intend to marry. When I'm of age, I'll buy a farm and live on it, perhaps with Mary. They say," she confided in a stage whisper, "that I'm very like her."

"I've never met Mary, Georgie, but you're definitely like her. What would you do with your life, if you were free to choose?"

"Be a farmer," she said without hesitation. "I like the feel of the earth, causing things to grow, the smell of a well kept barnyard, the sound of cows mooing — well, it doesn't matter. I'll never be allowed to be a farmer."

"No matter whom you marry, you could emulate Marie Antoinette and have a little farm to play in."

"*Play?* Pah! Besides, I like my head on my shoulders. She was a very silly woman."

"My father is a farmer in Wales, but I confess I couldn't wait to leave the barnyard and the cows. They have to be milked, you know, at a dismally early hour."

"I know that, dolt!" She went suddenly misty-eyed. "Oh, I do love cows! And dirty hands."

"They have to be clean to milk," Owen said prosaically. "Also warm. Cows dislike cold hands on their teats."

They entered the house by a back door Owen had not dreamed existed, and began to climb a chipped, battered staircase.

"What could you possibly like better than a farm, Owen?"

"Academia. I'm a scholar, and hope one day to be an Oxford don. My discipline is in the Classics."

She mock-retched. "Erk! How indescribably boring!"

They had passed down several interminably long and musty halls, and now faced a door badly in need of paint. How extraordinary! The parts of Pemberley open to guests were magnificently kept up, but the unseen parts were neglected.

"The schoolroom," said Georgie, entering with flourish. "Girls, this is Charlie's tutor, Owen. Owen, these are my sisters. Susannah — Susie — is almost sixteen, Anne is thirteen, and Catherine — Cathy — is ten. This is our governess, Miss Fortescue. She's very jolly, and we love her."

"Georgiana, you cannot invite gentlemen to tea!" said jolly Miss Fortescue, not because she was overly circumspect, Owen divined, but because she knew it meant trouble for Georgie if word reached her mama.

"Of course I can. Sit down, Owen. Tea?"

"Yes, please," he said, unwilling to give up this wonderful chance to meet Charlie's sisters. Besides which, the tea was just what he loved — three different kinds of cake, sugared buns, and not a slice of bread-and-butter anywhere.

An hour with the female Darcys enchanted him.

Georgie was a nonpareil; if she could be prevailed upon to wear a fashionable dress and speak on socially acceptable sorts of subjects she would take London by storm even without those ninety thousand pounds. With them, every bachelor would be after her, some of such looks and address that Owen didn't think she would be able to resist their blandishments. Later on, he changed his mind about that. Solid steel, Georgie.

Susie was blonder than the others, though she had escaped colourless brows and lashes; her eyes were light blue and her silky hair flaxen. Extremely proud of her talent, Miss Fortescue brought out her drawings and paintings, which Owen had to admit were far superior to the usual scribbles and daubs of schoolgirls. By nature she was quiet, even a little shy.

Anne was the darkest in colouring, and the only one with brown eyes. A certain innate hauteur said she was Mr Darcy's child, but she also had Elizabeth's charm, and was very well read. Her ambition, she said without false modesty, was to write three-volume novels in the vein of Mr Scott. Adventure appealed to her more than romance, and she deemed damsels in castle dungeons silly.

Cathy was another chestnut-haired child, but whereas her brother's eyes were grey and Georgie's green, hers were a dark blue in which flickered the naughtiness of an imp — no malice. She informed Owen that her father had slapped her for putting treacle in his bed. Of repentance she displayed none, despite the slap, which she regarded as a mark of distinction. Her sole ambition seemed to be to earn more slaps, which Owen read as Cathy's way of demonstrating that she loved her father and was not afraid of him.

It was clear that the four girls were starved for adult company; Owen found himself sorry for them. Their station was that of high princesses, and like all high princesses, they were locked in an ivory tower. None of them was a flirt, and none of them considered her life interesting enough to dominate the conversation; what they wanted were Owen's opinions and experiences of that big outside world.

The party broke up in consternation when Elizabeth walked in. Her brows rose at the sight of Mr Griffiths, but Georgie leaped fearlessly into the fray.

"Don't blame Owen! It was me," she said.

"It was I," her mother corrected automatically.

"I know, I know! The verb 'to be' takes the same case after it as before it. He didn't want to come, but I made him."

"He? Him?"

"Oh, *Owen*! Honestly, Mama, you're so busy correcting our grammar that you never get around to scolding us!"

"Owen, you're free to have tea in the schoolroom at any time," said Elizabeth placidly. "There, Georgie, are you satisfied?"

"Thank you, Mama, thank you!" cried Georgie.

"Thank you, Mama!" the other three chorused.

Holding the door, Owen allowed Elizabeth to precede him. She continued up the interminable corridor to a more imposing set of double doors, and once through them, he found himself in what the Darcys called the public parts of the house, apparently because they were open to inspection by strangers when the family was not home.

"You are wondering why so much of Pemberley is not kept up," she said, leading the way to the blue-and-white Dutch Room, full of Vermeers and Bruegels, with two Rembrandts in proudest place, and, hidden by a screen, a Bosch.

"I — er —" He floundered, not knowing what to say.

"It will be refurbished after Cathy comes out — eight more years. Though it doesn't look very nice, structurally it's perfectly sound. What's lacking is a new coat of paint, and some replaced balusters and stair treads. A Darcy of generations ago decreed that the non-public parts of the house should be refurbished no more often than every thirty years, and that has become an unwritten law. When Cathy leaves it will be twenty-seven years since the last time, but Fitz says that will be long enough. I confess I'm looking forward to it, and won't let the colour be brown. So dark!"

"Does that include the servants' rooms?" he asked.

"Oh, dear me, no! The permanent servants live two floors up. Their rooms are done at ten-year intervals, like all the public parts of the house. They're cheerful and well-appointed — I always feel that servants should be made very comfortable. The married ones live in cottages in a small village only a walk away. People like my own maid, Hoskins, and Mr Darcy's valet, Meade, have suites."

"You must consume a great deal of water, ma'am."

"Yes, but we're lucky. Our stream is absolutely pure, having no settlements on it between here and its source. There is a huge reservoir in the roof — it stands on iron pilings. That gives our water the power to flow through pipes all over the house. Now that water closets have been invented, I've persuaded Fitz to install them adjacent to every bedroom, with some in the servants' quarters too. And now that powerful pumps are available, I want a supply of hot water to the kitchen and to some new, proper bathrooms. This is an exciting age to live in, Owen."

"Indeed it is, Mrs Darcy." What he did not ask was where all this potential waste was to go, as he knew the answer: into the river below Pemberley, where the stream would not be pure any more.

"Your daughters are delightful," he said, sitting down.

"Yes, they are."

"Have they no exposure to the outside world?"

"I am afraid not. But why do you ask?"

"Because they're so starved for news. Why aren't they allowed to read newspapers and journals? They know more about Alexander the Great than about Napoleon Bonaparte. And it seems a pity that they're not permitted to meet men like Angus Sinclair. He would surely do them no harm." He stopped, horrified. "Oh, I do beg your pardon! I must sound critical of your arrangements, and I don't mean to."

"You are absolutely right, sir. I agree with you wholeheartedly. Unfortunately Mr Darcy does not. For which I have my own sisters to blame. My parents permitted us free rein from a very early age. It did Jane and me no harm, but Kitty and Lydia should have been curbed, and were not. They were more than hoydens, they were flirts, and in Lydia's case, a tendency to associate unchaperoned with officers of a militia regiment led to shocking trouble. So when we had our own girls, Mr Darcy decided that they would not be allowed to mix in the world until they officially came out at eighteen."

"I see."

"I hope that your heart is proof against the charms of, say, Georgie?" Elizabeth asked with a twinkle.

He laughed. "Well, the man who would inspect a filly's teeth did she have half as many as ninety thousand pounds does not exist."

"I beg your pardon?"

"That was how Georgie put her situation to me."

"Oh, I despair of her! I cannot cure her indelicacy!"

"Don't try. The world will do it for you. Under that brave front lies a great deal of vulnerability — she thinks she's like her Aunt Mary, but in truth she's more like Charlie."

"And over-dowered. They all are, though Georgie is worst off in that respect. The others have a mere fifty thousand pounds each. It was not our doing, but Fitz's father's. The money was left in trust for any daughters Fitz might have. We fear fortune hunters, of course. Some are so charming, so irresistible!"

"Well, I cannot see Georgie falling in love with a fortune hunter — or Anne, for that matter. The most vulnerable is Susie. Cathy is more likely to dupe her seducer than run off with him."

"You cheer me immensely, Owen." The purple eyes gleamed at him as mischievously as Cathy's. "It is tea time. Can you eat a second tea?"

"Easily," he said.

"You are twenty-five, I believe?"

"Yes. Twenty-six in October."

"Then you're safe for at least another five or six years. After that, your figure won't run to second teas. Gentlemen set in their early thirties, finish growing from calves to bulls."

NINE

Mary's days dragged more and more as time went on. Now that her life was regular, she could mark off each interval between the delivery of fresh food as one day, though she could not be sure it really was. If it was, then at the end of thirty pencilled strokes on her wall (including those first estimated seven), she began to despair. Wherever her prison lay, no one had found it, though she was sure people would be looking for her.

Things had happened which caused a lump of terror to rise in her doughty breast; how much longer would Father Dominus bother to keep her alive? For all his talk about the Children of Jesus, she had seen no evidence of their existence beyond Brother Jerome, Brother Ignatius and Sister Therese, all hovering on the brink of puberty, and though Ignatius and Therese spoke freely of their fellow Children, it seemed to Mary that there was an element of the unreal about what they said. Why, for instance, did no child attempt to run away, if they did indeed have the freedom to venture out of the caves? Human nature was adventurous, particularly in the young — what escapades she and Charlie used to get up to when he was a boy! Somewhere she thought that perhaps Martin Luther had said were he to be given a child until he turned seven, he would have the man. In which case, how young were the Children of Jesus when they were taken? Neither Ignatius nor Therese was prepared to confide in her fully; much of what she had pieced together came from what they refused to say. Yet the old man fed his disciples extremely well, clothed them, doctored them, allowed them considerable liberty. That they worked for him without being paid indicated that he exploited them, as did his neglect of their education.

At first she had hoped that the book he was dictating to her would answer some of these questions, but after thirteen sessions he was still absorbed with the conundrum of God and the evil of light. A pattern was emerging: of a circular progress through his riddles akin to what was said of people hopelessly lost — that they walked in circles and always wound up where they started. And so it was with Father Dominus's book. He didn't seem to know how to get off the track he wandered and go in a straighter line.

He had also curbed her contact with Ignatius and Therese. Now she walked to the underground river on her own, while Ignatius stood guard at the beginning of the tunnel and returned her to her cell when she emerged. Their communication dwindled to greetings and farewells; clearly he had been told not to say anything to her beyond those civilities.

Removal of Therese was stranger. In her talks with Father Dominus not related to dictation Mary had realised that he despised the female sex, mature or immature. Affection would show in his face when he spoke of the boys, but the moment Mary introduced the girls into their conversation he would stiffen, the expression he wore would change to contempt, and he would brush her aside as if she were some noxious insect.

Then Mary's courses began to flow, and she was obliged to ask Therese for rags, as well as come to some arrangement about soaking and boiling them after use. It seemed Therese had to request the fabric for these rags from Father Dominus, who beat her with a stick and called her unclean. The rags were forthcoming, handed over by a tearful Therese together with the story of the old man's reaction, but that was to be her last contact with Therese. After it, Camille brought her daily necessities, and would not succumb to Mary's blandishments, though the frightened blue eyes held yearning.

That tipped the scales in Mary's attitude toward him. Until then her sense of self-preservation had prompted her to go softly, never to antagonise him, but such control was alien to Mary's frank nature, and the bonds that tied her tongue were frail. When next he appeared to give dictation, she flew at him verbally, since the bars on her cage did not permit of any other opposition.

"What do you mean, you awful old man," said Mary, snapping the words, "by calling an innocent child unclean? Do you doubt your power over a little girl's mind, that you would whip her with a rod? Disgraceful! That child manages a kitchen capable of producing good food for fifty stomachs, and how do you thank her? You pay her no wages, but that is no surprise, since you pay no wages to any Child of Jesus! But to *beat* her! To beat her because she asked for rags for my courses? To call her unclean? Sir, you are a bigot and a disgrace to your calling!"

He had reared up in outrage, eyes rolling in his head, but when Mary mentioned rags and courses, he flung his arms about his head, hands blocking his ears, and rocked in his chair.

For perhaps a minute she surveyed him angrily, then she sat down on her chair and sighed. "Father, you are a fraud," she said. "You think yourself a son of God, and you keep these children to worship and adore you. I acquit you of being greedy for profits from your nostrums, for I believe that you spend them on good food and other comforts for your followers. Your expenses must be considerable, even including fodder for your donkey train and coal for the fires I presume you need in your laboratory as well as in your kitchen. Nothing you have dictated to me thus far has told me why you are here, or how long you have been here, or what you intend to achieve. But you disappoint me bitterly, to take out your spleen on an innocent like Therese — and for no better reason than her sex. The female sex is God's creation in equal measure to the male sex, and how He has designed our bodily functions is His business, not yours, for you are not God. Do you hear me? *You are not God!*"

His hands had dropped from his ears, though the look on his face said he didn't like either Mary's subject matter or the tone of her voice. But he didn't get up and run; instead, he swung to face her, thin lips peeled back from perfect teeth.

"I am God," he said, fairly calmly, and smiled. "All members of the male sex are God. Females are the creation of Lucifer, put on earth to tempt, seduce, corrupt."

She snorted derisively. "Rubbish! Men are not God, any more than women are. Males and females both are God's creation. And did it ever occur to you that it is not women who tempt and seduce, but men who are weak and unworthy? If there is a devil in humankind, it is in men, who strive to corrupt women, then blame women. I have had some experience of the devil in men, sir, and I assure you that it needs no lures thrown out by women. It is already inborn."

"This conversation is pointless!" he snapped. "Kindly pick up your pencil, madam."

"I will do that, Father Dominus, if you give me a new subject. Thus far I have given you nigh on two hundred pages of text, and only the first fifty are fresh and original. After that, you merely go over the same ground. Move on, Father! I am very interested in the genesis of Cosmogenesis. It is time you told your readers what happened after you entered the Seat of God in your thirty-fifth year. Why, for instance, did you enter it?"

She had caught him; he stared at her in amazement, almost as if he had received another visitation. Mary breathed a silent sigh of relief. It was in his power to kill her, and perhaps for a few moments when she had castigated him so bitingly he had contemplated having Brother Jerome pitch her down her privy well to certain death, but, all unknowing, she had saved her life by showing him where he was going wrong. The brain that once must have been as formidable as any in the whole country was softening, a gradual process of which perhaps he had some awareness, yet knew not how to remedy it. Would he, back in his heyday, have whipped poor little Therese? Or thought the female sex unclean? Mary didn't know, but wanted to. Now, with any luck, she might find out, for he was grateful enough at her criticism to come to the conclusion that her life was worth sparing. He wanted to write this book, but he didn't know how. A mind that could invent lamps and cure-alls apparently did not have the ability to plan a verbal construction. As long as she guided him in his literary work, he would keep her alive.

"Proceed as follows," he said. "'Lucifer's greatest stratagem in his bid to control the destiny of men was his invention of gold. Consider its qualities, and be consumed with admiration for the subtlety of Lucifer's mind! It is his own colour, brilliant and yellow as the Sun. It never tarnishes. It is malleable and ductile enough to be worked into all manner of objects. It is as permanent as it is heavy. It contains no imperfection. As long as men have existed, they have worshipped gold, and in doing so, worshipped Lucifer. Men kill for it. They hoard it. They base the economic prosperity of their societies on it. They conquer for it. They demonstrate their wealth by loading it upon their own selves and the bodies of their women, who hunger for it as an adornment. It goes into the tombs of the chieftains and emperors to tell future generations how great the power of the dead man.

"'In my thirty-fifth year I was entrusted with the custody of the gold hoarded by a man given entirely over to Lucifer, though I did not see it at the time. This gold was in many forms — coins, jewellery, ornaments, objects. My master removed the precious stones from the jewellery and gave me the gold mountings, chains, pieces. I was to melt it down, remove any impurities, and cast the gold into ingots. Then I was to bring him the ingots. But the actual refining of the ingots had to be conducted in complete secrecy, so much so that my master refused to let me tell him whereabouts I would do this work.'"

His face had taken on a dreamy look; Mary scribbled with her pencil and said nothing, waiting out the pause.

"'He knew I would not betray him, for he owned my soul. I remembered the moors and caves of the Peak District, and found a huge cave that now functions as my laboratory. It was perfect for my purposes, even including, in close proximity, a hidden cave in which I could stable the donkeys which brought in my requirements during the nights. When I had set myself up, I gave my helpers poisoned rum to drink, then threw them down a hole into the darkness. For six months I toiled, melting down the gold into ten-pound ingots — a smaller size than is usual, but I needed something of a weight that I myself could carry. I was young then, and wiry.

"'And when my work was done, I went to explore the caves, and so found the dark Who is God. It was a revelation in many ways, far beyond the pillars of Cosmogenesis. For I looked on the gold ingots and saw them for what they were — the work of Lucifer. The property of Lucifer. The instrument of Lucifer.

And I understood that my master was Lucifer's servant in every way. Therefore he should not have his gold. I took it and I hid it far from the laboratory cave, and I never went back to my old master.

"'I remained with God in the darkness for many moons. How much of Lucifer's Sun time passed, I do not know. But when finally I emerged I was changed. Gold had no power over me, or any other of Lucifer's tricks. Stark white spiders weaved their colourless strands over the gold, a mouldering that threw Lucifer's power in his face as of no moment, a nothing. And there it sits to this day, in the darkness of God, rendered null and void.'"

Putting down her pencil, Mary stared at Father Dominus with awe and a new respect. "You are a singularity, Father," she said. "You are a bigot and a tyrant, but you have had the strength to withstand the lure of gold."

Working his muscles as if they hurt, he got to his feet. "I am tired," he said on a whisper. "Copy that, please."

"Gladly, but more gladly still if you would send me Therese."

But, as was his wont, he had disappeared in a twinkle, and she could not be sure he had even heard her.

What a story! Was it true? Father Dominus could and did lie, but somehow this tale of gold had the ring of truth about it. Yet who could this mythical master have been, to have accumulated so much gold that it took Father Dominus six months to refine it? And would he really permit the publication of something that described with no emotion the murder of a number of helpers?

Her dinner came — a beefsteak with mushrooms, creamed potatoes, and, for dessert, a slice of steamed treacle pudding. A reward for putting her dictator on the right road again, she divined. Not one to look gift horses in the mouth, Mary demolished the meal with real enjoyment, and felt the strength flow into her. Perhaps he wasn't mad, she thought, stomach full and attitude unusually benign.

Which did not last beyond the morrow, when Father Dominus came looking dishevelled and sleepless, sat down in his chair, and proceeded to give her a treatise on the chemistry of gold and how to refine it. It seemed she had to ask him how to spell every fourth or fifth word, so larded was it with abstruse terms, and that shredded his temper.

"Learn to spell, madam!" he shouted, jumping up in a rage. "I am not here to serve as your lexicon!"

"I can spell extremely well, Father, but I am not an apothecary or a chemist! When I ask you to spell a word, that word is strange to my experience! If your subject were music, I would not need to ask how to spell glissando or toccata, for I am a proficient in music. But what you have dictated to me today is a closed book."

"Pah!" he spat, and vanished.

Her menu went back to bread, butter and cheese, though she had exchanged the small beer for water — over the top of his objections. To Father Dominus, water meant typhoid and typhus; the three percent intoxicant in small beer as well as its brewing process made it safe to drink. And in that belief he was by no means alone; most families took their children straight from milk to small beer. Mary loathed it, and had only got her water after she pointed out to him that the streams flowing through the caves were as pure as water got.

From Ignatius, still appearing to let her out of her cage and let her walk into the river tunnel, she began to receive alarming signals that all was not well in the world of the Children of Jesus.

Lantern in hand, boots on her feet, she put her fingers on the rough wool of his sleeve and forced him to look at her face. "Dear Ignatius, what is the matter?"

"Not allowed to talk to you, Sister Mary!" he whispered.

"Nonsense! There is no one to hear us. What is it?"

"Father says we have to be out of the Southern Caves quick-smart, and there's so much to do! Jerome's too ready with his cane, and the little ones can't keep up."

"How little are the little ones?"

"Four — five — something like that."

"Where is Therese?"

"Gone today to the Northern Caves. Her new kitchen's ready."

"And what about me? Am I to be moved?"

He looked hunted, miserable. "Dunno, Sister Mary. Now go!"

When she came back he hustled her into her cell, picked up her boots, and disappeared around the screen. Mary's heart sank. That did not bode well, the confiscation of her boots, which Ignatius had taken to putting outside the tunnel entrance.

Father Dominus when he came was as restless as a child put on a stool to wear a dunce's cap, and his dictation when finally it came was worthy of a dunce's cap — disjointed, rambling, and bearing no relation to gold, God or Lucifer. In the end she asked him, voice as humble as she could make it, to spell out a list of abstruse terms for her, so that in future she would not need to break his concentration by requesting help. Thirty-two words into the list, he suddenly leaped up and whisked himself away.

For a while Mary tried to convince herself that all of this was the result of a geographical dislocation; it must surely be worrisome to have to supervise fifty-odd children in a move of some miles from a cave system that had been their home for years to a new one that perhaps they feared more, as it evidently contained both the laboratory and the packing cave. And the gold? No, she could not assume that. The gold was wherever God dwelled, and what he had said offered insufficient information to decide on a locality.

On the following day Brother Jerome appeared with her bread and water, though no butter, cheese or jam. Dark eyes watching her contemptuously, he held out a hand. "Gimme your work."

Silently she passed it through the bars, a miserably small set of pages compared to their earlier sessions, which had kept her so busy copying that she had little time for worry or idle thought.

One day steak, mushrooms and pudding, now bread and water, she thought. What is happening? Has that frail mind crumbled? Or is my new regimen merely a symptom of the fact that I am now miles away from the kitchen? Water aplenty can be collected everywhere, but bread and what one puts on bread come from a kitchen.

Father Dominus erupted screaming from behind the screen during her second day of bread and water, the pages she had given Jerome clutched in one hand.

"What is this? What *is* this?" he shrieked, beads of foam gathering at the corners of his mouth.

"It is what you dictated to me the day before yesterday," Mary said, her voice betraying no fear.

"I dictated to you for two hours then, madam — *two hours!*"

"No, Father, you did not. You sat on your chair for two hours, but the only usable information you gave me is written down there. You rambled, sir."

"Liar! Liar!"

"Why would I lie?" she asked reasonably. "I am quite intelligent enough to know that my life depends upon pleasing you, Father. Why therefore would I antagonise you?" She had an inspiration. "In fact, I thought you in sore need of sleep, and judged that tiredness caused this lapse in your concentration. Was I wrong?"

Two little pellets stared at her with the bluish, milky glassiness of skimmed milk, but she stared back unintimidated. Let him stare!

"Perhaps you are right," he said finally, and stormed off with no intention, it seemed, of dictating to her this day.

His mind was failing, of that she no longer had any doubt, but whether it might be called madness was moot.

"Oh, if only I could establish sufficient rapport with him to talk rationally about the children!" she said to herself, perched on the edge of her bed. "I still have no idea why he acquired them, or how, or what happens to them when they attain maturity. Somehow I have to cozen him into a softer mood."

Of Brother Ignatius there was no sign, nor did Jerome appear to replenish her supply of bread, down to half a loaf. An instinct had caused Mary not to waste water on washing her face or any part of her body: she might need what she had to drink, and that sparingly. With no dictation to copy and every book read at least several times, that day dragged, especially because she had not been let out for exercise. Sleep came slowly, was haunted by dreams, and lasted but a short time.

When Father Dominus appeared he was carrying a fresh loaf of bread and a pitcher of water.

"Oh, how glad I am to see you, Father!" Mary cried, smiling her best smile and hoping that it held no element of seduction. "I languish with nothing to do, and am looking forward to the next chapter of your Cosmogenesis."

He sat down, apparently having decided that her smile was not seductive, but instead of putting the bread and water jug on her shelf, he put them on the floor beside his chair. His message, she was sure, was to tell her that receiving this largesse depended entirely upon her own conduct during their interview.

"Before we start the dictation, Father," she said in her most winning voice — quite an effort for Mary — "there is so much I wish to understand about the darkness of God. Lucifer is self-apparent, and I agree with your philosophy wholeheartedly. But as yet we have not discussed Jesus, Who must be writ large in your cosmogeny, else you would not have christened your followers the Children of Jesus. There are fifty of them, you say, thirty boys and twenty girls. Those numbers must have a significance, for nothing you have said to date lacks import."

"Yes, you are intelligent," he said, pleased. "All numbers of import must end in no number — that is, what the Greeks called zero. A nought, we write in Arabic numbers. Not only is zero no number, but in Arabic it has no beginning and no end. It is eternal. The eternal zero. Five plus three plus two are ten. The line that never meets itself and the circle that always does."

He stopped; Mary blinked. What utter nonsense! But she said in tones of awe, "Profound! Amazing!" She hesitated for as long as she thought she dared, then said, very delicately, "And Jesus?"

"Jesus is the offspring of a truce between God and Lucifer."

Her jaw dropped. "*What?*"

"I would have thought that self-evident, Sister Mary. Men could not bear the formlessness and facelessness and sexlessness of God, but also refused to be completely taken in by Lucifer's wiles. God was getting nowhere, and Lucifer was getting nowhere. So they met on a rock in the sky that briefly turned into a star and forged Jesus. A man, yet not a man. Mortal, yet immortal. Good, yet evil."

Mary couldn't help the sweat that broke out all over her body, nor the shudder of revulsion that precipitated her off her chair. "Father, you blaspheme! You are anathema! Apostate! But you have answered all my questions, even those I have not asked. Whatever you want with those children, it is evil. They will never be let grow up, will they? The little girls talk of a school in Manchester run by Mother Beata, who will train them as abigails, but there is no school, no Mother Beata! What do you do with the boys? Of that I have heard nothing, for Brother Ignatius is too dull and Brother Jerome too cunning to tell me. Wicked! You are wicked! I curse you, Dominus! You stole your children too young to be under cruel masters, which means you bought them for gin-money from their godless parents, or from the Parish overseers! You exploit their innocence and think your duty acquitted because you feed, clothe and physick them! Like calves fatted for the table! You *murder* them, Dominus! You kill the innocent!"

He had listened to her diatribe in amazement, so stunned that he was speechless. What opened his mouth on a torrent of words was her accusation that he murdered the innocent; if she had needed any proof, his hideous tantrum proved it. Screaming shrilly, screeching, spitting, his body convulsed with the enormity of his rage, he called her bitch, strumpet, seductress, Lilith, Jezebel, the names of a dozen other biblical temptresses, then began again, and again, and again. While Mary, beside herself, shouted him down with one single accusation over and over.

"You kill the innocent! You kill the innocent!"

It seemed not knowing what else to do, he picked up the ewer and pitched it at the bars, showering Mary with shards and precious water. Then he turned blindly, blundering into the screen, and ran away shrieking curses on her head.

The screen tottered and fell, it seemed incredibly slowly, its upper border catching something beyond it and ripping that down too. An immensity of light poured in, so brilliant that Mary flung up an arm to shield her eyes. Only when she was sure she could cope with such intensity did she open her eyes to look upon a vista that, under different circumstances, would have awed her with its beauty. Wherever she lay at least a thousand feet above the surrounding countryside, which spread into the moors and weird rocks of peaks and tors. Derbyshire! Many miles from Mansfield!

A wind whistled into the cave, a wind that must have been excluded by a sheet of dark green canvas that now lay on the floor beyond the screen. So that was why her prison had been perpetually filled by a soft, moaning whine! Not a window left open on a crack, but a sheet of canvas that somewhere had not been entirely efficient, and gaped a tiny crack in the seal.

Oh! she thought, shivering, I will perish from the cold long before I can die of thirst!

She could not reach the cave mouth, of course; it lay a good twenty feet away, and the bars still confined her. The bread lay beyond her reach, the water was drying rapidly in that terrible wind. Where did they enter and leave? In the right-hand wall there was nothing, but in the left-hand one three tunnel maws loomed; her exercise route, and two others farther away. Beside the farthest was a pile of tallow candles and a tinder box; that must be the tunnel that led far underground in the direction of the Northern Caves. The middle one, she decided, communicated with the old kitchen next door. Oh, what had happened to Therese? To Ignatius? They were dangerously close to puberty, which Mary's instinct told her was Father Dominus's boundary. Once a child crossed it into manhood or womanhood, he or she was disposed of. All she could hope was that, coming at the hands of a skilled apothecary, death was swift and oblivious. No need, surely, to resort to violence. Though, after listening to those warped and twisted concepts of God and the Devil, some tiny part of her wondered if perhaps they were indeed fatted calves, and sacrificed at puberty to a lightless god. No, surely not!

But who, her relentless mind went on, can predict the quite unpredictable vagaries of a mind as diseased as Father Dominus's? Not every madman was a raving lunatic, though Father Dominus could upon occasion manifest himself a raving lunatic. At other times he seemed as sane as she was herself, capable of producing facts in a logical order, and even, once or twice, convincing Mary that his Cosmogenesis had some merit, given his experiences.

I need to *see* these children! she told herself, knowing that there was scant chance of its happening. I want to talk to them, not in furtive whispers with one ear tuned for Father or Jerome, but over sweet hot chocolate and delicious cakes, all the goodies that permit children to abandon their defences. I need to know that, having named them after a hybrid demigod half dark and half light, they are not spoiled in the sense that perishable food spoils; that their innocence is still there, still intact. If he needs them as mules to toil for him, and has not bothered to educate them in Cosmogenesis, then they will have survived. The danger is that these sole disciples need to be educated in his philosophy, or theology, or whatever it is he classifies it as. Certainly it is not a sane man's ideology, and arises out of inadequacies in himself. But what sort of brain could witness utter darkness and be moved to worship it as God? Or brand all light as evil?

Calmer after a while, she gazed around her little prison. Yes, the ewer on her table still held water, enough if she drank very sparingly to last for a number of days. Of food she had an elbow of stale bread. Well, food was not nearly as necessary for life as water. Admitting that her need now was far greater than ever before, she shook and rattled every bar in her cage, to no avail. They were mortared into the cave walls; if she had had any kind of implement, even a spoon, she might have tried to chip at the walls, but with the regimen of bread and water had come a demand for her spoon, her only eating implement.

Tears ran down her face; she sobbed for some time. Then, exhausted, she slumped upon the side of her bed and put her head in her hands. The pencil marks said she had been in this place for about six weeks, and it seemed she was doomed to die after all. No Child of Jesus would come to help her; they had gone to the Northern Caves, including Therese and Ignatius.

But despair passes, especially in the Marys of this world. Her shoulders squared, she sat up, jaws tight. I will not accept my fate *tamely*! she said to herself. I will drink two mouthfuls of water, then I will sleep. When my strength returns I will try to loosen the bars, this time at the big door they use to go in and out of my cell. Perhaps it is weaker.

A plan she followed precisely. But the big door did not yield, and its lock was beyond her, as was the lock on the shelf. If only she had her mending kit! The little hooky device that unpicked stitches might have worked the internal apparatus of the big door's lock. But she had absolutely nothing.

I have finally reached the end of my tether, she thought, but I refuse to give in. I am in the Hand of God, yes, but also in my own hand. As long as I have water to drink, I will not yield to permanent despair.

TEN

Lydia too had realised that she was a prisoner, not long after
Ned Skinner had delivered her to Hemmings and the clutches of
Miss Mirabelle Maplethorpe. More experienced than any of her
sisters, Lydia quickly recognised the woman's origins as a
bawdy-house. But never as one of the whores who did the actual
servicing. Miss Maplethorpe ran the whores and made sure they
serviced in whatever way a gentleman patron desired. What was
Fitz about, to employ a woman like her? Mama had been given
Mary; she was palmed off with a madam. Which perhaps meant
that Fitz regarded her with as much contempt as he did fear that
she might overset his plans. The bars on the windows indicated
fear, but Miss Maplethorpe indicated utter contempt.

Not that Miss Maplethorpe was uncivil: far from it. The
only thing Lydia was denied was her freedom. With an
unlimited supply of wine, port and cognac at her command, it
seemed that Fitz truly expected her to sink into a state of

permanent inebriation. Whereas the truth was that Lydia belonged to that peculiar sort of bibber who could, if they wished, stop drinking entirely. And now was definitely the time to stop drinking; she *had* to find out what was going on!

However, she decided to keep her sobriety a secret. At first she emptied the bottles out of her bedroom windows, but the fluid stained the bricks of the outside wall. Then she found that if she poked the neck of a bottle between the bars of a ground floor window, its contents fell into the earth of a garden bed and soaked away. She had plenty of time alone in which to do this, time she could pretend was spent drinking. No one, it seemed, *chose* the company of a drunkard.

She had been in residence for a week when Ned Skinner came a-calling — now! Now was her moment! Spilling a little brandy on her dress, Lydia lolled in a chair and waited. Sure enough, Ned strolled in with her keeper, bent to peer into her face, caught a whiff of the dress, and straightened.

"Foxed," he said.

"She always is. Come, we may talk next door."

As soon as she was certain they had settled in the adjoining drawing room, Lydia tiptoed to the communicating door, opened it a fraction, and listened. As she was looking at the backs of their heads, she was safe enough.

"How are you managing?" Ned asked.

"Oh, she's no trouble. Starts to drink at breakfast and keeps on drinking until she passes out, but she likes to be bedded too. My men are kept busy enough servicing her. Clever of you, Ned, to recommend I bring male helpers."

"Mr Darcy says her booze intake is to be regulated somewhat."

"Why, in God's name?"

"Her sisters are paying her a visit in ten days' time."

"I see. But as regulating her intake will cause tantrums, wouldn't it be better not to regulate it at all? Let her sisters see what she really is."

"Mr Darcy does not wish that."

"And Mr Darcy is your idol."

"Exactly."

"Have you found any trace of the other sister, Mary?"

"None whatsoever. She's vanished from the earth."

"I can assure you that she hasn't turned up in a brothel, unless it be south of Canterbury or north of the Tweed, and that's highly unlikely, given her age. Beauty is well and good, but thirty-eight summers make a female body stringy or blowsy, all depending. From what you say of her, stringy."

"Yes, she's stringy. Flat-chested too."

"Then no brothel anywhere," said Miss Maplethorpe.

"How long can you look after this one, Mirry?"

"Another two months. Then I must hie me back to Sheffield. Aggie is strict, but loath to use a horsewhip."

"Could you send Aggie as your replacement?"

"Ned! She's too vulgar. Mrs Darcy and Mrs Bingley would see through her. No, I think you must look inside a Bedlam."

"How will those women be any less vulgar? I'll ask Mr Darcy to advertise."

"Excellent. You'll find someone, you have the time."

"I must go, Mirry."

"Tell your idol that Mrs W. is safe and well. Indeed, she must have the constitution of an ox to have weathered so much poison. For taken in the amounts she takes it, booze is very poisonous. I have a bet that her mind will go before her body does. Would you like me to lace her port with a port-tasting potion from Father Dominus?"

"Who?"

"An old apothecary dolled up as a friar. He supplies me with a very good abortifacient, and the Old Master apparently had some of his poisons on hand. Also physicks to drive one mad, or induce a paralysis. I'm surprised you don't know him. Thick with the Old Master, he was."

"I was too young, Mirry, and when the Old Master was present, I hid. I must say you do not look your age, m'dear."

"Thank Father Dominus!"

"Mr Darcy would not approve, so no potions, Mirry."

"I do believe you worship that man as fools worship God!"

"Then do not blaspheme." He got up. "Now about the iron bars —"

Much though she would have loved to hear the rest, Lydia shut the door and raced to her chair, fell into it to loll with great realism. But no one entered. Not long after, she heard the sound of hooves on the gravel drive, and sat up indignantly.

Oh, they were villains! And though it seemed Fitzwilliam Darcy had some scruples, he was heartless. Well, she had always known that. Sending George off to one war after another! Oh, George, my George! How can I live without you? Sober! she thought savagely. That is how I will live — *sober*.

I am no mean actress, Lydia thought ten days later. What hoops I have made them jump! Especially that cow Mirry the Moo. Tears, tantrums, hours of screaming and screeching — it took real courage to go on with my performance when that yokel Rob threatened to choke me if I did not shut up. Well, I did not shut up, and Mirry the Moo was obliged to send him out of the house for fear that he really would choke me. I let my best language loose — peculiar, how people dislike that. In my opinion, scratches and bites are far worse, and I gave plenty of those.

Thus it was that when the splendid Pemberley equipage drew up at the Hemmings door a little after lunch, Lydia was almost beside herself with excitement. Now her keepers would get their well-deserved comeuppance!

The perfect lady's companion, Miss Maplethorpe stayed only long enough to see the visitors comfortably settled, then left them alone with Lydia. The moment the door shut behind her, Lydia sat up straight and dropped all pretence of drunkenness.

"Oh, that is better!" she exclaimed.

Jane and Elizabeth had been amazed to see the change in their little sister — she looked so well! Every vestige of puffiness had vanished from her face and figure, she was clean from head to feet, and clad in a fashionable dress of ice-blue lawn. Her flaxen hair was done up in a bun on the crown of her head with tendril-like curls framing her face, and whatever she had used to darken her brows was quite unexceptionable. She appeared what she had not appeared in years: a lady.

Jane looked at Elizabeth and Elizabeth looked at Jane; the improvement was remarkable, not to mention most welcome.

"Better?" Jane asked.

"I am sober," Lydia assured them. "I had to be sober, to tell you what is going on."

"Going on?" Elizabeth asked, frowning.

"Yes, yes, going on! Your heartless snob of a husband has abducted me, Lizzie — I am a prisoner in this awful place."

"How are you a prisoner?" Jane asked.

"Oh, for pity's sake, Jane, have you no eyes in your head? Don't the bars on the windows speak for themselves?"

"*What* bars?" Jane barked, even her tranquil temper tried.

Eyes screwed up against the glare of a fine summer's day, Lydia realised that she could not see the silhouette of the bars through the diaphanous curtains. In such a hurry that she tipped her chair over, she ran to the nearest window. "Come, they are here! Come and see the bars for yourselves!"

Jane and Elizabeth followed, anxious expressions on their faces. But now that she was at the window, Lydia could see no bars. Where were the bars?

"Oh, how cunning!" she cried. "The cruel, scheming lot! Oh, they make me out to be a liar! Jane, Lizzie, I swear to you that until today there have been bars over every ground floor window in this house!" Eyes glittering, fists clenched, Lydia ground her teeth, a hideous sound. "I swear it on my husband's dead body! *There were bars!*"

Elizabeth pushed the window up and examined the bricks on all sides of it. "I can see no places where there might have been bars, dear," she said gently. "Come and sit down."

"There were bars, there were! I swear it on George's grave!"

"Lydia, it was your imagination," said Elizabeth. "You have not been yourself of late. If you are sober now, surely you must see that this window was never barred."

"Lizzie, I am not drowned so deep in drink that I have taken to imagining things! These windows were barred. All of them!" A desperate note crept into her voice. "You must believe me, you must! I am your sister!"

"If you are truly free from the effects of the wine, dear, why can I smell it on your breath?" Elizabeth asked.

"I had a glass or two with my breakfast," Lydia said sulkily. "I needed it to scrape up my courage."

"Dearest Lydia, there are no bars," said Jane in her softest tones. "You are looking very well, but you still have a long way to go before you are cured of your drinking."

"I tell you, I am a prisoner! Mirry the Moo won't let me go outside without her!"

"Who?" asked Elizabeth.

"Mirry the Moo. I call her that because she's a cow."

"You do an injustice to a very nice lady," said Elizabeth.

"No lady, she! Mirry the Moo is the proprietress of a bawdy-house in Sheffield."

"*Lydia!*" cried Jane on a gasp.

"She is, she is! I overheard her talking to Ned Skinner ten days ago, and she made no secret of it to him. What's more, he knew all about her. They were talking of dosing me with poison, or something to paralyse me, or send me mad. All of which means that Fitz knows about them too."

"I think it is time you produced some proof of these wild statements," Elizabeth said grimly.

"With the bars gone, I've lost my proof!" Lydia began to weep. "Oh, it isn't fair! If you don't believe me, who will? Lizzie, you're a sensible woman — surely you can see that I'm a threat to your precious Fitz?"

"Only by your intemperate behaviour, Lydia. How can you expect to be believed when you accuse Fitz of murder and call him names even the most depraved of women would not? I cannot credit these allegations about Miss Maplethorpe — or Mr Skinner! — because you look so well cared for — cared for properly for many days. No, I do *not* believe you, Lydia."

By the time that Elizabeth had finished speaking, Lydia was in floods of noisy tears.

"Come, dearest, weeping won't help," said Jane, hugging her. "Let us ring the bell. A cup of tea will do you more good than all the wine in creation. You grieve for George, we know that."

The comprehensive look Miss Maplethorpe gave Lydia when she came in spoke volumes. "Oh, dear! Has Mrs Wickham been trying to tell you that there are bars over the windows?"

"Yes," said Elizabeth.

"A part of her delusory state, Mrs Darcy."

"She says you keep a house of ill fame in Sheffield," said Jane.

That made Miss Maplethorpe laugh. "How did she ever get that into her head, I wonder?"

"She says she overheard a conversation between you and Mr Edward Skinner." Jane sounded so aggressive that Elizabeth was startled.

"How extraordinary! I've met Mr Skinner only once, when he brought Mrs Wickham to Hemmings."

"Where did you live before you came to Hemmings? What kind of work did you do?" Jane asked with rare persistence.

"I administered the women's Bedlam on Broadmoor, then I cared for a relative of the Marquess of Ripon," said Miss Maplethorpe. "I came with glowing recommendations, Mrs Bingley."

"A *women's* Bedlam? I thought men and women were cared for in the same institution," said Jane, apparently unimpressed by the glowing recommendations.

"That is so," said Miss Maplethorpe, looking a little harried, "but it is still necessary to have a supervisor for the women."

"I didn't know there was a Bedlam on Broadmoor," said Jane.

"Indeed there is! There is also a Marquess of Ripon," said Miss Maplethorpe tartly.

"One reads in the letters of Argus that mad people in a Bedlam are shockingly mistreated," said Jane. "Like animals in a menagerie, only worse. Sightseers pay a penny to tease and torment them, and the staff resort to torture."

"Which is why I left Broadmoor to go first to the Marquess, whose relative died, and then to come here." Miss Maplethorpe's face had gone to flint. "And that is all I have to say, Mrs Bingley. If you have further complaints, I would appreciate it if you addressed them to my employer, Mr Darcy."

"Thank you. Might we have some tea?" Elizabeth said hastily. She took Miss Maplethorpe to one side. "I have a question too, Miss Maplethorpe. Is Mrs Wickham's mind permanently deranged?"

"It is too early to tell. I trust not."

"But if it is, what kind of care will she need?"

"The kind she receives now at Hemmings, but, alas, those bars would have to become a reality. It appears that she is — er — very fond of the company of gentlemen. I have already had to persuade her to return home on several occasions. If this is a new sort of symptom, I am sorry to have to tell you of it, Mrs Darcy."

"Pray don't think it comes as a shock," Elizabeth said. "She has ever been so."

"I see."

"She says she isn't drinking very much."

"That is true. She has improved."

"Thank you!"

Casting Miss Maplethorpe a speaking glance, Elizabeth returned to Jane and Lydia, whose tears had ceased.

Though by nature she was shallow, wild — and self-centred, apart from her devotion to the late Captain George Wickham — Lydia had sufficient intelligence to understand that she had boxed herself into a corner. The one thing she had not counted upon was the silent removal of the bars; in their absence she could see that her own conduct did not predispose Jane and Lizzie to believe her tale. Resolving to keep sober had improved her outward appearance — and her underlying health — so much that she did not look the victim of an abduction. Quite the opposite. And tears, she soon saw, would not benefit her. Her plans to be freed must now depend upon her own actions; neither Lizzie nor Jane would support her, let alone conspire to spirit her away from Hemmings. Therefore no more tears, no more references to abductions, imprisonment, or Ned Skinner.

Though it was not the tea hour, Miss Maplethorpe sent in an excellent tea to which all three sisters applied themselves with enthusiasm. Lydia chatted away quite brightly, allaying what fears Jane and Elizabeth still felt. Fancy Jane flying at Mirry the Moo! But it had not lasted, of course. Jane always believed the best of people, even if they were standing on the gallows.

Since she knew nothing of Mary's disappearance from Ned Skinner's custody, Lydia concentrated upon that subject.

"At first I thought she would simply appear after indulging in a fit of abstraction," said Jane.

"She was prone to those," said Lydia. "Always had her head in a book and desperate for access to bigger libraries."

"But it is now four weeks since she vanished," Elizabeth said, "and I for one no longer think there is anything voluntary about her absence. Fitz agrees. He has managed to have two-thirds of each shire's constables put to searching for her, and the advertisement has circulated from one end of England to the other. With a hundred pounds reward. Many people have lodged information, but none has led, even remotely, to Mary." Her face had gone very stern. "We begin to fear now that she is dead. Fitz is convinced of it."

"Lizzie, no!" Lydia cried, taken out of her own troubles.

Elizabeth sighed. "I still hope," she said.

"*And* I," said Lydia. "Mary could give lessons in stubbornness to a mule. What worries me is leaving the search to the constabulary — Jane, Lizzie, they're bumbling fools!"

"We agree," said Jane. "For that reason, Lizzie and I tend to make Fitz's life a misery. Though Charlie and Angus still go out every day."

"Angus?" said Lydia.

"Angus Sinclair, publisher of the *Westminster Chronicle*. Lizzie says he is in love with Mary."

"Jane, no! Truly?"

The ladies remained another hour, then left in plenty of time to reach Bingley Hall by sunset; Elizabeth was staying there that night, and looking forward to seeing the boys, if not Prissy.

"What do you think about Lydia?" Jane asked as the chaise negotiated a particularly bad section of road.

"I'm puzzled. She looks very much better for her weeks at Hemmings. I didn't think her deranged."

"Despite the bars."

"Yes. But what puzzles me most, Jane, was your attack on Miss Maplethorpe. So unlike you!"

"It was the look she gave Lydia when she first came in," Jane said. "You were seated at more of an angle than I, so it's possible that your interpretation of the look wasn't the same as mine. What I saw was derision and contempt."

"How extraordinary!" Elizabeth exclaimed. "Her manners were all that might be expected, Jane. Very ladylike."

"I am convinced it is an act, Lizzie. Nor do I believe that she ever saw a Bedlam." Jane laughed. "Mirry the Moo! If that is not just like the old Lydia of Longbourn days!"

"I'm sure that Matthew Spottiswoode and his York agency would have gone into Miss Maplethorpe's background thoroughly."

"Then we must visit regularly, Lizzie."

When Elizabeth returned to Pemberley she did something she had never done before; she sent for Edward Skinner, who, said Parmenter, was at home.

Their interview got off to a bad start, however, when it took Ned an hour to report. Elizabeth mentioned his tardiness, at her most imperious.

"I beg your pardon, Mrs Darcy, but I was engaged in some manual labour when your summons arrived, and had to make myself respectable," he said without a vestige of apology in his voice.

"I see. What do you know of Miss Mirabelle Maplethorpe?"

"Who?"

"Mrs Wickham's companion at Hemmings."

His brow cleared. "Oh, her! I only met her the once, and scarce recollect being given her name."

"In which case, you know very little of her?"

"Nothing whatsoever, ma'am. Mr Spottiswoode knows more."

"Then I shall apply to Mr Spottiswoode."

"That would be best, ma'am."

"You've been at Pemberley longer than I have, so you must be aware it's a hive of gossip. Have you heard any rumours about Miss Maplethorpe?"

"Only that Mr Spottiswoode was lucky to find her."

"Thank you, Mr Skinner. You may go."

And I have not advanced a friendship there, thought Elizabeth. Why does Fitz esteem him so?

She went in search of Matthew Spottiswoode, an easy business, as he never left his desk unless accompanied by a Darcy. Elizabeth was as fond of him as she was put off by Ned Skinner, and could not credit that he was guilty of any transgression in the matter of the hiring of Lydia's companion. Only Jane's peculiar reaction to the woman had spurred her to make enquiries, for Jane was the world's least suspicious creature. Of course Elizabeth might have gone to Fitz, but he was her last possible resort. They could not meet these days, it seemed, without quarrelling, and, having been so shockingly insulted by Lydia, he would not welcome an older sister's questions. Lydia was also costing him a great deal of money.

"Matthew," she said, entering the steward's office, "tell me what you know about Miss Mirabelle Maplethorpe."

A man in his late fifties, Matthew Spottiswoode had spent his entire life in service to a Darcy of Pemberley. First, Fitz's father as an under-steward, and then Fitz as an under-steward followed by elevation to the stewardship itself. His education was somewhat lacking, yet eminently suited to his profession, as he was brilliant at arithmetic, wrote a literate letter in a copperplate hand, kept impeccable books, and had the sort of brain that stored away facts which he could trot out at a moment's notice. He was a happily married man who lived on the estate and had the felicity of seeing all his children in service to Pemberley.

"The lady who is caring for Mrs Wickham?" Mr Spottiswoode asked now, having no trouble identifying her.

"The very same. Mr Skinner sent me to you."

"Yes, I hired her through the employment agency for ladies in York that I am accustomed to use — Miss Scrimpton's." He looked at his mistress shrewdly. "It was a very hasty business, but I was singularly fortunate, Mrs Darcy. The agency had just that moment accepted Miss Maplethorpe as employable. Since Mr Darcy was very anxious that Mrs Wickham be settled at Hemmings immediately, I went through Miss Maplethorpe's recommendations, and found them so suited to our needs that I did not bother to look farther afield. Miss Scrimpton had no other lady on her lists even remotely suitable."

"Kindly tell me about her recommendations, Matthew."

"Well, she had letters from persons such as Sir Peter Oersted, Viscount Hansbury, Mrs Bassington-Smyth and Lord

Summerton. Her two actual employers were first — for many years — the Bedlam on Broadmoor, where she supervised the female inmates and their nurses. A very glowing document! Her second place was in eastern Yorkshire, caring for a relative of the Marquess of Ripon. This patient, a lady, had just died. The persons who gave her personal letters of recommendation had all suffered a relative in the Bedlam." He coughed apologetically. "You understand, Mrs Darcy, that those having insane relatives are peculiarly sensitive about the fact. I did not feel it politic to bother them, as their letters were all genuine, I do assure you."

"I see. Thank you, Matthew."

Well, that was that. Miss Maplethorpe was cleared of all suspicion. Jane must have imagined the look — or, more likely, Lydia had been insufferably rude to her companion, and not endeared herself.

The noise of merriment from the schoolroom made her smile; she opened its door to find Owen having tea with the girls, and wondered if he had succumbed to the charms of Georgie. But if he had, she decided later, he was concealing it well enough to be called crafty, and she did not think him crafty. The real reason behind the visits, she realised, was pity. Well, something had to be done, no matter what Fitz said! Owen may not be in danger of falling in love, but her girls were so inexperienced that she could not say the same for them. Susie positively melted when Owen looked at her, and Anne was not much better.

*   *   *

Ned Skinner left the house a worried man. What on earth had pushed Elizabeth Darcy to make enquiries about Mirry? Not anything Lydia could have told her, and the job on the bars had been excellent. The workmen had quietly replaced every brick with a hole in it.

The bars would have to remain off, a shame. Mrs Darcy and Mrs Bingley would visit Lydia often, and Lydia, Mirry had informed him in a wrathful note brought by courier, was *pretending* to be drunk! That indicated that she was not at all dependent upon the bottle, the scheming little hussy!

What could be done about Lydia? As far as Ned was concerned, only one fact mattered: that she was out to ruin Fitz's public career. She had said it, and she meant it. But it could not be allowed to happen, no matter how drastic the solution might have to be.

Of course Fitz and Spottiswoode were unaware of Mirry's true identity. Men like Fitz, Ned knew painfully well, were too exalted to understand how some aspects of the world functioned. His own function was to shield Fitz from all things beneath his notice, and when Fitz — in a tearing hurry — not like him at all — decided Lydia had to have a companion, Ned had known how to engineer the choice. A true lady's companion, Ned knew (though Fitz did not), would never be able to restrain a tartar like Lydia.

The woman Ned had in mind was Miriam Matcham, who ran a brothel in Sheffield that he had known from birth. Though she informed him that she could give him only a few months, she was paid more than her brothel duties earned her in a year. She put him in touch with a man who could forge all manner of documents, and together they invented a history for Mirry. Broadmoor was wild and remote, why shouldn't it have a Bedlam? And who in Derbyshire would know whether it did, or didn't?

Now Mrs Darcy, of all people, was asking questions! Poking her nose where it didn't belong. As if Lydia herself were not enough of a problem! Cunning as a fox, unscrupulous and immoral, without the steel of a Mirry or the brain of an Elizabeth Darcy.

He went to Hemmings to find out what exactly was going on, a long ride that instinct told him not to break by staying at an inn, though he had not, as yet, put together the pieces of a murderous jigsaw in his mind. He slept for some hours in a field where Jupiter could graze, then went on. And for every mile of the way his mind dwelled on Lydia, how to solve the terrible problem she had become. If she could stop drinking at will, then she was very dangerous, could not be shut up the way Mrs Bennet had been, in a delicious haze of comfort and cronies. His thoughts continued to skirt around the ultimate alternative, but by the time he reached Hemmings the pieces made an appalling sense, and he was convinced it was the only alternative. Remained but when, and how.

"Oh, Ned, I am so glad to see you!" Miss Maplethorpe cried when he slid into the house through the back door, having left Jupiter in a grove of trees with a loosened girth, a horse blanket against the dewy chills, and sweet grass to tear at.

"Is she, or is she not, permanently drunk?" he asked in the kitchen, with no ears listening.

"As far as I can tell, she's more often sober than drunk, but she's an actress would make a fortune on the stage. At the moment she's sober and strutting around as if she owned this place. But what am I to do if she decides to go for a walk?"

"Go with her, Mirry."

"And what do I do if she decides to drive into Leek? Or Stoke-on-Trent?"

"Go with her. But that isn't what you're asking in truth, is it? You want to know if you can use force."

"Yes, I do."

When she deemed his silence overly long, she dug him in the ribs. "Well? Am I to use force, or not?"

"Not. I don't know what you did to make *both* her sisters smell a rat, but you did something. Lydia's not some scragged moggie out of the gutter like your girls in Sheffield, Mirry. You should be walking on eggshells."

"Oh, shit! I *knew* it was too easy!"

"So much money for too little work, you mean?"

"Yes. Give me proper instructions, Ned, or whistle for your lady's companion. Then see what happens! Your fine madam will be in some fellow's bed quick as lightning! You know how I keep her at Hemmings. My — er — helpers are nigh exhausted servicing the bitch."

"Well, that's why you brought them, after all. Instructions — let me see … If the little hussy goes out in the carriage, you go with her. If she walks, you walk with her. And feed your fellows

Spanish fly or whatever else they need to keep on fucking her." He began pulling on his gloves, so big that they had to be specially made for him. "Only remember that all it will take to bring you down is one enquiry to the Marquess of Ripon."

"I don't give a bugger about the Marquess of Ripon! Remember, my name's not Mirabelle Maplethorpe."

"Perhaps the informant would have something to say about Miss Miriam Matcham."

"I wish you'd find someone else to do your dirty work, Ned!"

He paused with his hand on the door, and laughed. "Be of good cheer, Mirry! I hear that even in New South Wales they have bawdy-houses. No, no, I'm teasing! You're safe with Ned Skinner."

When he reached Jupiter he didn't tighten the girth; he took the saddle off completely, changed the bridle for a halter and tied the horse so that it could move to graze but not emerge from the shelter of the trees, the bases of which were hidden from the house by a tall hedge. Jupiter taken care of, Ned lay at full length and dozed for a while. He came awake in a trice; there was noise from the house, men coming and going as if hurried.

Darkness fell. Ned Skinner continued to watch. Yes, he was right! They were quitting the place! A wagon arrived and was loaded with the best of the furniture and carpets, drove off with two of the five men travelling on its box. At midnight Mirry emerged with a birdcage in one hand and a frilly parasol in the other, just as the carriage came from the stables. She stepped into it, followed by her maid, and two more of her henchmen sat on its box. The equipage rolled away, leaving Lydia and one man behind. No, Lydia was to be left alone. The fifth man soon appeared in the trap, geeing his fat pony to an awkward trot. He probably had the silverware, thought Ned cynically.

What could Lydia be doing, not to have raised the alarm? There were lights in the drawing room and lights in an upstairs bedroom; she was there, then, but drunk or sober? Drunk, he decided. Sober, she would have screamed the place down.

The thing was, what to do? He had to come to a decision right at this moment, well before a new dawn arrived and Lydia embarked upon a walk to — Bingley Hall? Yes, Bingley Hall. Of course she would encounter someone on the road, someone who would either convey her to her destination or to the constabulary in Leek. Ah, but there was no constable in Leek! Like his fellows, he was searching for Mary. No matter. Once she was seen, Lydia would be entirely removed from his control.

The overriding drive in Ned's life was his love for Fitz. No one else could command his devotion. And what did it matter if half of what he did for Fitz was unknown to Fitz? Love carried no sort of conditions in Ned's mind; it was something so pure, so powerful that it needed no acknowledgement. Lydia Wickham was out to ruin Fitz's public career — a great man brought down by a silly, brainless bit of a thing not fit to lick his boots.

Tonight. If it were to be done at all, it must be done tonight, while she was alone in the house, deserted by servants and companion. Did she have any jewellery? Any money? He doubted the latter, but jewels were a possibility. Two of her sisters were very wealthy, so they could have gifted her with some pretty pieces. Not that it really mattered, only that it would seem more logical. Furniture missing, carpets missing, silverware missing, jewellery missing ...

He brought out his watch and saw that the time was a little after one. Almost an hour before he had to decide.

"What do you say, Jupiter old man?" he asked the horse.

Hearing its name, it lifted its head to look at him, nodded, and went back to its grazing. Jupiter says yes, he thought. Good old Jupiter says yes.

The idiots hadn't even locked the house behind them! Ned pushed the front door open and entered softly. A slight glow from the drawing room enabled him to locate a candelabrum; he lit a fresh candle from a burning wick and went to the stairs, which did not creak. Hemmings was a good house.

The sound of snores guided him to Lydia's bedroom; even if of late she had been sober, tonight she was certainly drunk. Sure enough, there she was, sprawled on the covers of her bed, in a pink muslin day dress. A pretty wench, he thought, gazing at her without a flicker of desire. Such a profusion of near-colourless hair spilling around her — a nuisance, considering what he had to do.

There were plenty of pillows. He chose the stiffest of them, over-stuffed with down, climbed onto the bed and straddled her, the better to come at her head. It was not an ideal way to kill anyone, for the deep mattress yielded more than the pillow did. Only a very strong man could do it, but Ned Skinner was superlatively strong. He put the pillow over Lydia's face and held it there, sitting his rump on her to immobilise her despite her feeble little struggles. For a full quarter of an hour by the mantel clock he did not relax, then judged her dead. Suffocation was slow, he was aware of that.

Removing the pillow revealed that her eyes had bulged a trifle, their whites webbed with red veins, and her mouth was open on sadly discoloured teeth. He sat heavily on her chest now, to make sure that she could not draw a breath. She did not, for Lydia Wickham was dead. Fitz was safe from this latest Bennet peril.

In the morning a butcher or a grocer would arrive, wonder why there was no answer to his knock, then his calls, and finally his hollers. After that, discovery was inevitable. Two branches of candles burned in the room; by their light he searched for money and jewellery. Her empty purse lay on the dressing table, together with an empty grey tin box that had probably held her jewels. How splendid! They had stolen everything.

Half past two by his watch; dawn would come in about two hours. Jupiter made ready for the road, Ned Skinner mounted and cantered off. He was going straight home, but not by the customary route. He skirted around Pemberley, and finally came down on it from the north. Only someone actually following him would have known where he had come from; and no one had followed. As always in the aftermath of such sickening deeds, he kept his mind absolutely fixed upon the memory of Fitz's beardless cheek pressed against his own infant pate. The first lovely thing in an awful life.

Curiously, it was Ned himself who brought the news of Lydia's demise to Pemberley, and that lay at Elizabeth's door.

The southern Peak District had become the focus of the search for Mary, for that was where the caves were located, and everyone had decided that Mary was imprisoned in a cave. Only the most visually spectacular of them were known; visitors thronged to go through them, each holding a candle-lamp, every group blackening their beauty a little more from the smoke. But many caves never saw a candle, and no one dreamed of their existence or extent.

When Ned rode in on Jupiter, he saw Mrs Darcy in the stable yard, and tipped his hat to her courteously. To his surprise, she beckoned him over when he had dismounted.

"Mr Skinner, could you spare the time from your search to call in at Hemmings and see how Mrs Wickham is doing?"

The hair rose on the back of his neck; had his eyes been a lighter colour she might have noticed their pupils dilate, but their blackness saved him. The request had taken him completely aback. For a moment he simply stared at her, amazed, then he turned his reaction to good purpose by looking at her in puzzlement.

"Do you have a feeling, Mrs Darcy?" he asked.

"A feeling? Of what sort?"

"Oh, I don't know, exactly. A presentiment or some such?" He looked apologetic. "I suppose it was the look on your face, ma'am. With all the to-do about Miss Mary, I confess I had clean forgotten Mrs Wickham."

She thought more kindly of him, and put a hand on his arm. "Dear Mr Skinner, perhaps I do have a presentiment. How acute of you to see it! I hate to ask you to make the ride, but Angus and Charlie are staying somewhere, and it is a week since Mrs Bingley and I visited her. Miss Maplethorpe promised to write, but has not. I worry that something is amiss."

"Think nothing of it, Mrs Darcy. Jupiter and I will start at once. He's a good lad, my horse. The only one can carry me."

Thinking of the horse, she had a qualm. "Are you sure? Ought not Jupiter to rest?"

"No, ma'am. He and I are up to the ride."

And he managed to make his escape before the sweat on his brow became noticeable. Oh, the wretched, wretched woman! A thorn in Fitz's side for twenty-one years now, and a thorn in Ned Skinner's side too. Still, he reflected, making sure Jupiter had a drink of cool water, Lydia had to be discovered any time now, and this was probably the best way. Despite which thought, he rode the miles to Hemmings with a hideous weight in his belly and a grey veil before his eyes. Let her have been found already, *please*!

Luck was with him. The afternoon was drawing on when he rode into the Hemmings driveway and saw several vehicles choking it. A group of respectable-looking men were gathered just outside the front door; he dismounted and joined them.

"What's amiss?" he asked.

"Who are you to make it your business?" asked a man officiously.

"Mr Darcy of Pemberley's personal aide, by name of Edward Skinner. What's amiss?"

Fitz's name worked wonders, of course. The officious man shed his arrogance at once. "Constable Thomas Barnes of Leek," he said, fawning. "A tragedy, Mr Skinner! Robbery, murder and mayhem!" A phrase he had been waiting half a lifetime to utter.

"Mrs Wickham?" Ned asked, concerned. "Very fair, youngish."

"Is that the lady's name? Dead, sir. Done to death."

"Oh, dear Jesus! She's Mr Darcy's sister-in-law!"

Huge consternation reigned. It was some time before Ned could get a lucid story out of them, interspersed as it had to be with his own explanation as to why Mr Darcy's sister-in-law was living so far from Pemberley. Most were present only to poke and pry, and took absolutely no notice of Constable Barnes. They soon took heed of Ned Skinner, who told them to leave very softly, but with such a look in his eyes! Brrr! That reduced the group to Dr Lanham, Constable Barnes, and two shire odd-job-men who held their tongues.

Their reconstruction of events was considerably plumped out by Ned's account of who should have been at Hemmings, and were not. A few skilful remarks from Ned soon led them to the conclusion that Miss Maplethorpe and her staff had set upon poor Mrs Wickham, done her to death, and absconded with everything of value the house held. Also, as Ned pointed out after a walk to the stables, a barouche carriage, two matched thoroughbred horses, a pony and a trap. What was worse than anything else, these villains had been *Mr Darcy's* employees!

"I must return to Pemberley as soon as possible," said Ned at the end of half an hour. "Dr Lanham, may I leave it to you to convey Mrs Wickham's body to Pemberley tomorrow?" A few guineas changed hands. "Constable Barnes, may I ask you to write a full report for Mr Darcy?" A few more guineas changed hands. "Thank you, gentlemen, particularly for your tact and discretion."

And all that went better than I could have hoped, thought Ned, riding away. The story of ruthless employees will spread far and wide. Serves you right, Mirry! Your cowardice has convicted you, for all that the lawyers prate of being innocent until found guilty.

He was happy, very happy. Fitz was freed from all threat, and no one would dream of associating *him* with Lydia's death.

He reached down to pat Jupiter's steaming neck. "You were right, old man. That was the time to kill her, while someone was on hand to take the blame. Steady on, now! Just to Leek for you, my dear good boy. I'll hire a chaise-and-four at the post house and travel like a lord the rest of the way. You've done enough."

When he finally reached Pemberley a little before midnight, he was surprised to find Parmenter up and waiting for him with a message from Mr Darcy.

"The master wishes to see you this moment," the old man said, oozing curiosity. "I am to bring you dinner in the small breakfast room when you've seen Mr Darcy. Is Miss Mary found?"

"Not to my knowledge. And thank you for the dinner. I could eat any horse save Jupiter."

Fitz was in his parliamentary library, and alone — a relief. That probably meant that Mary had not been found, but what could Fitz have to say to him? A Fitz who looked white and worn, plucked at the strings of Ned's heart — who was lumping fresh cares on him? Was it that wretched wife?

"Ned, I have disturbing news," Fitz said.

Ned went to the port decanter and filled a red wine glass full to its brim — it had been a very long and anxious day, and Jupiter was in a strange inn's stables, though the grooms had been threatened with murder if they so much as *looked* the wrong way at Jupiter.

"Tell me your news first, Fitz. I have ill news too."

"Matthew Spottiswoode has had a letter from Miss Scrimpton — the tabby who runs a ladies' employment agency in York. It seems Miss Scrimpton encountered the Marquess of Ripon somewhere in York, and ventured to tell him that Miss Mirabelle Maplethorpe was proving as good a companion to her client as she had to his deceased relative. But Ripon denied all knowledge of insane relatives, dead or alive, and of Miss Maplethorpe. Whereupon Miss Scrimpton discovered that there are no female inmates in the Bedlam on Broadmoor, which is for the most violent of males only."

Fitz got to his feet, held out his hands. "What can it mean, Ned? Is someone trying to get at me through Lydia? But it all happened so quickly — none of it makes sense!"

"It makes some sense to me," Ned said grimly. "I have to tell you that Miss Maplethorpe is an imposter — or, at least, that her being an imposter fits well with her activities at Hemmings." He stopped, drained his glass, poured another. "No, I'm not reduced to guzzling your best port, Fitz, but my news is the worst. Mrs Wickham has been murdered."

"Jesus!" Fitz sank into his chair as if his legs had lost all power, the lock of stark white hair that had recently appeared in his jet-black mop falling over his brow. His eyes were wide, but only shock gave him pause; his intelligence was superior and still functioning. "You imply, murdered by Miss Maplethorpe?"

"Yes, assisted by the five men she had with her as helpers. I thought it odd that she was the only female apart from her maid, but she has a certain authority about her, so I didn't question it beyond wondering. After all, she came recommended as a lady with experience of — er — *wild* patients. They were all in the plot, apparently."

"Plot? How do you know of any plot?"

"Mrs Darcy seems to have had a feeling that all was not well at Hemmings, Fitz. This morning she asked me to go there and see that all *was* well. By the time I got there, the local doctor and constable had arrived. I was able to fill in the gaps in their knowledge of events. What happened we will never quite know, but we think that the original plan was for a simple robbery.

The best of the furniture is gone, the carpets, the silverware, the barouche and its horses, the pony and trap, and, we think, some jewellery. As to how — the local doctor says she was suffocated with a pillow by one man, while another sat on her chest."

Fitz had slumped; he made a retching sound. Ned poured a big glass of port, and handed it to him. Finally, his own glass filled again, he sat down. "Drink it, Fitz, please, else it will have to be cognac." Watching Fitz drink, he saw a little colour return to his face, and sat back, relieved. Fitz would do now. "Did Mrs Wickham own any jewels?" he asked.

"It seems so, yes. A sapphire and diamond set Elizabeth never wore, and gave to her when she moved to Hemmings. Poor woman! Oh, poor, poor woman! Apparently Jane gave her a rope of pearls. As Lydia has had no opportunity to pawn them, Miss Maplethorpe must have taken them if they aren't there." He got up and began to pace restlessly. "What an awful year this has been! Two of my wife's sisters gone. One is certainly dead. The other? I must presume her dead too."

"Not yet, Fitz. One gathers they were very unalike. Mrs Wickham imprisoned in a bottle, Miss Mary game for anything." He grinned. "I never knew Miss Mary conscious, but she fought even when unconscious." He stretched, winced.

"I am a selfish brute, Ned! Eat, and then go home to sleep."

"Mrs Wickham returns to Pemberley tomorrow with the Leek doctor. It will be late, but the doctor will see it done."

"Thank you. You must be sore out of pocket."

"That does not signify."

"It does to me. Render an account, please, Ned."

*   *   *

As soon as Ned had gone, Fitzwilliam Darcy got to his feet and walked to Elizabeth's rooms. When he scratched softly on her door, she opened it herself and stood back for him to enter, giving him a keen glance.

"I knew it was you. Ned brought bad news, didn't he?"

"Yes." He went tiredly to one of a pair of armchairs and sat down, patting the seat of the other. "Sit down, Elizabeth."

"Is it very bad?"

"The worst. Lydia is dead."

How peculiar! It had struck him like a thunderbolt, whereas she looked almost unaffected save for her eyes, which widened. "Oh! I must have had some idea of it, because it comes the way an old friend does, an old friend one hasn't seen for years. I've been waiting, but knowing too. I just — felt that all was not right. Ned noticed it this morning."

"You don't usually suffer from premonitions."

"I agree, I don't. Every time Charlie was ill, I was wrong!" She produced a smile and glued it to her mouth, which felt as if set in stone. "I used to bury him regularly. But he always got better. I used to fancy that he didn't care for life over-much, but knew that if he died I would die as well, and it was knowing that made him recover."

"A rather muddled explanation, my dear."

"I daresay it is. Despair and Charlie were tied together in those days, yet look at him now. He has shed his childhood like an old skin. I am so happy for him — and for you, Fitz."

Only a few candles burned, making a halo of fiery light around her head and throwing her face into shadow. He screwed up his eyes in an effort to see her clearly, and thought, My sight is going. "I have been unkind to Charlie," he said, voice not as steady as he wished. "Unkind to you as well, Elizabeth."

"You are unkindest to yourself, Fitz. Tell me everything that happened — and please, I beg you, don't spare me. Once George Wickham was dead, it was only a question of time before Lydia died. *How* she loved him! Of all five of us, she loved best and most. Without him, she had no reason for being."

"It wasn't suicide, even in the remotest way. She fell victim to a nest of thieves, though I smell several rats. Suffice it to say that Miss Maplethorpe was an imposter, her manservants her minions, and that they planned to rob Hemmings — furniture, silver, carriage, horses, and jewellery. The things you and Jane gave her when she went to Hemmings. Lydia must have surprised them in the act, and they murdered her. Apparently she was drunk at the time. The doctor said she reeked of wine and spirits. They suffocated her with a pillow, so they may have wanted to make her death seem a natural one. Certainly that is out of the question."

"Jane took against Miss Maplethorpe," said Elizabeth. "Jane, who never takes against anyone! The day we saw her, Lydia wasn't drunk, though pretending to be in front of Miss Maplethorpe. She was full of some tale about bars over the windows, but there were none, nor had there been. I looked closely. The hold on sobriety is frail, I am told, so perhaps, not succeeding in persuading Jane or me about the bars, she went back to her old ways. I don't know, except that, like you, I smell rats."

"Elizabeth, there *were* bars over the windows," Fitz said, his face horrified. "They were supposed to be removed before Lydia was sent to Hemmings. It had been the home of a madman. Why didn't Miss Maplethorpe explain?" He took her hands, she thought absently. "I keep asking myself, why Hemmings? How could a nest of thieves plan such a thing when Lydia was moved there in such a hurry? It was *less than a week* between that dreadful scene in the dining room and her removal to Hemmings! Yet they were ready with the lady's companion, and their plan — how is that possible?"

"And Lydia was *murdered*? Fitz, it makes no sense!"

"Perhaps Miss Maplethorpe enlisted with Miss Scrimpton's agency prepared to take the first opportunity that came her way — at the moment my mind inclines that way, for it does make *some* sense. The jewels were worth about three thousand pounds, if Jane's pearls are the ones I believe she gave away. The furniture and silver would not be worth more than a thousand pounds, though the carpets were rather fine — I bought them new for two thousand. The barouche and its pair of matched horses represent the most valuable thing they stole — about four thousand. The pony and trap was negligible."

"A total of about ten thousand pounds," said Elizabeth.

"Yes. A good haul, I suppose, even for professional thieves, who will certainly know where to dispose of their loot for the best price. If they lose about a third to the fellow who buys from them, then they have indeed prospered. Miss Maplethorpe will pay her men two hundred pounds apiece, and emerge about five thousand pounds the richer. It may be that she saw far grander pickings, since my name was associated with the position. I don't know, except that she certainly displayed no patience. Scarcely a day on the agency's books, and she was on her way to Hemmings."

He began to stroke the smooth skin of the backs of her hands rhythmically; it calmed and soothed him, and he wondered why they had taken to quarrelling every time they met. A part of the trouble, he knew, was his inability to tolerate her perpetual teasing, the habit she had of making fun of him. In the days when his passion had burned white-hot, he had suffered it, divining that for some reason beyond his understanding she thought it did him good to be teased, tormented, made fun of. But the longer they were married, the harder it had become to bear this capricious flightiness, and finally he had begun to round upon her each time she belittled him. At this moment, however, she was not moved to mock, so it was very pleasant to be with her, feel his blue devils dissipate.

"You have a very powerful mind, Fitz," she was saying. "Bend it to this conundrum. There must be a better answer! When you find it, we can rest." She moved her head, the halo dissolved, and he saw that her beautiful eyes were filled with tears. "Poor, poor little Lydia! Such a bad business, right from the beginning. Who believes in fifteen-year-old love? We did not, Jane and I. Nor did Papa, though he was too indolent, too indifferent to his duties as a parent to curb her. We judged her elopement moral laxity, but I see now that it was the only way she could keep her George. She loved him with every part of her! And he was such a villain, such a liar. His father did him no service, to raise him alongside you as if the pair of you were equals. His expectations were nonexistent, while you were heir to one of the largest fortunes in England. I remember him from Longbourn days as naive, grossly under-educated — yes, I know he went to Cambridge, but he learned nothing there, or at his school. Certainly his entire plan was to use his looks and charm to marry money, but at every turn he was foiled. So I suppose with Lydia came a certain measure of security, through our connection to you."

"You don't believe that I was instrumental in sending him to his death?" he asked.

"Of course not! He was a soldier by profession and died in battle, so Lydia said."

"Only three sorts of soldier die in battle, Elizabeth. One is the brave man who dares all. One is the hapless wretch who stands in front of a ball or a bayonet. And one is the lazy cur who finds a secluded spot to sleep the battle away — without first ascertaining whether his spot is in range of the enemy's artillery."

"Is the third way how George Wickham died?"

"So I'm told by his superiors. But Lydia will never know that now." He got up, kissed her hands. "Thank you for your understanding, Elizabeth. Her body is coming to Pemberley. We'll bury her here."

"No, it must be Meryton. Jane and I will take her."

"With Mary still missing? Are you sure?"

"You're right. Oh, she will hate to be buried here!"

"She can always vent her spleen at me by haunting Pemberley. She'll have plenty of company."

A groom from Pemberley located Charlie, Angus and Owen in Chapel-en-le-Frith, a village as old as its Norman name, and situated an easy ride from the cave district, which was why Charlie had chosen it. As the groom caught them before they set out for a day spent underground, they abandoned their plans and rode home.

Apart from forging a strong friendship, Charlie and Angus had a liking for caves in common — a liking that Owen refused to share. As his revulsion was more fear than detestation, he was, the other two informed him frankly, a dashed nuisance, especially when the cave under exploration was more a tunnel than a chamber. So Owen rarely went caving; he preferred to pass his time at Pemberley with the Darcy girls. With them he felt useful; he could ride (astride) with Georgie, function as a candid critic of Susie's art, help Anne with her Classics, and try to talk Cathy out of some harebrained prank sure to see her sent supperless to bed. As luck would have it, the day they were sent for was a caving day for Owen, who had ridden from Pemberley at dawn and joined his two friends for breakfast. Now they were all returning to Pemberley — what a relief!

All three were mystified by Fitz's curt summons. The groom knew nothing, and had been ordered not to ride back with them, which suited the trio very well — they could speculate aloud in peace. From which it could be deduced that they did not ride in an abstracted worry, but rather with an eye to any likely hole in a hillside or gorge, of which there were many, though not all proved to be more than a single small room. Angus had devised a system whereby they didn't make the mistake of exploring the same opening twice; those they had examined bore a bright red rag firmly fixed outside.

"There's one without a rag," said Angus suddenly. "Oh, I wish we had better maps! I have written to General Mowbray for army survey maps, but so far not a squeak from the man. Which probably means they do not exist." He marked the cave as best he could on his map, noting the look of the terrain in the vicinity. "It's somewhat off the beaten track as caves go, Charlie," he said anxiously.

"Don't fret, Angus, it will be attended to as soon as we go a-caving again," said Charlie in a soothing voice.

Angus was not looking very Puckish these days, Charlie thought. His hair had less apricot in it, and the creases in his cheeks were threatening to become fissures. Any doubt he had experienced about the depth of Angus's affection for Mary had vanished; the man was head over heels in love, and quite demented by worry. Over five weeks, and not a sign of her anywhere. If she were still alive, she had to be held in a cave. Of course she might have been spirited several hundred miles away, but *why*?

* * *

Under the lee of a curling cliff they encountered a bizarre procession coming toward them on foot, and courteously drew off the bridle-path they were following to let it pass. Perhaps thirty small forms clad in brown habits, hoods pulled right over their heads, walked two abreast behind a little old man clad in the same fashion, save that his hood was pulled back and he wore a large crucifix on his chest. He looked somewhat like a Franciscan friar. In the rear came two bigger children pushing a hand cart loaded with boxes that clinked as if they contained bottles.

"Hola, Father!" called Charlie as the friar drew level with him. "Where are you going?"

"To Hazel Grove and Stockport, sir."

"For what reason?" Charlie asked, not sure why he asked.

"The Children of Jesus are on His business, sir."

"And what business is that?"

"Follow me." The friar stepped aside. "Children, walk on," he said, and the children obediently walked on.

How miserable they seem! Angus thought, watching them as they passed. Shoulders hunched, cowls entirely hiding their faces, and their eyes fixed upon the ground. Flinching and shivering as if in distress, even emitting faint moans. Then he saw that the friar was moving toward the hand cart, and followed.

"Halt!" the old man cried. The procession halted. One gnarled hand indicated the boxes. "Pray open any of them that you wish, sir. They speak of the purity of our intentions."

A box of blue bottles was labelled *Children of Jesus Cough*

328

Syrup and a box of green bottles were a remedy for influenza and colds. A sluggish brown liquid proclaimed itself an elixir for the cure of diarrhoea. A box of clear bottles contained red liquid that said *Children of Jesus Paint for Boils, Ulcers, Carbuncles & Sores*. A box of tins were an ointment for horses.

"Impressive," said Charlie, concealing his smile. "Does this mean you make nostrums and potions for diseases and ailments, Father?"

"Yes. We are on our way to make deliveries to apothecary shops."

Charlie held up a tin of horse ointment. "Does this work?"

"Pray take it and give it to your stable master, young sir," said the friar.

"How much do you charge for it?"

"A shilling, but it will retail for more. It is popular."

Charlie fished in his waistcoat pocket and produced a guinea.

"This is for your trouble, Father." He managed a trick he had learned from his father, of looking very sympathetic, yet all steel underneath. "It's such a beautiful day, Father! Why do your boys wear their cowls up? They should be getting some sun."

Rage danced in the pebbly blue eyes, but the answer was smooth and reasonable. "They have all suffered from bad masters, sir, and I have to physick them with a lotion that reacts badly in the sun. Their skins would burn."

Angus intervened. "Father, have you seen a lost lady in your travels?"

The rage died, the eyes widened innocently. "Of what kind is this lady, sir?"

"Tall, thin, about forty, reddish-gold hair. Handsome."

"No, sir, definitely not. The only lady we have seen was poor Moggie Mag. She was bringing home rabbits for her cats and lost her way, but we set her upon it."

"Thank you, Father," Angus said. "Whereabouts do you and your children live?"

"In the Children of Jesus orphanage near York, sir."

"A long way to walk," said Charlie. "Given that there are no monasteries anywhere in this part of England, where do you stay?"

"We beg for alms and we camp, sir. God is good to us."

"Must you go as far afield as Stockport to hawk your wares?"

"We do not hawk, sir. The apothecaries of this part of England like our remedies best. They'll take everything we can manage to bring with us."

The three men prepared to ride on, but the friar held up a hand to detain them, and addressed Charlie.

"When I thank God for this guinea, sir, I would like to mention its donor's name. May I ask it?"

"Charles Darcy of Pemberley." Charlie tipped his hat and rode off, the others following.

"The Children of Jesus," said Angus. "Have you ever heard of them, Charlie? I haven't, but I'm not from these parts."

"I've never heard a whisper of them. Still, if they really do hail from York, that would account for my ignorance."

"Except," said Owen thoughtfully, "why are they on a bridle-path? A bridle-path through wild and desolate country? Surely this is not the main route from York to Stockport? They look like Roman Catholics and may be trying to avoid several kinds of odium and petty persecution — the kind of thing that happens to gypsies. The friar said they camped and begged for alms, which likens them to gypsies."

"But no one could mistake them for gypsies, Owen, and they're little children — boys, I hazard a guess. One very small fellow must have had a bee inside his cowl, and dropped it long enough for his companion to shoo the bee. A boy, and tonsured. People in rural fastnesses tend to be kind — 'tis in cities that the quality of mercy is shoddy," Charlie said. "I shall ask my father to make enquiries about them. As an MP, he must know the location of all orphanages."

"They're not Romans, Charlie," Angus said, splitting hairs. "Monastic orders don't sell a remedy for impotence, and most of the boxes on the cart were full of that. It also answers why the old man can sell his Children of Jesus wares as far afield from York as Stockport. 'Twould seem to me that his remedy works, else he'd not concentrate upon it." He grunted. "Children of Jesus! One of the very many Christian sects that afflict northern England, do you think, Charlie?"

"I do, though the prize for the most perspicacious question must go to Owen — what are they doing on this bridle-path?"

Once the three riders were out of sight, Father Dominus again halted his progress.

"Brother Jerome!" he called.

Lifting his skirts, Jerome came at a run, leaving Ignatius to mind the cart.

"Yes, Father?"

"You were right, Jerome. I should not have brought the boys out into daylight, no matter how deserted our route."

"No, Father, not wrong, just mistaken," said the only literate Child of Jesus, who took care to be obsequious in all his dealings with the old man. "They have been naughty, they needed a special punishment, and what better than a day in the light of Lucifer? It is besides the shortest way to the shops."

"Have they been punished enough?"

"Given that we have encountered Mr Charles Darcy, I would say so, Father. Ignatius and I can take the hand cart on by ourselves once the boys are back in the Northern Caves. They may not *like* living there as much as they have the Southern Caves, but today's ordeal will reconcile them," said Jerome, at his oiliest.

"Brother Ignatius!" Father Dominus called.

"Yes, Father?"

"Jerome and I are going to take the boys back to the Northern Caves now. You will remain at this end of the tunnel with the hand cart until Brother Jerome returns. There is food and beer enough on the cart."

"What about Sister Mary?" Ignatius asked.

"What about her?" Jerome asked.

"She will be taken care of, Brother, have no fear," said Father Dominus.

Brother Jerome, who aspired to donning Father Dominus's habit when the old man died, understood the implication of that statement, but Brother Ignatius did not.

"Back to your cart, Brothers. Children, walk on!"

They resumed their progress, but not for long. At the hill gorge where sat the aperture Angus had marked on his map, they produced dirty tallow candles from their robes, lit the first one from Father Dominus's tinder box, and filed inside, for it was narrow to enter, though much wider within. Last to come was Brother Jerome, who first made sure he obliterated all traces of their leaving the bridle-path, then pulled out some bushy shrubs by their roots and put them across the aperture until it was entirely filled in. From outside, the cave had disappeared. Inside, sufficient light still percolated to make Ignatius's wait with the hand cart a bearable one, and he had a lantern for the night hours. It suited him to stay there, peacefully alone, though it never crossed the limited terrain of his mind to spend some of those hours freeing Sister Mary, not very far away. The walk in daytime had pierced him to the marrow, just as it had the little boys; only Jerome and Father could tolerate the brightness of Lucifer's Sun, and that because God had specially armed them to war against evil.

The Children of Jesus had twenty miles of utter blackness to walk, but Father Dominus had catered well. At intervals there were stocks of imperishable food and candles, and water was never far away as the underground streams carved through the soft limestone.

Just a mile beyond the entrance loomed a side tunnel that led to the old kitchen and Mary's cell, but they ignored it to tramp on. Sometimes even the smallest boy had to bend double, while the bigger ones crawled on their bellies, but the way remained patent from one end to the other, though not in a straight line; its kinks and twists were tortuous. The walk took a whole day, but they never stopped beyond short pauses to eat, drink and replace candles.

Eventually the walkers emerged into a series of windblown caverns dimly lit during daylight hours by narrow holes, many of them made at Father Dominus's command, for the ground was a crust only feet thick, half of that a clayey subsoil; every hole had been planted outside with a bush that survived the constant wind, and no one dreamed that the Peak District caves extended so far north.

The entrance the Children normally used lay behind a waterfall on a tributary of the Derwent, and here outside the ground was solid rock that did not betray a footprint or the iron tyres of a hand cart.

The work to join the laboratory cave and the packing cave to the dozen chambers behind them had taken many years, for Father Dominus had first laboured alone, then after sending to Sheffield for Jerome, with some assistance. As the older of the boys grew strong enough, they too were put to the task, which finally began to quicken significantly. The ventilation holes consumed most of their time, and were always dug from the bottom upward, first with a pick, then, when the subsoil was reached, with a sharp-edged spade. The mystic in Father

Dominus would much have preferred to keep the darkness, but he needed the caves to house his children in closer proximity to the place where they manufactured his cures.

What he had not counted on was a minor rebellion: the children refused to move, and in the end had had to be driven like sheep at dead of night across the moors, weeping, moaning, trying to run away. They hated the laboratory cave and the packing cave, and, though they could neither read nor write, were quite intelligent enough to understand that this move meant longer hours at their smelly, disgusting, sometimes dangerous work. Even after Therese was in her kitchen — much better appointed too! — they tried every night to return to their beloved Southern Caves. Then Father Dominus had an inspiration: to take the boys out into the light of day and force them to walk for miles. Jerome had objected, afraid that, even on a deserted bridle-path, they would encounter someone, but the old man dismissed the possibility with a sniff. He was too much an autocrat to respect sage advice when it was given. But of all people, Charles Darcy! That could spell ruin, after what Jerome had told him about Sister Mary, who was in all the newspapers. Fitzwilliam Darcy's sister-in-law! And the woman had cursed him, called him apostate!

Huddled in his cell at the very top of his caves, Father Dominus rocked with grief, for near-blind though he was, this was one message writ in vivid scarlet upon the withered parchment of his brain — somewhere God had abandoned him, and Lucifer in the person of Mary Bennet had triumphed. His world was crumbling, but at least he knew why. Mary

Bennet, Mary Bennet. Well, he and Jerome would survive. It was back to Sheffield for them, until all the fuss died down and he could return to build anew. God's darkness riddled the Peaks, God could be found again. But this time, no children. They made his task too hard.

There was a fine tremor in his left hand that echoed the one afflicting his head. A new phenomenon. *Give me time, give me time!*

Brother Jerome appeared, hesitating in the entrance to his cell. "Father? Are you well?"

"Yes, Jerome, very," he said briskly. "Have the boys settled?"

"Like lambs, Father. It was the right thing to do."

"And the girls?"

"Obedient. The boys have told them."

"Sister Therese ... Can Camille take charge of the kitchen?"

"Yes, Father."

"Return to Ignatius first, Jerome. Deliver the potions, but when you and Ignatius reach the waterfall, it will be time to see that he meets with an accident. Then, later, you can send Sister Therese to Mother Beata."

"I understand, Father. It will be as you wish."

Despite the few mourners, Lydia's funeral was sadder than her mother's. Elizabeth, Jane, Kitty, Fitz, Angus, Charlie and Owen gathered in the old Norman church on the estate, and then at the graveside. For once Jane was not washed away by tears; she was too angry at Miss Mirabelle Maplethorpe's perfidy.

A reward of five hundred pounds had been offered for the lady's apprehension. Unfortunately no one with an artistic eye had ever seen her, so the notices that went up in town and village halls and post offices bore no picture of her.

June was now well advanced, and Mary had been missing for nearly six weeks. Though none confessed to pessimism, everyone secretly felt that it was highly unlikely she was still alive. So on that sunny, halcyon day when Lydia was laid to rest in the Pemberley burial ground, the identity of the next one to be laid there was very much in the forefront of all minds.

The youngest, yet the first of us to go, thought Elizabeth, leaning heavily on Fitz's arm. Charlie had made as if to take her when the graveside ceremony ended, but stepped back quickly when his father kept possession of her and led her away toward the house. The friction between his parents had always grieved him, but he had been so ardently on his mother's side that he could see nothing good in his father. Now he sensed a new array of emotions in Pater, softer and kinder than during, certainly, the past year, when Mama had begun fighting back. Though, thank God, she had abandoned her tendency to poke what she considered harmless fun at him — she was so convinced that he needed levity, owning none, and that she could inculcate it in him. Whereas Charlie knew that would never happen; Pater was proud, haughty and terribly thin-skinned. Did Pater and Mama actually think that he and his sisters didn't know their parents had taken to fighting like a pair of cats?

Cheated of his mother, he took Kitty's arm, and left Jane to Angus, who did not know the ordinarily weepy Jane. *Murder!*

It mazed the mind, that such a pathetic soul as Lydia could have been done to death.

A shadow loomed: Ned Skinner, as ever self-effacing, yet there in case Pater had need of him. Something about that association did not sit well with Charlie, but what it was, he had no idea. As if they had always known each other, when that was manifestly impossible. Pater had been about twelve at the time that Ned was born. Charlie knew a little more of Ned's background than anyone else save Pater; that his mother had been a blackamoor whore in a brothel somewhere, and that Ned's father had been the leader of a ring of criminals that had its headquarters in the same brothel. He had found these facts in Grandfather's papers, but nothing further; someone had torn sheaves out of Grandfather's diaries. When he complained to Pater, Pater said Grandfather had done it himself, in a fit of dementia just before he died. None of which answered why Pater and Ned were such warm friends, when it went so badly against the grain of Darcy of Pemberley to make a close friend out of such a man as Ned Skinner. Pater was stiff-rumped, no one who knew him could deny that. So why Ned?

Never having known Lydia, Charlie could not grieve for her, but he did understand his mother's grief. And Aunt Jane's. Aunty Kitty, a shallower woman, seemed to regard the death as at least partly a blessing, for it meant she could spend the summer at Pemberley after all. The people with whom she associated had not been on Pater's invitation list this year, since he was expecting great things from the Commons and Lords.

"I am delighted that Kitty is here," said Elizabeth to her son and to Jane. "She'll give Georgie a little much-needed town bronze. I don't quite know why, but Georgie loves her."

"She's a widgeon, Mama!" Charlie laughed. "Georgie likes any person who isn't run-of-the-mill, and Aunt Kitty is so elegant."

"I hope she can persuade Georgie not to bite her nails," Jane said. "It ruins her hands, which are quite beautiful."

"Well, I'm off to find a cave that Angus has lost," Charlie said, kissed his fingers to the ladies, and vanished.

"I'm glad Lydia is buried here," said Jane. "We're close to her, and can put flowers on her grave."

"She had few flowers in her life, poor little soul. You're right, Jane, it is good that she's buried here."

"Don't pity her for lacking the things she pitied us for having," said Jane. "Lydia loved life in army towns, she loved riotous parties and the company of men — the *intimate* company of men. She pitied us for leading staid, virtuous existences."

"All I can remember is how she loved George Wickham."

"Yes, but despite her declarations to the contrary, Lizzie, she had a fine old time of it when he was away." Jane looked angry. "No word of her assailants, I suppose?"

"No, not a whisper."

When the body of a lad about fifteen years old came floating down the Derwent River, it attracted attention only because Miss Mary Bennet, closely connected to Pemberley, was missing.

A shire constable was sent to look at the bloated, horrible remains, which the local doctor said could have drifted downstream for miles, for the lad had been dead at least three days. The doctor was of the opinion he had drowned, as he bore no marks of foul play. The body sported only two oddities: the first, a bald spot had been tonsured into the crown of his hair; and the second, he was circumcised. Otherwise the lad was well nourished and bore no evidence of a hard master, which made it unlikely that he had been a worker in a factory, mill or foundry, or a soldier. As the corpse was naked and therefore without a name, the constable wrote it down as "Male Youth. A Jew." He forwarded his report to the superintendent and sent the body for burial as a pauper. No need to worry about consecrated ground: no Christian, this one.

However, when a second adolescent body was found at the foot of a cliff not far from the first, news of it was conveyed to Mr Darcy, together with the constable's report on the first. Fitz called in Charlie and Angus, but not Owen, who, consumed with guilt, had gone home to Wales, leaving some sore hearts in the schoolroom and a militant sparkle in Georgie's eyes.

Fitz looked grim. Then he explained why he had summoned them. "Youths and children die with quite depressing regularity," he concluded, "especially at this time, when the Poor Laws are so abused. But this pair are out of the usual way. Both are about the same age — fourteen or fifteen. Pubescent, but not long such. One is male, the other female." He shifted in his chair uncomfortably. "Neither bore the stigmata of enforced child labour — no weals from injudiciously plied whips or crops, and no broken skin. The lad has gone to a pauper's grave already, but the girl has had a rigorously prosecuted post mortem at my instruction, and she has no broken bones or scars from old injuries. Both were well fed and healthy to look at. The girl was healthy in all respects. No stroke or apoplexy felled her untimely."

"So she didn't fall from a cliff," said Angus, whose Argus ears were pricking.

"She did not. She was put there to make it seem she had, and I suppose were Mary not missing, a constable wouldn't even have been notified. She would simply have gone straight to the paupers' burying ground."

"Pater, when you sent for us after Aunt Lydia's death, we encountered a very peculiar group of people," said Charlie, looking at Angus. "However, I think Angus should tell you. If I do it, you'll think I exaggerate."

"Not at all," said Fitz, surprised. "You recount events well, Charlie. But let Angus tell of this, if you like."

"We encountered a procession of — we think — male children led by an old man," said Angus. "He called them the Children of Jesus, and said they came from an orphanage of that name near York."

Fitz frowned. "An orphanage run by religious?"

"Roman Catholic, perhaps. They looked Franciscan, though the shade of brown was wrong."

"The Children of Jesus orphanage, run by quasi-Franciscan friars and located near York. Such an institution does not exist, near York or anywhere else north of the Thames, I would think. 'Children of Jesus' doesn't sound right. It would be 'Sacred Heart of Jesus' or 'Mary Immaculate' were it Roman. Romans are not fixated upon Jesus as an entity the way some Protestant sects are — I mean the ones which talk so much of Jesus that there is hardly a mention of God. The name 'Children of Jesus' sounds as if it were made up by someone unschooled in theology."

"Then we were right to doubt them!" Charlie cried. "It was the old man — a very fishy person. Never looked one in the eye."

"We were riding down a bridle-path," said Angus, "that Charlie knew of, certainly, but we met no one except the Children of Jesus on it. How would a friar from York know of it? The old man said he was an apothecary, and was very quick — *too* quick! — to show us his wares, stacked on a hand cart. Perhaps fifty boxes of elixirs and nostrums of all descriptions — look anywhere you like! he said, and gave Charlie a tin of horse ointment. The labels all read 'Children of Jesus' this or that. Who knows? Perhaps the old man believes 'Children of Jesus' gives his remedies a certain cachet." He cleared his throat and looked apologetically at Charlie. "I haven't had a chance to tell you, but I rode over to Buxton to visit the apothecary shop, and was surprised to find the proprietor very keen on 'Children of Jesus' products. Swears by them! So do his customers, who are prepared to pay almost anything for 'Children of Jesus' choler elixir." He looked impish. "It cures impotence. If the old man opened a shop in Westminster and sold that alone, he would make a fortune."

When the laughter died away, Charlie spoke. "I think the old man is mad," he said. "There was an eldritch quality to him, and I never saw thirty-odd little boys so demure and well-behaved as his were, not in all my life. They so winced and quivered when I asked to let them remove their cowls that I'm sure they didn't want their faces on display to him. I think the old man terrorises them. Oh, how afraid I was of some of my schoolmasters! Though I fancied him mad, an even greater fear. The only things that ever petrified me when I was a little boy were you, Pater — sorry! — and the occasional lunatic who crossed my path. Sane people are terrified of mad people because their conduct can't be predicted and they can't be reasoned with. To little boys, that old man might be Satan."

"To the apothecary in Buxton, he was Father Dominus," said Angus. "I haven't quite finished recounting my adventures, Charlie. Father Dominus always comes during daylight hours to be paid, but the goods are invariably delivered in the middle of the night, and by children in religious robes. My informant had never heard of a delivery during the day. He seemed to think that the children were refugees from bad masters whom Dominus had taken under his protection."

"Curious," Fitz said, steepling his fingers and putting their tips against his mouth. It made him look like a prime minister. "Where do they come from, since it isn't York?" he asked. "If normally they go by night, that might account for their strange behaviour when you met them in broad daylight, but they must hail from somewhere, and there they will be known."

"I'm sorry I lumped you in with lunatics, Pater."

Fitz glanced at his son with a smile in his eyes. "I do have sufficient imagination, Charlie, to realise why a little boy would lump me in with lunatics. I must have been extremely forbidding."

"A lot less so these days, Pater."

"We must divide up our forces to deal with this," Fitz said, amusement gone. "Angus and Charlie, you'll concentrate on the caves. It may be that Father Dominus uses a cave in his wanderings, and if Mary is still alive, we must presume she's being held in a cave. Whether there is any connection between her and the Children of Jesus is unknown, but if you work assiduously, perhaps some evidence will come to light. Angus, how long can you remain here?"

"As long as I have to, Fitz. I have good deputies to deal with matters in London, and my journalists must be having a mouse's time with the cat away in Derbyshire. Unpolished prose."

"Good. We must pray that things come to a head before all of us have to go, whether we want to or not. If Mary isn't found before Oxford goes up and Parliament comes out of its summer recess, then I think there's very little hope for her."

"What of the orphanages?" Charlie asked.

"They go to Ned. It's just such a job as he relishes, up on that monstrous black horse and riding from one place to another," Fitz said dispassionately.

"By the way, Pater, while Angus was riding to Buxton, I was engaged in making some enquiries of my own," said Charlie. "I asked about a procession of children who may or may not have

344

been clad as religious. Farms, hamlets, villages, I asked. But the procession, even as a group rather than a line, never emerged at either end of our bridle-path. The only settlement in the direction from which they were coming is Pemberley, and we know they were never at Pemberley. I think that means they came down to it from Stanage Edge, though they were never in Bamford. And its far end is Chapel-en-le-Frith."

"You are implying they entered a cave?" Fitz asked.

"Either that, or they crossed the open wilderness between the caverns and north of The Peak."

"Did they look as if they were carrying food? Water?"

"Under their robes, Pater, who knows? Water is easily found anywhere, but I've never heard of a group unencumbered by tents or caravans camping in the open. The moors are cruel."

"That they are. I shall ask Ned what he's heard."

Nothing, as it turned out when Fitz spoke to Ned.

"No matter how popular Father Dominus's remedy for impotence may be, Fitz, I'll go bail he's up to no good. Yet it makes little sense, does it? Here's a fellow with genuine cure-alls aplenty up his sleeve, hauling in fat profits, apothecaries clamouring for all he can supply them, while he's tramping a bridle-path that leads to naught save Pemberley. In charge of a group of children who seem not to be ill-treated. What's his goal?" Ned asked, frowning.

"Charlie deems him a madman, and that may be the simple truth. Nothing about the business makes a shred of sense. In fact, it makes the circumstances surrounding Lydia's death look clear as crystal. Now you say you can find no sense either, Ned."

"More important, where is this factory of his? And he must have a warehouse. An orphanage would be a very clever disguise, wouldn't it?"

Fitz looked alert. "You're right, it would. Orphanages are at the discretion of the Parish, but not every Parish has one. I know certain philanthropists endow orphanages. I think we may discount workhouses and poorhouses — they contain indigents of all ages. I've written to all the religious denominations owning a central authority, and will receive answers in the fullness of time, but there may be institutions quite unconnected to any religion."

"Rest easy, Fitz! Jupiter and I will ride from place to place, even as far afield as York. Orphanages and charity homes are not as numerous as apples on a tree."

"Unless the tree be a pear."

"When you joke, Fitz, you're worn out," Ned said, smiling. "That wretched lock of white hair! I swear it grows wider daily."

"Elizabeth thinks it makes me look distinguished."

"All the better in a prime minister, then."

"You'll need plenty of gold. Here." Fitz tossed Ned a bag of coins, deftly caught. "Find them, Ned! I'm grieved to see Elizabeth pining."

"Peculiar, isn't it?" Ned asked.

"I beg your pardon?"

"Well, this whole business started over Mary's letter to Charlie — the one I purloined and copied. You were so upset about it! But looking back from whereabouts we are now, it hardly seems worth a tenth of what you made of it."

"Don't rub it in, Ned! I was too sensitive about the possible outcomes, busy thinking months — sometimes years — ahead. I should have waited on events, I see that now. You were in the right of it when you said I was making a mountain out of a molehill "

"I don't remember saying that," Ned said, wrinkling his brow.

"You didn't use those words, but that was what you meant. I ought to listen to you! You're usually right, Ned."

Ned laughed, a big sound. "It's the poker up your arse, Fitz. Makes it a painful business to back down."

From another man, a mortal insult: from Ned, a loving truth. "Punctilious to a fault, eh? Pride in my ancestry was ever my besetting sin."

"And ambition."

"No, that's a later besetter. Still, if I had waited on events I wouldn't have asked you to watch Mary, and we would have lost her at Mansfield."

"I lost her anyway."

"Oh, cease and desist, Ned! Though if we do find her, she may write her wretched book with my blessing. I'll even pay for its publication."

"The result will be the same, whether you pay or the publisher does. No one will read it."

"*That* was what you said!"

ELEVEN

There were about three tablespoons of water left in the bottom of her ewer, though thirst had not been the torment Mary had busily imagined. The cave was bitterly cold, especially at night; the screen may have been put there to conceal what lay outside her bars, but the canvas had excluded the wind that blew eternally, save for that ever-present moaning whine. Her only defence was to draw her heavy velvet curtain closed, but it was far from adequate. In winter she would not have survived a week. However, there could be no denying the fact that this chill did not provoke a consuming thirst. If she paced her cell, she grew warmer — but thirstier.

She now wore every item of clothing they had left her, dirty as well as clean: four pairs of woolly socks, four flannel nightgowns, one flannel over-robe. No gloves, and her hands were very cold. The scrap of bread had been eaten already, before it grew too stale to gnaw. Easier to follow the passage of time now that she could see daylight. Her stomach must have shrunk, for she felt no hunger pangs.

To her horror, rats came to feast on the loaf of bread Father Dominus had kicked aside on his last visit to her; when they had finished it they didn't leave, just cruised the dark hours waiting for a far tastier meal — her own dead body. They did not look like the few rats she had seen before. They had been black and fierce, whereas these were small and grey, easily intimidated. Creatures of the moors, obviously.

It was only now that time hung so heavily upon her that she realised how busy and occupied she had been during most of her incarceration. Producing a page of perfect copperplate devoid of any error was a vastly different task from ordinary writing, when one could cross out a word, or over-write it, or pop in a caret-mark and put a forgotten word above. Much and all though she had condemned Father Dominus's ideas, setting them down error-free on a page had taxed her, as it would have taxed any but a professional scribe, one of those persons who copied out an aspiring author's prose to render it fit for a publisher's eye.

Now it seemed as if all her woes had descended at once. She had nothing to occupy her time, and that fact loomed largest on her list. It was like being back caring for Mama, existing in a limbo of idleness, yet far worse; she had no music to console her, and no books she had not read at least a dozen times. Add to that inertia her lack of food, exercise and water, and — oh, dreadful!

The days when she had found prayer a compensation had long gone, though now, with naught else to do, she prayed, but to pass the time rather than with any confidence that prayers were things God answered. Were I Mama, she thought, I would find release and comfort in sleep; Mama had always been able to do that. But I am not made in Mama's mould, so I cannot sleep the hours away.

So to keep her mind off the cold, she began to dissect her conduct since Mama's death had liberated her, and came to the conclusion that all her efforts had been ludicrous. Not one thing had gone to plan, which hinted at one of two things: either Satan was conspiring against her, or else her aspirations, her ability to be practical, and her own person, were wanting. Since it hardly seemed likely that she was important enough to earn so much of Satan's attention, the second alternative was obviously the correct one.

I was obsessed with Argus, and I thought if I wrote a book confirming his theories and observations, I would impress him so profoundly that he would be eager to meet me. Well, I will never know now whether things might have fallen out that way. I do have a crusading spirit in respect of the poor and downtrodden, but who am I to think that anything I do can help them? I see now that my research was not thorough enough, even including the allocation of my financial resources. I should have corresponded with several publishers first of all, and learned how much exactly my book would have cost me to publish. And, since I had reconciled myself to living with Lizzie at Pemberley when my funds were all used up, why did I deny myself at least a few of the comforts a gentlewoman expects when she travels? Some of it was to appear no better off than those I wished to interview for my book, but I am ingenious, I could have devised a scheme whereby I travelled quite comfortably, yet seemed when divorced from the activity of travel to be, say, a penurious governess. Some of it lay in the sheer euphoria of being free at last to do as I pleased, but more of it lay in an abysmal ignorance of the world at large. There was never a need on my part to have so many guineas in my reticule, for I had my letter of credit and could have withdrawn two or three guineas at a time.

Hindsight, Mary Bennet! Experience has given you wisdom, but the vagaries of chance have put your life at peril. It seems you cannot even ride the public stage-coach without disaster, and what is that compared to your present predicament?

A sensible woman would have accepted Mr Robert Wilde's very sincere proposal of marriage, but what did you do, pray? Why, you looked at him as if he had grown another head, and then snapped it off! But you know the reason for that full well — you could see that it would have been an inappropriate union — he younger than you, wealthier, more appealing to the opposite sex. And face it, Mary, you were right to refuse him! He will find a more suitable wife, one whom he can love without being ridiculed, which would have been his fate had he married you.

From Robert Wilde her mind skipped to Angus Sinclair, who had said no word of love. He had offered friendship, and that she had felt able to accept. It was he whom she missed upon her travels: the kindred sense of belonging, the receptive ear turned her way to listen to whatever she said. Yes, she had missed him acutely, and known that were he with her, the adventures would have taken on new dimensions. Mr Robert Wilde's face she found hard to remember, but Mr Angus Sinclair's sprang immediately into her mind like a portrait done by a master.

She was missing dearest Lizzie too, though Jane not as much. Jane cried so, and tears accomplished nothing, changed nothing. The only tears Mary respected were those of the deepest, sharpest, most harrowing grief, and one could not compare those tears to the tears of Jane. No, Lizzie was the sensible and sensitive one — why was she so unhappy? When I get out of this, Mary resolved, I am going to discover the cause of Lizzie's unhappiness.

At night, huddled in her chilly bed, a slightly angular ball trying to warm just one spot, she wondered about the origins of her prison cell. Seizing the opportunity during one of Father Dominus's more approachable moods, she had asked why he had ever needed to construct such a thing, only to be rebuffed. Not by a refusal to enlighten her — that would have been more understandable. No, Father Dominus had denied ever building it! When she pressed him for an explanation, he had said he owned no theories about it at all, and changed the subject. So who had made a cage in a cave? A cave, what's more, that lay far from any accessible chamber, if she could believe Ignatius and Therese. Who had built it, and why? Robbers? Refugees? Kidnappers? She would never know, it seemed. But to wonder liberated her mind a little, let it drift into sleep. And when she was free, she would try to find out.

When I get out of this, she kept saying to herself — never *if* I get out of this. Three tablespoons of water left, and she was still saying when, not if.

The new dawn was a sunny one, she saw when she tugged her curtain back for the morning look, then closed it to cut the wind. Cold, so cold! Her lips were dry, their skin crusted and flaking. Do I, or do I not?

"I do not count on Thee to provide, O Lord, except to give me strength and ingenuity," she said, and drank the last of her water.

No sooner had she set the empty ewer down than there was a roar in the bowels below her, a huge shudder that threw her flat; dazed, she climbed to her feet and saw that the wooden seat of her commode had twisted, splintered. The hole beneath it was still there, but instead of the sound of running water came a column of dust that billowed about her.

Another noise followed, this one inside her cell — harsh and metallic. She ran to the curtain and pulled it back to reveal the bars. They had buckled! When she tried to open the big door, it swung inward on its hinges, squealing, its lock sheared where the mortise entered its socket. Mary ran through it — if more of this subsidence was to come, let her be outside the cell, not in it! Then, remembering how cold she was, she steeled herself to return to the cell and take her two blankets. More layers to warm herself.

"Thank you, dear Lord," she said then, safely outside again.

There were two more openings in the left side wall of this foyer cavern, as well as the one she had used for exercise. She looked into each, and saw blackness. A stack of tallow candles of the cheapest sort lay beside the far tunnel, together with a tinder box well stuffed with dried mosses almost as fine as wool. But not for one moment did Mary contemplate either. She was no Ariadne with a ball of twine wending her way through the Labyrinth of the Minotaur, and after that upheaval in the depths, who knew what had happened in the tunnels?

No, she would enter the world directly, from the aperture, no matter how precipitous the terrain outside. She went to the edge of the opening. Not a cliff, thank God! A pile of rocks spread downward and, at the top of the cave, a massive boulder leaned; it must have helped the dark green canvas conceal the cave to anyone on the moor below. She was nothing like a thousand feet up, she saw now, but rather about three hundred feet. The wind buffeted and tore at her, but the landslide was dry, and she had some protection from the blankets once she managed to wrap them around her shoulders. The position of the sun told her that she was looking north across a desolation of moors, conical peaks and ragged rock formations; nowhere could she see a house or settlement of any kind. Therefore when she reached the bottom she must turn toward the south and, some instinct said, the west rather than the east. If habitation there were, it would lie that way. Oh, for her boots!

The rocks were difficult to negotiate, and bit into her hands when she had to cling for dear life with toes groping for a foothold below. Ten minutes into her descent saw her quite warm from the effort; off came one blanket, which she tossed downward as some protection against wearing her socks out.

Her strength had dwindled alarmingly, but Miss Mary Bennet was not about to be defeated by her own bodily shortcomings. She kept scrambling down, occasionally falling, but always halted by a protruding boulder too soon to sustain injury.

It seemed to take forever, but at the end of about an hour Mary was standing on rank, strappy grass that only the hungriest sheep could fancy. Her socks had held up under the harsh treatment, but they wouldn't last if her walk was one of many miles. This *had* to be the Peak District of Derbyshire, she thought, and wished she knew whereabouts Pemberley lay. But as she did not, she set her course around the base of the low hill in which her cave sat, and hoped that some sort of civilisation lay close at hand.

At first it did not look auspicious; the countryside seemed as wild and deserted as it had to the north, and Mary's spirits sank. No road, no track, no path … But after she had tramped about five miles, wincing as the sharp-stoned ground cut into her feet, her sensitive nose scented the foetid commingling of barnyard aromas — pigs, cows, geese, horses. Yes, yes! This way did lead to habitation! *To people!*

Farmer William Hawkins saw a scarecrow coming down the lane, staggering and tottering. Tall, skinny, dressed in rags, with the hair of a fairground clown, reddish and sticking up, and a face like a fairground skellington, just the bones. Transfixed, he watched until the scarecrow came close enough to see it was a woman; then he realised who she had to be, and whooped so loudly that Young Will came bolting out of the barn.

"'Tis Miss Mary Bennet," said Farmer Hawkins to his son. "Oh, look at her feet, poor soul! Arms up, Will, we'll chair her to the house. Then you can climb on the pony and go find Mr Charlie — he's hereabouts, searching them caves."

Mary was put into a wooden armchair by a kitchen fire, given water and then broth. By the time that Young Will found Charlie and Angus, Mary had regained sensation in her limbs, felt warm, cosseted, *alive*. The broth was skimmed off a true farm soup, always on the hob, added to with whatever came to hand that day, and it was delicious. Only a little of it had made her feel sated, but she knew that would pass; in a few days she would be eating huge meals to heal her body's travails.

Then Angus burst through the door, his face wet with tears, his arms out to enfold her in a hug. Much to her astonishment, Mary found this treatment exactly what she might have wanted had she dreamed of wanting it, which she had not.

"Oh, Mary, if you but knew the despair we have all felt these past weeks!" he said into her hair, which smelled of tallow and dust, and somewhere underneath, of Mary.

"Set me down, Angus," she said, recollecting herself. "I am very glad to see you, but I cannot stand for long, even with a gentleman supporting me."

Obedient to her every whim, he put her in the chair. "I can imagine that our despair is as nothing compared to yours," he said, understanding she was not yet ready for declarations of love. "Where have you been?"

"In a cave, the prisoner of a mad little old man who calls himself Father Dominus."

"So he *is* up to no good! Charlie, Owen and I met him with about thirty little boys, carrying his wares."

"The Children of Jesus," she said, nodding. "Where is Charlie, if he was with you today?"

"Gone home to fetch a carriage for you." Remembering his manners, Angus turned to the Hawkins family and thanked them for their kindness to Miss Bennet. They would, of course, have the hundred pounds reward. "No, no, Mr Hawkins, I insist!"

Mary's head was nodding. Angus moved behind her and let her head lie against him, as the chair back was low. She was still asleep when Charlie and the carriage arrived, so Angus carried her to it and bundled her in furs; she felt very cold. Mrs Hawkins had peeled off her socks and washed and dressed her feet, but Angus and Charlie were anxious to get her home, where by the time they arrived Dr Marshall would be waiting.

"Are you well enough to give us all your story, Mary?" Fitz asked a day later as the group assembled in the Rubens Room before dinner. Though she was too thin, it was clear that her basic health was unaffected by her ordeal; a hot bath, her hair washed by none other than Hoskins herself, and the loan of one of Lizzie's gowns made her look quite breathtaking, Angus decided. Too thin she might be, but the clean lines of her flawless bones was better emphasised. Only heavily bandaged feet bore testimony to her sufferings.

If Mary had one virtue greater than others, it was her reluctance to complain coupled to her dislike of occupying the central position on a stage. So without self-pity or florid embroidery, Mary told her story. She had no idea that Ned Skinner had been taking her to Pemberley when Father Dominus struck; in fact, she remembered nothing between being evicted from the Friar Tuck and waking some days later in the cave, a prisoner. Both the ladies and gentlemen found it hard to credit that she had been stolen for no better reason than to act as a scribe for a book about his outlandish beliefs.

"Though originally he stole me to experiment upon me," she qualified, resolving that nothing she said would paint him madder than he truly was. And what was madness anyway? "He told me that I had been dying from a swelling of the brain — apparently his skills as a physician were developed enough to diagnose this from my appearance as I lay on the bank where he found me. It seems he had concocted a remedy for swelling of the inner organs, but had no one upon whom to test it. So he stole me, fed me his concoction, and cured me. *Then* I became his scribe. At first his Cosmogenesis, as he calls it, fascinated me — a truly original concept wherein God is the darkness, and all light is evil. His term for the author of evil is not Satan or the Devil, but Lucifer. How much Cosmogenesis owes to his encroaching blindness I know not, but certainly it contributed. Though he never said so, I gathered that light was painful to him. Ignatius said once that whenever he set out to collect payment from apothecary shops, he wore spectacles with lenses darkened by smoke."

"So the boys we encountered behaved as they did because they abhorred light," said Charlie. "I put it down to fear of him."

"Fear of him is something new as far as the children are concerned, and even so, it is the girls who fear him more. Events occurred that provoked him into calling them unclean."

"What happened to *you*, Mary?" Fitz asked.

She looked wry. "My undisciplined tongue, of course. I had kept it under rigid control, understanding that to antagonise him might earn me a death sentence. But when he informed me that Jesus was the result of a cynical collaboration between God and Lucifer, I could not remain silent. I called him wicked and evil, and he ran away, cursing me. That was the last time I saw him. I was left to die — and would have, had the subsidence not occurred."

"I think he decided to abandon you after he met us," said a horrified Charlie. "I told him I was Charles Darcy of Pemberley and asked after you. He must have panicked."

Mary's interrogation at Fitz's hand continued for several hours, yet neither he nor Angus felt that, at its end, they knew much about anything except Cosmogenesis. Surely she must have had some kind of contact with the children! But no, she maintained that she had not.

"Give it up, gentlemen!" she said at last, tired and a little angry. "I cannot embroider the facts. You have seen thirty little boys, I have seen only the two you saw pushing the hand cart. Believe the testimony of your own eyes, not my hearsay, for hearsay is all it is. I was kept in a barred cell, and moved no farther from it than a tunnel that led downward to an underground river. Wherever the children were kept gave them no excuse to see for themselves the woman of whom Therese and Ignatius talked. When I asked Father Dominus about the cell, he denied building it. Whoever did, he said, did so before his time. All I can tell you is that the poor children were shifted to some new location, and disliked it. Father's reasons for the move are unknown to me, but they were not very recent. It seems an old plan of his."

"Let us cease and desist," Fitz said, eyes on Mary's face. "You have had enough. You were right to think a subsidence occurred. Though the public caves were not affected, the movement was felt everywhere, and for the time being all inspections of the caves are cancelled. We must presume that within the area are many caves as yet undiscovered, and that somewhere in them are the Children of Jesus. The question is, did the subsidence occur where they are, or completely elsewhere? The old man's dementia is apparently increasing, so we cannot know whether he has locked them up, or still lets them roam free. Provided, that is, that they are still alive."

There was no point in shielding Mary from anything. Fitz told her — and, perforce, Elizabeth, Jane and Kitty — about the two dead bodies. This, coming hours after learning of Lydia's death, almost overset Mary. To her own surprise, she held out her hand to Angus, and was given it. Such a comfort!

"The dead girl must be Sister Therese," she said, blinking at tears. "I am sure of it. I never did believe there was a Mother Beata. I think that once the girls matured, they were to be killed. Yes, the girl's body belongs to Sister Therese, and I insist that she be buried in decent circumstances. Mourners, a stone at her head, consecrated ground."

"I'll see to it," said Angus. "Fitz has bigger things to do, Mary. How, I don't know, but we have to find those poor children. If Father Dominus's madness has progressed beyond human values, then he won't care about the children."

"Did he give you any reason why he has the children, Mary?" Elizabeth asked. "It seems he fed them well, clothed them — doesn't that suggest he loved them, at least in the beginning? I know you say they're terrorised, Charlie, but if he had always had that effect upon them, they would not have joined him. From what you say, Brother Ignatius loved him, Mary."

"Brother Ignatius was simple. I think Father Dominus deliberately kept all his children simple — certainly they were never taught to read or write. He told me that he stole them from bad masters, but if Sister Therese and Brother Ignatius bore no sign of ill-treatment, perhaps he stole them at a very young age from their parents, or — or even *bought* them from their parents or the Parish overseers. Parish care can be cruel, depending upon the rapacity of the overseer. It would not have been hard to acquire them at a very young age if there was money in it. As to whether he would have killed all of them upon maturity, we'll possibly never know, for Ignatius was the oldest of the boys, and Therese the girls." Mary sighed and clutched Angus's hand harder. "If he is mad, and I for one don't doubt that, then to be adored by these simple little people must have contributed to his high opinion of himself. Don't forget that they worked for him, and were paid nothing. The gospel of St Mark says, 'Suffer the little children to come unto me.' If

Father Dominus believed himself chosen, one can make some sense of it."

"Much will be answered if we find them," said Fitz.

"May I say something about their being found?" Mary asked.

Fitz stared at her, smiling slightly. "By all means."

"Don't look in places where the caves are well known, but farther north. If the first body was Brother Ignatius, then he floated *down* the Derwent, yet was still north of the caves people visit. In the bowels of my prison was a stream, I could hear it flowing strongly, then saw it on my exercise walks. Until I talked to Angus and Charlie, it hadn't occurred to me that these underground rivers are far under the ground. So my stream was much deeper than I had imagined. Go to the north, where all is desolation. These children are like moles, they can't tolerate the light of day. Search by night."

The gentlemen were staring at Mary in admiration, and Angus was bursting with pride.

"What a head you have on your shoulders!" he said.

"If I do, then why do I get into such dreadful scrapes?"

Fitz took over, disliking loss of purpose. "The moon is coming up for half, so we can search at night for quite some time. I have spyglasses, and may be able to locate more. It's quite a dry summer, which means less cloud."

"I shall have prayers said for the children in churches of all denominations," said Elizabeth. "They'll haunt my sleep until they're found, but if they're found dead, I'll never sleep well again. Fitz, may I have the funds?"

"Of course," he said at once. "Like you, Elizabeth, they haunt my sleep. I'll call in Ned and put him to work as well. His eyes are very sharp, and he works best at night. In the meantime, those from Pemberley who search will carry tents and camp on the moors. Riding back and forth takes up too much time, though we'll keep horses with us. I must ask the ladies to limit their use of carriages and riding horses, for I want the grooms as searchers. Huckstep will come with us and leave a deputy here with two grooms. I'll also commandeer footmen and gardeners if you tell me how many you can do without."

"Take whomsoever you want," said Elizabeth.

"Though," she said to her husband later that night, "I don't believe that method will answer this conundrum. Mary was freed by a natural convulsion in the earth. My prayers will do as much good as your men."

"I believe in God," he said ironically, "but a God of sorts only. My God expects us to help ourselves, not make Him do all the work. Faith is too blind, so I'll put my trust in men."

"And in Ned Skinner most of all."

"I have a premonition about that."

"Why did you oppose Mary's crusade so bitterly?"

His manner grew stiff. "I am not at liberty to say."

"Not at liberty?"

"The more so, now our son is prospering."

"Cryptic to the last."

He kissed her hand. "Goodnight, Elizabeth."

*   *   *

"Well, Lizzie," said Jane over breakfast next morning, "though we cannot actively help the men in their search, there are still things we can do." The large amber eyes looked stern. "I am going to assume that the children will be found alive and safe. That their health will be unimpaired."

"Oh, splendidly said, Jane!" cried Kitty. "They will be saved, I'm sure of it too."

"You're leading up to something," Elizabeth said warily.

"Yes, I am." Jane answered. "Lydia has left a hole in my heart that only time and apprehension of her murderers will mend. But consider this, Lizzie! About fifty children between four and twelve who probably don't remember any life except the one they've had with Father Dominus. What will happen to them when they're found?"

"They'll go to the Parish if theirs can be located, or to orphanages wherever there are vacancies," said Kitty with composure, spreading butter thinly on unsweetened wafers.

"Exactly so!" cried Jane, sounding wrathful. "Oh, my temper has been sorely tried of late! First Lydia is done to death by thieves who can't be found, now we have fifty-odd children who have never known the joys of childhood!"

"There are few joys of childhood to be found on the Parish, or in the orphanages, or walking England's roads because they have no parish," said Mary dispassionately. "The comfortably off are privileged, and can give their children joys — if, that is, they don't spoil them on the one hand, or beat them mercilessly on the other." She got up to help herself to a second plate of sausages, liver, kidneys, scrambled eggs, bacon and fried potatoes. "All too often, children of any class are regarded as a nuisance — seen, but not heard. Argus says that it's cheaper for pauper females to feed their babies gin than milk, as they're too dried up to give them suck. The poorest children I saw on my brief travels were infested with vermin, had rotten teeth, crooked backs and shockingly bowed legs, bore atrocious sores, were hungry, wore rags and went barefoot. Joys, Jane? I don't think poor children have any. Whereas children of our own class tend to have too many, which makes them *expect* joys — *and* gives them a perpetual discontent that follows them all of their lives. *Comfort* should be ever-present, and joys merely an occasional treat. Save for the only joys that truly matter — the company of brothers, sisters, and parents."

How could we have forgotten Mary? Elizabeth wondered. Just such an encomium as she would have come out with in Longbourn days, save that this one is wise. Where, along her way, did she pick up wisdom? She never used to have any. Her travels and travails, I suppose, which doesn't say much for the sheltered life of females of the first respectability. Jane is wincing because she knows very well that her sons are grossly over-indulged, especially when their father isn't home to discipline them. And then they go to Eton or some other public school to be tormented and thrashed until they're old enough to turn into tormentors and thrashers. It is a vicious circle.

"We're drifting off the subject," said Jane with unusual asperity, "which is the Children of Jesus."

"What do you want to say, Jane?" asked Elizabeth.

"That when the children are found alive and well, the gentlemen will lose interest in them immediately. Fitz will donate one of his many secretaries to sort them out, return them to their proper parishes, or their parents, or put them in orphanages. Except that we know orphanages are already overcrowded. There won't be room for them, especially because, from what Mary says, they won't know their parents or their parishes. So they'll end up more miserable than they were under Father Dominus's care, for at least he fed and clothed them, and they seem not to have suffered illness."

"You want to build an orphanage," said Kitty, revealing that she had unsuspected powers of deduction.

Elizabeth and Mary stared at their flighty widgeon of a sister in amazement, Jane with the pleasure of finding an ally.

"Quite so!" said Jane. "Why separate the poor little things when they have been together for years? Mary, you're the one who Angus said had a head on your shoulders. Therefore you are the one who should deal with the practicalities — how much it will cost to establish an orphanage, for example? Kitty, you frequent all the best houses in London, so you should seek donations to the Children of Jesus orphanage. I will engage to speak to Angus Sinclair and beg that he publish their plight in his journal. I will also speak to the Bishop of London and imply that one of our aims is to eradicate any Papist, Methodist or Baptist tendencies the children may have picked up from Father Dominus, whose theology, Mary says, is apostate. The Bishop of London is no proselytiser, but it is an irresistible opportunity for the Church of England."

Jane's eyes were glowing as huge and yellow as a cat's, and her face was quite transfigured. "We will break new ground in the care of indigent children! I'll choose the staff myself, and supervise all aspects of the orphanage's progress in future years. You'll share this duty with me, Lizzie, which is why I suggest that the orphanage be situated halfway between Bingley Hall and Pemberley. I think Fitz and Charles should buy the land and pay for the building of a proper institution. No, I refuse to hear of our using an existing house! Ours will be designed for its specific purpose. The money Kitty brings in will be invested in the Funds to provide income for wages, food, clothing, and a proper Church of England school as well as a library."

By this, Elizabeth was gasping. Who would ever have guessed that Jane, of all people, possessed so much zealotry? At least it would keep her from having too much time to spend missing Charles. Only she, Elizabeth, foresaw opposition from the gentlemen. Mary thought the orphanage a splendid idea, but deplored its small scope and thought they should be building several. Kitty sat bending her not very powerful mind to the problem of how to obtain donations from the Mighty, very attached to their money. And Jane was utterly convinced her plan would succeed.

"To think that all of this originated in Mary's strange obsession with the poor," Elizabeth said to Angus, who rode to Pemberley to (he had explained to Fitz and Charlie) write an urgent letter to London; his real reason was to make sure his Mary had not decamped. "It's been like a pebble thrown upon a snowy slope," Elizabeth continued. "Instead of coming to a harmless halt, it's rolled, gathering a huge coat of snow, until it threatens to overwhelm us. I'm glad that Jane seems to have tossed off all desire to weep herself into the vapours, but at least when she did that, we all knew where we stood. Nowadays anything may happen."

Angus laughed until Elizabeth's reproachful expression told him she couldn't see a funny side. "Jane is probably right," he said then. "We would cheerfully have handed the children to the Parish overseers and forgotten them. Logic says that they were too young to know what a parish is when they were abducted — or sold — and may not remember any parents. So a Children of Jesus home is actually an excellent idea. I imagine Mary is in favour?"

"And that's all that really concerns you, you lovesick Scot! Yes, of course she is, though she envisions orphanages being built all over England," said Elizabeth, smiling. "However, I cannot see Fitz consenting to schemes that would beggar him in a year."

"He shouldn't have to, or be asked to. The mills of any government grind even slower than those of God, for exceeding fine takes time, especially in Westminster. I see Fitz's most pressing task as flogging his parliamentary colleagues into a radical program of changes to the lower end of society. He can always trumpet what happened in France — the Lords are prone to listen to that argument. All people resist change, Lizzie, but change will have to come. Not all of it will be in favour of the poor, thanks to take-out payments in many parishes. Some have hardly an employable man or woman on their lists, so attractive is the thought of being paid a pittance *not* to work. The poor-rates are soaring."

"Go and find Mary," she said, tired of the poor.

His contrary beloved did look pleased to see him, but not in the guise of a lover. Yet. Some of her reactions since her return had given him hope, but his innate good sense warned him against endowing them with too much significance. He could only imagine what it must have been like for her during her imprisonment, and thus far had not been able to talk to her for long enough to discover just how deep in fact were the wellsprings of her unquenchable determination. So he attributed her reactions to a realisation of her feminine weakness, when in reality she had come to no such realisation. Mary *knew* she was not a weak female; Angus still harboured a man's illusions about it.

"We found the subsidence," he was able to tell her. "It seems the caves extend much farther than anyone had counted on, but now their extent will remain unknown. The innermost caverns are quite blocked by immense falls of rock. What is something of a mystery is why the subsidence occurred at all."

"And the underground river?"

"We can hear it, but it's changed course."

"When do you move north and search by night?"

"Tonight. The day has been relatively cloudless, so we have hope that the moon will shine. We've amassed a number of what Fitz calls spyglasses. He's asked farmers with flocks grazing in the region to bring them farther south. Less moving forms to confuse us when we search by night."

"My goodness!" said Mary, impressed. "It sounds like an army manoeuvre. I never thought of sheep. Don't they sleep at night?"

"Yes, but any untoward noise startles them."

"Are there deer?"

"I imagine so."

"The children won't be easy to see in their brown garb."

"We are aware of that," he said gently.

It had been agreed that the search parties (there were three, one each for Fitz, Charlie and Angus) should concentrate upon the bases of peaks, hills and tors, but also carefully inspect the banks of the Derwent and its tributaries. It was the biggest river in the region, and flowed strongly, even in summer. Since Brother Ignatius (if indeed it were he) had been found floating on it, that argued some proximity, if not to the river itself, then to some tributary or underground stream that fed into it.

The first night was an eerie experience, for few settled men, be they labourers or gentlemen, were used to moving through the night on foot, and surreptitiously at that. While it was up, the half moon radiated a colourless light that drenched the landscape without enlivening it; even after the moon set, a glow suffused the heavens from the light of more stars than most had ever dreamed existed. With their eyes used to the darkness, it was easier to see than Angus, for one, had thought possible. The few deer could be identified as what they were, especially if a man had a spyglass. What were more surprising were the dogs that roamed in search of quarry — rabbit, shrew, rat and, earlier in the year, lambs. Once they had been pets or working dogs, Fitz explained, either abandoned or in search of better food than their masters had given them, and they were savage, all signs of domesticity lost.

Then Charlie had a bright idea, which was to dress the small child of a Pemberley groom in brown robes and ask him to walk near the river bank for some distance, then turn and walk into more moorish terrain. The seven-year-old had no fear, and thoroughly enjoyed his perambulations, especially because he was allowed to stay up far past his usual bedtime. Tracking him gave the searchers some idea of what they would see if a Child of Jesus appeared.

A week went by and the moon waxed to full, still in relatively cloudless weather; so bright was the beautiful silver orb that one could read by it, and that despite the belching chimneys of Manchester, not far away. As luck would have it, the wind favoured them by blowing the smoke eastward into Yorkshire.

Then the moon, rising later each night, began to wane, and no child had yet been seen. That made it more likely that the poor Children of Jesus were now imprisoned; despair began to invade the hearts of the searchers, so buoyed up with enthusiasm when the search had begun.

Ned Skinner wanted none of search parties; he preferred to work on his own, and had his own theories as to where to look. While the three groups of men were still what he considered too far south, he was mounted on Jupiter and prowling high up the Derwent, particularly where a strong tributary fed into it. Fitz hadn't wanted him to ride, protesting that his outline against the starry sky would give his presence away, but Ned took no notice. That was the chief problem with the three search parties as far as he was concerned: they went on foot, leading their horses, and it made them far too slow.

He had his own spyglass, a more powerful instrument than any Fitz owned; it had belonged to a sea captain much attracted to voyaging into the kinds of places where a sailor might need to check whether the natives on a beach were carrying human heads. From horseback height its range was over long distances, yet at close quarters it was crisp and clear, for it telescoped for accurate focus, and this was by no means the first time it had come in handy during Ned's nocturnal adventures.

The moon was waning now, so it was rising later. However, the twilight didn't fully bleed away until shortly before the moon came up, and Ned had no intention of leaving his hiding place until twilight was gone. He had taken over a cave, but it was a simple, probably wind-hewn declivity in an outcropping of soft rock. It had room for him and Jupiter, and he had made several trips to stock it with food for him and the horse. No sweet grass on the moors!

Full darkness had fallen when he ventured out, the eastern sky already silvering to herald the imminence of moonrise. Perhaps at no other moment would even his sharp eyes have discerned the white glint of falling water on the tributary, miles to his west. His thumbs pricked; he stiffened in the saddle enough to transmit his change of mood to Jupiter, which shook its head. He reached forward to pat its neck.

"Easy, old man," he said quietly.

They moved at a trot until the waterfall came entirely into view. about fifty feet high, and containing a good volume of water that widened at its base into a broad pool. Its only possible source could be a large spring, probably not far above the cliff over which it tumbled. Were it closer to other spectacular attractions it would have drawn visitors, but it sat amid some miles of uninspiring hills, gorges and moors. The Peak, away to the south, was about as far as visitors went unless they were poets, writers, painters or other peculiar folk enamoured of desertion wherein to rove and roam. At night, suchlike were usually tucked up in a warm bed at an inn or a farmstead. Certainly none such were abroad this night. He had it all to himself.

Finding a patch of shadow from an overhang, Ned slid from Jupiter's back and prepared the animal for one of the waits he inflicted upon it occasionally. Then, quieter than a stalking cat, he edged toward the pool, keeping in the shadows.

The pool's margin was limestone, polished to a slight sheen in a yard-wide ribbon that led from the side of the waterfall to the grass, in which it persisted for about a hundred more yards before dwindling to invisibility. A path worn by little feet! On the border between the grass and the limestone he paused, head cocked, listening, but could hear nothing alien over the sound of the falling water. He reached into the left pocket of his greatcoat, and into the right, to make sure his pistols were ready, and his knives. Following the path to the edge of the waterfall, he discovered that it dived behind the curtain of water, and was dry because the wind blew the spray eastward.

He passed through a huge opening to enter a vast cavern lit by amazing lamps as well as candles reeking of tallow. Fairly level, the floor was filled with plain wooden tables at which little robed figures stood over basins and bowls, mortars and pestles, apparently engaged in mixing substances together, or grinding them to powder. At one side of the cave and close to the entrance was a huge alcove containing a very hot coal fire, iron rods holding iron cauldrons and pots over the shimmering, shivering surface. A strange-looking cupola blocked off the top of the alcove, its pinnacle sprouting a wide metal tube that led, braced on brackets, to the outside air behind the falls. Whatever its principle, it was efficient, for there was hardly any smoke in the cavern. Near it were condensers for distillation, and a whole table devoted to filtering liquids through cheesecloth or cloth. The Children of Jesus laboratory, wherein Father Dominus made his cure-alls!

In this dim environment the children had pulled off their cowls — all boys, Ned decided, for they all bore the little bald spot of a tonsure on the crowns of their heads. Girls were never tonsured that he had heard of. Almost thirty of them, with a big lad roaming from table to table — features coarse, eyes pitiless. They were afraid of him, and flinched or shuddered when he approached. Not Mary's Brother Ignatius, he decided. This one had no heart.

Getting past Brother Jerome (for so one boy had addressed him) was difficult, but Ned succeeded when the youth went to the fire and roared for more coal — that must be an exercise, the lugging of sacks of coal! At its rear the cave tapered down to a high, quite wide tunnel. A short passage, it opened into another vast, artificially lit cavern, in which were more tables. These contained bottles being filled through funnels from ladles dipped into ewers — the girls! Longer hair, no tonsures. They were working in a frenzy, though no one supervised. That meant Brother Jerome must have charge of all of the children. Where was Father Dominus?

The air was filled with odours, all sorts from disgusting to sickly-sweet; did Father Dominus make women's perfumes as well as the traditionally foul things that cured ailments? Somewhere in the mélange Ned's nose identified one particular smell, a smell he knew, sniffed regularly. *Gunpowder!* Ye gods, what was the old bugger up to? The moment he inhaled it, Ned knew why the caves in the south had subsided: Father Dominus in the guise of Guy Fawkes had blown them up! That meant he must have been using them too, and realised when he met Charlie that he would have to abandon them. What better way than gunpowder? He was an apothecary, he would know how to make it. Even I, thought Ned, could make it if I knew the correct proportions of the ingredients, which are just sulphur, saltpetre and powdered charcoal. So simple, so destructive ...

Where was the gunpowder? Then he saw that the passageway between the laboratory and the bottling cave was wider than it looked; its sides were stacked with small barrels. But where was the trail of powder that led to the detonating cask? Gunpowder was black as pitch, the floor covered in black dust — was the whole floor the trail? No, it would fizzle. Though air got in, the bottling cave felt more stifling than the laboratory one. Producing noxious fumes and smoke from a big fire, the laboratory would have to be closest to the outside air.

First thing to do, he decided, was to eliminate Brother Jerome. Sooner or later he would come down the passage to see what the girls were doing. Ned moved into the most lightless spot near the end of the short corridor, and pulled out a knife. It would have to be quick and efficient; let the youth shout once, and Father Dominus might appear. Brother Jerome would be easy to deal with, but Father Dominus was as intelligent as he was crazed, and until he could find the fuse trail, Ned wanted the old man oblivious to his presence. For he had to get the girls out; that was what Fitz would want him to do above all else. The boys were on the far side of the kegs of explosives, and would fare at least a little better. The girls would either be buried under falling rock or immured in blackness to perish slowly, perhaps in agony from injuries. An insupportable thought.

Sure enough, here came Brother Jerome. He never knew what had happened to him, so quick the knife that went in under his rib cage and twisted up to the left to pierce his heart. He dropped like a stone, voiceless.

Ned stepped out of the shadows and walked up to the nearest of the tables, at which six little girls were counting pills into small round boxes. The pills were lavender in colour, a sure sign they were for kidney trouble. Everyone knew that.

"Don't be afraid," he said quietly, "and don't cry out. I'm here to save you. Do you see those kegs stacked in the passage? They're full of gunpowder. If you're here when it blows up, you'll die. I want you to go among the other tables and tell the girls to move into the waterfall cave — truly, I mean you no harm!"

They stared at him round-eyed, never having seen a man so big or so burly, and perhaps something of his strength resonated within them as comforting, for none cried out, or tried to run. A more ruthless man than Ned Skinner would have been hard to find, yet in that moment he radiated truth as well as strength. What he could not know was that they were hideously aware of gunpowder and its dangers, for they had made it, seen two of their number die, and suspected that they would all become its victims. They had noticed the change in Father Dominus, and feared him desperately. Father had taken to calling the girls wicked, unclean, polluted, and ranted that women were creations of Lucifer. Sister Therese had vanished; at first they had thought she had gone to Mother Beata, but then Brother Jerome began to boast that he had twisted her neck, and that they believed implicitly.

Soon all the little girls were hurrying through the keg-lined corridor, spilling out of it among the boys, who looked bewildered, though some looked displeased. When Ned appeared in the wake of the last girl, they bleated and milled about, a few boys trying to slip past him into the passage. But he could always deal with boys.

Out came a pistol; he brandished it. "Go on, get out into the fresh air! This place is going to come down! Stay here and you'll be blown up. Out! Out!"

Since the only path to freedom led into the open air, they began streaming under the waterfall and into the night, while Ned went back to locate the gunpowder fuse.

As he walked he cocked his pistol, flipped the frizzen back off the powder pan and into position for the spark, then curled his finger around the trigger, carrying the firearm straight and fully horizontal; once the powder in the pan was exposed, the weapon couldn't be tilted in case the hole carrying the spark to the charge became blocked.

Some paces short of the passageway stood Father Dominus, face twisted up in fury and frustration, a blazing torch in his left hand.

"You interfering fool!" the old man screamed. "How dare you steal my children?"

Ned shot him in the left chest, deeming that the easiest way out of an invidious situation. But Father Dominus had a fanatic's strength, and hurled the torch backward into the passageway despite his mortal wound. "I am dead, and you will die with me!"

No, thought Ned, unperturbed. I'm too far from the blast, and moving at a run toward the waterfall. But the vagaries of cavern design carried some of the stupendous explosion forward into the laboratory cave, which collapsed together with most of the hill, honeycombed by Father Dominus's caves. Ned felt the boulder strike his legs and pelvis, and a colossal agony; I am done for after all, he thought, but it is worth it, to have done this one last good turn for my dearest Fitz.

The explosions echoed across the moors and came clearly to the searchers working their way slowly around The Peak.

The three leaders had gathered for a conference when the great booming noise reached them.

"That's no cave subsidence," said Fitz. "Gunpowder!"

They had horses with them; Charlie and Angus ran to get their parties mounted while Fitz rode north grim-faced, his own men after him as soon as they could. Ned had intended starting at this end, Fitz was thinking — pray God he's all right! Pray God the children are all right!

Leaderless and rudderless, the children hadn't fled the scene save to run beyond the range of falling boulders; they were huddled together, weeping, when Fitz and his group rode up, and let themselves be wrapped in blankets the men carried, given water liberally laced with rum.

Fitz moved among them in search of a cognisant face, and chose a little girl about ten years old because she was acting rather like a mother hen toward the others.

"I'm Fitz," said the man who never let people outside the near family use his Christian name. "What's your name?"

"Sister Camille," she said.

"Have you seen a very big man named Ned?"

"Oh, yes! He saved us, Fitz."

"How did he do that?"

"He said the passage was stacked with gunpowder and we would die unless we ran outside. Some of the boys tried to stop us, but Ned waved his pistol at them and we all ran. The gunpowder *exploded* just the way it did when we were making it. Sister Anne and Brother James were killed then, and my eyebrows got burned off. So when Ned told us it would blow up, we knew it would. I think Ned didn't expect us to believe him."

Fitz's heart had plummeted. "Is Ned still inside, Camille?"

"Yes."

Charlie and Angus were riding up with their men, rejoicing at the sight of all those little brown-robed figures.

"Bad news," Fitz said to the other two. "Ned found this cave, and got the children out just in time. Father Dominus had stuffed it with gunpowder — he actually forced the children to make it! A boy and a girl were killed in the process. Can you credit the depth of his villainy? Ned hasn't come out." He drew a breath, balled his hands into fists. "I must go in to look for him. Charlie, tell Tom Madderbury to ride to Pemberley. We'll need the barouche for Ned — I doubt we'd get him into a fully closed carriage. Also carts and wagons to bring the children. Hot food in hay boxes for the children. They'll sleep after water laced with rum, but we can't keep them here. The best place to put them is the ballroom — have Parmenter light fires at that end of the house to make sure it's dry. And tell Madderbury to make sure everybody knows the children will be part-blind from living in dim light. Their full sight will come back, but it will take time. We must have the wooden stretcher with the slight curve for Ned in case his back is broken, splints of other kinds, bandages, wadding, compresses, laudanum as well as the strongest opium syrup. Make sure Marshall is waiting for us. He can see the children too."

Charlie went off at once; Fitz turned to Angus. "It wasn't difficult to shed Charlie, but now I must ask you to step back, Angus. I must go in alone."

"No, I insist I go with you."

"Angus, you can't! There's no point in losing more than one man if more landslides are to come. It wasn't a natural convulsion, but the result of an explosion, and we don't know enough about the effects of explosions in enclosed places to run unnecessary risks. If I think it's safe, I'll tell you. And keep Charlie out."

Seeing the good sense in this, Angus waited outside, and when Charlie would have rushed in after his father, persuaded him that one death, if death there had to be, was preferable to two. Only reminding Charlie of his mother deterred him.

The waterfall was gone, though the pool was still there, and the cavern entrance was revealed as yawning. A torch in his left hand, Fitz entered a world of rubble and rocks; like most Peak District caves, it was dry and windblown, of little interest to sightseers. He didn't understand that it had been hidden by a waterfall, so wondered why no one had ever noticed it.

"Ned!" he called. "Ned! Ned!"

Where he stood was reasonably safe, he thought, but where once there had probably been a vast cavern was now an immense heap of boulders interspersed with smaller, sharper rocks, and much rubble. Strain his ears though he did, he could hear no trickling earth or groans from overtaxed stones: nothing to suggest a further fall. He moved onward, treading lightly, warily.

"Ned! Ned! Ned! Ned!"

"Here," said a weak voice.

Following the sound, Fitz discovered Ned lying half under a boulder that concealed his legs and lower torso from sight.

"Ned," he whispered, sinking to his knees.

"Are they safe? Did they all get out?"

"Every last one. Don't speak, Ned. First we have to get this almighty stone off you."

"I doubt that will make any difference to the outcome, Fitz. I'm done for."

"Nonsense!"

"No, the simple truth. Bladder and bowels are squashed flat. Hip bones too. But you can try. You won't rest if you don't try, will you?"

The tears were pouring down Fitz's face. "Yes, Ned, I have to try. It is my nature. We'll dose you with opium first."

Charlie appeared at his father's shoulder. "Pater — no, I refuse to use that ridiculously pretentious term, even if it is Darcy custom and tradition! Papa is good enough for most men, and good enough for me. Papa, what is to be done?"

"Papa is good enough for me too, Charlie." Fitz got to his feet, heedless of his tears. "Have we any opium with us? I think we can lever the stone off him with two or three stout men and stout iron poles. Have we any poles with us?"

"Poles, yes. Yes. We had no idea whether we might have to shift rocks, so we included them." He looked wry. "And a keg of gunpowder." He knelt on one side of Ned, his father on the other.

"What happened to Father Dominus, Ned?" Fitz asked.

"I shot the old bastard in the heart. Should have gone down like a stone, but he didn't. Carrying a torch, threw it into the passage. Must have heard me, and piled up powder in front of the detonating keg. I swear there was none when I walked through it back to the front cave." Ned groaned, reached for Fitz's hand. "I'm glad I lived to see you again."

"Take heart, you'll see years more of me."

They decided not to move him until the barouche came, which was at dawn, lending some natural light to the shambles inside the cave. Fitz hadn't left Ned's side, though Charlie moved back and forth; Angus had inherited the duty of caring for the children.

Madderbury, the groom who had ridden to Pemberley, returned with the carriage, and informed them that enough carts and wagons would shortly arrive for the children. Dr Marshall had been summoned, and would bring a nurse with him.

Three strong men wielding poles levered the boulder off Ned in one move, which left Fitz and Charlie staring in horror at the mess below Ned's waist. He cannot survive, thought Fitz. But by sliding the six-foot-long wooden stretcher under Ned's body they managed to lift him and lug him to the conveyance; the open nature of the barouche enabled them to lift him over the doors and put the stretcher diagonally from one seat to the other, the only way the vehicle could accommodate his formidable length. Fitz sat with him, opium ready, while Charlie sat on the box to make the coachman's task more difficult with his constant orders to mind this, and avoid that.

It took many hours, though the summer's day had not yet ended when finally the barouche reached Pemberley. Dr Marshall was waiting. One look at the injuries saw the doctor praising their good sense in keeping Ned as flat as possible. The crush nature of the injuries had prevented massive bleeding, but, "There is no hope," he said privately to Fitz as soon as the initial examination was over. "I did a year in the Peninsula with Sir Arthur Wellesley, so I've seen this kind of injury before. The wound is ragged, open, and contaminated by bowel contents. He's lost blood, so I won't bleed him myself. However, he won't take more opium until he has spoken to you and Mr Charlie. No one else. And he asked that it be soon. He knows he's dying."

Why does Papa weep so for him? wondered Charlie as, still in all their dirt from the search, they went to the room where Ned Skinner lay.

The big frame looked quite shrunken in the bed. Fitz drew up a chair and sat close by his head, his hand reaching for Ned's, plucking at the coverlet. Bidden be seated, Charlie put his chair just beyond his father's, for Ned had turned to look at Fitz, and Charlie wanted to see his face. Ned smiled, suddenly looking quite absurdly young, though he was eight-and-thirty.

"Charlie has to know," he said, voice clear and strong.

"Yes, Ned, he must know, it's right and fitting. Do you want to tell him, or shall I?"

"It's not my place, Fitz. You tell him."

It came out baldly: "Ned and I are half-brothers."

"That doesn't surprise me, Papa."

"That's because you're a Darcy. A man could never ask for a better brother than Ned, Charlie. Yet I couldn't acknowledge him. Not my doing, but my father's. He made me swear a terrible oath that I would never reveal the relationship. With Ned, too young at the time to swear any oaths, he preferred to convince him he was unworthy."

"*Grandfather? Harold Hunsford Darcy?*"

"Yes, Harold Darcy. Thank God every day that you never knew him, Charlie. A truly evil man. He ran dens of thieves, cutthroats — and brothels! — in Sheffield, Manchester, Liverpool, many other northern cities. Why? To *amuse* himself! He was so bored by the life of a gentleman that he took to crime. Indeed, he fancied himself a master criminal. Most of his activities he ran from his favourite brothel in Sheffield. Ned's mother, a Jamaican, was his passion — yet he forced her to whore for him. She died of the pox when Ned was three. Pater died of the pox too, though my poor mother never knew that. His was hideously malignant — it killed him in six months, raving and demented. Mama was never well after bearing Georgiana, and died too. All the deaths happened in the same year. He wrote me a letter on his deathbed, and exacted the oath when he gave me that awful document. It exulted in his deeds, and told me of Ned's whereabouts. After I buried him I went to Sheffield and took Ned, and gave him to be reared by respectable people. I was seventeen, Ned was four. Whenever I could, I spent time with him. So strange, Charlie! I looked into that dark little face with its curly black hair, and I loved him with might and main. Far more than ever I did Georgiana. Anyway, after Harold died I glued my world back together again in Humpty-Dumpty fashion, with pride and hauteur my mortar. But having Ned to love, I was never quite alone."

Charlie sat, numb and winded. So much answered! "Uncle Ned?" He touched Ned's shoulder very delicately, since his father held the hand. "Uncle Ned, you did a wonderful thing. Nearly fifty children will live because of you." He managed a smile. "And live well, I pledge it."

"Good." Ned lay frowning for a long moment, then opened his dark eyes that were, Charlie could see now, so like Papa's. "I have to wipe the slate clean." He spoke suddenly, and in gasps. "Wipe it clean."

"Then wipe it, Ned," said Fitz.

"I murdered Lydia Wickham. Smothered her. Drunk. Out to it. Felt nothing. Too drunk."

"Why, Ned? Not for my sake, surely."

"Yes, for your sake. Easy to see you'd never be — rid of her. Never. Why? You'd done naught save give — that pair — money. On the cadge — always. So she thanked you by setting out to ruin you. You, the best man ever. When our father — died — you came to get me — give me a home — send me to school — spend time with me like an — equal — not you so high — and I — so low. I loved killing her!" He stared across Fitz to Charlie. "Look after your father. Won't — be here to do it. You must."

"I will, Uncle Ned. I will."

Fitz was weeping inconsolably.

"Lydia had to go, Fitz," Ned said more strongly, not gasping. "A foul-mouthed strumpet with naught on her mind except money, booze, fucking. So I set it up cunning and I killed her. Mirry and her men played into my hands — flew the coop. S'what I wanted, give Mirry the blame. Same brothel, new management. Miriam Matcham is her name. She's murdered a dozen whores in her time, likes to watch some soulless pervert kill them. Just like our dad … Yes, Mirry Matcham will hang a dozen times over, so let her hang for Lydia. It will please Mrs Bingley." He closed his eyes. "Oh, I'm tired! Why am I so tired?"

"You'll be buried at Pemberley as a Darcy," said Fitz.

The eyes opened. "Can't have that. Won't have that."

"Yes!" said Charlie.

"See, Ned? Your nephew echoes me."

"Not fitting."

"Yes, it is fitting! Your stone will say 'Edward Skinner Darcy' for all our world to see. Beloved brother of Fitzwilliam, Uncle of Charles, Georgiana, Susannah, Anne and Catherine. *I* wish it."

"I do not. Charlie, please …"

"No. It is right and fitting."

"Jupiter!" Ned cried suddenly, trying to lift his head. "I left him in a cave — give you directions — "

"He came home before you did, Ned."

"Look after him. Best horse ever."

"We'll look after Jupiter."

The pain, which he seemed to have held at bay by an Herculean effort of will, returned to rack him, and he screamed until given the strongest opium syrup. A little later he died, apparently asleep and in no pain.

Charlie broke his father's hold on Ned's hand and led him from the room.

"Come to my library," Fitzwilliam Darcy said to his son. "We must talk before either of us sees your mother."

"Do you really want to acknowledge Ned openly?" Charlie asked. "No, no, I don't disapprove. I simply want to be sure that it wasn't a passing fancy said to please poor Ned."

"I *must* acknowledge him! He has done murder for me, though I swear on your mother's head that I didn't ask him to do it, or so much as hint at it. If the truth be known — he was too broken to live to tell all, I suspect — he has murdered other people for my sake. So that I might be prime minister of a Great Britain." He put an arm across Charlie's shoulders, partly affection, partly lack of strength. "Well, that is not going to happen. I shall remain in Parliament, but on the back benches. From the back benches I can wield as much influence as I'll ever need. Your mother called it pride, but I would rather call it hubris — overweening pride. My head was filled with the desire to be prime minister, but perhaps one day you can be that. However, I'll understand if you don't choose a political career. In truth, politics are shabby and shoddy. I must apologise to you, dear Charlie, for making your life a misery when you were a child. In many ways I was as tyrannical as

Father Dominus. But all that is gone. Ned Skinner shall not die in vain."

"How much do we tell Mama?" Charlie asked, taking Papa's full weight with a brimming heart. I have crossed the ditch filled with sharpened stakes that lies between boyhood and manhood: from now on, I am my father's son.

"We will accede to Ned's wishes. Miriam Matcham and her men can take the blame for Lydia's murder. We'll obtain proof that she looted Hemmings and fled the night Lydia died, and we'll have Miss Scrimpton's testimony to her false credentials. Though, as you are well aware, a Darcy of Pemberley's testimony alone is quite enough to send Miriam Matcham and her minions to the gallows."

"Whatever you think is best, Papa. Here, sit down."

"We will bury Ned as befits my brother. I have none other, Charlie, and wish I could have given you a brother, even base-born. But I was too proud to whore, and I had my father's horrific acts to point out to me what can happen to men of wealth and birth when they become bored. I went into Parliament, you have your Greek and Latin scholarship, so we have no need to walk in Harold Darcy's footsteps." He laughed wryly. "Besides which, I married into the Bennet family — quite enough to keep any man from boredom!"

"I begin to see why you opposed Mary's crusade," Charlie said. "You were afraid of what she might unearth about Harold Darcy if she started ferreting in Sheffield, which isn't so far from Manchester. What did you do with Harold's letter?"

"I burned it, and have never been sorry I did. As a boy I detested him, which may be why he became so attached to George Wickham, who toadied him shamelessly. I think George expected a huge bequest in the will, but it would have amused my father to inflate George's hopes, then puncture them, especially with a living as a clergyman! If anyone knew how far that lay from George's heart, it was my father. He delighted in that kind of cruelty. Though George never knew of his nefarious activities — had he, I would never have got rid of him. When George didn't succeed with your Aunt Georgiana, I think his sharp eye soon spotted my love for your mother — why else would I have paid his debts and forced him to marry Lydia? Being married to Lydia suited him, as it kept him under my nose, and ensured that I would keep on paying his — and Lydia's — debts."

"Much of what you've said to me, Papa, must also be said to Mama, including a little of Lydia. But not who really murdered her."

"Wise man! That will remain our secret."

"What about Harold Darcy?"

"Perhaps an expurgated version?"

"Yes, Papa. Explain the who and why of Ned, and a fair number of Harold's perfidies, but not the worst. Except that I insist you tell her of your oath to Harold about Ned's relationship to you. She feared and disliked Ned, perhaps thinking that he had some hold over you, and that secretly you railed against that hold. She must be shown that you loved him as brothers love. Mama always understands relationships founded in blood."

Fitz began to weep again; Charlie put an arm about his father's bowed form and hugged him. What a difference it made, to know that the demigod was human after all!

"I'll tell Mama. The more personal things you must tell her yourself when you're able." Emboldened by this radically softer, more approachable Papa, Charlie decided to dare all. "It grieves your children very much when you and Mama quarrel, but even more when we can skate on the ice between you. Can that state of affairs be mended?"

"Don't press your luck, Charlie. Good night."

TWELVE

Exhausted, Fitz did not wake until mid-morning of the next day, to find Elizabeth sitting by his bed, busily writing at a little table. But the face he saw was Ned's, and he came to consciousness with a despairing cry.

"Ned! Ned!"

She put down her pen immediately and moved to sit on the edge of the bed, reaching for his hand. "Hush, Fitz! I'm here. Ned is at peace, do you remember?"

Of course he did, now that sleep was banished, but he couldn't staunch the tears. "Oh, Ned, Ned! How can I go on without Ned, Elizabeth?"

"I suppose the way I would, were it Jane. Only time can mend some wounds, and then never quite. I felt my father's going badly, and mourned a long time. You were so good to me then! I had poor, sickly little Charlie — isn't it amazing, Fitz, how he has grown? When he came to see me yesterday evening

I was — stunned. It seemed as if he went out to look for the children still a boy, and came back a man. Even his face has changed. The beauty that so plagued him is gone — vanished into thin air! He's very, very handsome, but the epicene quality is absolutely gone."

She was talking, he understood, to give him time to compose himself, but this grief defied society's rules. It would be many days before he could fully command himself.

"What a feast for Caroline Bingley could she see me now," he said, taking the handkerchief she held out.

"Just as well then that I sent her packing."

He managed a watery laugh. "Yes."

"Ned worked very hard for you," said Elizabeth. "Jane is more settled now that she knows who murdered Lydia. Charlie has notified the Sheffield constabulary, and this woman Matcham and her minions will be arrested. If it were not for Ned's work, we would never have known. I wish I could have thanked him, especially thanked him as my brother. So does Jane."

"What are you writing?" he asked, to change the subject; it hurt to talk about Ned.

"Oh, just lists for Mary, who is orphanage mad. It was a way to fill in time until you awakened."

He groaned. "Will orphanages be any easier to bear than a book about the ills of England?"

"Probably not, except that the worst Mary of all to bear would be an idle one. Poor Angus! He's so deeply in love with her, and she won't see it."

He sat up, mopped his face, blew his nose. "I went to bed in all my dirt, and need a bath. Would you ask Meade to prepare it for me?" He looked at her, smiling. "We must talk, but not yet. After Ned is buried and things settle down. Our son was impudent enough to say that our children are tired of skating on the ice between us, and somehow we have to melt that ice. In a few days. Is that satisfactory?"

"Yes," she said, rising and moving the table away. "I'll leave you to your ablutions, my dear."

"I love you, Elizabeth."

"And I, you."

"I only said I wished I had never married you to hurt you, to elicit some kind of response. It was a terrible thing to say."

"Later, Fitz. Have your bath."

She gave him a wonderful smile and went out of the room, her papers in one hand.

Jane and Mary were in the pink morning room, a delightful small apartment reserved for the ladies. Of Kitty there was no sign.

"Fitz is awake," Elizabeth said, coming in. She tugged the bell cord. "I'm in need of coffee. Anybody else?"

Having ordered coffee for three, she sat down at the table, littered with papers. "Where's Kitty?"

"With Georgie," said Jane. "Today is how to be queenly, I think, or perhaps how to be charming."

"She certainly needs tuition on both," said Mary with a snort.

Of course the subject of Ned Skinner had already been talked to death, but it continued now Elizabeth had joined them.

"And to think how much I disliked him!" said Jane for the tenth time. "All the while, he was making his investigations on our behalf. Lydia can rest in peace now that her murderer won't escape retribution. William says that England hangs many more felons than the rest of Europe combined, but they *should* hang if they kill innocent people. I just wish Father Dominus had lived to be hanged. Especially considering what he did to poor Ned."

"Which reminds me," said Mary, tired of Jane on the subject of Lydia and hanging. "You have eight children at Bingley Hall for the summer, Jane, yet it seems you spend your days *and* your nights at Pemberley. They're already as wild as savages out of a jungle — what will they be like when finally you go home?"

Jane looked insufferably smug. "Oh, I've solved all of the difficulties inherent in children, Mary dear. When Lydia died I sent for Caroline Bingley. After Lizzie's insult she couldn't darken Pemberley's doors, but she does so enjoy her summers here in the North. She has been staying with me since just after dear Lydia's funeral. The children are *petrified* of her, even Hugh and Arthur. She *spanks* them! I can never raise a finger against them, I confess — they stand there looking so contrite and adorable! But that doesn't wash with Caroline! Down come the trousers, and she spanks them *hard*! Of course they are howling as if being killed before the first smack lands — it is the sight of her huge hands." Jane sighed. "But I will say this. They are much better behaved after Caroline takes over."

"Does she spank the older ones?" asked Mary, fascinated.

"No, she canes them."

"And Prissy?"

"She makes her walk for hours with a book balanced on her head, or practising her curtsies, or conjugating Latin verbs."

"Does this mean you intend to stay here?" Elizabeth butted in.

"No, just that I may come and go as I please. Caroline really enjoys disciplining children," said Jane.

"Now why does that not surprise me?" asked Mary.

Looking after twenty-seven boys and eighteen girls sat so ill with the Pemberley servants that, after a week of it, they rebelled.

"I am very sorry, Mrs Darcy," said an anguished Parmenter to Elizabeth, "but Children of Jesus is a misnomer. Children of Satan would be far closer to the mark."

Elizabeth understood much that her butler had not said, but decided to appear tranquil, unimpressed. "Oh, dear!" she said placidly. "Tell me what has happened, Parmenter."

"*Everything!*" he wailed. "We have done precisely what you wished, marm, down to closing the ballroom shutters and limiting the number of candles. We took the cots for the extra summer servants out of storage, put fresh straw in the mattresses, and made them up with clean sheets, blankets, nice cotton quilts. The old nursery commode chairs have been put behind a screen that the children knocked down immediately. Every toy in the attics was brought down, and now lies in pieces. Truly, marm, *nothing* has been overlooked! We set up trestle tables and benches for them to eat at, with knives, forks and spoons. Glasses for lemonade. And our thanks? Bedlam, marm, I swear! They do not like the food, and throw it all over the place. And they will not use the commodes! They squat like stray dogs to do their business, then throw *it* at the walls! They pulled the mattresses off the cots and slept on the floor amid puddles of — of — I leave it to your imagination. Oh, marm, the *filth*! Our lovely ballroom is ruined!"

"I assume that they refused to be bathed?"

"Absolutely, marm. In fact, they refuse to take off their robes, which stink to high heaven!"

"I see. In which case, Parmenter, lock every door and window opening into the ballroom, and do not unlock any of them until I am present and specifically instruct you."

And off marched Elizabeth to find her sisters — but only after visiting Mr Matthew Spottiswoode.

"Matthew, I do not care what you are doing, kindly abandon it!" she commanded, surging into his office.

As word had long spread of doings in the ballroom, he did not attempt to protest, simply folded his hands on his desk and gazed at her enquiringly. "Yes, Mrs Darcy?"

"I want twenty of the biggest, hardiest nursemaids Lancashire can produce. I say Lancashire because I very much doubt that any big or hardy enough exist in Derbyshire. Offer them a king's ransom to drop whatever they are doing and come to Pemberley at once — and I mean *yesterday*!"

"Certainly, Mrs Darcy. Though I very much fear that, even for a king's ransom, it will be some days before my quest bears fruit," said Mr Spottiswoode, eyes limpid, mouth perfectly straight, all laughter on the inside. "I take it you would like me to engage upon this myself?"

"Yes! And start in Manchester! Failing that, Liverpool."

Alone among the sisters, Elizabeth had some appreciation of the causes underlying the behaviour in the ballroom. She had no doubt that until their removal to Pemberley, the children had been closer to angels than mortal children usually are. Knowing this, everyone had expected the angelic conduct to continue. Whereas Elizabeth saw the last week as evidence of a new and different kind of terror. What, after all, did they know of any life save that which Father Dominus had inflicted upon them? And the many years of love would surely far outweigh the fear of him and Jerome that had come so very recently. If I were an eight-year-old Child of Jesus, she thought, walking Pemberley's stunning cream-and-gilt corridors, what would I make of being bundled out of the only home I have ever known by a band of men, then locked inside an utterly alien environment? I think I would register my disapproval in every way at my disposal! And have we — Mary, Kitty, Jane, I — come near them since they arrived? No, we have not, doing what all women in our circumstances do — wait for servants to clean them up and any messes they make. But servants are — oh, a law unto themselves! If they dislike the work they are put to, they take out their spleen on whatever defenceless is at hand. In this case, the Children of Jesus themselves. No servile hand will have been raised against them, but one cannot say the same for servile tongues. They have been roared at, screamed at, reviled. I know it, I know it!

Well, she vowed as the end of her hike loomed in view, it is time to change all that. Not with sweetness and tenderness — they are not yet ready for those. But with authority from the people they will sense own the kind of authority Father Dominus did. With instructions aimed at teaching them how to go on. We did not rescue them to see them cast upon the world rudderless and poverty-stricken, which means that it is our responsibility to start their education here and now.

Jane, Mary and Kitty were enjoying a comfortable prose in the Pink Parlour; it continued exactly as long as it took Elizabeth to storm in.

"Jane," she said wrathfully, "this is all your idea, so present me with no excuses as to why your sensibilities and delicate feelings preclude your participation! Kitty, doff that silly frivolity of a dress and don something made of mattress ticking! This instant, do you hear me? Mary, as you are responsible for thrusting the Children of Jesus into Pemberley's bosom, turn your redoubtable skills at achieving things to good purpose!"

All three sisters gaped at her, jaws dropped, eyes huge.

"I am flattered to be deemed redoubtable, Lizzie, but I am in complete ignorance as to your good purpose," said Mary. "Pray tell me what is amiss. Something is."

"The Children of Jesus — Children of Satan, Parmenter calls them! — are behaving worse than savages. My servants are at their wits' end, and if the four of us do not set them an example, I am going to be looking for some dozens of new servants, starting with a butler!" said Elizabeth between her teeth.

"Oh, dear!" whimpered Kitty, paling. "I do not have any dresses made of mattress ticking, Lizzie."

"Jane, if you cry, I *swear* I'll smack you! And harder than Caroline Bingley smacks your darling little Arthur, horrid child that he is! Meet me at the main entrance to the ballroom in half an hour, dressed for *war*."

"I do believe that Lizzie exited in a puff of smoke," said Mary, scenting a challenge and feeling hugely invigorated. "Well, girls, don't dither! Kitty, if you have nothing you paid less than two hundred guineas for, I suggest you borrow a dress from one of the below-stairs maids. I'd give you something of mine, but it would trip you up."

Jane had leaped to her feet, looking terrified. "I want to cry, but I dare not!" she said on a wail.

"Good!" said Mary with satisfaction. "Kitty, move yourself!"

Elizabeth was waiting, laden with starched white aprons and four whippy canes. Face like flint, she doled three of the canes out and kept one. "I hope these will be for show only," she said, removing a large key from the pocket of a voluminous apron Kitty had last seen on Mrs Thorpe, the under-housekeeper. "Put on an apron, please. A party of footmen is coming with dust shovels, brushes, scrubbing brushes, rags, buckets of soapy water and mops — at least, they had better be coming! From what Parmenter says, everything from food to faeces is decorating the walls and floor inside. Mary, I am your commanding officer in this sortie, is that understood?"

"Yes, Lizzie," said Mary, utterly cowed.

"Then let us proceed." Elizabeth inserted the key in the lock, turned it, and opened the door.

A distinct odour of excrement assailed their nostrils, but too little time had passed for the food detritus to spoil, a mercy. What looked like a large number of brown-wrapped bundles were sliding and skating on the polished hardwood floor, kept glossy for dancing. None of the bundles took any notice of this influx of women, which gave Elizabeth time to close and lock the door, then return the key to her pocket.

For a reason unknown to her, Parmenter had placed the extra-large dinner gong just inside this door; Fitz had brought it back from China, liking its exquisite bronze work, only to find that Parmenter would not be parted from his old gong, and "lost" the new one. When her eyes lighted upon it, Elizabeth smiled with genuine enjoyment, and brought her cane down on its chased surface.

BOOM! When the reverberations of that crashing roar died away, the ensuing silence was perfect. Every brown bundle was stopped in mid-action.

Elizabeth produced the wicked noise of a whippy cane hissing through the air and strode to the middle of the floor, careful not to tread in any suspicious matter.

"Take off your robes!" she thundered.

They hastened to shed their robes, revealing that Father Dominus had not believed in underwear. Or baths. Or rags for wiping the bottom. Their skins should have been whiter than milk, but instead were a dingy grey that had tidal marks around armpits and groin where they had sweated as they toiled.

Another key turned in the lock; in came a dozen manservants bearing the appurtenances necessary to clean the floor and walls.

"Thank you," said Elizabeth. "You may put them down — I will look after things here. Herbert, please assemble every tin bath Pemberley possesses — if there are not enough, borrow more from Pemberley village. Make sure when the time comes that the laundry can supply sufficient hot water to half-fill them. With that I want the Paris soap, sponges, and soft scrubbing brushes." She turned from the wooden-faced Herbert to an equally expressionless Thomas. "Thomas, I want someone driving a fast cart to go into Macclesfield immediately. He is to buy thirty pairs of under-drawers, trousers, shirts and jackets to fit a ten-year-old boy. Also twenty pairs of under-drawers, petticoats, dresses and jackets to fit a ten-year-old girl. Shoes can wait. I want the clothing back here yesterday, please."

How true it is, thought Elizabeth, keeping her face stern, that human beings stripped of their clothes feel hideously vulnerable. The horrible little beasts of a moment ago are now clay ready for moulding. She made the cane hiss again.

"Now Miss Mary, Miss Kitty and Miss Jane are going to show you how to clean and wash a floor. Miss Mary will take fifteen boys, Miss Kitty fifteen girls, and Miss Jane those left over. You will have to do the counting, ladies, as the children cannot. I want to supervise everybody, but I need an assistant. Camille, come here, please. *Quickly!*"

Mary made short work of counting her fifteen boys, and

Kitty, relieved that she had inherited girls, was not slow to follow; only Jane dithered until she received a minatory look.

"What do you call the yellow water that comes out of your body, Camille?" she asked.

"Wees, Miss — Miss —"

"Miss Lizzie. And what do you call the brown sausages that come out of your body?"

"Poohs, Miss Lizzie."

"Thank you." Elizabeth straightened. "Attention!" she bawled, sounding so like Miss Sackbutt of Meryton schooldays that her sisters jumped and shivered. "Camille, push that little chair with the hole in its seat over here, please."

"Now I happen to know," she hollered, "that Father Dominus would never have permitted you to wee and pooh all over his caves! So why are you treating this beautiful room with less respect? This is called a commode chair, and beneath the hole in its seat is a chamber pot for wees and poohs. In future you will use my commode chairs — and keep them spotlessly clean! If you do not, I will rub your nose in your own wees and poohs! *After* I have given you six cuts with this cane! Do you understand?"

Every grimy head nodded.

"Splendid! In future these commode chairs will be put outside on the terrace, where they will be sheltered if it rains. You will have privacy for your motions. In the meantime, you are going to clean this room of the food, wees and poohs. Miss Mary, Miss Kitty and Miss Jane will show her group how to do this, and it will be done properly. Dust shovels first to scoop up the solids, then we scrub, wipe, and mop. *Hop to it!*"

While that went on, Elizabeth removed the brown habits to the terrace, and instructed Herbert to have them taken away and burned. The commode chairs went out under shelter, after which the commanding officer talked to Camille about food.

The Pemberley chef had supervised the children's menu himself — a mistake. Therese had cooked for over fifty people, but her only instructor had been Father Dominus. Whereas the tyrant in the Pemberley kitchen had a fit of the vapours if one of his sauces was too buttery — or, worse, not buttery enough. Elizabeth sent for Mrs Parmenter.

"Use one of the under-cooks capable of making plain food," she instructed. "Absolutely no wine, exotic herbs or any other flavouring that alters taste. Roast meats, stews, soups, a little chicken to introduce them to something other than red meat. For dessert, tarts, puddings, jellies. Plain bread, and plenty of it. Confine foods like eggs and bacon to breakfast. And cut it all up for the time being. These poor children cannot use a knife and fork, they are used to a spoon. Give them small beer to drink, it is what they are used to."

All of which was as nothing compared to giving each child a bath. Elizabeth deliberately chose one of the smallest children to go first; a boy named William who looked about four years old.

"Oh, he's adorable!" Jane whispered, eyes brimming. "Such a dear little man!"

"I'm glad you like him. You may have the honour of giving William his first bath," said Elizabeth.

By the time the hot water reached the ballroom it was an ideal temperature for a bath, not far above lukewarm. The cakes of soap came from Paris and were perfumed• with jasmine; the sponges came from the Red Sea and produced a deliciously tickling trickle of water down the spine. Well aproned, sure of William's pleasure, Jane picked him up and popped him into the shallow tin bath.

That was the end of peace. William let out a screech of outrage, sank his teeth into the edge of Jane's hand, and proved he could walk on water.

"Mary, I think Jane needs help," said Elizabeth.

"No, I do not!" growled Jane, jaws clenched. "I'll beat the little monster yet!" *Smack!* Down came Jane's hand on William's flank. "Now sit in the water and be still, you imp of Satan!"

By this time Mary was engaged in her own struggle with Timmy, and Kitty was discovering that girls were equally opposed to being assaulted by soap-and-water. Nothing daunted, Elizabeth grabbed Camille by one arm and threw her into a vacant bath, brush ready to scrub away eleven years of accumulated dirt.

Mrs Thorpe, who had stayed to witness with her own eyes Mrs Darcy conquer, drummed up a dozen hefty maids to assist, and gradually, fighting, screaming, resisting all the way, the forty-five Children of Jesus had their first bath. By the time it was over and the howling children were wrapped in huckaback towels, every grown woman was soaked to the skin.

Now remained the horror of teaching the children how to put on under-drawers, let alone the other layers of clothing society demanded. They wanted their robes, and wept for them desolately, but the caves were a thing of the past, and so were their robes.

Foreseeing trouble, Elizabeth took William and showed him how to pull down his under-drawers and trousers (they swam on him) before sitting on a commode, and gave the boys a dispensation to go out into the garden and wee there. This meant the girls felt discriminated against, which necessitated a lecture on having to sit to wee while boys didn't.

"Oh," groaned a sopping Elizabeth as she lay back in a chair in the Pink Parlour and drank her tea thirstily. "Only now do I understand how privileged we are. We bear however many children God ordains, but we hand them over to nurserymaids and see nothing of their bad side, let alone deal with wees and poohs."

"Yes, today should teach us what it is like to rear children without servants," said Mary, munching cake.

"Though," said Kitty, "the Children of Jesus are a special case, not so? They have never been trained in any way, whereas I imagine that even the poorest mother must organise herself to deal with her situation more comfortably than the kind of thing we saw today. I would think that her older children must be put to helping her with the younger and the babies."

"Well said, Kitty!" Mary poured herself more tea.

"And well done, girls," said Elizabeth warmly. "Our labours are not yet done, but today was the worst. By the time that the twenty nursemaids I have asked Matthew to find arrive here, we will have instilled some of the daily routines into our charges." She got to her feet. "Tea came first, but now I am going to go to my room, lie down, take a nap, and dress for dinner. *After* a bath!"

"Never say that word to me again!" cried Jane with a shudder. "To think that I actually smacked a child!"

"Yes, you'll hurt long after he doesn't," said Mary wickedly.

Sherry or madeira in the Rubens Room restored the ladies to some semblance of themselves; Kitty's recounting of events in the ballroom revealed that she was no mean raconteuse, and had the gentlemen doubled over with laughter.

"Lizzie alone seemed to have some idea of what was to come," Kitty ended, looking down at her shell-pink lace gown with fervent love. "She told me to wear a dress of mattress ticking! And after ten minutes in the ballroom, I swear I wished I owned one! As it was, I wore an awful old thing of beige cambric, then sent it to be burned. 'Twas good for nought else, I assure you."

"It is clear to me," said Mary, "that the children cannot be accommodated in the ballroom for much longer. It pleases me that their spirits have not been broken, and they mouth 'light of Lucifer' and 'the dark of God' like meaningless cant, so they were never drilled in Cosmogenesis. However, that is not what I wished to say, which is that until an orphanage can be built they have to be put somewhere suitable. I am not foolish enough to think that such things grow overnight, like toadstools. Angus, you are a man of eminent good sense. What do you suggest?"

"I have no suggestions," he said, startled.

"Fitz, you are an MP and therefore must know *something*. What do you suggest?"

"That we utilise Hemmings, since my lease on the property still has months to run. I've told Matthew to engage carpenters to put tiered beds in three of the bedrooms — one for the girls, two for the boys. Which leaves three bedrooms for the nursemaids, if you will consent to engaging a mere nine instead of twenty. The large drawing room will make a good schoolroom, the small one a staff room. The dining room will seat all the children on benches at refectory tables. The two teachers can live in the cottage, the general servants in the attic. And so on, and so forth."

"Brilliant, Papa," said Charlie, grinning.

"Does this mean you'll build the orphanage, Fitz?" Angus asked slyly, while the ladies listened breathless.

"Do I have any choice? But I shall bludgeon Charles Bingley into contributing, never fear! I've found eight acres of quite unfarmable land just this side of Buxton, close enough to halfway between here and Bingley Hall. However, we'll cast our net wide enough to catch fifty-three more children, and build to house one hundred in all." He coughed, looked at the ladies with amusement and apology. "Under ordinary circumstances I would retain my innate scepticism about such a large institution — that its staff would embezzle, perhaps also ill-treat the children. But with our ladies supervising every sneeze and snuffle, I doubt anyone will get away with much."

"That is splendid news, Fitz," said Mary, very pleased.

"As you say, Mary, an MP has to be good for *something*."

Angus saw nothing of Mary for the next three days; all her time was given up to the children, since even nine nursemaids proved hard to find at such short notice.

It isn't fair, he told himself; in the days when she lived in Hertford, I saw more of her than I have here at Pemberley. Some kind of task always has first call on her time, including these wretched children — and her without a maternal bone in her entire body! Jane does it melting with sensibility, Kitty does it because she is easily dominated, and Elizabeth does it because, of all of them, she is the true mother. But Mary does it from that huge sense of duty — does love enter into her life at all? At this moment I tend to think it does not. She is kind, but not loving.

Prey to the blue devils and atypically morose, he was jerked out of what was threatening to become a mire of self-pity by the appearance of his beloved, who doffed her apron and demanded that he take her for an airing.

"For I am tired of wees and poohs," she declared as they left the house in the direction of Mary's favourite glade, which happened to be Elizabeth's favourite as well.

"Infantile talk is depressing," he said.

"So is human waste," she answered tartly, and ground her teeth. "I find myself more attuned to the prospect of educating them in literacy and numeracy than in weeing and washing. How can they shun anything as delightful as water?"

"You find it delightful because your nurse gave you your first bath before you could remember," he said, spirits soaring just to be with her.

"They must commence their schooling as soon as possible. I believe that there is a warehouse in Manchester that sells desks, slates, slate pencils, chalk, blackboards, copybooks and the like." She stuck out her chin and looked militant. "Now that I don't have to pay to have my book published, I have plenty of money — yes, I have abandoned all thought of writing a book. I'll crawl before I can walk, and what better place to crawl in than a schoolroom? One of the most disgraceful aspects of childhood at Longbourn was Papa's reluctance to see us well-educated. So we went to the Meryton school to learn reading, writing and arithmetic, but after that we were not given a governess. Had we, then Kitty and Lydia might not have turned out so wild, or I so narrow. The daughters of gentlemen *should* have a governess. Instead, Papa spent the money on his library, Mama's clothes, and our dinner table."

Head whirling, Angus fixed on the most pertinent fact among these confidences. "May I ask you a question, Mary?"

"Of course you may."

"Pay for your publication? Is that what you were planning to do when you finished your book?"

"Yes. I knew it was going to cost many thousands — almost all that I had, in fact."

"Mary, you silly chicken! First of all, if a publisher knows you are determined to pay to have a book published, then he will take you for every penny you have. But you must *never* pay to have a book published! If it's worth reading, a publisher will be willing to incur the expense of publication himself. In effect, he takes a gamble on the author — that the book will attract enough readers to make a profit. If it does make a profit, he will pay you what is called a royalty on each copy sold. The royalty is usually a small percentage of the book's price." He glared at her. "Oh, you are a silly chicken! Do you truly mean that you scrimped and pinched your pennies on your travels because of your book?"

A delicious pinkness had suffused her cheeks; she hung her head, apparently willing to be apostrophised as a silly chicken. "I wanted it published," she said gruffly.

"And nearly got yourself murdered! I could shake you!"

"Pray do not be angry!"

He waved his hands about wildly. "No, I am not angry! Well, a wee bit — but only a wee bit. Och, Mary, you would drive a sane and sober man to madness and the bottle!"

The sight of Angus in such straits was quite fascinating, but it also caused her to experience a sudden empty panic in her middle regions — what if one day she angered him so much he walked away? She gulped, backed away from the thought. "Would you be able to drive me into Manchester for the schoolroom needs?" she asked.

"Of course, but not tomorrow. In case you had forgotten, we bury poor Ned Skinner Darcy tomorrow."

"No, I had not forgotten," she said, voice low. "Oh, and we made Fitz and Charlie laugh!"

"And thereby did them a very good turn. Death is always in our midst, Mary, you know that. Anything that lightens grief, even for a moment, is a blessing. While Ned has lain waiting for the vindication he couldn't have in life, you and your sisters have dealt with those he saved. He could not do aught else than applaud your kindness and hard work. In one way, they are *his* children."

"Yes, you are right."

They walked on in silence as far as the glade, where the sun, directly overhead, turned the water in the little brook to solid gold save for the diamonds of its tumbles.

Mary gasped. "Angus, I have just thought of something!"

"What?" he asked warily.

"Father Dominus told me that he had a hoard of bars of gold. I know the caves have collapsed, but do you think you could look for the gold? Imagine how many orphanages it would build."

"Not as many as you think," he said prosaically. "Besides, the old villain must have stolen it from the government. Gold is marked on each ingot — that's the proper name for a bar of gold — with the brand of its owner, and that owner is almost inevitably the government."

"No, he said he melted it down from coins and jewellery that had been entrusted to him by some far bigger villain. He melted it down and poured it into ingots himself. More than that I do not know, save that it definitely was acquired by nefarious means."

"I think he was bamming you."

"He said each ingot weighed ten pounds."

"Which, being gold, isn't very big in size. Gold is hugely

heavy, Mary. Ten pounds of it would be nowhere near the size of a house brick, I assure you."

"Please, Angus, please! Promise me that you'll look!"

How could he refuse? "Very well, I promise. But don't hope, Mary. Charlie, Fitz and I are going back to see if there's been a fresh subsidence, and to look at the hill itself. If we find any gold, rest assured that we'll claim it on behalf of the Children of Jesus. Who, I suspect, would be entitled to a large percentage of any treasure-trove. If, that is, it can be proven that the real owner is not the government."

Her face took on a martial expression. "Oh, no, the children cannot have it! They'd spend it on the wrong things, like any poor people gifted with unexpected fortune. It will build orphanages." Her chest heaved on an ecstatic sigh. "Just fancy, Angus! Perhaps my incarceration had a divine purpose — to unearth ill-gotten gold and set it to work on gifting the poor with the things that really matter — health and education."

"She is determined," Angus said to Fitz after Ned Skinner Darcy was laid in his resting place.

"If such a treasure exists, Angus, Father Dominus didn't earn it from selling a cure for impotence, no matter how successful it was. The gold may be ill-gotten, but from where or from whom? The government does ship consignments of gold coins around the country, but none has been plundered that I or any other MP remembers. Which is why I doubt the story. Except that I know of one man who might have amassed so much, and all of it ill-gotten. A man long dead who, as far as I know, had no association with Father Dominus. Yet it's true that when that man died, his ill-gotten gains could not be found anywhere, apart from precious stones prised out of jewellery."

Fitz's face bore a look that forbade questions — a pity. Who did Fitz know had that kind of mentality? For he spoke as if he had known the man personally. As many layers as French pastry, that was Fitz. Who had changed radically, but for the better.

When he informed Angus that he would refuse the prime ministership, Angus was staggered.

"Fitz, you wanted it heart and soul!" he cried.

"Yes, but that was before all this. Some secrets I will carry to my grave, though I've come to love and esteem you greatly over this summer, and hope that we'll be brothers-in-law. We Darcys have been pristine of reputation, and we'll go on being pristine. Were I prime minister, I might be tempted to use my powers in unscrupulous ways. Well, I don't choose to walk down that road. I'll refuse to contend for the post, and so I have written to the men supporting my candidacy. I'm sorry if I've misled you, my dear Angus, but I've misled no one more than I have myself."

"Yes, I understand, Fitz."

That had been several days ago. Now it was gold, thanks to Mary, in her element driving back and forth to Macclesfield after teachers and nursemaids.

Now that they knew about the existence of the waterfall, which Fitz remembered seeing when out hunting deer, it was easier to understand how Father Dominus had kept the

Children of Jesus away from prying eyes. Hardly one in a thousand Englishmen could swim, so pools and waterfalls were phenomena to be admired at a distance, even by poets, writers, painters and other peculiar folk. Charlie was too slight to ride Jupiter, so his father had taken the animal, which accepted him with pleasure. Probably, Charlie thought, Ned and Papa shared some smell, or sat in the saddle the same way despite the weight difference. Who knew the mysteries of animals?

There were relics of the occupants in among the chaos of rocks and boulders: bottles, tins, labels floating on the placid surface of the pool. They ventured inside, but Fitz didn't want to see the spot where Ned had lain for so many hours, so they kept away from it.

Saddest discovery of all lay in a cave branching off the laboratory. Familiarity with the enormous masses of collapsed stone had imbued all three men with confidence when moving among the chaos; there seemed to be little chance, a week and more after the explosion, of further subsidence, especially given the continued dry weather — even in Manchester it was not raining.

A smell of decay had perfused the air inside the laboratory, a smell that stimulated Angus to explore the wall beyond the fire alcove more closely than anyone had thus far. Behind a boulder he found a tunnel that had not collapsed; heedless of shouted warnings from Fitz and Charlie, he entered it. Ten feet farther on it opened into what had been yet another huge cavern, now mostly obliterated. Here the stench was almost intolerable, emanating from the carcasses of donkeys.

Fitz's and Charlie's curiosity had overcome their caution, but none of the three wanted to linger there.

"The poor things died of injuries, or were partly buried," Angus said. "Many more probably lie completely covered."

"At least it tells us how Father Dominus brought in his supplies," Fitz said, leading the way back to the laboratory. "A donkey train! Given that a number must have had to carry various donkey edibles, I wonder how many beasts Father Dominus had?"

"Fifty at least," said Angus. "One for each person, with a few more for good measure. It would be interesting to know whereabouts he shopped. I'll set enquiries afoot, if only to gratify my own curiosity. My money is on Manchester."

"Did the children drive them?" Charlie asked.

"Occasionally, perhaps, if a few were used to deliver drugs, but from what Mary has said, I imagine Brother Jerome usually managed the business alone by stringing them together."

"Mary is rather close-mouthed about her experience," Fitz said, frowning.

"Yes, she is." Angus extinguished his torch and walked out into the fresh air. "I know not how her mind works, I confess. Most females are agog to tell of their adventures down to the very smallest detail, but she seems not to trust that our reactions will reflect her own standpoint. I suspect this may have something to do with a childhood and young womanhood spent in a repressive atmosphere."

"Angus, I congratulate you!" Charlie cried, beaming. "To have read that aright, you must love her very much indeed.

Mary's papa was the only male influence in her life during Longbourn days, and he detested her. I believe the result of that is her mistrust of men. She's so intelligent, you see, that it goes against her grain to accept the male sex as superior."

All of this philosophising lay too far from Fitz's heart to bear; he gave a snort and said, "If the old man hid any gold here, it's buried for time immemorial. I suggest we climb the hill and see what else came down."

There were dimples and hollows in the surface of the hill where something underneath had collapsed, but as they ascended higher they became aware of stout bushes growing where bushes would not have grown had Nature done the planting.

"Look, Papa," said Charlie, uprooting a bush. "There's a roundish hole that goes far down, getting narrower."

"Ventilation wells," said Fitz. "The amount of light one of these admits would be negligible."

The higher they ascended, the less evidence of subsidence they encountered until, near the hill's rocky crown, there were no dents or dimples in the ground, though the bushes still grew to conceal holes. Wedged in one they had found the carcass of a sheep, and decided that Father Dominus had patrolled regularly to remove ovine bodies before shepherds found them. Which may have given the hill a bad name among shepherds, and caused them to avoid it as grazing for their flocks.

"I don't understand," said Angus as they paused beside a bush. "All he had were fifty-odd children, yet under here he might have housed a thousand, given the number of ventilation wells. Why bother with these upper caverns, or are they mere tunnels? If they're tunnels, he had some reason to keep going."

"We'll never know what drove him, Angus," Fitz said with a sigh. "We don't even know how long he suffered his madness beyond what he told Mary about an enlightenment in his thirty-fifth year. Certainly he retained his skills as an apothecary, and they were considerable, else his nostrums would not have worked, and we know they did. I believe Mary has not told us everything she knows about Father Dominus — look at how long it took her to speak about the possibility that he had hoarded gold. Somewhere during his life he must have had a business or a shop, and at a different time in his life he must have had access to gold — if Mary is to be believed."

"No!" snapped Angus. "If Father Dominus is to be believed!"

"I cry pardon."

"It is rather delicious to speculate on the old boy's life," said Charlie, playing peacemaker. "What if at one time he did have an apothecary's shop, a wife, children? And if so, what has happened to them? Did they die in some epidemic, leaving him gone mad?" He giggled. "It would make a good three-volume novel."

"Perhaps they're still alive, and wondering whatever happened to their dear papa," said Angus, grinning.

Charlie pulled out the last bush on the hill. "I'm going down to have a look," he said after peering into the hole. "This one is wider, I'll fit."

"Not without rope and torches," said Fitz.

"Not at all!" Angus cried.

But Charlie was already loping down the hill.

"Fitz, you must stop him!"

The fine dark eyes looked ironic. "You know, Angus, it will do you good to father a few children. I'm sure Mary is up to the task, so don't let her wither on the vine, please. Lady Catherine de Bourgh had Anne when she was forty-five. I grant you that Anne was no recommendation for a late child, but she did show it is — er — possible. Mary is barely thirty-nine."

Face crimson, Angus spluttered out an incoherent reply that had Fitz laughing.

"What I'm saying, my friend, is that sometimes it is necessary to let go the leading-strings, no matter how your heart cries out against it. I'll let Charlie explore knowing the dangers, just stand up here myself praying to every god I know."

"Then I'll pray too."

Back came Charlie leading Jupiter, laden with rope, torches, bags. "Papa, this beautiful animal is game for anything! I wish I rode heavier! Then you wouldn't have him. Such a gentle nature!"

"You'll never have him, Charlie. He's my last link to Ned."

Fitz tied one end of a long rope around his waist with Angus three feet in front of him; the two men took the strain as Charlie descended into the depths holding a torch and a tinder box. At thirty feet the rope suddenly slackened; Charlie was on the floor of the cave, and safe thus far.

"Not too deep!" came his voice, thin but audible. "It's the second-to-last cave, quite small. I think it must have been

Father Dominus's room — it has a table, a chair, a desk, another chair, and a bed. Like a monk's cell, not even a rush mat on the floor. There are two openings, almost opposite each other. One's sense of direction is uncertain down here, but I'll look into the unscreened opening first."

"Charlie, be careful!" was wrenched from Fitz.

The two men waited what seemed an eternity.

"It's just a tunnel leading downhill," came Charlie's voice at last. "The other is curtained off with black velvet from above the top of the aperture — the material drags on the floor, as if he wanted to keep all light out. I'm going in."

"The nadir of parenthood," Fitz said between his teeth. "Take heed, Angus. No one can escape it."

They waited then, speechless, ears straining for Charlie's voice, dreading a vast rumble.

"I say, Papa, it's amazing! Father Dominus's temple to his god, I think. Utterly black. Haul me up!"

The Charlie who emerged from the hole was covered in dust and cobwebs, and minus his torch and tinder box, left below. He was smiling from ear to ear. "Papa, Angus, I've found Mary's gold! The temple cave was small and absolutely round — it was a great help to be a classical scholar, for it leads me to think that he interpreted this particular cavern mystically. Round like a navel stone or a Roman temple to a numinous god, with its altar in the exact centre, and round too. It was covered with a black velvet cloth and it consisted of innumerable little bars of gold. An offering to his Cosmogenic god, I suppose."

He reached into his shirt and withdrew a small brick which glittered with that magical glow only pure gold can achieve: fire without fire, heat without heat, light without light. "See? Ten pounds is about right," he said, thrilled with himself. "And not a government mark to be seen! Or any other mark, for that matter."

They sat down, both to recover from the strain of waiting for Charlie, and the shock of learning that Father Dominus had told Mary the truth.

"How many of these bricks are there?" Angus asked.

"Impossible to tell without dismantling the altar — is it hollow, or packed solid? He had made it round by putting each bar at an angle, so I hazard a guess that it's solid save for the natural spaces this way of stacking produces," said Charlie, eyes bright. "The whole altar measures about three feet in diameter, and three feet in height. What an offering!"

"Better that, than one of his children," said Angus grimly.

"We have to think this thing through," said Fitz, drawing a circle in a patch of dust with a stick. "First of all, we cannot make this find public, either now or at any time in the future. I will approach the government, of which I am a member until such time as Parliament goes into session." He scowled. "That means we have to move the gold to Pemberley ourselves. Interesting, that lead has been mined in the Peak District for centuries! If we can lift it out of the temple chamber and wrap it securely on sleds, we can pretend it's a hoard of lead from Father Dominus's failed experiments to alchemise it into gold. Lead is valuable enough that it will seem good sense on our parts to garnish it on behalf of the Children of Jesus. We will simply say that it was already wrapped in job-lots, and we preferred to get it out of the caves ourselves for fear of more collapses."

"Thus appearing responsible citizens," said Angus with a grin.

"Quite. I'll have the Pemberley carpenters make two sleds — they ought to suffice, given the dimensions of the altar. A pity the donkeys were killed. They would have been ideal." Fitz turned to his son. "I am afraid you have to go back down the hole at this moment, Charlie. Would I fit?"

"I think so, but Angus definitely not."

"Angus very definitely not! Someone has to remain up here to haul us out. Jupiter can do the work, but not without guidance. You and I are going down to count the number of ingots. On that figure depends the extent of our transportation."

It was a gruelling task for two men not used to manual labour, but being together was a mental fillip; they could urge each other on, twit each other when one flagged, make a joke out of a trembling limb or eyes blinded by sweat.

"One thousand and twenty-three ingots," said Fitz, lying flat out on the ground looking up at the twilit sky wherein Venus shone as Evening Star, cold, pure, indifferent. "Christ, I am a broken reed! No work for a man of fifty, let alone a sedentary one. I will ache for weeks."

"And I for months," said Charlie with a groan.

"We availed ourselves of a pair of scales in the old man's cell and discovered that one ingot weighs a full ten pounds avoirdupois. For what reason I know not, Father Dominus chose not to use troy weight, which is usual for precious metals — only twelve ounces to the pound. At two thousand, two hundred and forty pounds avoirdupois to the ton, we have about four and a half tons of gold down there."

Charlie sat up with a jolt. "Heavens, Papa, that means we have shifted over two tons each!"

"A mere matter of feet, and not the bottom layer," said Fitz austerely. He looked at Angus. "Had we been forced to work in torchlight, it would have been intolerable, but we found two extraordinary lamps in Dominus's cell, also a barrel of some kind of oil that fuels them. Mary is right when she says his mind was first-rate. I've seen nothing like them anywhere. It may be, Angus, that your company could patent and manufacture them if we bring one up after we're done."

"I think the patent should be awarded to the Children of Jesus," Angus said.

"No, they will have all the gold except for a reward payable to Mary. Take it, Angus! Otherwise I'll break both lamps and no one will benefit."

"Then why not Charles Bingley?"

"It's in my gift," Fitz said royally, "and it goes to you."

I will never break him of it! thought Angus. No one will. "Very well, and I thank you," he said.

"Four sleds," said Charlie, interrupting. "We'll need some donkeys, not to pull the sleds, but to brake them."

"How do you know about sleds, Fitz?" asked Angus.

"They're used in Bristol, where the quays are hollow from warehouses beneath. The load is better distributed on a sled's runners than on the four points where a wagon's wheels touch the ground. Runners will help getting the load downhill too, where the subsidences are greater."

"I take it we say nothing to the ladies?" Angus asked.

"Not even a hint of the most obscure kind."

"But we will have help loading the wrapped packages onto the sleds?" Charlie asked anxiously.

"Yes, but only Pemberley men, and the most trusted. We'll need a winch to bring the parcels up from the chamber, and a basket small enough to pass through the ventilation well without sticking. The basket will have to be perfectly balanced, and equipped with little wheels. That will enable us to wrap the ingots in it, then wheel it through into Dominus's cell. Charlie, make sure you bring plenty of gloves when we return. Each package will have to be well-roped besides well-wrapped."

"What a mind you have, Papa!" said Charlie. "Every detail."

Fitz's rare smile flashed out. "Why do you think it was so easy for an obscure MP from Derbyshire to aspire to the prime ministership? Few men are willing to deal with the minutiae, and that is a flaw in character."

"When do we begin this Herculean task?" Angus asked, rather ashamed that his muscular build negated his sharing in it.

"Today is Wednesday. Next Monday, if the sleds can be made and the donkeys located by then. We will hope to complete it in five days."

* * *

When they set off down the hill, Charlie let Angus lead Jupiter and deliberately fell behind to be private with his father.

"Papa, is this Grandfather's loot?" he asked.

"I imagine so."

"How then did Father Dominus lay hands on it?"

"A question I suspect Mary could answer, at least partially, but chooses not to. Miriam Matcham's statement to the Sheffield authorities refers to a Father Dominus who supplied poisons and an abortifacient to her — he would have been ideal for an abbess. Since her mother inherited the brothel from Harold Darcy, it seems likely that Father Dominus originally belonged to Harold Darcy. Perhaps he was a trusted confederate. Certainly over the years Harold must have accumulated huge quantities of gold jewellery and coins, none of which ever came to light, though the precious stones did — he had a little cask full of loose but faceted rubies, emeralds, diamonds and sapphires. No pearls were ever found, or semi-precious stones. Given Dominus's skills, it may be that he was commissioned to melt down the gold. Still, it's all conjecture."

"Good conjecture, Papa. I wonder why Mary keeps his secret?"

"If you ask her, she may tell you, but she will never confide in me. As she sees it, I treated her with contempt, and I did."

"In the old days she would have told me, but not now. I am too close to you," said Charlie ruefully. "There is a kind of invisible barrier between men and women, isn't there?"

"Yes, alas." Uncomfortable at the turn the conversation had taken, Fitz went elsewhere. "What we do know is that the old man never tried to exchange any of the gold for money, or otherwise betrayed his whereabouts to Harold Darcy."

"What a shock it must have been to Grandfather!"

"That too we may be sure of. Around my twelfth birthday there was a marked change in my father. He became wilder, much angrier, cruel to Mama and to the staff. Unpardonable!"

"Papa, your childhood was hideous!" Charlie blurted. "I am so sorry!"

"That was no excuse for my being so hard on you, my son. I have more to apologise for by far than you."

"No, Papa. Let's call it equal, and begin again."

"That is a deal, Charlie," said Fitz huskily. "Now only remains to mend my fences with your mother."

The gold was removed over the course of five days with remarkably little fuss. It never occurred to Pemberley's faithful retainers to question their master's story of four and a half tons of lead, nor would it have occurred to the most naive among them that Fitzwilliam Darcy and his only son were capable of the hard labour involved in lifting, wrapping and roping one hundred pounds many times over. No glint of gold showed through a rent in the light canvas, nor did any parcel fall apart while being manhandled. After some rather exhilarating rushes down the hillside, the contents of the sleds were loaded into wagons and so to Pemberley, where they sat in the big "safe house" — a stone barn Fitz used to store items of value. In the fullness of time several wagons conveyed the parcels to London and a curious destination — the Tower.

The public caves had been reopened for inspection; once more tourists could wonder at the maw of The Peak cavern, wander inside to see the rope-maker's walk and the ancient houses that had, from time to time, sheltered the people of Castleton from unusually remorseless weather, or, in lawless times, bands of marauders.

Much to Elizabeth's delight, Fitz had ordained that his girls should in future dine with the family, and actually spent a little time with them. Cathy's tendency to play pranks dwindled, Susie learned to hold up one end of a conversation without turning the colour of a beet, and Anne displayed an eager interest in all matters political and European. Georgie tried very hard to conduct herself like a lady, and had consented to having her nails painted with bitter aloes — it tasted vile — while heroically managing not to wash the hideous remedy off.

"What happened between Susie, Anne and Charlie's tutor?" Fitz asked his wife, frowning direfully.

"Absolutely nothing, except that they fancied themselves in love with him. I think that shows good taste," Elizabeth said tranquilly. "He gave them no encouragement, I assure you."

"And Georgie?"

"Actually rather looking forward to her London season now that Kitty has painted alluring pictures for her delectation. She's such a beautiful girl that she'll take magnificently if she loses her Maryisms, which Kitty assures me she will. Witness her struggle to conquer the nail biting."

"It has been a terrible summer," he said.

"Yes. But we've come through it, Fitz, and that's the main thing. I wish I had known that you and Ned were brothers."

"I would have told you, Elizabeth, could I."

"He always reminded me of a huge black dog guarding you from all comers."

"He filled that role, certainly. Many others too. I loved him." He looked directly at her, dark eyes on hers. "But not as much as I love you."

"No, not more. Just — differently. But why did you stop telling me you loved me after Cathy was born? You shut me out of your life. It wasn't my fault that I could give you no son other than Charlie, or that he was so unsatisfactory. Still, you don't find him unsatisfactory now, do you?"

"No better son could any man have than Charlie. He's a perfect fusion of you and me. And it's true I shut you out of my life, but only because you shut me out of yours."

"Yes, I did. But why did you shut me out?"

"Oh, I was so wearied by your endless mockery of me! The quips and smart remarks, the poking sly fun — you couldn't forgive it in Caroline Bingley when she denigrated you, yet you denigrated me. It seemed I only had to open my mouth, to be ribbed for my pompousness or my hauteur — things that are innate, for better or worse. But that was nothing compared to your lack of genuine enthusiasm for married life. I felt as if I made love to a marble statue! You didn't return my kisses, my caresses — I could feel you change into that thing of stone the moment I entered your bed. You gave me the impression that you loathed being touched. I would gladly have kept trying for a son, but after Cathy I could bear no more of it."

She was aware of a tremor as fine as a cat's purr, swallowed painfully, looked not at him but out the window of her sitting room, though it was long after dark and she could see nothing save the dancing reflections of candles. Oh, how *sure* she had always been that she could lighten Fitz's nature, make him see how ridiculous he could be, with his icy demeanour and his stiffness. Only over this last year had she given up on poking gentle fun at his rigidity, and that had been from anger and disgust. But now she finally understood everything there was to know about leopards and their spots. Fitz would *never* be able to laugh at himself! He was too obsessed with the dignity of a Darcy. Charlie might succeed in breaking Fitz's ice, but she never would. Her touch was too remorseless, her sense of humour too irresistible. As for his other accusation — what could she say to defend herself?

"I have nothing to say. I concede defeat," she said.

"Elizabeth, that isn't enough! Unless you speak, we can never heal the rift between us! Once, a long time ago, when Jane was so ill after the birth of Robert, she said in her delirium that it was only after you saw the glories of Pemberley that you changed your mind about accepting me."

"Oh, that one, unguarded remark!" she cried, pressing her hands to burning cheeks. "Even Jane doesn't know when I'm funning! I didn't mean it the way it sounded, and had no idea Jane took it so seriously." She walked on her knees from her chair to his, and gazed at him with soft, glowing eyes. "Fitz, I did fall in love with you, but not because of Pemberley! I fell in love with your generosity, your kindness, your — your *patience*!"

Looking down at her, he knew himself lost all over again in those lambent eyes, that wonderful lush mouth. "I wish I could believe you, Elizabeth, but the statue doesn't lie."

"Yes, it does." Perhaps if she didn't need to look at him, and that was far easier here at his feet, she could tell him. "I'll try to explain, Fitz, but don't make me look at you until I'm done. Please!"

He put one hand on her hair. "I promise. Tell me."

"I was utterly revolted by the act of love — it still revolts me! I found it cruel, animal, anything but an act of love! It left me physically hurt and spiritually bereft. The Fitz I love is not that man. He can't be that man! The humiliation, the degradation! I couldn't bear it, and that's why I turned into a statue. Eventually I prayed that you'd stop visiting me, and eventually you did stop. But somehow nothing was solved."

Fitz looked at the fire through a wall of tears. The one thing he had never dreamed of! That what to him was evidence of the strength of his passion appeared to her as a rape. They go into marriage so virginal that its fleshly side is an utter mystery. Yet, coming from that family, I didn't deem her so sheltered. The mother must have been a Lydia in her youth, and her daughters had all seemed anything but unaware of love's physical side.

"I suppose," he said, blinking the tears away, "that we men assume our wives will recover from the shock of the first time, and grow to enjoy what God really did intend to be highly enjoyable. But perhaps some women are too intelligent and too full of sensibility to recover. Women like you. I'm very sorry. But why did you never tell me, Elizabeth?"

"I didn't think that man would understand."

"Separating him from me,"

"You're many men, Fitz, with many secrets."

"Yes, I do have secrets. Some I'll tell you, but not all. Just rest assured that the ones I keep from you are not concerned with you in any way. Those I'll confide in Charlie, who is my heir and my blood son." He began to stroke her hair rhythmically, almost as if he didn't know what he did. "That man, as you call him, is absolutely a part of me! You can't separate him from the whole. I was an unfeeling brute, I can see that now, but from ignorance, Elizabeth, not from deliberation. I love you more than I did Ned, more than my son or my daughters. And now that I'm going onto the back benches, you'll have no rival in Westminster."

"Oh, Fitz!" She lifted her head and pulled his down to kiss him, slow and languorous. "I love you just as much."

"Which leaves us with the basic problem," he said, moving over in the chair so that she could squeeze in beside him. "Is it at all possible to breathe life into the statue? Can I be Pygmalion to your Galatea?"

"We must try," she said.

"It's probably a good thing that this state of affairs has lasted so long. I'm a man of fifty, and have far more control over my primal urges than a man of thirty. It's up to me to breathe life into you." He kissed her again, as he had done

431

during the halcyon days of their engagement. "You need something I'm not prone to give — tenderness."

"I have hopes for that man as well as for you, Fitz. We've all changed over the past year, from Mary to Charlie."

"Shall I come into your bed, then?"

"Yes, please." She heaved a sigh and put her head on his shoulder. "I have hopes for my own happiness, but I fear greatly for Mary's. If she weds Angus, married life will come as a shock to her." She giggled. "However, she's not as ignorant as I was. Do you know, Fitz, that when we gathered at Shelby Manor for Mama's funeral, she actually said to me that she wished Charles Bingley would plug it with a cork for Jane's sake? I was appalled! She was so pragmatic!"

"She'll walk all over poor Angus."

"I very much fear that you're right about that. Yes, she's changed in many ways, but she's still the one-sided, stubborn and determined creature she always was."

"Give thanks for one thing, Elizabeth. That Charlie told her she screeched. Think of the songs we have been spared!"

THIRTEEN

Refusing to act as a formal chairman, Fitz held a round table conference about the gold. Present were Elizabeth, Jane, Kitty, Mary, Angus, Charlie, Mr Matthew Spottiswoode and Fitz himself. He explained very carefully to the four ladies that each had a vote, that each lady's vote was the equal of a gentleman's, and that, since Mr Spottiswoode owned no vote, their votes therefore were in the majority: they could, if united, outvote the gentlemen four to three. This confused Jane and Kitty, but thrilled Elizabeth and Mary. It appeared, however, that despite refusing to act as a chairman, Fitz had every intention of conducting the meeting. He rapped a paperweight on the literally round table.

"Each orphanage will be known as a Children of Jesus orphanage, and we will be known as their Founders, with a capital F. Since we have an odd number of votes — seven — it's not necessary to have a formal Chairman Founder," Fitz announced.

Flutters and whispers broke out.

Fitz rapped the paperweight.

Silence fell.

"There are one thousand and twenty-three ingots of gold, each weighing ten pounds," Fitz said, rather like a schoolmaster. "To Matthew's and my surprise, we discovered that Father Dominus chose avoirdupois for his ingots, not troy weight, which is customary for precious metals. Therefore the ingots weigh a full sixteen ounces to the pound, instead of twelve ounces, which is troy weight. This increases their value by one-quarter or four ounces. A druggist as skilled as Father Dominus must have known what he was doing. My theory is that he cast an ingot of a weight no government would, and also of a portable weight. Even a child can carry ten pounds avoirdupois."

"He made the children carry it, you imply?" Mary asked.

"Within the caves, certainly." He waited for other remarks, then went on. "Because of her vast colonies and trade routes, our own Britain is the source of the gold for a number of European countries desirous of establishing a gold-based currency. They buy the gold from Britain."

"How do you pay for gold?" Charlie asked.

"With raw materials and other goods Britain needs but cannot produce. Coal we have aplenty, but our iron is running out, so are our supplies of steeling metals and copper. We cannot grow enough grain to feed the populace any more — the list is virtually endless. However, gold is in short supply too, though some is coming out of India and some other of the old East India Company countries. But that means that we

Founders around this table are in an excellent position, as it cannot be proved that *our* gold was ever government gold."

They were hanging on his every word; when he paused this time, no one spoke.

"I believe we can sell our gold to the Exchequer for six hundred thousand pounds, and no questions asked. It's worth far more."

Loud gasps went up; Charlie whooped.

"Very well, let us assume that we'll have six hundred thousand pounds in trust for the Children of Jesus orphanages," Fitz went on. He gave Mary a minatory glare. "And before you go off half-cocked, Mary, kindly hear me out. To spend money on the construction of an orphanage is one thing, but the cost of a building and its land doesn't mean we can build a hundred of them, or even half a hundred. Before even one additional institution can be contemplated, we must first arrive at the cost of keeping the original orphanage going. If one hundred children are to be properly fed and clothed, comfortably accommodated, adequately supervised, and satisfactorily educated, we will need three teachers and one headmistress, ten nursemaids and a matron, four cooks, and at least twenty general servants. Otherwise you'll have a typical Parish orphanage, in which the staff are too few, too poorly paid and too discontented to be fair or kind to the children, where education does not happen at all, and the children are put to work in place of general servants. It's my understanding that you wish to conduct an institution which will serve as a model for all other orphanages. That means you'll want to prepare the children to set forth at fourteen on productive and lucrative careers, rather than unskilled. Am I correct?"

"Yes," said Mary.

"Then your original orphanage will cost you about two thousand pounds a year in staff wages alone. You must allow about twenty-five pounds per child per year for food and clothing. That's another two thousand, five hundred pounds. Many items from bedding to towels will wear out at least once a year. And it goes on, and on, and on. I mention these figures to give you some idea of the expenses incurred in running one institution. Take them in and keep them in your minds."

He glanced to right and to left, avoiding Angus's eyes for fear he'd laugh. "If we invest our six hundred thousand pounds in the four-percents, they'll yield an income of twenty-four thousand pounds a year. I would suggest that four thousand be re-invested to allow for rises in prices as time goes on. So your income for running expenses will be twenty thousand pounds per annum. I strongly urge that you err on the side of caution, my fellow Founders. Build a second orphanage, by all means, but no more. Then you'll always have the money to keep them solvent, for once you apply to any other sort of body for additional funds, you'll lose control, autonomy. In conjunction with Matthew and my solicitors, I'll draw up deeds of trust that prevent any future trustees looting the funds. It will be Angus's task to commission external auditors."

I am so happy! Elizabeth was thinking, her mind far from the business at hand. Why did I fear it so much? Oh, how lovely it was to be in his arms, hold nothing back! He was so gentle, so tender, so considerate. He led me like a little child, explaining to me why he did this or that, the pleasure he felt in doing them, encouraging me to let go of my fear and feel the pleasure too. I am voluptuous, he says, and now that I know what the word means, I'm not offended by it. His hands stroke me so perfectly! How did he put it? He sent that man — no, I mustn't think that way! — he sent that *part* of himself to sleep for ten years. As time goes on it gets easier, he said. And I sent myself to sleep too. Or rather, I never awoke. But now that we're both awake, it is a whole different world.

"*Lizzie!*"

Blushing scarlet, Elizabeth recollected her surroundings and looked anywhere but at Fitz, who was smiling as if he knew what she had been thinking about. "Oh! Yes?"

"You didn't hear a word I said!" Mary snapped.

"I am sorry, dear. Say it again."

"I think we should build at least four orphanages, but no one agrees with me — not even Angus!" She turned on the hapless Scot in fury. "I hoped for your support at least!"

"I'll never support you in foolishness, Mary. Fitz is in the right of it. If you built four orphanages, you couldn't split yourself into four segments, which means the institutions wouldn't be properly supervised. You'd be cheated, taken advantage of. What we view as charity, others will view as rich pickings. There's an old saying, that charity begins at home. Well, many who work in charity institutions have adopted that as their credo — but not in any admirable sense." Angus looked heroic at successfully defying Mary: Mary looked taken aback.

"Bitten by a tartan moth, Mary?" Charlie asked wickedly.

"I can see that no one masculine agrees with me," said Mary sulkily.

"And I do not agree with you either," said Elizabeth. "I suggest we build two Children of Jesus orphanages — the one near Buxton, and a second near Sheffield. Manchester is too vast."

And so it was arranged.

The forty-five existing Children of Jesus had settled in at Hemmings and discovered all the horrors of reading, writing, and sums. In one respect Mary retained her common sense; the senior teacher and the head nursemaid were to be sparing with the rod, but not spare it entirely.

"Having been so isolated and regimented, they are bound to go the opposite way for a while," she said to teacher and nursemaid, both petrified of her. "They must be given good principles now, not later. Their true characters will emerge under our kind regime, but we must not hope for forty-seven angels. There will be imps — William is one — and possibly a devil or two — Johnny and Percy. Set them predictable standards, so that they will all know which deeds will be praised, which condemned, and which will earn the birch rod. The sort of child who cannot be disciplined by the birch rod will have to be threatened with expulsion, or some other dire consequences." She looked around. "I see that there is a pianoforte here. I think we should offer music lessons to children who like music. I will look for a music teacher. In our

Children of Jesus institutions, we will offer pianoforte and violin." She looked fierce. "But not the harp! Fool instrument!"

And off she marched to the carriage. It was a long way to visit Hemmings. Once ensconced in the vehicle, she leaned back against the squabs and sighed in sheer pleasure.

Who could ever have believed what would come out of her brief odyssey? The days when she had dreamed of Argus seemed lost in the mists of time, so much had happened. I suffered a schoolgirl's passion, she thought. His ideas inflamed me, and I took that as evidence of love. Well, I still don't know what love is, but most definitely it isn't what I felt for Argus. Who hasn't corresponded with the *Westminster Chronicle* since I went away. I wonder what kind of summer he has had? Perhaps his wife has ailed, or a child. Those are the kind of things that destroy private passions. I can wonder, but I don't feel anything beyond a natural sorrow for his plight, whatever it may be. He has done great work, but what else can be done, when Fitz says the Parliament won't act? The Lords rule Britain because the Commons is stuffed with their second, third, fourth and so on sons. Nothing will happen until the Commons is filled by true commoners: men whose roots do not lie in the Lords.

She must have dozed, because the carriage had passed through Leek and was now on the Buxton road. Waking, she didn't remember quite what she had been thinking. Well, time to think about her own future. Fitz had seen her yesterday and apologised to her sincerely — how changed he was! Not proud or haughty at all. Of course any fool could see that he and

Lizzie were on much better terms; they floated around like newlyweds, exchanged speaking glances, shared private jokes. Yet at the same time they had developed that irritating habit only people who had been married for many years possessed: they said the same thing at one and the same moment, then smirked at each other.

Fitz had told her that she would receive a reward for her discovery of the gold — fifty thousand pounds. Invested in the Funds, she would have an income of two thousand pounds a year — more than enough, he assured her, to live exactly how she wished, anywhere she wished. If she wanted to live unchaperoned, he wouldn't object, save to caution her against living in a city. How much of her original nine and a half thousand pounds did she have left? he asked her. She was proud to be able to tell him, almost all. Then use it to buy a good house, he said. Promising to think about everything, she had escaped, very uncomfortable with this sympathetic Fitz. For she had discovered that she thrived on opposition, and now no one was opposing anything she said or did. Only in the number of orphanages were people against her, but she had come around to their way of thinking: two, and two only.

Oh, it was too bad! Independence had been a challenge when everybody was against it, but now that, in effect, she could do whatever she liked, independence had lost some of its glitter. However, dependence was infinitely worse! Fancy needing another person the way, it was all too obvious, Lizzie needed Fitz, and he, her. As a child she had never enjoyed the closeness Lizzie and Jane had, or Kitty and Lydia. Mary in the middle, and overlooked. Now Mary was in the middle again, in a far better way. Lizzie, Jane and Kitty all admired her as much as they loved her, and they loved her now more than they used to. Being a rational creature, she admitted that she had earned their love, had expanded her always-present nucleus into something huge and well-rounded. But none of that was an answer to her dilemma: what was she going to do with her life? Could she fill it with orphanages and other good works? Highly satisfactory, yet not — *satisfying*.

Buxton had come and gone by the time she had arrived at one conclusion: that she would be responsible for the Sheffield orphanage alone, leaving the Buxton one to Lizzie and Jane. If she did that, she wouldn't be perpetually on the move in a carriage between the two. After a while, she suspected, the children's faces would become blurred, and she would lose track of which child was which in which institution. Having families, Lizzie and Jane could share the duties in an alternating fashion. The Sheffield orphanage was being built in Stannington, so perhaps she could have a house at Bradfield or High Bradfield, on the edge of the moors. That appealed; Mary liked beautiful aspects. She didn't need a manor house. Just a roomy cottage with a cook, housekeeper, three maids and an outside handyman cum gardener. Renting in Hertford, she had learned that no servant liked a heavy load of work, and that all servants had ways of evading work. The thing to do, she decided, was to pay well and expect value for money.

It was time, for instance, to sit at the pianoforte again; she hadn't even practised in weeks. That would fill in some spare time. A library. Her new house would have a magnificent library! Once a week she would spend the day at the Sheffield orphanage. Yes, once a week was sufficient. Were she to visit more often, the staff would grow discontented, feel that they had no independence. That word again! Everyone needs a measure of it, she thought. Without it, we wither. So I must not seem to be the superintendent, just what in fact I am — a benefactress. Though they will never know which day of the week will see my arrival!

What puzzled her most was her yearning for Hertford, for the tiny life she had led there after Shelby Manor had been sold. Yes, she was missing the receptions and parties, the people — Miss Botolph, Lady Appleby, Mrs Markham, Mrs McLeod, Mr Wilde. And Mr Angus Sinclair, in whose company she had spent nine wonderful days. Longer, actually, than she had during the weeks at Pemberley, where so many people gathered for every meal, every conversation, every orphanage meeting, every *everything*. At Pemberley he wasn't hers the way he had been in Hertford, and that hurt. Such talks they had enjoyed! How she had missed him when she set out on her adventure! And how glad she had been to see his face when her ordeal was over! But he had stepped back into the shadows, probably feeling that, now she was reunited with her family, she had no need of him.

But I do! she cried to herself. I want my friend back, I need my friend in my life, and when I move closer to Sheffield I'll never see him except on visits to Pemberley when he's there, which isn't often. Just for the summer guest parties. This year he has stayed longer because of me, but not in any personal way. To aid his friends Fitz and Elizabeth. Now he's talking of going back to London. Of course he is! London is his home. While I was in Hertford he wasn't far away, but the North is an interminable and arduous journey from London, even by private carriage. I will *never* see him! What an empty, horrible sensation that causes in me! Like losing Lydia, only more so. She was important to me as a *duty*; I didn't admire her or think her a nice woman. And Mama's death was like being sprung from a trap. I didn't even miss Papa, who regarded me with contempt. Oh, but I'll mourn Angus! And he isn't even dead, just no longer in my life. How terrible that is.

She wept the rest of the way home.

Indeed, the party was breaking up. Fitz and Elizabeth had decided to accompany Charlie to Oxford, then go to London, Fitz to attend Parliament, Elizabeth to open up Darcy House in preparation for Georgie's coming-out in the new year. Angus had elected to travel with them, but it didn't occur to anyone to ask Mary. With Georgie and Kitty in the coach, Elizabeth wouldn't be alone. How strange it would seem not to have the dark presence of Ned Skinner lurking out of sight! thought Elizabeth. He protected me, and I never knew it.

The orphanages had commenced a-building, but neither would be fit for occupancy until late spring, and Mary admitted that there were many decisions to be taken that could only be taken by one of the Founders. Her days at Pemberley would not be idle ones.

So at the beginning of September she waved them off on their journey to Oxford and London, then, abhorring inertia, summoned Miss Eustacia Scrimpton to have a little holiday at Pemberley in order to discuss the appointment of senior staff. Naturally Miss Scrimpton came with alacrity, and the two ladies settled down to discuss what sort of qualifications were necessary to fill such desirable vacancies.

"You will have your pick, dear Miss Bennet," said Miss Scrimpton, "considering the generosity of the salaries. We will call them salaries for the senior staff — it makes them feel very important. Wages are for the lowly."

By the time that Miss Scrimpton departed for York a week later, all was in train to advertise in the best papers nearer to the time.

Mary gravitated to Matthew Spottiswoode, who had good ideas too, some of them at the suggestion of the builders.

Coal fires, fires in the dormitories, hot water for ablutions, said Mary, brooking no opposition.

"Those will make a Children of Jesus orphanage kinder than Eton or Harrow," Matthew said with a smile.

"No doubt it is good for the over-indulged sons of the Mighty to shiver," said Mary, bristling, "but our children will have done their share of shivering by the time they join us."

"Quite so," said Matthew hastily; my, she was fierce!

Choosing the actual children was a difficult task indeed, since only forty-five of the two hundred were, so to speak, already enrolled. One hundred and fifty-five were but a few grains in the sandpiles of colossal poverty and neglect. Apart from the obvious qualification of having no parents, no lucky child could be on the Parish. No less a personage than the Bishop of London had written to give Mary the names of two gentlemen with some experience in this kind of activity.

Now what to do? Mary asked herself when December came and Christmas loomed. Lizzie had sent her what seemed a wagonload of boxes and bandboxes, all containing clothes for her. *Clothes!* What an outrageous waste, Mary thought in disgust, opening box after box upon gowns of finest lawn and muslin, exquisitely soft wools, silks, taffetas, satins and laces for the evening. So *that* was where her favourite shoes had gone! Lizzie had stolen them as templates for the shoemakers! Oh, the waste! What was wrong with black, even if she was out of mourning? For Lizzie had decreed that they would not go into mourning for either Lydia or Ned.

Still, there was a very pretty dress of lilac lawn oversewn with multicoloured sprigs of flowers, and a pair of lilac slippers apparently meant to go with it. *Silk stockings! Silk underwear!* However, if she did not wear these beautiful things, Lizzie could not; Lizzie was nearly a head shorter, and much plumper in the bosom. Her feet were much smaller too. Waste not, want not, said Mary to herself the next morning as she donned the lilac dress and slid her silk-clad feet into the slippers. Lizzie had assigned her a maid, a nice child named Bertha, and Bertha had a knack for dressing hair. Since Mary refused to adopt the fashion of cutting the hair around her face so it could be twisted into framing curls, Bertha took the whole red-gold mass and piled it on top of Mary's head, but softly, so that it looked as thick and wavy as it really was.

"I will say this for you, child," Mary said gruffly, trying to avoid looking at herself in the mirror, "when you do my hair, I don't feel the pins and combs."

It took all her courage to venture from her room to eat her breakfast, but everyone she encountered gave her a dazzled smile that she couldn't interpret as condescending or amused.

Her appetite was still hearty, though once she had regained her usual weight she seemed to stop growing stouter. Of course that was because she was a busy person, active, prone to walk even long distances; she disliked riding a horse, never having done so at Longbourn. Nellie had been their only steed, and she was a plough horse, too broad in the back to fall off, and too slow to cause any panic. But whenever Mary saw Lizzie or Georgie atop one of Fitz's beasts, her heart soared into her mouth.

True winter had not yet arrived. When it did, Mary guessed, Pemberley became rather like a snail, withdrawn into itself. Best walk while she still could.

The silk under-things felt exquisitely comfortable, and the soft slippers seemed sturdy. They didn't rub at her heels or toes. Her feet were so long and narrow that her store-bought shoes and boots always gave her blisters. Yes, wealth has its compensations, she decided as she draped a heavy lilac silk shawl around her shoulders. Leaving the house, she headed for the woods across a little stone bridge so artfully built that it looked as if the Romans had put it there.

Discovering no blisters thus far, she turned off the path into her favourite glade, where in spring Lizzie said daffodils turned it into a tossing yellow sea, for it got the sun. Time to rest; she sat upon a mossy rock at the edge of the big clearing, gazing about in delight. Squirrels frantically gathering a last nut or two, a fox lurking, winter birds.

And back came her private grief, the one thing that marred her busy and productive existence: she missed Angus, wished him here, exclusively hers now that the rest were gone. So much to tell him! How much she needed his advice! For he was wise — wiser than she. And strong enough to oppose her when she should be opposed.

"Oh, Angus, I wish you were here!" she said aloud.

"That's good," he answered.

She gasped, sprang up, whirled around, gaped. "*Angus!*"

"Aye, that's my name."

"What are you doing here?"

"I'm on my way to Glasgow, where the family businesses are. They don't run themselves, Mary, though I admit I have a younger brother who keeps the steam engines chugging and the foundry chimneys reeking. We always spend Christmas together, then I do something very mad and *sail* back to London through the wintry seas. Like all Scots, I love the sea. 'Tis the Viking in us." He perched on a rock opposite hers. "Sit down, my dear."

"I was wishing so hard for you," she said, sitting.

"Yes, I heard. Is it lonely now they've all gone?"

"Yes, but it isn't Lizzie or Fitz or Charlie I miss. Jane doesn't visit, though I don't miss Jane either. I miss you."

His reply was oblique. "You look delicious," he said. "What brought on this transformation?"

"Lizzie sent me what seems a ton of clothes. An appalling waste! However, if I don't wear them, no one else can. I'm taller and thinner than the others."

"Waste not, want not, is it?"

"Exactly."

"Why have you missed me in particular, Mary?"

"Because you're genuinely my friend, unrelated to me by blood or marriage. I've harkened back to our time in Hertford, when it seemed that we talked about everything. Nothing stands out, except that I so looked forward to seeing your face when you joined me in the high street, and you never disappointed me. You didn't try to cozen me or wheedle me out of my expedition, even though I can see now how foolish it was. Of course you knew that at the time, but you never dampened my enthusiasm. And how idiotic I was over Argus, poor man, whoever he may be. Truly, I am so grateful for your understanding! Nobody else understood, even remotely. No matter how mistaken it was, I *had* to make that trip! After seventeen years cooped up at Shelby Manor, I was a bird finally flying free. And the ills of England — Argus — gave me a valid reason to explore a wider world. For that reason I'll always love Argus, though I don't love him."

"In which case it's time I made a confession," he said, face serious. "I hope you'll find it in your heart to forgive me, but even if you don't, still I must tell you the truth."

"The truth?" she asked, eyes gone grey.

"I am Angus, but I am also Argus."

Her jaw dropped; she gaped at him. "*You* are Argus?"

"Yes, for my sins. I was bored, Mary, and idle. Alastair ran the family businesses, and the *Chronicle* had begun to run itself. So I invented Argus, with two objects in mind. One was to keep myself busy. The other was to draw the attention of the comfortably off to the plight of the poor. That second motive was never as important to me as the first, and that is the truth. There is a spirit of mischief in me, and it gave me intense satisfaction to dine in the best houses and listen to my hosts rave about the vile perfidies of Argus. A delightful feeling, but not as delightful as walking the corridors of Westminster to encounter members of the Lords and Commons. I gathered ideas from all these people, and I wallowed in the mischief I made far more than in the social conscience I was helping to engender."

"But those letters were so real!" she cried.

"Yes, they're real. That is part of the power of words, Mary. They are seductive, even on paper. Spoken or written, they can inspire the downtrodden to revolt, as happened in France and in America. It is words that separate us from the beasts."

Anger didn't seem to want to come; Mary sat in shock, trying to remember what she had said to Angus about Argus. How much of a fool had she sounded? How much of a silly, love-starved spinster? Had he, with his self-confessed spirit of mischief, taken pleasure in duping her?

"You made a fool of me," she muttered.

He caught her words, sighed. "Never deliberately, Mary, I do swear it. Your transports over Argus filled me with humility and shame. I longed to confess, but dared not. If I had, you would have spurned me. I would have lost my dearest friend. All I could do was wait until I judged you knew me well enough to forgive. I beg you, Mary, forgive me!"

He had dropped to his knees, and lifted his clasped hands to her imploringly.

"Oh, do get up!" she snapped. "You look ridiculous. If I didn't know better, I'd think you were proposing marriage."

"I *am* proposing marriage!" he yelled. "I love you more than life itself, you idiotic, stubborn, pragmatic, opinionated, blind, deaf, adorable wench!"

"Get up, get up!" was all she said.

Defeated, he dragged himself back onto his rock and gazed at her, utterly confounded. She hadn't lost a scrap of her composure, though apparently she didn't mind being called names. How very beautiful she was, with her hair done properly and clad in a gown that became her fetchingly. Her lips parted.

"You are Argus, you say — that is a shock. And you love me — that is another shock. You want to marry me — a third shock. I must say, Angus, that when you start on serious subjects, you do not seem to know when to stop."

Inside herself, a coal of wonderful warmth was glowing, but she had no intention of telling him about its existence until he had suffered more than thus far he had. Oh, my dearest friend! If we are married, you will always be there for me. I do not know if that is love, but it will certainly do as a substitute.

Her face must have betrayed a little of that coal, for he

relaxed suddenly, produced the dimples in his cheeks that hovered on the verge of fissures. "The time to stop," he said, "is when we've sorted everything out to our mutual satisfaction. I have loved you since our first meeting in Hertford — oh, the mortification of knowing I was Argus while you extolled the wretched figment's virtues! My self-esteem shrank to nothing because I, the rich and powerful Angus Sinclair, was no more to you than a contact with your hero, Argus."

"That did not last very long. On our first walk I began to see that I'd made a friend who wasn't going to force me to send him away by declarations of love and proposals of marriage. And by our ninth walk, as well as all the dinners and parties, I did not know how I was going to get on without you. Even today, after declarations of love and proposals of marriage, I find I cannot send you away."

"If you forgive me, it's because you love me in return," he said, leaning forward eagerly. "Will you forgive me?"

"I have already done so. *Does* that mean love? I must take your word for it. What I do know is that I must have your constant, perpetual friendship if I am to be happy. I will marry you to keep you as my dearest friend. And when I drive you mad, you must tell me. I find I am the sort of person who does indeed drive other people mad. Poor Miss Scrimpton was gibbering when I let her return to York, and Matthew Spottiswoode has taken to hiding whenever he thinks I'm coming. Charlie says I am an eccentric. I see no point in trying to dissimulate, Angus. I am a very difficult and wearying person," said Mary without a trace of self-pity or sorrow that she should be that way. The truth was the truth, why repine?

"That's why I love you," he said, almost bursting with happiness. "In some ways we're alike — we take pleasure in poking and prying, for one, and when we sink our teeth in, we can't let go, for another. Also, I'm a little mad myself. Were I not, I wouldn't sail the North Sea in winter. But my greatest joy, my dearest Mary, is that life with you will never be dull."

"I feel exactly the same way," she said, rising. "Come, it's time we walked back. I want to know all about Argus."

Yes, he was bursting with happiness — but was she? I may never know that for certain, he thought. Her composure is like a stone wall. How do I batter it down?

They had dinner *à deux* that evening, which rather perturbed Parmenter, always disconsolate when the family was away. Darcy House had its own servants. The easy camaraderie between Miss Mary and Mr Sinclair didn't suit his ideas of propriety, but he knew Mr Fitz and Mrs Darcy would find nothing untoward in two fortyish people spending the evening alone together. So when they repaired to the plushly purple little drawing room which held a Fra Angelico, a Giotto, a Botticelli and three Canalettos (hence its name, the Italian Room), Parmenter finally gave up. Having put out the port, the cognac and the cheroots, he left them to their own devices.

"I wonder which Darcy collected this glorious art?" Mary asked, accepting a port to keep up her courage.

"I have no idea, except that I'm positive they were sold for a hundredth of their value by some impoverished Italian."

Angus didn't bother looking at the paintings; he was too absorbed in watching Mary, who was wearing a low-cut taffeta gown of marmalade shot with vermilion. That long and graceful neck, he was thinking, needs no gems to improve it, but diamonds would draw attention to it. Such a perfect curve!

"I thought Elizabeth was the most beautiful woman I knew," he said, "but she can't hold a candle to you."

"Nonsense! You are besotted, Angus, which warps your taste as well as your judgement. I am too thin."

"For the fashion, perhaps. But spareness suits you where it would reduce most women to scraggy old hens. Caroline Bingley springs to mind."

"You may smoke if you wish. I am not supposed to drink port, but I like it more than I do wine. Less vinegary."

He shifted from his wing chair to a sofa and lifted one brow at her. "I don't feel like blowing a cloud. Come and sit here with me. I haven't kissed you yet."

She came to sit with him, but slewed sideways just too far away for kisses and cuddles. "We must talk about this."

He sighed. "Mary, when you stand before God, you will demand to talk about *that*! I knew you were going to have something to say, because you always do. Sooner or later, my exasperating love, the kisses are inevitable. Also greater and more daring intimacies. I suppose you're as ignorant as other maiden ladies?"

"I don't believe so," she said, considering the question. "There were all kinds of books in the Shelby Manor library, and I read them all. So I know quite a lot about bodies and copulation — connubial duty is the seemly phrase, not so?"

"And how do you feel about that side of marriage?"

"I don't suppose you'd be content with friendship?" she asked hopefully.

He laughed. "No, I insist that you do your connubial duty." He reached out to take her hand. "What I hope to see is the night when it becomes a pleasure, rather than a duty. May I kiss you? It *is* permitted between an engaged couple."

"Yes, it is far better to begin as we intend to go on," she said, composure undented. "You may kiss me."

"First," he said, pulling her very close, "it's necessary to be in — er — intimate proximity. Do you mind?"

"It would be better if you took off your coat. I'm embracing naught but clothes."

He removed the coat, a struggle, as it had been made by Weston and fitted like a kid glove. "Anything else?"

"The cravat. It scratches. Why is it so starched?"

"To hold its shape. Is that better?"

"Much." She unbuttoned his collar and slid one hand inside his shirt. "How nice your skin feels! Like silk."

His eyes had closed, but in despair. "Mary, you cannot act like a seductress! I'm a man of one-and-forty, but if you keep on provoking me, I may not be able to control myself!"

"I love your hair," she said, running her free hand through it. She sniffed. "It smells wonderful — no pomade, just expensive soap. And you will never be bald." Her other hand crept down to his chest. "Angus, you're very muscular!"

"Shut up!" he growled, and kissed her.

He had wanted this first contact with her lips to be tender and loving, but the fire was lit in him, so the kiss was hard and passionate, probing. To his amazement she responded ardently, both hands working at his shirt, while his hands, despising idleness, did an expert job on the laces down the back of her dress. Her sweet little breasts somehow fell into his grasp, and he began to kiss them in an ecstasy of bliss.

Suddenly he pushed her away. "We cannot! Someone might come in!" he gasped.

"I'll lock the door," she said, lifted herself off the sofa, stepped out of her dress and petticoats, kicked them away, and stalked in her silk underwear to the door. Click! "There. It's locked."

Her hair had fallen down; the last petticoat was tossed into a corner, the camisole and drawers lying on the floor in her wake like exhausted white butterflies.

He had used the time to good advantage himself, and took her back into his arms as naked as she was, save that she let him peel off her stockings. Oh, what heaven! No composure now, just gasps and purrs and moans of delight.

"You'll have to marry me now," she said a long time after, when he got up to put more logs on the fire.

"Come to Scotland with me," he said, kneeling at the fire, his head turned so that he could smile at her. "We can be wed across the anvil in Gretna Green."

"Oh, that's the perfect way to get married!" she cried. "I was dreading a family wedding, all the curious coming to gawp at us. This is far the best way. But isn't Gretna Green a long way east? I thought the road to Glasgow would be farther west."

"I'm in a carriage, dear inquisitive love, and between here and Glasgow lies a body of water called the Solway Firth. The road to Glasgow as well as to Edinburgh goes through Gretna."

"Oh. It's appropriate that one Bennet daughter should have a runaway marriage at Gretna Green."

"I cannot believe you," he said, utterly lost in love.

"I must have more Lydia in me than I suspected, dearest of dear Anguses. That was the loveliest thing I have ever done. Let's do it again, please!"

"One more time, then, you insatiable wench." He pulled her onto the floor and cushioned her head on his shoulder. "After that we have to make ourselves respectable and go to bed. Each in our own room, mind! Parmenter will have a stroke as it is. A short sleep, alas. At dawn we start for Gretna Green. If by any chance I've quickened you, we had best hurry, else all the old tabbies will be doing their sums."

Fitz came into Elizabeth's room looking concerned. "My dear love, I think there might be bad news from Pemberley," he said, sitting on the edge of her bed, a letter in his hand. "A courier has just brought this for you."

"Oh, Fitz! It must concern Mary!" Fingers trembling, Elizabeth snapped the seal and unfolded the single sheet of paper, then began to read its few lines.

She emitted a sound between a howl and a shriek.

"What is it?" Fitz demanded. "Tell me!"

"Mary and Angus are on their way to Gretna Green!" She thrust the letter at him. "Here, read for yourself!"

"If that doesn't beat all!" he breathed. "They have not a soul there but themselves. Stolen a march!"

"How will they ever get on?" Elizabeth asked, feelings mixed.

"Very well, I hazard a guess. She is an eccentric, and he is a man who likes unusual things. He'll let her have a free rein until she bolts, when he'll curb her firmly but kindly. I'm delighted for them, I truly am."

"So am I — I think. She says she has written to Charlie with the news. Oh, why are we in London? I want to go home!"

"We can't until the Season is over, you know that. I do have hopes that Georgie will continue to behave herself, but if we aren't here —!"

"Yes, of course you're right. You don't think Georgie will accept the Duke, or Lord Wilderney?"

"No, she's too much a Darcy to care for peers. I think she may choose Mr John Parker of Virginia."

"Fitz! *An American?*"

"Why not? He has the entrée — his mother is Lady de Main. He's also extremely wealthy, so he doesn't need Georgie's dowry. Still, it's early days. The Season hasn't yet really commenced."

"Our first chick will probably fly the nest," Elizabeth said, rather disconsolately.

"We have four others."

"No," she said, blushing. "Five others."

"Elizabeth! No!"

"Elizabeth, yes. In June, I think."

"Then we'll go home in April, Season or no Season. You won't want to grow too heavy in London, it's damp and smoky in spring."

"I would like that very much." She heaved a sigh of satisfaction. "Next year will be a quiet one. The year after that, we'll have to bring out Susie."

Jane descended on London shortly after the news of Mary's sensational elopement reached her, free to do so because Caroline Bingley had finally found a useful occupation: turning the Bingley boys from harum-scarums into beautifully comported gentlemen. Though she did quite a lot of complaining, secretly she loved it. Nothing gratified her more than wielding power. Not that she had things all her own way. The Bingley boys were foes worthy of her steel.

"Louisa and Posy are free to do what they have yearned to do for years," Jane said to Elizabeth the day after she took up residence in Bingley House.

"And what is that?" Elizabeth asked dutifully.

"Sell the Hurst property in Brook Street and move to Kensington," said Jane.

"No! Among what Fitz would call the old tabbies?"

"Better to be the only Persians in a society of tabbies than be reduced to hanging on Charles's sleeve for every guinea," Jane answered, smiling. "Mr Hurst left them with very little apart from the property, and that would have been mortgaged had Charles not put his foot down. Its sale has given them a comfortable income that will not require Louisa in particular to economise on her clothes or sell her jewels."

"Well, Caroline was ever the driving force. Does she know?"

"Oh, yes."

"What did she have to say?"

"Very little. Hugh had chosen to short-sheet her bed the night before she received Louisa's letter, and Percival broke rotten eggs into her favourite walking boots." Jane looked demure. "By the time she had found the culprits and exacted vengeance, Louisa's news was a trifle stale."

"How can you bear her at Bingley Hall day after day, Jane?"

"With equanimity, actually."

"So what brings you to London?"

"I want to say farewell to Louisa and Posy, as I doubt I'll ever have much time to visit Kensington."

"And Charles is coming home," Elizabeth accused.

"Yes, he is. Oh, it will be delightful to see him!"

"And so the babies will begin again," Elizabeth said to Fitz that night, curled up next to him in bed.

"It is their business, my dear."

"I would not mind, were it not for her health."

"At forty-six, how many babies can she bear?"

"Oh! I never thought of that." She sat up and linked her arms about her knees. "You are right as always, Fitz. We are all growing old." She looked wistful. "Where do the years go?"

"Provided that you survive this child, Elizabeth, I don't care," he said, stroking her cheek. "When do you plan on telling our children that there will be a new addition to the family?"

"Not until February, I think. Just before Georgie's coming-out ball."

"Is that wise? Why not now?"

"If I tell them then, it will take the edge off Georgie's nerves. With a duke and an earl refused, I don't wish her to face that ordeal feeling that every debutante's eye is upon her."

"It is their mamas who are jealous, my love."

And so the news was broken, though not without some discomfort on Elizabeth's part.

Charlie was delighted, hugged and kissed his mama, shook his father warmly by the hand and announced that at his advanced age he would feel more like an uncle than a brother.

Susie and Anne were pleased, but not quite sure what to make of decrepit parents who produced babies. Cathy was furious; the family had to endure an outbreak of pranks that only ceased after Charlie shook her until her teeth rattled and told her roundly that she was a selfish little beast.

Georgie was so thrilled that she sailed through her ball and marked the occasion as memorable by declining to become Mrs John Parker of Virginia.

"*Why?*" asked Elizabeth, exasperated. "To refuse so many advantageous offers is ridiculous! You'll get a reputation for the worst kind of capriciousness and receive no offers at all."

"With a dowry of ninety thousand pounds?" Georgie asked smugly. "I do not intend to marry yet, Mama — if at all. I am enjoying my season, especially breaking hearts. You were twenty-one when you married Papa, and had had other offers. Besides, I refuse to have a betrothed underfoot while I am busy watching our new precious mite grow into a person."

Well, that answers one question, thought her mother: Georgie is not in love with any of her suitors.

What she didn't know (and Georgie had no intention of telling her) was that every week Georgie wrote to Owen Griffiths, who had not yet succumbed to her charms, but would, she was sure. She had worked out how to have her cake and eat it too, even if Queen Marie Antoinette had failed. When time had proven that she was a dedicated spinster, she intended to buy a farm on the outskirts of Oxford; then she could be a farmer and Owen could be an Oxford don.

Word came from Glasgow that Mr and Mrs Angus Sinclair would shortly be embarking upon a ship to sail to Liverpool, as both orphanages were nearing completion, and Mary wanted to be on hand to drive both teams of builders mad. Everyone knew that builders might be relied upon for ninety percent of the works, but never bothered with the last ten percent. These two projects, vowed Mary, would be finished down to the last nail and the last touch of paint in the most obscure corner.

Angus had finally succumbed to the need a wealthy man was supposed to have for the status of a country seat. Alastair and his brood occupied the Scottish mansion, and some weeks of Mary's company had reduced them to abject terror. The very thought of Mary resident in Scotland had Alastair's wife in the throes of vapours and Alastair himself on the verge of emigration to America. So to learn that Angus intended to live in close proximity to the Sheffield orphanage caused rejoicing in every Sinclair breast north of the Border. They could escort him and Mary on board the ship with light hearts and sincerest good wishes. Let Angus live among the Sassenachs!

He found seven thousand acres outside Bradfield on the edge of the moors; they included a forest, a park, and a proper number of tenant farms. Because the mansion could be sited atop a tall hill, Mr and Mrs Angus Sinclair agreed that the property should be named Ben Sinclair.

In the meantime, said Angus's letter to Fitz in London, would Fitz object if they stayed at Pemberley until Ben Sinclair became a reality?

Everyone gathered at Pemberley or Bingley Hall for the summer of 1814, eagerly awaiting the birth of two longed for, very worrying babies. The only defector was Owen Griffiths, who was not sure if he could withstand Georgie's charms did he see her in the flesh, so prudently went home to Wales. His paper upon the movements of Caesar in Gaul had circulated far and wide, so perspicacious was it upon things like the inaccuracy of Caesar's mileage; the academic Powers That Be were now hailing him a formidable future scholar. If the formidable future scholar kept Georgie's letters in a neat bundle tied with a satin ribbon the colour of her eyes, that was his business, no one else's. When he wrote to her, he addressed her as his dear Scruff. Her letters to him said "dear Owen."

Elizabeth's pregnancy had been uneventful yet burdensome; she swore to Fitz that this one was a giant. Her labour was exhaustingly long, though uncomplicated, and resulted in a huge boy child with curly black hair and Fitz's fine dark eyes. Provided that he was fed by two wet-nurses, he was a quiet and placid baby, but alert.

"God has been very good to us," Elizabeth said to Fitz.

"Yes, my sweetest lady. Ned has been returned to us, and this time he will rejoice in his name. Edward Fitzwilliam Darcy. Who knows? Perhaps he will be prime minister."

Mary's pregnancy was more eventful, chiefly due to the book Kitty had sent her. It was written by an aristocratic German obstetrician who had definite ideas upon motherhood, despite (as Angus protested) his inability to experience the phenomenon in person. Everything she consumed was measured or weighed, its proportion of the whole diet regulated, and her own bodily condition monitored ruthlessly.

As the months wore on Angus grew increasingly sure that an expectant Mary was a fair indication of her ability to don the mental trappings of a married lady. She had hopped into the connubial bed with all Lydia's glee, rendering him profoundly grateful that her child-bearing years were nearing an end. Otherwise, he reflected, she would probably have followed Jane's example and fallen again every time he hung up his trousers for the next twenty years. Therefore he could be confident that his bride was up to the physical demands of marriage.

As to the intellectual and spiritual demands — she took them in her stride too. Who else would have seized upon the ideas of an unknown German *accoucheur* as if his book were an obstetrical bible? Who else would have accepted pregnancy as a matter of course, made no attempt to hide herself away, and, as her girth increased, shoved her belly into people's midriffs thinking she was as thin as ever? Unaccustomed to witnessing blatantly pregnant ladies, those she met, including the staff of "her" orphanage at Sheffield, were forced to pretend she was indeed as thin as ever. When "her" children told her she was getting fat, she told them outright that she was growing a new baby inside her tummy, and made them a part of the process. Her frankness appalled the staff, but ... Hers *was* the hand that fed.

As if that were not enough, she insisted upon journeying to London to see how Angus lived there, and participated in the pleasures of choosing furniture, carpets, drapes, wallpapers and paints for the interior of Ben Sinclair. Much to Angus's relief, her taste in these things proved better than he expected, and, besides, when it veered away from his own tastes, she deferred to him with equanimity. She met all his London friends, and held sway at several dinner parties with that distressing bulge uncamouflaged.

"The worst of it is," she informed the insufferably stiff and proper Mrs Drummond-Burrel with a peal of laughter, "that I cannot pull my chair into the table, and end in wearing everything from soup to sauce."

Perhaps the time was right for change, or perhaps it was just that Mary was Mary; Angus didn't know, save that even the most waspish among his acquaintances hungered for more of her refreshing candour, particularly after they realised that her grasp of politics was highly developed and she cared not a jot that ladies were not supposed to be political. Shorn of his anxieties on her behalf, Angus understood that over the space of one short summer Mary had changed from a dandelion into a most exotic orchid. What he suspected he would never know was how much of the orchid had always lain dormant underneath.

Entering her eighth month, she returned to Pemberley to make sure the child would be born surrounded by its family. So by the time that she began her labour early in September, Angus had a very good idea of what his married life was going to entail. His wife intended to be his partner in all his enterprises, and expected him to be a partner in all her enterprises. It was as clear to him as it was to Fitz and Elizabeth that the Sinclairs were going to be in the vanguard of social change, particularly education. Mary had found her métier — universal education. Over the wrought-iron gates to the Children of Jesus orphanages at Buxton and Stannington stood the motto Mary had coined: EDUCATION IS LIBERTY.

To the surprise of everybody save Angus, Mary bore her labour pains with patience, tranquillity and copious notes she wrote in a diary between contractions. Twelve hours later she produced a long, slender boy child with a magnificent pair of lungs; he screamed the house down until shown the purpose of a nipple, then mercifully shut up. Mary was following the dictates of her German bible still, and nursing him herself. Luckily she was brimful of milk, whereas the more buxomly endowed Elizabeth was dry.

"God has been very good to us," she said to Angus, who was a ghost of himself after twelve hours spent pacing up and down the Great Library with Fitz and Charlie for company. "What do you wish to call him?"

"Have you no suggestions?" he asked.

"None, my dearest friend. You may name the boys, I will name the girls."

"Well, with a head of hair that would set a haystack on fire, it will have to be a Scots name, my wanton wench. Hamish Duncan."

"What colour other than carrots could his hair have been?" she asked, stroking the baby's thick ginger fluff. "A dear wee man! I must arrange for Dr Marshall to circumsise him."

"*Circumcise?* I'll have no son of mine circumcised!"

"Of course you will," she said, unperturbed. "All manner of horrid substances collect beneath an intact foreskin, including a natural exudate called smegma that looks like cottage cheese. The foreskin is removed by all Semitic peoples — Jews, Arabs — as hygienic principle. I imagine that if grains of sand got under it they would hurt dreadfully, so one can see why desert peoples originated it. Graf von Tielschaft-Hohendorner-Göter-und-Schunck says that the wall paintings in Egyptian tombs reveal that the ancient Egyptians circumcised. He recommends that all male children be circumcised irrespective of their ancestry. I have followed his advice to the letter, had an easy pregnancy and delivery in my forty-first year, and so must defer to him in this too."

"Mary, I forbid it! What will they say of him at school?"

"No, you don't forbid it," she said comfortably. "You will consent because it is the right thing to do. By the time he goes to school, I will have taught him how to argue more successfully than a clutch of Privy Councillors."

"The laddie's doomed," said Hamish's father morosely. "Our son will be branded an eccentric long before he goes to school."

"There is merit in that," said Hamish's mother thoughtfully. "He will have his own niche. Nor, with us as parents, will he be brought up too narrow, as I was."

"Certainly he won't lack character, or be a shrinking violet. But, Mary, I absolutely forbid circumcision!"

Mary squealed with delight. "Oh, Angus, look! He is *smiling*! Diddlums, tiddlums, coochy-coo, smile for Papa, Hamish! Show him how much you are looking forward to being circumcised!"

FINIS